RUBY RUINS

JEWELS OF ILLUMINATION BOOK TWO

JMD REID

© 2021 by JMD Reid

All rights reserved. No part of this book may be reproduced, stored in a retrieval system or transmitted in any form or by any means without the prior written permission of the publishers, except by a reviewer who may quote brief passages in a review to be printed in a newspaper, magazine or journal.

The final approval for this literary material is granted by the author.

Edited by Poppy Reid

Second Edition

Print ISBN: 978-1-949382-68-6

This is a work of fiction. Names, characters, businesses, places, events and incidents are either the products of the author's imagination or used in a fictitious manner. Any resemblance to actual persons, living or dead, or actual events is purely coincidental.

PUBLISHED BY FALLBRANDT PRESS

www.FallbrandtPress.com

BOOKS BY JMD REID

Jewels of Illumination

Diamond Stained
Ruby Ruins
Obsidian Mind
Emerald Strength
Amethyst Shattered
***
Jewels of Illumination Box Set: Books 1-3

Masks of Illumination

Mask of Guilt - May 2021
Mask of Vengeance - June 2021
Mask of Hope - July 2021
Mask of Betrayal - August 2021
Mask of Redemption - Sept 2021

Assassins of Illumination

Fractured Soul - Oct 2021
Shattered Soul - Nov 2021
Sundered Soul - Dec 2021

The Storm Below

Above the Storm
Reavers of the Tempest
Storm of Tears
Golden Darkness Descends
Shattered Sunlight

To my Uncle Dave for slipping me a copy of the Hobbit and opening up my love for fantasy!

MAP OF KASH SLUMS

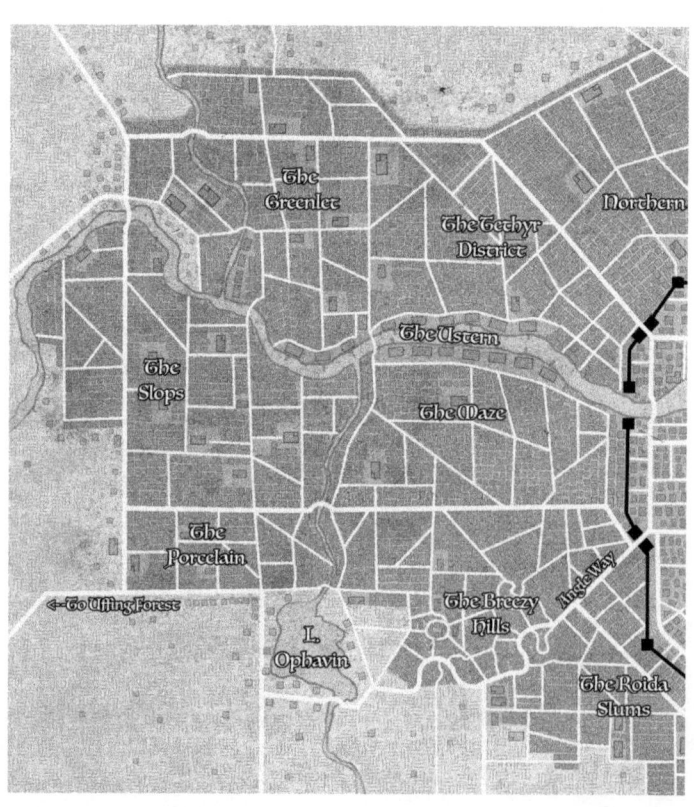

MAP OF OLD KASH

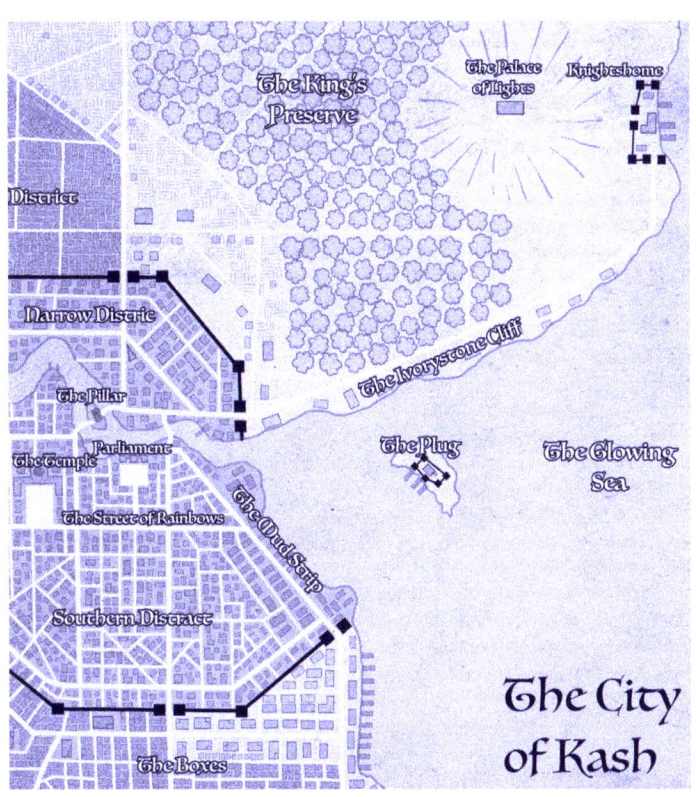

1

Forty-Third Day of Forgiveness, 755 EU

Obhin's black-gloved hands flexed and relaxed with building excitement. He marched along the sluggish flow of the Greenwine through the northwestern neighborhood of Kash. The stench of the waste dumped into the river from the canneries on the west bank filled his nose. The day's heat, summer having started three days earlier with the Feast of Restitution, ripened the foul odors. His boots thudded on the uneven cobblestones, his chainmail coat ringing about him. The locals, the poor who lived in the slums, gave him strange glances. His eastern blood, giving him dusky-brown cheeks, caused him to stand out in the mostly Lothonian neighborhood of pale faces.

The woman at his side didn't help him blend in.

Avena had eschewed the traditional garb of women in Kash and the rest of the Kingdom of Lothon. She didn't wear one of her dresses—dark brown or blue or soft gray—with their layers of rustling petticoats. She wore a man's trousers, hand-me-downs from Bran, and a man's long shirt beneath a padded gambeson. The quilted tunic was often worn under armor. However, its layers of cloth provided some protection against weapons both edged and blunted.

"Do you really think Creg knows something about what happened to Carstin?" Avena asked as she pulled out the heavy linen glove from a satchel she wore on her left hip. A binder, a rod of metal, hung on her right. The glove was long, its cuff extending to well past her elbow. It had small emeralds embedded in it, and a mesh of copper wire woven into the fabric's weave to connect the gems.

"Don't know," Ōbhin said as he marched with purpose. His face was set, the scar on his right cheek stretched taut. She matched his stride. "But only he and Handsome Baill will know, and Creg's the one we've found."

For nearly a Lothonian month, the last fifty-two days, Ōbhin had been looking for the survivors of his old gang of bandits. Most were dead, killed when their leader, Ust, had attacked Dualayn's manor that terrifying night. A few had escaped. Whiner Creg, as the skinny man was nicknamed, might be stained Black with his crimes, but he was a survivor.

Facing pain, he'd talk. Give answers.

Avena pulled the glove over her right arm. It was her prototype, a jewelchine invention of her own. They both worked for one of the most renowned inventors of jewel machines in Lothon. His skills had embroiled him in the machinations of the Brotherhood crime syndicate when he'd uncovered a lost relic from the blood-stained ruins. The organization needed something from that Recorder.

Ōbhin feared what would happen to his employer when Dualayn found it.

Avena worked the glove up beneath the sleeve of her long shirt, tugging with care as they marched ahead. The road left the Greenwine behind as they moved deeper into the heart of Greenlet, as the slum was called. It was one of the many villages the expanding borders of Kash had swallowed in the last few decades. Remnants of the original buildings, made of frames of wooden beams with wattle and daub walls covered in whitewash, stood between cheap tenements raised of mud-fired brick and factories belching black smoke into the air as they produced everything from textiles to canned food.

Jewelchines revolutionized the world with a headlong rush.

"I hope that works as you promise," Ōbhin said.

"It has its limitations," she said, "but it'll make my arm as strong as yours. Stronger." She flashed him a broad grin, her cheeks pale and fair. She was Lothonian and went around with her face uncovered like it was nothing improper.

In Ōbhin's distant home of Qoth, women guarded their faces with the same modesty a Lothonian lady did her breasts.

Avena wore her brown hair in a braid down her back, mauve ribbons entwined through them, leaving her round features exposed. She was youthful, twenty springs, a few years younger than Ōbhin. Her girlishness faded as she pressed two fingers into the heel of her palm. Green light glowed from the network of embedded jewelchines.

"I never would have thought of connecting a chain of smaller jewelchines to make a unified effect," she said. "The Recorder holds so much. Dualayn is so close to unearthing something important."

"Good," Ōbhin said. He glanced down at his black gloves. Wearing such an ill-omened color was a self-imposed mark of his past crimes. Now he was Dualayn's chief guard. By protecting the man and his employees, Avena included, Ōbhin had unburied some of who he'd used to be before he'd destroyed his life. He no longer walked through the dark, but twilight.

Maybe one day, I'll find that path back to Qoth, he thought.

The street led to a square. A public house, the original that had dominated the heart of Greenlet before Kash invaded with its cheap buildings and rapacious factories, stood on one corner. It was built in the old style, its wooden beams strong, if stained, walls painted a deep green. Each of its three floors was wider than the one Below it. A sign swung above, marking it the Green Grasser.

The door opened and a laborer sauntered out in a patched overcoat, a dark-blue felt hat perched on his head. It was shabby, old and worn. He slouched down the street and spat on the cobblestones. Ōbhin's eyes slid past him to examine the intersection. One of the many rickety tenements rose on the other side of the public house.

"Across the street," Ōbhin said as the pair entered the intersection, "that's the house Runty Ed said he's in."

"Can you trust that sneak thief?" she asked.

Ōbhin shrugged. "We'll find out. The boy's pretty scared of me." Ōbhin had caught Runty Ed and a friend trying to rob Dualayn's manor house a few months back. The thief ran with the Breezy Hill Boys, one of the many street gangs populating the overcrowded city. "He said a man with a runny nose and who's as skinny as a broom has been shacked up in there."

Several youths lounged on the steps of the tenements. All of them wore patched pants and ratty shirts, none tucked in. They had green bandannas tied about their throats. Wearing green, white, or blue was a statement in Kash. A hundred or so years ago, a civil war had split the nation. The Blues had won. In the past few months, the Greens and Whites had been rioting in Kash. Sometimes it seemed like a mob erupted every other day as they protested the newest tax passed by Parliament and signed into law by King Anglon Exustin.

One of the boys whistled as they approached the house across. Ōbhin ignored them and threw open the rickety fence with a loud clatter and creak of rusting hinges. He marched for the front door, Avena at his side. Her face held the fierce expression of a wolverine.

She was the only person he could trust on this raid. He didn't want word getting back to the Brotherhood. He couldn't trust any of his men. One of them was worse than a spy. A changeling who'd killed and replaced one of Ōbhin's new friends and now pantomimed as him.

"There's a jewelchine lock," Avena said, nodding to the amethyst jewel set in the door. "It's warded."

He drew his resonance blade, a curved tulwar with a single edge. A graceful weapon with an emerald, wrapped in gold wire, was set in the pommel. The jewel wasn't for decoration but powered the sword. He pressed a spot on the crossguard with his gloved thumb.

The sword hummed to life as the emerald shone with verdant light.

"Won't work," she said.

"Resonance blades can cut through anything."

"Not amethyst barriers."

He grunted. He'd learned that fighting the monstrosity who'd used to be his old bandit leader, Ust. "Then the wall. I can cut through it fast."

Avena punched the door with her gloved hand. The emerald flared bright as she struck the amethyst set in the door. Purple energy rippled over the door, flashing into existence. The amethyst flared at the same time it popped out and clattered on the floor inside. The barrier died.

She smiled in delight. "It worked."

"That's impressive, Avena," he said in awe. It took a brawny man, someone stronger than Ōbhin, to do that.

She thrust the door open. The jewelchine alarm blared, the sound deafening Ōbhin's ears.

The howling of the heliodor alarm slammed into Avena's ears, her cheek muscles tightening in a wince. Barely heard over the caterwaul, someone cursed upstairs. The excitement of danger ignited her veins, that thrumming rush. The emptiness that liked to lurk inside of her, the guilt from surviving when her twin sister had not, drank it in.

She always found exhilaration around Ōbhin. A thrill always tingled through her soul. Whether from whispering their shared secret of the true nature about the thing that had replaced Smiles or fighting to protect Dualayn from the machinations of the Brotherhood, she savored the rush. But that wasn't the only reason she enjoyed spending time with Ōbhin.

He trusted her strength.

He didn't look down at her for the weakness other men saw in her sex. *She* was the one person he trusted to accompany him on the raid to capture Creg, to find answers in the events that happened leading up to Ust's attack.

"Let's go!" she shouted as footsteps thudded upstairs. "Elohm's Colours, let's grab him."

Ōbhin led the way while her exhilaration surged even hotter through her. They would finally have a source to learn what Ust had known. Concrete and certain answers to questions. No more floundering in the fog.

Her right hand seized her binder from her belt, drawing a steel rod the length of her arm. The pulsing of the emeralds through the long-sleeved glove she wore gave her the strength of a brawny strongarm, but it had its limitations.

It didn't strengthen her back or legs. She'd almost broken her spine discovering that.

Ōbhin burst into the house, disturbing the dust drifting through the air. A couch rested in a sitting room to the right, old and neglected, the horse-hair stuffing bursting out of the cushions. Its frame was dented and gouged, the shine vanished. Stairs lay to the right, runners battered by years of use. Ōbhin pivoted for it. She raced after him.

A face appeared at the top of the stairs, nose running. A slender figure with a wild look, skin pale, a jerkin of studded leather armoring his torso. Rust tarnished the steel rivets. He raised a crossbow.

Ōbhin cursed in his native tongue and dived right. Avena's body moved before she could even recognize the threat held in the bandit's arms. She threw herself to the left, her feet acting by instinct. A loud twang snapped through the air over the blaring alarm.

A dark shape blurred through the air and slammed into the wooden floor. She hit the floor on her shoulder, her padded gambeson blunting the impact. She rolled up into a crouch and activated her binder. Purple light burst from the gem set in the weapon's recessed butt.

"No need for this, Creg," Ōbhin called. He stood to the right of the stairs, a stoic warrior. He had the brown skin of an easterner. Not one of the Tethyrians, who abounded in Kash, but from the more distant Qoth, a land of mountains. A scar twisted his right cheek. He wore his black hair cut short, face shaved smooth.

Sable gloves *still* adorned his hands.

"We're just here to talk. Find out what Ust knows."

"Suck on a pus-filled roach, traitor!" Creg growled. "I don't answer to the Brotherhood no more. Black-filled bastards want my head. I ain't givin' it to 'em."

"We're not with the Brotherhood," Avena called, feeling dirty just at the thought. The Brotherhood of Masons and Builders were one of the two major crime syndicates plaguing the city of Kash. They and the Free Associate of Rangers warred through street gangs for control of all manner of illicit activities from Tethyrian narcotics to trafficking girls and boys for their customers' dark appetites. Their tendrils spread out across the Kingdom of Lothon.

"That fat healer you work for's bendin' over and takin' it up the arse from the Boss. So you're as good as workin' for those pus-infected spawn! So you want me, gotta come up here and take my Black-damned head yourself!"

Avena hated how right Creg was. Dualayn *had* made a deal with Grey Kalon, the current leader of the Brotherhood. Early spring, a band of highwaymen had abducted Avena and Dualayn. The thugs had brought them to speak with Grey and his unusual associates. It had been how Avena met Ōbhin.

He'd killed Dualayn's bodyguard because he fought *with* Ust's band. Now Ōbhin was polishing his soul clean of the Black crimes he'd committed, finding the gleam that all humans possessed. Any could reflect Elohm's Colours if the grime was scoured clean.

Even that odious Creg upstairs.

"We have to rush him," Ōbhin whispered. "Ideas?"

She glanced around the room, not spotting any other stairs. The ceiling looked rickety. With Ōbhin's resonance sword, he could quickly cut a hole through it, but it would be hard to scramble up it. The ceiling was out of her reach though Ōbhin's greater height *might* let him snag it. Before any more ideas popped into her head, the blaring alarm ran out of power.

Used a small gem, she thought, her ears ringing.

Shouts echoed outside. Boyish. Enthusiastic. She glanced at the door to see a group of the youths, some almost her own age, forming up outside, a dozen or more holding makeshift weapons and all sporting green bandannas.

She realized why they wore green. Not to mark them as loyal to the Greens political faction, desiring a return of a dynasty of kings who had extinguished their bloodline in a civil war over eighty years ago, but to mark them as the local street gang. They pulled their bandannas up to cover their noses and mouths.

"Green-Face Boys!" she hissed to Ōbhin.

"Niszeh's Black Tone." He cursed to one of the pagan gods his people worshiped. "He paid them off."

"We're in *Rangers* territory," she said.

Ōbhin scowled and spat. "Can you hold them?"

He could do it with ease. A dozen boys against a resonance blade wielded by a trained swordsmen would be cut to ribbons. They'd be left bleeding and dying, limbs severed, bodies hacked apart with the same ease she'd find in slicing through warm cheese.

Ōbhin didn't want to kill these boys. The horror lurked in his eyes. He trusted her to find him another solution.

"Yes!" She glanced at the stairs. "What about the crossbow?"

Ōbhin darted into sight of Creg at the top of the stairs.

TWANG!

Ōbhin already moved, ducking back into cover as the crossbow hurtled down and impaled the floor near its brethren. Ōbhin pounded up the stairs before Creg could reload. She heard a vile curse from above. A crossbow hurtled down at Ōbhin. He raised his left arm in warding. The heavy, wooden stock slammed into the chain covering his forearm. Metal rattled. He grunted, kept running.

She scrambled to the right and rushed at the door, gripping her binder tight.

It would be an effective club even without her enhanced strength. However, its amethyst jewelchine had an additional effect that triggered on a hard impact. It tangled up those struck in bonds of purple energy for a quarter of an hour or so, squeezing limbs tight to torso and tripping up legs.

It took a great level of strength to break free.

She reached the front door and faced the mass of ruffians and young hooligans rushing at her. She kicked the door shut and fell into the fighting stance Ōbhin had taught her; weight on her back foot, her right foot pointed towards the direction of attack, her body turned sideways to provide the smallest profile to her enemies.

Boys shouted outside as she raised her binder into a guard position.

2

Ōbhin's head throbbed from the stock of Creg's thrown crossbow clipping his temple as it tumbled past. A wet heat trickled down from the ache. Boots thudded on the landing on the second floor. Creg appeared again, another crossbow held in his hand. Ōbhin cursed, diving against the stairs' wall.

TWANG!

The crossbow's limbs snapped forward. The bolt blurred past him, the wind of its passage kissed across his cheek. It slammed into the wall below. Creg snarled and retreated down the hallway, his boots pounding on the hardwood. A door slammed shut.

Ōbhin's heart pumped thundering fear through his veins. At close range, no amount of chain would protect him from a bodkin-tipped crossbow quarrel. He felt naked. Caution slowed his climb, his resonance blade out before him. He took each step with care while banging and shouts echoed below.

Avena had skill with her binder. She could tangle up the ruffians with the energy. She had come far from the riot last spring, spending every day drilling with his guards.

With that fake Smiles.

Ōbhin's hackles raised. He wanted to learn more about the thing masquerading as Smiles, and what Ust's men had done with Carstin's body.

Most of all, he burned to know where Dje'awsa lurked. The dark sorcerer who had unleashed the dead in the foggy streets of Kash and transformed Ust into a monster with blood magic and strangely cut gem utilizing the dark power of forbidden obsidian.

"You don't want to fight me, Creg," Ōbhin growled as he reached the second-floor landing. The hallway ran in several directions from here, doors lining them. He stared at the three through which Creg could have retreated. He advanced to his right. "You know you can't beat me even without my resonance blade. You're good with the backsword, but you're not better than me."

Fighting roared from below now as he crept down the hallway. The pounding of his own heart, pumping screaming blood through his ears, almost drowned out all other sounds. Beads of sweat worked down from his scalp to soak into his eyebrows. Some dribbled through, hot salt stinging his eyes.

Which door? If he chose wrong, Creg would pop out and put a bolt in his back.

A door creaked behind him.

~

The front door burst open. Avena acted.

Emerald light burned from the network of gems in her earthen gauntlets, mixing with the purple glowing from the bottom of her binder. She swung. Metal streaked and slammed into the shoulder of the first Green-Faced Boy who charged through the doorway.

His collarbone broke with an audible snap. He screamed in pain. Purple light flared about him, draping diagonally about his torso like a sash. It pinned his left arm to his side while his right spasmed, dropping the sap—a bag full of dense sand used to knock out a mugging victim—to his feet. He fell back into his friends.

"That Black-cursed quim broke my shoulder!" he howled as his friends shoved him to the side.

A scrawny youth with a rusty fish knife cleared the scramble. He thrust his blade at her chest. She retreated. Her binder flicked out and smashed into his arm. Bone snapped, twisting his arm the wrong way at the elbow. He screamed and dropped the fish knife. His friends boiled in behind him, knocking him to the side, the binding energy squeezing about his torso.

Two bigger youths swung heavy cudgels at her at the same time. She flowed into a guard stance as her feet danced. She blocked one with her binder. Purple energy burst across his weapon and snagged the nearest part of him: his head. It drove his own stave into his head, striking him hard and sending him reeling.

The other slammed his makeshift mace into her side. The gambeson's padding absorbed some of the blow, but she grunted, staggering to the side. The bruise already swelled across her lower ribs, radiating throbbing pain up her left side.

Her exhilaration swallowed the sensation as she pivoted and slammed her binder into his upper thigh. He grunted as the purple energy engulfed both legs and yanked them together. Off-balance, he crashed to the floor, pounding a fist against it in a snarl of pain.

The others rushed at her, leaping over their fallen comrades. She danced back through the room, swinging her binder in vast arcs before her. She changed her fighting tactics with so many around her, seeking to hold them at bay as they struggled to surround her. Brass knuckles gleamed on fists punching towards her. Saps swung in viscous arcs at her head. Staves blurred in powerful swipes.

Her feet moved, a graceful jig that pulled her away from them while her binder cracked into limbs. She broke arms and legs, tangled up limbs in purple energy. They fell to the ground, tripping up their green-masked comrades.

"Get that pus-filled quim!" howled a tough on his back, clutching a shattered knee, his legs bound tight.

"Someone seize her from behind!"

"Tooth, break her skull in."

"Stop being a Black-cursed coward and batter that wench down!"

She savored the power. Her earthen gauntlet let her inflict even more debilitating damage. So long as she didn't hit heads, she wouldn't kill any of them. She would leave them with broken bones, unable to thieve for months or longer.

Maybe they'd find an honest profession.

She smacked a boy, whose blond hair proclaimed Roidanese blood, in the side. Her brown braid danced behind her as she whirled to hit the tough coming up behind her from the fireplace. He didn't have a weapon in his hand. Only a closed, dirty fist. She readied for his punch.

It didn't come.

He threw thick soot into her face. Pain stung her eyes. The world went dark as she squeezed them shut. Grit abraded the sensitive surface of her eyes. Tears sprang from the corners. She squeaked out in shock, her footsteps faltering.

A hard blow slammed into her stomach. Air burst from her lungs. She staggered and fell to her knees, struggling to breathe. To see. Spittle spilled over her chin as she gasped, pain radiating up through her abdomen.

"That'll teach you your place, wench," snarled an angry voice.

Ōbhin threw himself to the floor in a clatter of rattling mail.

His resonance blade punched through the floor like it was made of the thinnest Demochian silk. A quarrel buzzed over his head and smashed through the cheap window at the hallway's end. The bubbled glass shattered, glittering shards spilling across the floor.

Ōbhin pressed himself up to his feet and whirled around to see Creg darting into a door on the left side of the hallway. There was only one other door on that side near Ōbhin. He darted for it and kicked it open. Cheap, dry wood burst in splinters. He rushed through the wreckage into a long room running the length of the hallway. Creg was at the other end by a bed. Several crossbows, cocked and loaded, lay on it. He had another one in hand, aimed at the door he'd *expected* Ōbhin to come through.

Creg pivoted and leveled the weapon at Ōbhin. Tension squeezed about the Qothian's throat. Twenty cubits between the two. Ten strides at a running pace. He'd never make it before the trigger pulled. However, a chest of drawers stood along the wall on the edge of a throw rug only three cubits away; the only cover between Ōbhin and Creg.

Ōbhin growled, "How many of those do you have stashed through the house?"

"Enough," Creg said. He sniffled, snot bubbling around his right nostril. "Heard you were lookin' for me."

"I'm wondering why you're resonating with the Rangers' filthy Tone now."

A sneer crossed the scrawny man's face. "The Rangers welcome a man with skill. The Boss thought to dump his piss-filled chamber pot on me 'cause of Ust."

Ōbhin darted for the chest of drawers.

TWANG!

He slammed into the side of the chest of drawers. The crossbow struck the wall behind Ōbhin. Creg cursed as the Qothian burst out from behind his cover to cross the rest of the room at a sprint. The scrawny man lunged for the bed and his waiting crossbows.

Ōbhin's right foot stepped on the small throw rug.

Nothing lay beneath it.

The rug rustled as Ōbhin's weight plunged through it into a small hole. His left boot still stood on a solid floor, but his right slammed down and broke through the lath-and plaster ceiling of the first floor. He dropped to his knee, jagged wood scraping against his leather boot.

Creg grinned and picked up his next crossbow.

Avena swung blind before her, a hard and brutal attack that held nothing back. She screamed through the pain radiating up her stomach. It turned into a choking cough, soot thick in her mouth. A curse burst before her then her weapon crashed hard into a solid body.

Her attacker landed screaming on the floor. She blinked and wiped at her eyes with her left sleeve. She gained her feet, panting. Sooty tears spilled down her cheeks. Raw, red veins ran through the stained whites of her eyes. She gazed across the blurry sitting room and adjoining kitchen.

Thugs and street ruffians lay in bound, groaning piles. The one who'd blinded her groaned at her feet. He looked to have been the last one still able to fight. She panted and groaned, leaning on the butt of her weapon, struggling to regain her breath.

A booted foot burst through the ceiling.

Avena gaped at it. Ōbhin's boot. She recognized the brown hue and the worn creases. She heard him grunt, his leg swinging as he struggled to yank it free. A spike of fear for the swordsman shot through her, a terror she hadn't felt in many years.

Flashes of that horrible waiting outside Dualayn's lab filled her, helpless to do anything as she worried if the first man she'd loved would live or die.

Deeper memories from the day Evane died dredged up that awful emptiness from her soul's depths. Both galvanized her into action.

She'd vowed to never stand by helpless again. She'd let Evane drown. She'd hadn't known how to assist Dualayn in curing Chames. She wasn't a helpless girl any longer. She was a woman of twenty winters.

She rushed for the stairs.

Creg aimed up the crossbow with a large grin on his face. He moved in an almost lazy fashion as Ōbhin struggled to rip his leg free. The top of his boot was caught on a broken slat. Desperation pounded through Ōbhin's veins as Creg grinned, a line of yellowish snot running to his crusty upper lip.

"Always did think you were better than me," he said. "Now, let's tal—"

Ōbhin had only one attack left. He threw his resonance blade.

The humming sword tumbled through the air. Fear flashed across Creg's face, painted by the spinning emerald. The bandit swung his crossbow to bat the blade aside. The sword sliced through the left arm of the crossbow. The force of the cocked string snapped the severed part back, slamming it into Creg's shoulder. The swinging stock of the weapon crashed into the side of the sword.

Resonance blades cut only with their edge.

The blow sent the blade spinning to Ōbhin's right. It buried into the wall beside the door Creg had waited by. The tulwar sunk to the crossguard, the projections of steel stopping the blade from spearing through the wall.

"Black-cursed bastard," snarled Creg as the blow from the ruined crossbow sent him stumbling onto the bed. His left arm hung twisted, pain burning across his face.

Ōbhin heaved with both hands planted on the floor and snapped the piece of wood caught on his boot. He jerked his leg free of the hole. Chainmail rattled as he rushed for his blade embedded in the wall. Footsteps banged up the stairs. Avena cried out; her words were muffled by the hot blood pounding through Ōbhin's ears.

Out of the corner of his eye, he caught Creg throwing himself off the bed. The man drew his backsword, a single-edged straight blade favored in Lothon.

The bandit howled and rushed at Ōbhin, raising his weapon high to deliver a powerful strike.

"Ōbhin!" Avena's words were clearer.

His black-gloved hand gripped the leather-wrapped handle of his resonance blade, the emerald shining bright. He wrenched it free of the wall and turned around to see slicing death coming for him.

"I'm coming!" shouted Avena as Ōbhin slashed his sword before him.

It was an instinctive swing, and a bad one. Ōbhin's training recognized it as his blade cut through the end of Creg's sword. Momentum didn't stop. It was conserved. He severed through half the sword; the top half now tumbled in a deadly arc at him.

He was trained to fight with a resonance blade. He knew his opponent's weapon was still lethal after being severed. So his feet were already dancing beneath him, his body twisting sideways out of instincts drilled into him on the dueling sands. The severed end of the sword flashed past him even as he flowed into his next attack.

A disabling slice to Creg's leg.

Avena gave a frightful shriek behind him. A bone-crunching blow echoed followed by the thudding of a body hitting the floor. Ōbhin's heart clenched as he finished his cut, severing through Creg's right leg above the knee.

Ōbhin whirled around as the bandit howled in pain. Creg fell with a painful thud on the ground. The coppery scent of blood filled the air. It spurted from the stump of the bandit's leg, splashing Ōbhin's boots.

Ōbhin finished his turn. His heart stopped.

The end of Creg's sword had tumbled through the open doorway and slammed into Avena's head. A half-cubit of blade had punched through her temple above her left eye. Blood oozed around the steel while her body twitched and spasmed on the floor.

Horror punched Ōbhin in the guts. His hand holding his sword trembled as he stared in dumbfounded shock.

"Avena?" he croaked.

3

"You cut off my Black-damned leg!" howled Creg. Something struck Ōbhin in the back, rustling his chainmail. The lower half of the backsword clattered at his feet.

Ōbhin stared at Avena as an avalanche of guilt engulfed him. The crushing horror swept about him like the rush of snow spilling down a mountain slope. It choked him. He didn't remember turning off his resonance blade and sheathing it. He didn't hear Creg's curses while the blood pumped from the stump of his leg.

"Avena?" croaked from Ōbhin's lips, a sound of boyish fright.

I heard her coming, lashed through his mind. *She was racing up the stairs to help me. I stepped aside and let this happen. It wouldn't have penetrated my armor. I could have taken it on my shoulder and been fine.*

He knelt over her, staring in horror at her twitching body. Her eyes danced beneath her eyelids. He could see a bit of spittle bubbling at the corner of her mouth. He ripped off his black glove, not caring that he exposed his hand before a woman, and held it over her mouth and nose.

He felt the warmth of her breath on his hand.

"Aliiva's motherly love," he gasped, crying out to the Tone of Mothers whose touch soothed. Topazes were the gem that resonated with Aliiva's harmony. The jewels that healed.

Dualayn!

His employer's name crashed through the heavy snows of guilt smothering Ōbhin. If she survived long enough, Dualayn was the only man in the world with the skill to save her. His topaz healers and knowledge of anatomy *might* be enough.

Had to be enough.

A mad hope seized Ōbhin. He scooped up Avena in his arms with care, wincing as her head lolled. The end of the backsword thrusting out of her skull quivered. Her entire body convulsed in his arms for a moment.

"Just hold on, Avena," he snarled, not realizing he spoke Qothian, his native tongue. A language she couldn't understand. "Aliiva, let your loving Tone sustain her and, Vatsim, let your music sing strength through my limbs."

He left Creg howling obscenities. Nothing else mattered to Ōbhin. He raced with single-minded madness. He crashed down the stairs and leaped over the groaning, bound bodies of the Green-Faced Boys. He burst onto the street, passersby gasping in shock. A woman screamed. A man shouted.

Their words spilled like rainwater over oilcloth.

He ran.

His legs stretched out before him, chainmail armor rattling as he raced through the slums. He held something more precious than his life in his arms. He glanced down at her face, more blood trickling out around the sword. It spilled over her eye. She wept a crimson tear.

His boots thudded on worn cobblestones. The summer sun glinted off the piece of the backsword, dazzling his eyes at times. He raced along the Greenwine and its sludgy waters. It flowed towards the Ustern, the mighty river bisecting Kash in half. People parted out of his way like waves before the prow of a sailing ship, fleeing the murderous intensity in his gaze.

Fear lashed at him to go faster.

Legs burned. He sucked in lungfuls of air. Drilling his guards, forcing them to run every day, had given him the endurance to push past the protesting muscles. He ignored the coppery taste building at the back of his throat.

Sustain her life, Aliiva. Please!

Avena had been the bright ray that led him out of his darkness. She hadn't let him sink back into a simpler life of drifting through misery. She had convinced him to stay on the harder path. Together, they would polish the guilt and filth off their souls, to let their diamonds shine brilliantly.

I can't have killed her.

The darkness pressed in on him as he ran. He could feel it threatening to devour his world. He'd returned to Niszeh's Black Tone, allowing disharmony to control his life again. Becoming a cold killer ruled by apathy, a sword swinging without any care. A pawn of men like Ust and Grey.

He reached Greenway Bridge and raced over the stone structure built across the Ustern. He heard shouts from the guardsmen wearing the white stag on their green and blue tabards. They chased after him, shouting at him to stop.

"Filthy Tethyrian! What did you do to that girl?"

Killed her, thought Ōbhin. His eyes flicked down to her. More blood trickled out to stain her face. She still bled. That had to be a good sign.

Her body twitched as he ran. The spasms rippled down her arms and torqued her body in his grip. He pounded across the bridge with long strides. The guards were shouting behind him, their voices growing distant. He passed wagons, the teamsters, wearing white or green armbands, glancing at him with bored ease.

None helped the guards. They were seen as extensions of the Blues who'd won the war and ruled the country.

He crossed the bridge into the Slops, another slum created when Kash spilled out of its ancient walls and sprawled up the Ustern from the bay. The stench of pig dung filled his nose, wafting from the holding pens where sounders of swine awaited slaughter in the new assembly line abattoirs.

The lanes wound through this district, a mad meander. Children playing in the street shrieked as he rushed by. Boys waved sticks and girls clutched skirts to hide their faces. He could see the first hint of green hills. Lake Ophavin lay to the south. The pastoral areas were where many of the wealthy built homes and complained about the encroachment of the city's slums.

It had been a quarter of an hour since she'd been injured, and his leg muscles had transmuted into heavy lead. Halfway there. Now he raced through the Slops. Laborers stared at him with exhausted expressions, faces smeared with soot. Women gasped as they gossiped on the porches of rickety tenement buildings.

He hardly noticed any of it. He raced through the city, passing shops and carts selling wormy turnips or day-old fish. Her spasms worsened as he neared the edge of the slum, the buildings thinning into houses with small gardens, the homes whitewashed and mostly in good repair. The women here shrieked as they hung laundry on lines or beat dusty rugs. Children peered at him through the gap between fence slats.

When he entered the familiar lane that wrapped around Lake Ophavin and led to the south shore where Dualayn's estate lay, he fought to hold onto her spasming form. He passed the high fences of the wealthy, walls made of river stone or high-quality brick. Cultivated vines grew up some, and all were topped by rows of spiked wrought iron, deadly obstacles for any would-be thief despite the artistry many possessed.

Guards at the gates peered at him with suspicion before relaxing. A few cried out to Ōbhin, recognizing him. He knew most of the guards of Dualayn's neighbors. He ignored the offers for help as he raced down the hard-packed dirt lane.

He darted around the approaching carriage of Lord Dynith Marey who sat high in the Parliament's House of Nobles. The groom wore a stiff coat of dark-red with a blue ascot about his throat.

Ōbhin counted houses now. He passed the Chabrith House then the Marey Estate.

Three to go.

He raced past the Vinhastin Estate with its walls made of pink stone and grounds dotted with white geese that filled the air with their honking.

Two to go.

The estate of Lady Demett flashed by, walls covered in a thick layer of cream ivy, iron spikes poking through the foliage.

One to go.

He pushed through the last reserves of his stamina, sweat pouring down his brown face. It stung his eyes. He kept running as Avena's spasms worsened. Froth beaded her lips. Fright clutched at his chest as he raced past the Tophreyn Estate. Then there was a gap filled with the blackberry hill, a small tor topped by trees and covered in the eponymous bushes. They were in full flower, a riot of pink blossoms dotting the thorny slope.

Ōbhin focused only on the brick walls and the large main gates. Fingers lounged out front. The older guard had become Ōbhin's second-in-command. He was smoking a blackroot cigar and staring down at his boots. The man looked up.

Avena bucked hard in Ōbhin's arms, almost spilling from his grip.

Horror crossed the older guard's bluff face and bulbous nose. The dark cigar fell burning from his lips. It struck his jerkin and spun off in a shower of sparks. He straightened up as Ōbhin closed the distance between them.

"Elohm's Colours, what happened to her?" Fingers asked, voice half-strangled. "Smiles, get the Black-damned gate open!"

He rushed towards Ōbhin and then stopped a few paces away. He opened his mouth to say something then snapped it shut as he whirled around. "Smiles, I said to get this Black-damned gate open!"

The wrought iron gates of the estate swung outward, pushed open by the thing masquerading as Smiles, a guard Ōbhin's age. Ōbhin feared his friend was dead, his body dumped in a shallow grave. The thing pretending to be Smiles looked like him, even acted like him down to the man's jovial manner and easy smiles.

The creature's grin melted away in a simulation of horror and fright so honest and real that Ōbhin almost believed it was the real Smiles.

"Avena," the fake-Smiles gasped, his dark eyes widening. He had a mop of light-brown hair, a tall man with a narrow nose. "Elohm's Colours, there's a half-cubit of steel in her head. How is she alive?"

"She just is!" growled Ōbhin, exhaustion burning through his body. "Get Dualayn! Now!"

Smiles bolted across the wilting grass and up the hill towards the large manor house. Ōbhin followed after, Fingers jogging at his side. On the slope to his left, Joayne stopped pushing her charge's wheelchair. The withered Bravine, Dualayn's long-invalid wife, slumped uncomprehending in her seat.

Avena thrashed hard in Ōbhin's arms. He stumbled, clutching desperately to her.

"We're almost there," he said, terrified of dropping her. He didn't understand how she could be still alive after the half-hour it had taken him to run here. He pushed himself as fast as he could, so he couldn't lose her now. "Just hold on. Aliiva, sustain her with your Tone a little longer."

Smiles threw open the new doors of the manor house, replaced when Ust had battered them down. He rushed inside, his shouts echoing. Fingers muttered prayers to Elohm, the singular god revered by the Lothonians and others who dwelt on the Arngelsh Isles.

As Ōbhin neared the doors, the manor house's marble exterior rising above him, relief surged through him. Dualayn crossed the entrance hall from his laboratory, Smiles trailing behind him like a frightened puppy.

The rotund, older man wore his usual dark waistcoat, this one a blue verging on midnight. He rubbed his soft hands before him, his plump face paling as Ōbhin slowed to a stop on the porch. He sucked in breaths while Dualayn pulled out his monocle to study Avena's injury.

"Colours, no," he said. "That is deep in her brain."

"Can you . . . help her?" Ōbhin snarled through his exhaustion. A dizzy wave swept through him.

"I will do my best," Dualayn said. "Oh, child, what have you done to yourself?"

He touched her forehead with a gentle caress, a father stroking his daughter. A scream echoed from upstairs. One of the maids, Smiles's wife Jilly, raced down them while a pile of laundered linens spilled around her feet.

"Avena!" Jilly cried and threw herself at the thing pretending to be her husband. Smiles wrapped her up in an embrace, comforting his "wife."

"This way," Dualayn said. "Hurry."

Ōbhin followed the scholar and healer across the repaired entrance hall and around the base of the staircase to the open door to his lab. Avena jerked again, her body twisting. She let out a terrible groan of pain.

"Why is she thrashing?" Ōbhin asked.

"She's bleeding in her brain," said Dualayn. "The fluid can't escape the skull, so it's putting pressure on her brain which, in turn, is affecting her body. She's lucky she was hit so high up. Lower down, near the back of the neck, is where her breathing and heartbeat are controlled."

"What's up here?" asked Ōbhin as he followed Dualayn into the lab.

"Emotions, memories, personalities. She might never recover. I have been reading the Recorder on brain regeneration—for my wife—and I've found out much, but there are still things I don't understand. I have ideas, things I shall try, but . . ." Worried pain flashed across Dualayn's face. "I want her to recover, too. I do, but you must be prepared for a suboptimal outcome."

"She'll die?"

"Perhaps. Or she might never fully recover. One half of her body might be paralyzed. Look at her face. You can see the right side is drooping with palsy."

Ōbhin stared in horror at how the muscles on half her face seemed to have relaxed, growing soft like rain-sodden clay. It pulled at her eyelid and cheek, her lower lip tugged down.

"Her personality might never be the same. Blows to the head are never simple, but I think I can repair her. I need your help with the first stage."

"Anything."

"Set her with care on my table, then we're going to wash our hands. Thoroughly. You'll have to remove those gloves."

Ōbhin nodded. He set Avena down on the wooden table, covered with a white sheet, that dominated the center of the lab. The air smelled heavily of lye, the scent almost burning his nose. Ōbhin pulled his hands away from Avena, her left side, opposite from her brain injury, twitching more than her right. He swallowed and glanced down at his gloves. Some of her blood had stained them, gleaming bright and crimson.

This is all my fault.

4

Dualayn emerged from the vault at the end of his lab holding two of the topaz healers, each the size of a woman's fist, and a handful of other topazes that were the size of marbles. Beyond, Ōbhin glimpsed shelves covered in all manner of gems: diamonds, emeralds, rubies, sapphires, amethysts, heliodors, and topazes. The seven wholesome jewels. Some were cut, others rough, and a few were wrapped up in wire, some sort of jewelchines.

Panic gripping him, Ōbhin was finding his mind seizing on anything to focus upon but Avena. He stared at the healers. Each was bound in gold wire, the best of the seven metals you could use with them. The cheaper the metal, the lesser the effect. Ōbhin didn't know what the smaller topazes were for. He was under the impression that healers required a big stone to put out enough power to do anything.

Dualayn set the gems on a cloth beside Avena's twitching body. He glanced at Ōbhin. "You didn't wash your hands. Come on, we don't have time for dawdling."

"Then let's do it," Ōbhin growled.

"We can't let any microbial into her," Dualayn said, his tone cracking. "What is the point in saving her if we deliver an infection that could kill her? Wash!"

Ōbhin had never heard the man sound so commanding. Dualayn marched towards the washbasin, rolling up the sleeves of his shirt. It had an aquifer jewelchine inserted into a porcelain spigot. Dualayn tapped the top and water gushed from the sapphire. He plunged his hands in them, wetting them, and grabbed a bar of lye soap. He scrubbed; subs appeared.

Ōbhin peeled off his gloves. He rarely took them off during the day. It wasn't proper for a man to be seen with his hands naked. The Lothonians had strange customs. Men bare-handed and women bare-faced. He didn't know what these "microbial" were, but he wasn't risking Avena's life.

Dualayn handed over the soap. Ōbhin scrubbed his brown hands with the white suds. He worked fast, the water vanishing down the drain, his thoughts drifting through recriminations. *I didn't know she was behind me,* part of him protested against the dark guilt pressing around him.

Finished, Ōbhin turned to find Dualayn anointing the small topazes with wood alcohol. The sharp, antiseptic scent stung the Qothian's nose. Then Dualayn picked up a scalpel, a small emerald inserted at the base wrapped in gold wire.

"A resonance knife?" Ōbhin asked.

"Yes. I observed the way the emerald on your tulwar is cut and wrapped by the wires." Dualayn drew in a deep, perhaps fortifying breath. "Now, I need you to hold her head still."

Ōbhin gripped the sides of Avena's head, his naked fingers sliding over her brown tresses. Dualayn grabbed the end of the backsword in tight hands and pulled. The steely grind of metal on bone clenched Ōbhin's jaw. Avena bucked as the blade came free, coated in a smear of her blood. More oozed out, mixed with a clear liquid.

Her spasms slowed. Stopped.

"Okay," Dualayn said, setting the length of blood-smeared metal down beside her and grabbing a healer. He activated it and pressed the jewelchine into her throat. "This will keep her alive for the next part." He tied the gem in place with a linen bandage, the orange light bleeding through the cloth.

"Next part?" Ōbhin asked, staring at the blood oozing out of the hole in her head, matting her hair.

"We're going to sit her up," Dualayn explained. "You need to hold her head still by the base of her head and her jaw. No higher."

"Okay," Ōbhin answered slowly. It sounded like no healing procedure he recognized. "Why?"

Dualayn picked up the scalpel. "I'm going to remove the top of her skull."

"What?" roared Ōbhin. "You'll kill her. Her brain will fall out."

"It's attached to her body by the spinal cords, the retinal nerves, the auditory nerves, and a few others. The level of anatomical knowledge I have learned from the Recorder is amazing. This was something the ancients used to do. Brain surgery, they called it. They healed traumatic injuries with skills and knowledge I barely grasp. I promise you, this is her only chance. I can't reduce the swelling without at least trepanning her. That's drilling a hole in her skull to let the fluids drain. This will, I hope, let me repair the damage directly. Now sit her up!"

Dualayn's command came with the intensity of a sword instructor. Ōbhin reacted like he would to the man who'd taught him to fight with a resonance blade in service of the Satrap of Qoth. With care, he sat Avena upright. Her head leaned back, not supported by her neck. He shifted his hand to the base of her skull, cradling her.

"I don't have time to shave her," Dualayn muttered. "I'm terrified this will be too late as is . . ." He sliced through her braid of hair with the scalpel. It fell to the table. Her shortened hair swayed loose about her head. He activated the scalpel's emerald.

It resonated.

Ōbhin fought against his pounding heart to hold her head still as Dualayn worked. Supreme concentration tensed every muscle in the older man's plump face. He cut the blade through her skull like it didn't exist. He worked slowly, pushing her hair out of the way while circling her head. Blood oozed from the line he cut, soaking into her tresses.

The muscles in Ōbhin's arms burned from the strain of holding her in place. His chainmail armor weighed on him. It clinked, the only other sound besides the humming of the resonance knife cutting through Avena's skull.

This is insane, Ōbhin thought over and over. *It'll kill her. You can't take a person's skull off. That's what protects their mind.*

Stray strands of her hair drifted off, severed as effortlessly by the vibrating knife as Avena's skull. He held the blade just so, controlling the depth of his incision. Dualayn moved around the table, standing shoulder to shoulder with Ōbhin to finish. He made the last cut a straight line made with delicate care. He crossed her temple. Blood trickled down to her eyebrows. He neared where he'd begun as he passed beneath her wound.

Finished.

He turned off the scalpel and set it down. He grasped the top of Avena's head and, with great care, lifted it.

Ōbhin stared with a strange mix of horror and fascination at Avena's brain. Two gray-lobes of white wrinkled and folded flesh joined by a small canyon. It reminded him of dried prunes sold by hawkers. Veins wound through the matter. Dualayn's scalpel didn't seem to have cut her brain. The only wound was the bleeding gash from the sword. Dark blood oozed out, the organ inflamed around it, swollen and bulging.

"Avena," Ōbhin croaked. His entire body trembled. He feared to breathe, terrified of dislodging the seat of her very being.

"I know," Dualayn whispered. "Okay, now lay her back down gently. Don't worry. Her brain won't fall out. Just go slow."

Like he lowered a newborn infant to the cradle, Ōbhin leaned Avena back. His hand held the back of her head, what remained of it, while Dualayn placed a small mound of clean linens for her to rest upon. Ōbhin settled her down on it and slipped his hand away.

He shook worse than he had after any fight. He felt drained by the act of witnessing the surgery. His chainmail rustled as he took a step back. His naked hands clenched. He struggled to breathe, his armor weighing at him.

His guilt.

Dualayn picked up five of the small topazes. He placed them on the wrinkled tissues of her brain, forming a circle around the injury. Staving off his despair, Ōbhin stared with questions. Something was missing.

"They're not . . ." Ōbhin cleared his emotion-choked throat. "They're not connected by wires. They're just jewels."

"I had always dismissed rumors I'd heard of Bofozujimnizemvev"—Dualayn said the mouthful of syllables with ease—"the Forbidden Kingdom. You must have heard of it."

"South of the Shattered Islands. They don't like outsiders much."

"No." He went to a drawer and opened it. He pulled out a tuning fork. "They were said to use 'proper harmonics' to activate gems. I thought it nonsense, of course." He struck the tuning fork against the edge of the metal table.

Its pure note, a high buzzing, resonated through the room. The five topazes on her head lit up with an orange glow. Ōbhin gasped and stepped back at the miraculous sight. Dualayn set the tuning fork up right beside her, the twin tines blurring from their rapid motion.

"Aliiva's motherly compassion," Ōbhin whispered.

"The Recorder spoke of using a specific frequency of sound waves to produce an effect in gems," said Dualayn. "I hope this is what they meant when they talked about brain regeneration."

Ōbhin took a step closer, reaching out a hesitant hand to Avena, then pulled back. He turned and grabbed his gloves he'd tossed onto the workbench. He pulled on the leather, covering his hands in black. Blood still stained the left, dried and crusting.

He trembled, his eyes looking everywhere but her. He took in the laboratory, fully seeing it for the first time since entering. The room used to be a dining hall. At the far end was the vault door that held Dualayn's collection of jewels. Besides the washbasin, cabinets lined the other walls full of all manner of items. Some were open, showing racks of jars and pots, others closed and locked. Among the visible containers, about half were sealed with wax while others were stoppered with cork. Diagrams decorated one wall, schematics for wire bending beside images of human anatomy, the outer layers of skin and muscles appearing to be flayed away to reveal the organism beneath. Another wooden worktable lay beneath the diagrams, covered in the small pliers, delicate chisels, and tiny hammers necessary to shape jewel machines.

The Recorder sat there, the strange and massive jewelchine that Dualayn had found in the Red Heart of the Forest, the center of the Upfing Forest. Every tree there, along with all the grass, had been stained red. It appeared centered around ruins that predated the Shattering, when Niszeh had destroyed the Harmony of the Tone, creating the Seven Good and the one Black.

To the Lothonians, they believed it was when Elohm's perfect people were ruined by the Black.

Either way, it had devastated lands far to the east, creating the Shattered Islands, and ended the legendary civilization that used to dominate the world. The Recorder, an amethyst and emerald gem somehow grown together in a spiraling helix *around* the wiring, held ancient knowledge.

Dualayn was studying it with a primer he'd received from the Brotherhood and their mysterious benefactor, the White Lady.

"You can go now," Dualayn said. "I have her, Ōbhin."

"What?" Ōbhin whirled around to stare at the older man. "No, no, what if you need more of my help?"

"I am fine on my own," he said. He was pulling down jars from a cabinet. "Now it's just a matter of keeping her alive to heal. I can do that on my own. This might take days. Even a week or longer. I'll take care of her. I don't need to be distracted by your worrying and pacing and muttering."

"You sure?"

"No one loves her more than I do," Dualayn said. "If Bravine and I had a daughter, I'd imagined she'd be like Avena. After my son died . . ." The old man drew a deep breath. "She almost was my daughter. If I hadn't failed with Chames, she would be. I won't fail her, Ōbhin. I promise you."

5

Ōbhin scrubbed Avena's blood off his glove with a fistful of grass, staining the green red. He spat on the leather and buffed more away. His eyes were distant, seeing past them to that moment in time. One little decision had irrevocably changed Avena's life.

For the last Lothonian month, two of his own people's lunar months, he'd spent most days in her company. When she wasn't working with Dualayn in the lab or tinkering with her own jewelchines, she was practicing and drilling with his guards. She was his confidant, the only one he could confide in when his loathing for the thing masquerading as Smiles grew too much. They were united in protecting Dualayn from his deal with the Brotherhood. When Dualayn uncovered the secret Grey and the White Lady needed from the Recorder, Ōbhin was certain it would end badly.

They had to protect him. His skills were remarkable. If he could heal her brain injury . . . No one recovered from injuries like that.

The creak of wheels drew his eyes to Joayne pushing Dualayn's invalid wife across the grounds. She did that whenever it was sunny, giving the woman fresh air. Bravine never seemed to notice. She just drooled, her mind destroyed by an inept physician after a fall broke her neck.

One simple decision. Choose the wrong doctor. Dodge the wrong piece of metal.

The front door creaked open. Ōbhin glanced behind, for a moment hoping it was Dualayn with good news before foolishness rippled through him. It was too soon. *It'll be days. Maybe even a week before she's up and about.*

She will recover. She's a fighter.

It was Fingers. The older guard, nicknamed for his swollen knuckles and his habit of popping them, stumbled out. He wore a gambeson, his binder hanging from a leather belt. He had a backsword on the other hip. His bulbous nose had lost its usual redness. His eyes were distant. He ran a hand through graying hair.

"How is she?" he asked Ōbhin, stumbling, almost drunk.

"Dualayn's trying something he learned from the Recorder."

"She can't die," Fingers croaked. "She's so young. Twenty . . . She should be married. Have her first babe sucklin' at her teat, not . . ." His eyes flicked to Ōbhin. "What were you two doin'? You rushed outta here like you were marchin' to battle. Now she's got a length of sword stuck in her head."

"Looking up an old friend," said Ōbhin. "Trying to figure out what happened to Carstin's body."

"Thought that damned sorcerer got it. The one who turned your ol' bandit leader into a monster."

Ōbhin shuddered at the memory of Dje'awsa. A foreign sorcerer with strange tattoos like jagged lightning bolts wrapped around his shaved head. He served the White Lady, as dark as she was bright. He used jewels in a way that could only be called magic. Right out of campfire tales. He'd turned the dead into shambling corpses and transformed Ust into a brute with inhuman strength and speed.

Dje'awsa used *obsidian*. The eighth gem. The one different from the others, brittle and birthed in violence. The gem associated with Niszeh and disharmony. They were forbidden to be used in civilized lands.

"Maybe," Ōbhin said. "I don't know. I wanted answers and now . . ." Now he stood motionless. His Avena was lying in there, maybe dying, and all he did was nothing. He had sworn to protect Dualayn and his people.

Protect her? He'd led her right into the fray.

"She wouldn't have stayed back," Fingers said. "Too stubborn by half."

Nearby, the skinny Bran lurked. He was the youngest of the guards, the youngest son of Joayne. He was gangly and his face pale. He was off-duty, wearing the red jacket he'd won while gambling at the Plucked Rooster. "She gonna be fine?"

"She's strong," grunted Fingers. "You go tell everyone that. Dualayn's got her in hand. Nothin' to worry 'bout."

Bran nodded and darted off.

"What are her chances?" Fingers asked, voice lower. This hopelessness filled his eyes once more.

"I don't know." The ground beneath his feet felt like loose sand. He remembered the earthquake that rocked Gunya, the Capital of Qoth. He had been on the Sands of Truth, facing Taim, when it struck. The ground had flowed beneath him. Became untrustworthy. Now he felt like he could plummet into darkness at any moment. "She might never be the same even if she wakes up."

"Elohm's bright Colours," breathed Fingers. He formed the prism before him, drawing it with his pointer digit.

"I didn't know you were so close with her," Ōbhin said. "You hardly say a word to her."

"She reminds me of my wife, you know. That same headstrong stubbornness." For a moment, a smile crossed Fingers's lips. "What I like 'bout Avena."

"Does she ever write you back?" Ōbhin asked. "Your wife?"

Fingers shook his head. "Why should she?"

He was estranged from his wife. He blustered that she'd cheated on him with the miller, or sometimes the baker, but the older man had confessed he'd hurt her and fled, ashamed and afraid he'd do worse. He sent her money and wrote to her every payday.

"I loved her the moment I saw her, you know," said Fingers. "It was a strikin' moment. She weren't from my village but from two over. Took a day's walk to reach it. Don't remember why I was even there, to be honest. It was the Feast of Auburn, and she were dancin' 'round the Plenty Pillar with the other unmarried girls. I saw her, and she stole all the color from the world. They all flowed into her. The only bit of vibrancy left."

Ōbhin shifted. He remembered the day he'd fallen in love with Foonauri. He'd been a boy of ten or so, playing when he'd spied on her wearing her maiden's mask, hiding her face for the first time as she began the transition from child to adult. Realizing he'd never see her face again unless she loved him had struck Otsar's passionate tone to resonate through his heart.

It had started Ōbhin down a road that led to murdering his rival for her and breaking his soul.

The first time he'd seen Avena, she'd been holding a knife in both hands, scared and yet standing up to the bandits—including Ōbhin—who'd been attacking her and Dualayn.

"You know what that's like," Fingers said.

"Yeah," Ōbhin admitted. "I know." He hated just standing here. There had to be *something* he could do.

I never should have taught her to fight.

Another voice whispered, *That wouldn't have stopped her from fighting.*

"I courted her and married her," Fingers continued. "I loved her more than life itself, but there were times when she just aggravated me. Made me angry." Pain choked his voice. "I tried so blessed hard. I did. I never wanted to hurt her even when she infuriated me. And then one day, I couldn't hold back. I hit her. Hard." His eyes grew raw. "I fled. What else could I do? You know what it's like to hurt someone you love? Not just emotionally, with words and shouts, but to *physically* do it? I couldn't believe I was capable of it. I hope she's happy. I know I complain 'bout her, but sometimes I imagine she's happy with the baker or the miller. With a man who don't knock her to the ground. I'm a horrible man, Ōbhin. It festers in me. I keep sayin' such terrible things 'bout her. She made me so angry that day, but when I pretend it was her fault and not mine, I don't drown. It's hard with Avena bein' 'round. I keep seein' Usrella in her face. And now . . ."

He looked on the edge of tears, about to spill his emotion. Ōbhin wanted to do something. He ached for some measure of control. For something he could do. He hadn't even found out the information they'd been looking for. He'd left Creg . . .

"Come on," Ōbhin said, resting his hand on Fingers's shoulder. He squeezed through the jerkin. "I need your help."

"With?"

A darkness surged through Ōbhin. "Talking with the man who did this. I left him with a severed leg. He can't have gotten far if he hasn't bled to death."

Savagery filled Fingers's eyes.

"I can come, too."

Ōbhin stiffened. He hadn't heard Smiles's approach. He turned around to see the friendly-looking man. He was a respectable distance away, wearing a padded gambeson. He had no sword but a binder on his hip. A smile grew on his face. Vicious.

"I would love to say a few things to the pus-filled roach that hurt her." The anger that came from Smiles felt so genuine. For more than fifty days, Ōbhin had yet to find a single slip-up in the thing's impression of Smiles. No one, not even Jilly, suspected him.

But Ōbhin and Avena had seen Smiles take wounds he shouldn't have been able to walk away from unscathed. They'd seen his flesh turn white and flow like potter's clay being molded by unseen hands.

"I need someone I can trust staying here," Ōbhin said, the lie coming easily. "Fingers is going with me, so who am I going to trust?"

"Cerdyn," said Smiles. "Even Dajouth *might* be trustworthy. He adores Avena."

"Pissant pants after her like a runt wantin' his turn to suckle at her teat," muttered Fingers.

"True," Smiles said, eyes sliding to Ōbhin. "Avena is like my Jilly. She inspires a man to rise and defend her."

"Please, Smiles, I need to know that she'll be safe," Ōbhin said, his stomach curdling. The real Smiles—*Phelep,* reminded Ōbhin, *that was his real name*—had been an easy-going and affable man. The sort of person with a ready joke or an ear that listened. Ōbhin hadn't known him long, and it galled him that he had to pretend with this thing.

But if Ōbhin was correct, the thing worked for Grey and was probably another of Dje'awsa's creations. It was placed here to protect Dualayn. For now, it was best to watch and not force the Brotherhood to act.

"I'll stay," Smiles said. He extended his hand.

Ōbhin gave a firm shake, nodding. "Thank you." *You're going to pay one day for murdering my friend.* "We'll be back soon."

The march to the house in the Greenlet passed in silence. The two men stalked with a fury that melted the locals out of their path. They were eyed suspiciously by a few of the guards, but many knew them by sight. Guard-Captain Thoph, who commanded the city guard in the nearby neighborhood, had even become friendly, coming around with pies his wife made.

On the porch of a nearby tenement, the Green-Faced Boys nursed broken limbs and sullen looks. None of them said a word. Ōbhin almost wished they did. The darkness inside of him itched for a release. His resonance blade would . . .

He battered down those thoughts. He couldn't give in to despair just yet. Avena still lived. Lausi's Hope still harmonized in his soul.

The first floor showed signs of Avena's battle. Broken cudgels and dropped saps littered it. The disturbance in the dust showed the battle raging through the room. He smiled, a moment of pride resonating within him.

He'd taught her to protect herself. With her earthen gauntlet and binder, she had incapacitated the street thugs.

"Where'd you leave the Black-damned bastard?" Fingers growled.

"Upstairs," Ōbhin said. He led the way, chainmail rattling. He took the steps two at a time. He passed a crossbow bolt embedded in the wall. He marched down the hallway to the open door. Avena's binder had come to rest against the wall. Her blood had dried to a small patch of brown.

Ōbhin picked up her rod, turning it in his gloved hand. Then he glanced into the room. A large pool of blood coated the floor, the surface covered in a coagulating film. A browning smear dragged off towards the right and then stopped.

"No," Ōbhin growled, stepping through the blood to where the trail ended.

"Sword scabbard's thrown to the side," Fingers noted, moving in behind him. "He must have used his belt as a tourniquet."

"And hopped out of here?" demanded Ōbhin.

Frustration boiled out of him. He whirled around and slammed his foot into the corner of the rickety bed. The frame cracked in a splintered groan, the hay-stuffed mattress sagging. An angry thought pounded in his mind over and over: *If I'd just let the piece of sword hit my shoulder!*

He fought to control himself. He needed answers. He would tear Kash apart to find Creg.

6

Anger simmered in Ōbhin after speaking with the sullen Green-Faced Boys.

After stalking out of the house, he confronted a few lounging on the porch of the rickety tenement they occupied, demanding answers.

"Your quim broke half our bones," complained the biggest one on the porch, his arm in a sling. "Why should we do more than piss on your boots?"

Fingers cracked his knuckles. "You got another arm and two legs that look fine to me. Pity if something happened."

"Just tell 'em, Dirk," a boy muttered, a large bruise running across his bare chest, the center a dark purple. "Elohm's Colours, wot do we owe that snot-nosed runt?"

"He's in with the Rangers, that's wot we owe," Dirk said. Ōbhin fought not to snort at the pretentious name. "They'll like to slit our throats if'n we talk."

The bruised one snorted. "They hauled him out of 'ere. He looked as white as grave mold. Doubt he'll live." He gave Ōbhin an accusatory look. "You hacked his leg off."

Ōbhin nodded, his hand resting on his blade's pommel.

"See, gettin' your bones broke is comin' off light," Fingers growled. "If you fought him, you'd all be lyin' in pieces instead of takin' your ease."

"Don't know where they took him," said Dirk. He sank back down to the steps. "Just paid to guard him. He was supposed to do somethin' for the Rangers. I reckon they'll want to piss on those who messed up their plans."

If Creg was with the Rangers, then they already knew about Dualayn. This was why he needed to protect the healer and keep him alive. Why had the Rangers sent Creg into town? What mischief was he supposed to cause? Did it matter now that he had his leg cut off? Had Ōbhin accidentally stopped a plot in motion? Maybe then some good would come if Avena recovered.

If . . .

"So, no idea where they hauled him off to?" Ōbhin demanded.

"Probably the Lair." The bruised one said.

"Ain't no Lair," another said, his leg in a splint. Pale vapor spilled from his mouth. His eyes were glazed. He had the look of someone smoking white dream, one of the narcotics that came out of Tethyr. He brought a pipe to his mouth and took another puff, a look of almost ecstasy crossing his face for a moment.

"It's a myth," another said, his teeth stained brown with Tethyrian weed, a root that was chewed to give energy and make you more alert, but it also made you antsy.

More prone to violence.

"They say the Rangers got them a hideout out in the King's Preserve," said the bruised one. "Called the Lair. Where they plot all their war with the Brotherhood. Not that they tell us. We're just supposed to sell their goods 'n keep the bastard Red Lips from sellin' here."

"When the Red Lips find out we're all banged up . . ." Dirk muttered.

"Well, if they took him anywhere, it's the Lair. Good luck findin' it. Them Rangers know those woods, they do."

Ōbhin hoped the Rangers had to bury the rotten man in the forest to the north of the city. He'd never find them in the King's Preserve. It galled Ōbhin that he couldn't find the answers he needed. Now the only other member of Ust's bandits left was Handsome Baill, and he'd vanished into the murky organization of the Brotherhood. Ōbhin itched to find him, too. He was the man who'd assassinated the last high refractor, the leader of Elohm's Church, and started off the current plague of riots that broke out every few days.

Ōbhin would scour the city, but he was one man. Kash was the largest city on the Arngelsh Isles, one of the biggest in the world. It dwarfed anything in Ōbhin's mountainous home of Qoth. Perhaps only the capital of the Democh Empire could rival Kash in size. The slums around it swelled with Tethyrian immigrants, poor factory workers, and farmers looking for work. The last was crushed by the new taxes, forcing them to sell off their land to men in favor with the Crown.

A rot swelled in the city, and finding one cancerous tumor would be difficult for Ōbhin.

In the days that followed, he tried. He talked to street thugs whenever he had free time from his duties at the estate. He paid Runty Ed and the rest of the Breezy Hills Boys to keep their ears listening. They were affiliated with the Rangers, so he hoped they'd hear something. It was how he'd found Creg to begin with.

And through it all, he worried about Avena. He saw her again and again with Creg's severed sword rammed into her brain.

The third day after her accident, he was swept up in a new round of riots. Farmers from the outlying village had sparked it when the King's Bounty, food given out to the poor, had run out in the Porcelain, a small slum between the larger Slops and the northern shore of Lake Ophavin. It had turned vicious; men struggling to feed families became violent, rushing the guards protecting the bread wagons.

More dead. More arrests. More property damaged and destroyed.

On the fifth day, the city seemed to have calmed down enough to let Ōbhin resume his pointless search for the sniveling man. Creg must have been in a shallow grave by now. That much blood loss should have killed him. However, until Ōbhin saw a body, he wasn't convinced. After drilling his men, he headed for the estate's main gate.

"Goin' out again?" Dajouth asked. The young man had blond hair that spoke of Roidanese blood, the kingdom to the west across the Border Fang Mountains. He clutched at the front of his shirt, groping whatever amulet he always wore beneath. "Eager to get brained in another food riot?"

The memory of the blow he'd taken two days earlier throbbed across the back of Ōbhin's skull. He'd staggered back with his black hair matted crimson. Someone had tried to steal his sword, but they hadn't hit him hard enough to daze him. Just enough to make his head ring.

"Thinking about it," Ōbhin said. "Better than waiting."

Dajouth glanced at the house. The young man, seventeen or eighteen, shook his head. "She's too pretty to be embroiled in this mess. If you wanna take a woman into the rough, you should find one like my ma."

Ōbhin glanced at the young man. "You'd take your ma into a den of thieves and thugs?"

"'Course." Dajouth grinned. "Why, she'd grab their ears and slam their heads together. Tough woman, was my ma. Avena's delicate."

"You let her hear you say that, and she'll thump you with her binder," Bran said. The youngest guard fixed eager eyes on Ōbhin. "I can go with you. Keep any sappers from rappin' the back of your head."

Cerdyn chuckled. The broad-shouldered guard was bare-chested in the summer heat, sweat beading on the shaggy hairs covering his torso. He was the biggest man in the guard. During Ust's attack, that strength had served well.

"I think I'll go see if there's any meat pies in the kitchen," Cerdyn said. "Don't get your head cracked in. I'd hate to work for Fingers."

"Will Kaylin remember your name today?" the impostor-Smiles asked. "You'd think you'd get a hint when she stares at you like a stranger day in, day out."

Cerdyn shrugged. Kaylin the cook had not been the same, or so Ōbhin was told, since her husband's death two years ago. She could remember how to cook, but any more than that seemed to slip away from her. She could be angry at you for entering her kitchen one moment and the next you were her new scullery boy and she'd snap at you to wash her dishes.

Cerdyn nursed an ache for her. He spent a great deal of his free time around her kitchen.

"Poor man," the thing pretending to be Smiles said. "When I first arrived, Kaylin had a temper, but at least she could remember your name."

"You knew her husband?" asked Ōbhin.

"A little. He must have died not more than a half-month after I started workin' here. My Jilly's been here longer. I guess he was a good man. Had to be to put up with Kaylin's anger. Glad my Jilly isn't one for shoutin'."

Ōbhin nodded as he looked away. It was so easy to forget that the thing wasn't Smiles. Ōbhin wanted to expose the creature, but who would it replace next? Which guard or servant would leave the estate only to be killed in secret?

I hope they didn't give your corpse to Dje'awsa, Smiles, thought Ōbhin.

"You're guarding the gate this afternoon, right?" Ōbhin asked.

"Me 'n Bran," Smiles said. "You forget?"

"Blows to the head do that," Dajouth said. He clutched tighter to his shirt. "You think she'll be different? Avena, I mean, when she gets better?"

"I don't know," Ōbhin growled. He marched towards the gate where Fingers stood watch. The man leaned against it, looking distant. He'd been silent since returning from their fruitless search for Creg five days back.

Pensive.

Ōbhin was halfway across the grounds, passing one of the rhododendron bushes adorned with lilac flowers, when Fingers opened the gate. A carriage trundled through and trotted down the driveway. The groom driving it wore the vestments of a priest, a prism dangling over the front and flashing in the sunlight.

Sighing, Ōbhin reversed direction and hurried after it to the manor's front door. Dualayn hadn't hired a new butler after Pharon's death in the attack, and none of the maids or other servants seemed to want to step into the role. An important visitor had arrived, and the proprieties drilled into Ōbhin as a palace guardsman wouldn't let him leave without greeting whoever this was.

Someone from the church?

Miguil, the estate's groom and Avena's former promised, emerged from the stables and jogged towards the front of the house to attend to the horses. The carriage slowed to a stop before the marble steps of the front porch. Ōbhin's long legs carried him past it, his leather boots thudding on the gravel driveway. He became aware of his shoddy clothing, a rough leather jerkin and linen pants, his face flushed from the exercise in the summer sun.

A poor impression for visitors.

"Your eminence," Miguil was saying as he helped Refractor Charlis, a high-ranking member of the church and a friend of Dualayn's, step down from the carriage. "Be welcome."

"Elohm's Blessed Colours fill you," the priest said. He was a bald, round-faced man who didn't seem to have a neck at all. His chin pressed into the rainbow robe that clad his body. Over that draped a white stole espousing his virtue: Honesty.

"Your eminence," Ōbhin added. "Dualayn is not seeing guests at this time."

"Yes, yes, he's in his lab," said the refractor. "Come on, child." He held out his hand to the other passenger in the carriage.

Ōbhin was shocked to see the young woman who stepped out in the yellow robes of a Daughter of Patience. It was Deffona, Avena's friend. The girl stepped down, her smile full of warmth. She didn't have the bags under her eyes he remembered from the times he'd seen her at the hospital her cloistered order ran. She wore a white wimple that framed her round face covered by a yellow veil that fell over her shoulders.

"Deffona?" Ōbhin asked.

"Blessed day to you, Ōbhin," she said, expression anxious.

"My new secretary," said Charlis. "I poached her from Eldest Daughter Anglia."

A look of momentary relief passed across Deffona's face. "It's been quite the challenge, and I do miss working at the hospital, but the refractor wanted to keep me close. He's such a powerful man, you know. He is trying to keep Parliament from passing another tax for the king." A giddy smile flashed across her face. "I even met the new high refractor."

Ōbhin gave a polite nod. He wasn't an Elohmite, so he cared little about who ruled their church.

"I'm working close with High Refractor Haphen on a bill that, I hope, we'll bring some measure of peace to the city," Charlis said. "I was hoping to have Dualayn's input on the details. His mastery of jewelchines is unparalleled."

"And we were hoping to see Avena," Deffona added, her voice quiet.

Darkness pressed on Ōbhin.

Miguil shook his head and said, "Dualayn won't let any of us see her. But we're all praying for her."

Miguil and Avena's plans to marry had been destroyed when she'd learned Miguil's true passion. She had little interest in being a disguise for a husband who'd prefer spending his time in the company of other men. Despite that, the pair had grown a friendship in the wake of Ust's attack and the death of Miguil's lover, Pharon.

"Such a tragedy," Deffona said, tracing the prism before her.

"Dualayn hasn't left her side," Ōbhin said as he led the two visitors up the porch to the new set of double doors, replacements for the old destroyed by Ust. They were carved with the seven gems forming a circle. Topaz took the top spot, the only gem bisected by the gaps in the doors. "He sleeps in there. Won't let anyone inside. He hardly even eats. Most of his meals are left untouched."

"He does emerge sometimes to eat, though?" Charlis asked as Ōbhin opened the door. Its hinges made hardly a whisper.

"He does."

They stepped into the cooler interior. The high ceilings helped to diminish the summer's growing heat along with curtains soaked in water before open windows. Ōbhin's small room, at the western end of the house, sweltered by day's end. Their steps echoed on the polished marble floor. The door to the lab was shut firm, a sign hanging out front asking for no disturbances. A tray of food, covered in linen, lay untouched on a small table beside it.

"Perhaps he'll emerge," said Charlis. "It is of rather pressing importance I speak with him."

"What exactly is this bill?" Ōbhin asked, then flushed. "My apologies for prying, your eminence."

"Oh, no, it's fine. The king is talking war with Roidan to seize all the gem mines in the Border Fangs. With the growing jewelchine revolution, the value of those mines climbs by the day. King Anglon is blinded by Black greed."

"It's behind the increased taxes," Deffona said. "Or so the refractor says."

Charlis nodded, his face somber. "Politics is no place for a servant of Elohm, and I am afraid some of His refractors and priests who've been appointed to the House of the Clergy are servants of coin. I chastise them, but bribes are flowing."

"It's so infuriating," Deffona huffed. "People are suffering. My order's hospital is groaning with those wounded in the riots. And there's sickness, too. The brown waters broke out in the Tethyr District."

Ōbhin winced at the news of the abdominal disease.

"Our new high refractor preaches peace, but the Greens and Whites swell the city." Charlis sighed. "And some idiot's started a rumor about a long-lost Briflon heir who will return and set things right." The priest rolled his eyes. "As if the three Briflon brothers hadn't exterminated their family fighting over who'd be king. It's just the sort of nonsense that scared people believe. They're ripe for a savior to swoop in and right all the wrongs. Kash is a ruby jewelchine dropped into a kettle. Soon, the steam will be hissing and there'll be another riot against our 'impostor' king."

"Is there any hope for peace?" Ōbhin asked.

"Some," Charlis said. "If I can get the support in Parliament. King Anglon and his queen are spending coin like a fool in a whorehouse."

"Refractor Charlis!" Deffona gasped.

He waved a hand. "I grew up in the Mud Strip, girl. The things I heard would make you blush." Then the priest took a seat on a chair placed for those waiting on word of their loved ones being cared for inside. "If I'm lucky, Dualayn will emerge, and I can talk with him."

Deffona glanced at Ōbhin. Her eyes took on a studious look. "I'm not sure I can stand to just do nothing. Would you kindly show me the grounds? I have never been here."

"Never?"

She shook her head. "Young acolytes are rarely allowed to leave the convent, and once I'd taken my vows, I was put to work in the hospital." She smiled. "Avena's visits were always a delight, even if the eldest daughter would scold me later for shirking my duties."

"Hard woman, her," muttered Charlis. "She was more like you when she was younger. Bright and cheerful."

"You knew the eldest when she was my age?" Deffona asked, blinking in some surprise. "And she *wasn't* the antithesis of fun?"

"Now, daughter, that's a bit harsh," said Charlis. The refractor leaned back in the chair. "She only ever wanted you to excel. I imagine she thinks of you as her real daughter."

Deffona blanched. "I'd hope my real mother would have treated me better."

Ōbhin shook his head. "I'm missing a piece or two of information."

"I was left on the hospital's doorstep as a babe," said Deffona. "Eldest Daughter Anglia didn't even join the hospital until I was nearly three or four. She had me spanked for the first time and had words with the other daughters about being too permissible with me."

Charlis made a surprised sound. "I knew her when she worked as Refractor Messian's secretary. He was my predecessor. I took his place, oh, twenty or so years ago when he decided the calling of a simple priest at a village church suited him. I selected my own secretary. Anglia spent some time in contemplation in a rural convent before she found a new away to serve Elohm. She was such a bright and friendly young woman. Messian adored her, you know." He flashed Deffona a smile. "She brought a certain brightness to the room."

"Wearing yellow does that," Deffona said. "We positively reflect light. Why, I imagine, give me a single jewelchine lamp, stick me atop the Gray Pillar, and I would reflect enough brilliance to light up the city."

"The imagination you have, daughter."

"And the patience to indulge in it." Deffona flashed Ōbhin a smile, her eyebrows arching in expectation.

After a moment he groaned, "Right, you're a Daughter of *Patience*."

"Hmm, Avena says you have quicker wit than that." Deffona glanced at the closed laboratory doors, the excitement in her face vanishing. "Refractor, may I walk the grounds? I fear that I cannot handle idle waiting."

"Losing that famed patience you just boasted about?" Charlis asked. "No, no, I understand. If my bosom friend's life lay in such peril, I would not be able to sit by so idly. Enjoy your walk."

Deffona nodded. "Ōbhin, would you be a gentleman and give me a tour?"

Ōbhin couldn't find a reason to deny her. "My pleasure."

"You have a politeness about you," Deffona said, taking his proffered arm. Her yellow robes rustled about her body. "A polish that a guard shouldn't have."

"It depends on the guard," he said as he led her to the front door.

"Intriguing," she said. "Avena mentioned you were a soldier or something in Qoth."

"Or something," he said.

"Yes, that's how she puts it. Like chiseling at granite to get a mere chip from you."

His brow furrowed as he opened the front doors. Summer sunlight fell dazzling on her robes. Blinking against the sudden glare, he said, "She speaks about me?"

"Often. It's not surprising."

"Well, I am training her and . . ." He hesitated. "Well, she is helping me track down some information." He cleared his throat. "I'm afraid she rarely speaks of you."

"Rarely?" The young woman deflated.

"She doesn't talk about unnecessary things with me," he added in haste. "You know, fighting and, er, our theories on Dualayn's research."

"Why the Brotherhood is so interested in it?" she asked.

He glanced askance at her. Deffona's face shone with innocence. It was about the only part of her body, save her hands, she showed. *She swathes herself in modesty and leaves her most intimate part exposed for any man to read her emotions.*

"She's talked a lot. You and her have secrets." She shuddered against him.

He studied the girl as they walked around the house, following the slope it rested on. They were passing the east wing that held the kitchen. The scents coming from there filled the air, the tang of soy sauce and spice of horseradish. Before them lay the grove gate, a small stand of trees beyond. It held a small clearing in the center with a few benches.

"And now you've carried her across half the city to get her help," said Deffona. There was something . . . girlish in her voice. Breathy. "A mad rush to save her life."

"What else could I do?" A memory of that panicked flight filled him. Avena had hardly weighed more than a feather in his arms, so frail as she twitched and spasmed. "I shouldn't have let her come with me."

"Could you have stopped her?"

He shook his head. They passed the side of the house and he turned them towards the lake. A cool breeze came off of it. The slums of the Porcelain lay at the far end, a black stain, but the southern end still had picturesque trees along its banks and reeds sprouting in its shallows. There were secluded spots along the shore. A heron waded, bill aimed at the water. Its beak flashed down to snatch out a red-and-white carp from the water.

"Will she recover?" Deffona asked, her voice tight now.

"Should be a few more days," Ōbhin said, trying to put more confidence in his pronouncement than he felt. "I think it's a good sign she's made it this far. Dualayn won't let her die."

"Good," Deffona said. "And you'll be caring for her, right?"

"Protecting her when her stubbornness throws her into the snowsnake's nest."

"Snowsnake?"

"Monsters they say live in the deepest snow of my homeland's mountains. Their bite freezes you, kills the flesh. Frostbite, we call it. They're said to be invisible and can strike through clothing if you're not careful."

"Well, I'm glad. You and her are like a rosebush." She glanced at Ōbhin. "One that's growing strong, I think. If a little . . . uncoordinated."

"Rosebush? Uncoordinated? What are you talking about?"

"Relationship. What me and you are doing right now. We're growing ours. It's newly sprouted. I'm not sure what shape it'll take, but with you and Avena, I see you two as a rosebush. With red flowers. Those are my favorite."

"Not yellow ones?"

She glanced down at her robe. "I wear enough of that sunny hue, thank you very much. Red would look brilliant on me."

"Still, I'm not quite following you. A rosebush?"

"That's what relationships are like. Various plants. They come in different sorts. Some relationships are foul and rotten, like those nasty corpse flowers they cultivate in Relasi. Sticky things that smell of death, or so I've read in books. Others are like nettles. Brush them, and you come away in pain. Or a rash from poison ivy. Others are bright. Daffodils that shine happy, or like those fine rhododendron bushes. Full of broad leaves and beautiful flowers."

"So I'm the thorns protecting Avena's beauty?" Ōbhin asked, thinking he understood her metaphor.

"Oh, no, she's the thorny one." Deffona giggled. "Too fierce and protective for her own good. You're the flowers."

"Me?"

Deffona glanced at him and smiled. "Oh, definitely. You don't know how handsome you are. The dusky and dashing easterner. Why do you think she's always around you?"

"Because we're trying to protect Dualayn and figure out what the Brotherhood is up to," Ōbhin said.

"That's just the excuse. Neither of you see it." Deffona shook her head. "From the minute she mentioned your name, I could tell. Miguil's a nice man, but they were the most dreary plant. Grass. So common. Serviceable. Dependable, maybe, but *boooooring*. She would have been miserable with him."

"They both would," Ōbhin said, his brow furrowing. He remembered that near kiss with Avena when they were drunk in that village not long after their meeting. He had kept his distance after that, and then other things seemed more important. Figuring out about Dje'awsa, keeping Dualayn safe, concealing the truth about Smiles.

Her presence always brightened him.

She wouldn't betray me like Foonauri, he thought.

You never imagined Foonauri could betray you, a dark voice said. His eyes drifted to his black gloves.

"She can do better than me," Ōbhin said finally.

"Does she want to do better? Think about it. I would love to see your roses blossom. They would be beautiful."

"And if the soil they grow in isn't fertile? If it's black and rocky?"

"Then it will be all the more beautiful for succeeding in such adverse conditions." Deffona studied the lake. Scarlet dragonflies hovered for moments before darting right or left over the reeds. "It's peaceful here."

"Yeah," he said, memories of Avena rippling through his mind. The way she smiled. Laughed. How she'd throw herself into a fight. How she'd convulsed in his arms. He'd gotten her hurt trying to figure out answers to questions that didn't matter.

Carstin was dead. His soul passed on. Did it matter what Dje'awsa did to his body? Was it worth getting Avena killed?

"Don't let your darkness keep you from finding something beautiful," Deffona said. She turned to him, her face round and bright. "No soul is too tarnished that it can't be polished bright."

"Avena likes to say that."

"Because it's true. That's Elohm's promise to us. That we can always be a better person than we think we can. But only if we try."

He gave an absent nod.

"Now, I am disappointed you haven't asked me what sort of plant Avena and I are." Deffona shook her head, her veil rustling about her shoulders. "A lack of curiosity is a terrible trait in a man."

"What type of plant are you?"

"Why, a blackberry bush, of course!"

"Avena's the thorns protecting your blossoms."

"Plus I'm sweet like their fruit."

Laughter bubbled out of Ōbhin's throat. He felt mirth for the first time since Avena's injury. The dark weight on his soul relaxed during that moment of shared joy with Deffona. A heron let out an angry caw and winged to the air away from the two chortling humans.

When they returned to the house, Charlis looked pleased. The tray of food was gone and the refractor was ready to leave. Deffona demanded promises from Ōbhin to be alerted as soon as Avena was out of danger.

Ōbhin agreed to deliver them.

He decided against searching for Creg after that. The man was either alive or dead, but he wasn't important. Ōbhin sank down into the chair outside the lab and realized what he'd been doing. Running away. A coward scared of facing more pain.

He could fight a mob of angry rioters, stand against a horde of shambling dead, and face against a magic-created monster like Ust, but what really mattered terrified him. Avena dying. What he felt for her. It was easier not to face it. To throw himself into something else.

He stared down at his black gloves and thought long and hard about what he felt. Avena didn't spark that instant blaze of heat that Foonauri had. He was a decade older now, twenty-two instead of a boy of ten. He'd loved and lost and suffered. His soul was streaked in grime and guarded against loss. The possibility of another woman betraying him terrified him.

Could Avena even do that? Could a woman that stubborn, that loving, that fierce, and that open be as duplicitous as Foonauri?

Was he worthy of finding out? What would happen to Avena the next time he took her into danger?

After that, when he wasn't training guards or doing his share of duty at the gate, he sat before Dualayn's lab and waited to find out her fate. He didn't know what would happen when those doors opened and she emerged—*if* she emerged—but he wouldn't run from his feelings. He would confront them.

Ōbhin vowed to stop being a coward.

7

Fiftieth Day of Forgiveness, 755 EU

She felt remote. Separated. A fleshless existence forced into a body. The weight of it surrounded her awareness. The sense of limbs. Of breathing. She experienced warmth. A weight on her eyelids. She struggled to open them. To move.

Fingers twitched. Toes curled.

The body felt more and more real. Less distant. She sank into it, merging with it. A heart beat. Blood pumped through veins. She smelled something familiar; the antiseptic sting of wood alcohol.

Her eyes opened as the alien sensation vanished. She wasn't separated from her body. She was awake, staring up at a stone ceiling. She caught a glimpse of locked cabinets. The creak of a heavy metal door opening and closing.

Dualayn stepped out of his jewelchine vault and into her sight. She shuddered, wanting to sit up, but her body felt so weak. Drained. She blinked. She felt no injuries. No throb of a bruise on her head.

"Father?" she croaked. "What . . . happened?"

"Avena," he said in relief as he hurried over to her and leaned over to study her. She realized she lay on the hard surface of his exam table. "Elohm's Colours, I think it worked. It *is* you."

"Who else would it be?" she asked. A fuzziness rolled across her body, prickling her senses. Her fingers spasmed. "What happened? I feel so weak."

"You've been unconscious, child. Poor Ōbhin has worn through the soles of his boots in worry. The whole household has."

"Ōbhin . . . We were . . . looking for someone." Memories rushed back into Avena. Those felt sharper than her body. "For Creg, that sniveling runt who worked for Ust. We found him in a house and . . . and . . ." She struggled to remember what happened after they entered the house. She caught flashes. Boys with green faces. Bursts of purple energy. Ōbhin's booted foot crashing through the ceiling. "I think there was a fight."

"What month is it?" asked Dualayn.

"Forgiveness," she answered. "The Forty-Third Day of Forgiveness, right?"

"It's the Fiftieth. You're off by a week, but that's not surprising since you've been unconscious the entire time."

"I took a blow to my head?" she asked. "Is that why I can't remember the fight?"

"You had this buried in your head," Dualayn said. He marched to his jewel-chine bench. She managed to sit up.

The effort left her dizzy.

When her vision cleared, he held up the severed end of a blade. He put his finger near the middle. "It had lodged that deep into the left lobe of your brain. Can you move your right hand?"

She raised it while processing what he said. It made no sense. She stared at the length of deadly metal, trying to fathom that burying into her brain and her still surviving.

"Good, good, and the palsy is gone from the right half of your face," he noted.

"That was in my head?" Avena croaked. "I should be dead."

"But you're not!" Dualayn had this look of giddy joy. "I regenerated your damaged brain, child. Using resonating topazes placed directly on it."

Avena's hands swept across her head. She prodded at her temple before her fingers slid into the fine silk of her brown hair. She stroked across her skull, feeling for any imperfections, finding no scar. Her hair felt different. Less weight.

"You cut my hair?" she asked.

"My apologies. You did have a lovely braid. Long hair is a woman's glory, so I do feel a tad bad for having to sever yours. But it was in the way."

"No, no. I'd rather be bald than dead." She smiled. "You truly removed the top of my skull to heal me? That theory on using topazes and a tuning fork?"

"The topazes' default mode is to spread healing energy," said Dualayn. "They repaired the swelling in your brain. So far, I can find no deficiencies in your memory or your abilities, but I must perform an exam."

She nodded. Despite the hollow pit in her stomach, a gnawing need for food, she was eager to learn more. The Recorder had revealed so much knowledge. What he'd uncovered alone was worth keeping protecting him. She had to recover to do that. To study with him and fight at Ōbhin's side.

He carried me all the way from the Greenlet. He'd crossed the breadth of the city. Not its longest measurement, for it stretchered wider west and east along the Ustern than it did north and south, but a feat that sent a giddiness through her. *That must have polished more of the murk off his soul.*

A yearning to see him almost overwhelmed her need to be examined for any problems.

Dualayn returned with a small diamond jewelchine housed in a tube of polished steel. It was another of Dualayn's inventions, though it hadn't caught. Diamond torches were just more expensive than a candle or an oil lantern. The rich might use diamonds to light their houses, and many cities were lighting their streets with them, but the commonfolk didn't have the extra coin on portable light, so had to go with cheaper alternatives.

"Okay, let's check your pupil dilation," Dualayn said.

She sat there as he shone the light in her eye, had her follow his finger, tickled her sides to get her to giggle, poked and prodded half her body to check her senses, and used a leather-wrapped hammer to tap her knees in the right spot to get them to spasm.

"What is the multiplication of twenty-eight and four?" he asked as he worked, the first of many questions.

She did the sum in her head. "One hundred and twelve."

"In what year did the Tri-Color War occur?"

"It started in 645, when King Kashen Briflon died, and ended in 652 when the last surviving brother, Gerey Briflon, perished killing his nephew Vash Briflon in the Battle of the Mud. They were the last two survivors of the Briflon dynasty."

"What is the property of heliodor?"

"It represents Elohm's Patience," she said. "His bright Yellow. It is the color that is associated with air and wind, with alarms and warnings. A heliodor can be left to be triggered, waiting for the right conditions before activating it."

"Good, good," he said as he went about his exam. "And who is the Archon-Supreme of the devas?"

"Reylis," she said, and thoughts stirred. The White Lady claimed not to be a deva, but she never denied being Reylis. "You once said that many of the pagan gods in the eastern lands have the same name."

"Similar names, even amid languages that have no familiar connection. Demochian, Qothian, and Tethyrian can all trace their origins back to a distant proto-language, but Ki'manese, Relasese, and the tongue of the Shattered Islanders is a separate family of tongues. Our Lothonian, Roidanese, Onderian, and those who live on the distant island of Busil are a third such family. Yet the names of gods, tones, spirits, and other such entities connected to the gems all are similar. The Tone of Fire is Otsar while the Passion of Fire is O'csari."

"Passions are what the Ki'manese people worship?"

Dualayn cocked his head as he prodded her armor. "Revere, perhaps. But you see the similarity."

"Raleth is the Tone of White and Reylis is the Archon-Supreme." A nervous writhe twisted through her. "Those seem . . . similar."

"There are names of other devas if you read older texts, but the church long thought revering them was too close to paganism centuries ago. Different villages might still remember them in their prayers, but only Reylis survived with official sanction. There is a Deva of Vengeance, I believe, named Oysar, and the Broken Mirror heretics in Ondere are said to worship them as the shattered pieces of Elohm. One god split into seven or eight parts or some nonsense like that."

Is the White Lady a deva? It sounded foolish. She couldn't be a divine being, and yet speaking with her a month ago had left Avena shaken. The woman spoke Honesty in everything save when she gave her name as Raya. Her nickname, she'd said, used by those she called friends. Not her true name, but a diminutive that could be drawn from Reylis.

"So Elohm's religion still survives in some forms in the pagan lands?" she asked. "And they have mistakenly worshiped His devas as gods?"

"That's *one* interpretation," said Dualayn. "You remember the name I told you about. The individual from Koilon."

Koilon had been a myth, one of the Anteshattering cities, until ruins were found in the Upfing Forest. Dualayn was certain they'd found the remains of it along with the Recorder. They had lucked out to dig into the library and found the Recorder immediately. Just as they'd started studying the relic, Ust and his bandits had "invited" them to meet with Grey Koilon, leader of the Brotherhood.

"It was a name similar to Otsar," she said, recalling the specific conversation Dualayn brought up.

"Ozsor," Dualayn supplied.

"Are you saying that these gods and tones were real people?"

"Mythology comes from somewhere."

"The Archon-Supreme is not a myth!" It was tantamount to calling Elohm a myth. She *knew* in her heart that a loving God had created the world. Her. Ōbhin. Everyone.

Dualayn smiled. "There's that fire. I think you are recovered."

She blushed. She didn't like what he was implying at all. She shifted. The White Lady couldn't have been one of these individuals from the distant past who inspired the name of all these pagan gods. The Shattering happened three thousand years ago. It was lost to recorded memory, only maintained in legends.

Mankind had fallen after it happened. Every history book Avena had perused at Dualayn's suggestion had given different dates. They couldn't even agree when Lothil Boat-Breaker led Avena's ancestors across the sea to settle the Arngelsh Islands, nor when Lothil's grandson, Boan Sword-Arm, had led the fight against the darklings infesting the forests and mountains before sealing them behind the Warding.

"Your recovery is remarkable," Dualayn said, drawing her out of her thoughts. He stared at her with a look of awe. "I think this is it, Avena. I'll soon be ready to heal her."

"You'll succeed," she said, hoping Dualayn could restore his wife's damaged mind.

Her own throbbed from weighty thoughts. Dizziness washed over her. Her mind felt remote, almost outside of her. She ran a hand over her forehead and it passed.

He helped her slip off the table. Her legs felt weak, a tremble racing through her muscles. She stared at her body. Her cheeks looked shrunken, cheekbones more pronounced. She ran a hand through the linen shift she wore and felt her ribs. She'd lost weight, but not enough that a few days of extra meals wouldn't recover, or so she hoped.

She had to resume her work with Ōbhin.

Did he get the information from Creg? Excitement galvanized her at that thought. She took the housecoat proffered by Dualayn and wrapped the light-blue wool around her body. She cinched it up tight before taking his arm for support.

"I am sure Ōbhin is eager to see you," Dualayn said. "He has taken to sitting outside my lab. Gave me a fright two days ago when I went to fetch my dinner. I didn't notice him until he let out a snore so loud I thought the house would shake."

She giggled as he opened the door to the entry hall.

Her eyes fell on Ōbhin. The scar on the handsome easterner's right cheek enhanced the deadly swordsman grace he never lost no matter what he did. He always moved with deliberation, even now as he stood to greet her. His dusky-brown face lit up at the sight of her. Life stirred in his dark eyes. Shining hope.

Awe.

She blushed beneath his intense scrutiny. He stared at her like she was impossible. A dream come to life. The beat of her heart quickened. A smile spread on her lips as, so it seemed to her, she witnessed him for the first time.

Joy burst inside of her.

Awe filled Ōbhin as he stared at Avena.

She looked frailer than he'd ever seen her. Her brown hair fell loose and short about her face, framing her round, pale features in a new way. A smile crossed her lips while her emotions blushed her exposed cheeks.

She stepped away from Dualayn. Her liquid eyes shone with her excitement. Ōbhin's heart felt light. It almost lifted him from the ground. Deffona's words whispered in his mind. Seeing Avena confirmed what the daughter had suggested.

For a moment, he thought she would fall. His hands reached for her and—

Black-gloved hands.

They froze before grabbing her. Shame burned through Ōbhin. What could hands clad in sable do but destroy what they touched? He could never do that to her. He had almost killed her with his recklessness. Going after Creg had not mattered one whit. Not when it had almost gotten her killed.

"Ōbhin?" she said, her voice tight. Her hands took his, her pale fingers squeezing about the stained leather.

"I am deeply sorry for getting you hurt," he said. "Aliiva's Tone resonates through me. I am glad you survived. I will not endanger you thus again."

"Will not endanger . . ." Stubborn anger tightened her expression. "Don't blame yourself for what happened. It wasn't your blade that stabbed me. It was Creg's. You listen to me, Ōbhin. I won't let you do that. I chose to be there. I can remember that much. I put myself in danger. You didn't have any say, so you can't have any guilt."

Her words were sweet, but Ōbhin knew the truth. He had to search for answers alone. He had to uncover what Grey and the Brotherhood wanted with Dualayn. Had to learn how to unmask the thing masquerading as Smiles without allowing it to steal another person's life.

He released her hands and took a step back. "I promised Deffona to inform her when you came awake. I'm glad you've recovered."

"Ōbhin," she said, her brow furrowing.

Though he marched away at a steady pace, Ōbhin fled the pain in his heart.

Ōbhin's sudden coldness stung her. She lowered her hands as Dualayn cleared his throat. "I am sure Deffona will be ecstatic to learn of your recovery."

Avena nodded.

"Come, come, let's get you to the kitchen. I am sure Kaylin will have something warm and filling for you."

"Yeah," she said, her thoughts churned up. *I disappointed him.* It stung hard. *I wasn't good enough to stand at his side. I thought with the earthen gauntlets and my training, I was.*

She would have to do better. Try harder. She would show Ōbhin that she wasn't as fragile as he thought. They had started this together, and she wouldn't let her weakness ruin that. She would be better.

She would show Ōbhin he could count on her.

"Avena!"

Jilly, Smiles's wife—*no, she's his widow and doesn't know it*, thought Avena—rushed down the stairs, her dark skirts swirling. The woman, a few years Avena's senior, swept her up in an embrace, rocking her. Jilly's cries attracted attention. Other maids drifted in. Shebani, Chobay, Deshvi, and plump Layni soon joined the hug. For a moment, Avena was all smiles as they kissed her cheeks and gushed over her.

"You need to eat," Jilly declared. "Dualayn, sir, why are you just letting her starve right here?"

"My apologies, madam," Dualayn said, a smile on his lips. "She keeps getting distracted with greetings."

The front door opened. Miguil and a few of the guards stepped in. Her former promised grinned, transforming his handsome face into something beautiful.

Dajouth pressed forward, his blond hair spilling about his head. "Avena, I am heartened to see the world is not diminished by the absence of your beauty." He spoke with the flowery tone he used with every woman. "I could feel your brightness shining through the walls. It called to me."

The fake Smiles slipped his arm around Jilly. He had that infectious grin, mimicking the real one so much. "It's a blessed day to see you up and about."

"It is," Jilly said, hugging the thing tight. She had no idea. She carried Smiles's child, conceived before his death and replacement.

Fingers held back as Bran wiggled through the maids to give her a hug. She smiled and embraced the boyish guard. Even gave him a kiss on the cheek. He blushed as he broke away only to be replaced by a hopeful Dajouth.

She hugged him but didn't give him a kiss. Normally, his flowery compliments grated on her, but not even the impostor's presence could dampen her elation right now. Not with the rest of her friends around her. The family that had come to replace what she'd lost to her mother's madness.

She glanced at Fingers standing in the doorway. He had such a look of relief on his face, an awe not dissimilar to Ōbhin's. She had always found Fingers off-putting. The way the man talked about his estranged wife infuriated and embarrassed her in turns.

Right now . . .

She smiled at him and held out her hand, beckoning. He swallowed and a dark look flashed across his face. Guilt or shame or some other emotion, she wasn't sure. Then he slipped out the door. It closed behind him with a clunk.

Just like Ōbhin, she thought. *Why do men have to be such great fools? Ōbhin should have yelled at me like he did after the riots. Does he think I'm that weak? And Fingers . . . How can he* possibly *think this was his fault?*

She would have to talk to them both. Later. The smells from Kaylin's kitchen were savory.

After she'd eaten a thick broth of wheat noodles and fish seasoned with soy and ginger, she was ushered up to her room on the second floor by the maids. She objected to being tucked in like a child, but Jilly and Layni overrode her protestations. In moments, they had her safely ensconced beneath the covers.

Exhaustion seized her, but sleep didn't come right away. Ōbhin lingered in her mind. She wanted to speak with him right now. To find out what he thought about her. Did he see her as some sort of burden? She refused to be one.

She would show him. *Tomorrow, I'll resume training with the guards.*

Next time they went into danger, she wouldn't get hurt.

8

Fifty-First Day of Forgiveness, 755 EU

Traces of exhaustion lingered in Avena the next day as she pulled on her boots for training with Ōbhin and the guards. She had to push herself through the lethargy that hollowed out her guts. She couldn't afford for Ōbhin to see her as weak. As a woman.

What's so wrong if he sees me as a woman? wandered through her thoughts.

Warmth rippled through her. She smiled. Would it be so bad if he saw her as a woman? He had the night he'd tried to kiss her. After, he'd backed away, respecting that she was promised to Miguil. Not any longer. She wouldn't marry a man she didn't love and who could never love her back.

Miguil had his secret desires that were condemned as sin by Elohm's Church.

Avena hadn't really thought of Ōbhin much that way. She'd been so focused on training, on learning from Dualayn, and protecting the healer from the Brotherhood and their foul creation: the simulacrum posing as Smiles.

She had to regain his trust. Being around Ōbhin made her feel alive, especially doing dangerous things. She didn't dwell on her past and the guilt she felt for standing by and watching her mother drown her twin sister in whitewash. Ōbhin filled something inside of her. Something ripped out that Black day.

Something Chames, her first love, had also given her.

"You'd like him," she whispered to Chames as she laced up her boots. "He's direct and honest. Once you get him to open up. If you earn his trust, he doesn't hold back."

Boots tied, she stood. Her legs were a little stiff. A week's sleeping had reduced her weight. She'd been ravenous. When she wasn't sleeping, she'd feasted. She'd broken her fast on a heavy meal of fermented beans coating toast with thin slices of fried ham, and not the canned variety that flowed out of the factories and sold to the poor of the city.

She grabbed her binder and thrust it through a loop in her belt. The iron rod's weight felt comfortable on her side.

She marched forward, her short hair swaying loose about her shoulders. That was . . . different. She'd been braiding her hair since childhood. She'd never cut it so short, only trimming it to keep it from falling too far down her back. Now it tickled her neck and brushed her cheeks with every step.

It irked her. She liked twining ribbons in her hair. A nice mauve went well with her brown locks. She pondered new ways to style it as she descended the stairs. *Maybe I can gather it into twin tails on the sides of my head like Onderian children.*

She'd seen children like that roaming through the Onderian quarter where the people from the Lothon's southern neighbors lived in Kash. They came to find work and new beginnings in the largest city in the Arngelsh Isles. The girls looked cute with their short hair gathered up in the two tails that thrust from the sides of their heads.

At least it won't itch my neck, she thought as she reached the bottom of the stairs.

She nodded to Jilly and Chobay as they swept the entry hall. Dualayn was back into research. He had a do not disturb sign out. She sighed, wanting to get in there and tinker more on her creation. She had ideas for a bodysuit of emeralds to strengthen every bit of her. A network of them that she could don and doff. There would be vulnerabilities with the wire. If they were cut, it would short out the entire network.

And there's the problem of joints. Too much flexing could snap them. Maintenance would be necessary.

As much as she exercised and trained, Avena couldn't quite match even scrawny Bran in strength. They were similar in weight, Bran having only a stone on her, and he wasn't much taller, but he had just enough of an edge on her. Against Cerdyn or Fingers, she didn't stand much of a chance in a direct contest of brawn.

She needed brains. To think when she fought. Her jewelchine invention was one such tool.

The others were gathering for the daily exercises at the fourth hour from dawn, midday still two hours away. A gray overcast hid the sun, keeping things cool until it burned through and allowed summer to shine.

Ōbhin stiffened when he saw her.

The pain in his face stung. She had failed him badly. She had been there to watch his back, and instead her injury had allowed Creg to escape. They'd lost their chance to find out some solid answers in a way that wouldn't endanger Dualayn by angering the Brotherhood.

"Is it wise to be out of bed so soon?" Fingers asked, his brow heavy and face tight. He popped his knuckles as he studied her approach.

"I'm fine," she answered.

"She's fine," Smiles said, rolling his eyes. "Only a week ago, you was spasmin' in Ōbhin's arms, a piece of metal as long as my arm thrust into your head. But now you're 'fine.'"

"Yep." She forced herself to smile. "If you'd been hit in the head, nothing would've happened."

Smiles's grin grew and then he burst into laughter. "True, true. My Jilly can tell you that there ain't nothin' betwixt my head. Why I can take a thumpin' and keep goin'."

"You're not training with us any longer," Ōbhin said.

Avena stiffened. "I'm recovered."

"Doesn't matter." He turned his back on her, his leather jerkin creaking around his torso. "I never should've taught you to fight. It's not a woman's place."

"A woman's place?" she demanded. "When did you get to decide where my place is?"

"It's my guard to run."

The others tensed. Bran swallowed while Dajouth released a nervous laugh.

"I know she's a pretty thing, but she's a better fighter than me or Bran. She's as good as Smiles."

Ōbhin shrugged. "It was a mistake. Men fight, women tend the house. Way it's supposed to be."

"I see," she said, her voice frigid. Pain tore through her soul. She no longer wanted to win back his approval. Anger bubbled in her. "Then don't let me stop you. Go on, do your exercises."

"You're still here."

"And?" She planted her hands on her hips. "I think you made it quite clear that I'm not a part of your guard, so you can't give me orders. I can stand here if I want to."

Ōbhin shrugged, still not looking at her.

That infuriated her even more. Was she *that* weak? How badly had she messed up? She couldn't remember the fight. It was all hazy. A patchwork quilt stitched together wrong. What mistake had she made?

Smiles muttered, "Not what a smart leader would do."

She gave him a sharp look. The simulacrum's memory of Smiles's life seemed complete. It made her doubt what she'd seen the night of the attack. The real Smiles had said those words over a month ago when only she and Ōbhin had been around to hear them.

"Never give an order you know won't be obeyed," were Smiles's words on the subject.

Right now, Ōbhin was being an idiot by giving her orders she would defy.

Bran and Dajouth flicked nervous eyes back and forth between her and Ōbhin while Smiles rubbed at the back of his neck. Cerdyn didn't seem to care, and Fingers just studied her with concern, the digits of his right hand tracing over the swollen knuckles of his left.

"Calisthenics!" barked Ōbhin. "We'll start with push-ups."

Avena never could do as many as the men most days, but she normally could manage as many as Bran. Today, she could hardly do any.

Her arms felt noodly and weak. She panted and gasped as she forced herself to push up and down, lifting and raising her torso. Ōbhin was upfront, not looking at her as he grunted through his exercises. She glared at him when she wasn't fighting the burning pain in her arms.

She collapsed after fifteen. Half her normal amount. A dizzying wave washed over her. She pushed it down and waited for the others to finish. Then they launched into the jumping exercises. She gasped and wheezed by the time they finished, only just managing to keep up with them.

Running, however, broke her. She didn't even make it around the perimeter once. She grew dizzy as they jogged past the reed-lined shore of Lake Ophavin. The world swayed about her. She gasped, bent over, and seized her knees to keep from collapsing. Her stomach growled.

Fingers fell out and studied her as she struggled to catch her breath. Sweat poured down her face. The day's heat was mounting. The sun burned through the thin clouds. She swallowed excess spit, the back of her throat tasting coppery.

"You know he's scared," Fingers said.

"He's disgusted with me," she hissed. "Did you hear what he said about me?" The pain welled. "I thought I'd proven myself. I had, right? That I could fight. That he could trust me to watch his back."

He cocked his head. "That's important to you, huh?"

"I want to protect us all!" she snarled. "Why should my sex bar me from doing it?"

"Don't see how it is," he said.

"Ōbhin disagrees."

"No, he's scared," Fingers reiterated. "Boy don't handle it well."

"He's a man."

"Maybe to you." Fingers spat. "You're all boys to me. And a girl. Too young and serious. Bah, you and Ōbhin should be sneakin' off to kiss, not whackin' at each other with pipes."

"What business is it of yours?" she demanded. Fingers hardly ever said a word to her.

"Just tellin' you, he's scared."

"And *that's* a reason for him to turn his back on me? I survived." She swallowed. "How badly did I mess up that day? I can't remember it all. It's just pieces shattered in my mind. I can glimpse bits here and there. None of it makes sense."

"Girl, you didn't—"

"Don't 'girl' me!" she snapped. "I'm twenty. A woman."

Fingers released a long exhale. "Give him a few days. You really scared him. He wants to run. You keep chasin' him, it'll just make him run faster."

"What are you talking about?" Her legs quivered, sore muscles wanting to collapse. Her clothing trapped in the heat. The sunlight warmed the back of her neck, her short hair sticking to her sweaty skin. "Scare him? How?"

"You know how. It wasn't your fault, but that don't change it." Fingers rubbed the back of his neck. "Wanna reassure him, then make sure you're mended before you try 'n show him you're not weak. You look like you're 'bout to pass out."

"Feel like it," she muttered.

"No shame in takin' some time to recover," Fingers added.

She studied him. "I thought you hated women."

"Don't hate women. Just my wife." He sighed. "And I don't even hate her, which makes me the fool. Makes it hurt all the more. Elohm's Colours, girl, go. Sleep. Get well. Give Ōbhin time to realize he's an idiot, and then you two can go back to your plots."

The tips of her ears burned. "We're not plotting."

Fingers snorted. This fatherly smile crossed his lips. "Go on, girl. Don't wanna see you hurt neither. Ōbhin weren't the only one scared to see you with a piece of metal stuck in your head."

"You?"

"Bah," he growled. "Smiles. He almost pissed his pants, and Dajouth didn't have no flowery thing to say for days, to the delight of every maid and cook."

"Do you have children, Fingers?"

He stared at her for a long time before he said, "No, thank Elohm. I'd be a lousy father."

"I'm not so sure." Her stomach rumbled. "I think I'll eat an early lunch and then take a nap."

"He don't hate you," Fingers added. "Or think you're weak or that being a woman is holding you back."

"He said it," she muttered. As much as she wanted to be back working with Ōbhin, training, plotting, and venturing out on secret missions, she wouldn't swallow those words.

"Make him sweat when he apologizes. My wife always did that." Pain flashed across his face. He jogged on, leaving her standing there.

She felt bemused by the entire conversation. Confused. Was Fingers trying to say that Ōbhin, in an infuriating and demeaning way, wanted to protect her? *I didn't fail him, he just doesn't want to see me hurt. Like I want that for him.*

She headed inside.

If he expects me to wait around dreading dark news while he goes and does something reckless . . .

First things first; she had to recover. Then she would figure out how to make Ōbhin see reason.

Fifty-Fourth Day of Forgiveness, 755 EU

Ōbhin hadn't seen much of Avena. She'd been spending time in her room for the last three days, taking care of herself. He hated the pain he caused her, but it was better to drive her away than to see her bleeding out on the floor again.

When he closed his eyes at night, the pool of her blood spread through his memory. A growing tide of crimson surrounded her head while the length of steel thrust into her skull. He'd get her killed. He'd mess up and lose the only thing keeping him from sinking back into the darkness.

He didn't know when it had happened. He told himself he was doing it to protect Dualayn and the others, but he knew that while Dualayn was a good man, it was Avena that he'd come to focus on. He didn't know when the shift in priorities had occurred. Maybe when she'd coaxed him out of the darkness.

Some days, he almost felt like he could take off his sable gloves and don a better color. A nice purple, the color of a warrior. Purple represented Qasigh, the Tone of Fatherhood. It was no coincidence that amethyst jewelchines produced shields and bands of restraining energy. They resounded with a father's love and desire to protect his family, just as healing topazes resounded with the Tone of Motherhood, spreading compassion and care, the tender love of a mother.

He could be rid of the Black and walk in the light. To do so, he had to keep Avena alive. He couldn't do that if he led her into danger.

When he'd turned his back on her, it had ripped out his heart. Pain pulsed through his soul. He never wanted to give her anguish, but he saw no other way. What sort of man protected by hurting the ones he cared for?

Loved.

He loved her. He knew it now. And he would never have her. Never be worthy of her. She could do so much better than him.

As he organized his men for their morning exercises, his gaze slid to Smiles. *I could just cut you down. That would protect everyone. Then I could leave.*

He was doing it again. Fleeing. Why was it so easy for him to be a coward?

Anger flared at his stupidity. He should just go to her. Talk to her. Reason with her.

She's too stubborn to back down, he told himself. *I never should have taught her to fight. She's a woman. It's a man's duty to bleed in their place. We're strong so we can protect them. We brave the wilderness and face the black-faced bears, the white leopards, and the winter snows to keep the home and hearth safe.*

He struggled to believe those words as another part of him whispered: *She didn't need your help fighting all those Green-Faced Boys. Trounced them all.*

He focused on the memory of her lying bleeding. The cost of his failure. If he'd taken her to any man but Dualayn, she *would* be dead.

The front door opened, the creak echoing across the lawn. His gaze flitted past Jolayn pushing Bravine and her wheelchair past a small group of sheep grazing, and landed on Avena stepping out of the manor. Mauve ribbons gathered her hair into two small tails above her ears. He tensed, fearing she meant to join their training again.

Then he noticed the dark-red dress she wore.

He relaxed.

She wasn't dressed for training. She must have finally accepted that she didn't belong with Ōbhin. She was better than swinging a sword or a stave. She didn't need to risk her mind. She'd invented a jewelchine. How many people in the world could claim that? Dualayn had no heir. She was practically his daughter. She would inherit his knowledge, even his fortune.

She'll make something bright with this world. It'll resound with the Seven Harmonious Tones, drowning out Niszeh's discord.

He watched her march down the path from the house, descending the gentle slope of the hills. One of the sheep baaed at her passage. It was skinny, shorn a few weeks ago. She marched back straight, her skirt swishing with her passage. The summer sun caressed the softness of her cheeks, her lips. She passed out of sight for a moment behind a rhododendron bush in full bloom. She emerged on the other side, nearer to the main gate.

Cold fear screeched through the warm melody singing through him. She marched for the gate alone. His feet moved before he could stop himself. He crossed the distance to her in long strides. She whirled at the sound of his approach, her expression hardening. Her chin lifted.

He didn't want her to hate him, only to stay away from him and remain in safety where she belonged. However, he could suffer her anger, her loathing, if it meant protecting her. He slowed to a stop before her, his tulwar swaying as it hung from his heavy belt.

"If you're going out, you need an escort."

She arched her eyebrow. Her hair gathered in the two short tails on either side of her head made her seem younger. Vulnerable. "I've ventured into Kash alone before. I'll be fine."

"Kash isn't the same as it used to be. I'll send one of my men with you."

"Is there a riot?" She glanced to the east. The grove of trees beyond the estate hid the curtain walls of central Kash. "I haven't heard the bells calling the guard."

"Doesn't mean there won't be one."

She patted her satchel as she said, "I'll be fine, Ōbhin. I don't need you to worry over me."

Avena took a step forward. He seized her arm, the sable of his gloves contrasting with the red of her dress. She shot a fierce gaze at his hands before her dagger-sharp eyes flicked up to his. She ripped her arm free of his black grip.

"I'm not *yours* to command! I go where I will! You don't have to worry about me. I'm not going unarmed."

He wanted to seize her by the scruff of the neck, haul her inside, and tie her to her bed, but she was already marching to the gates. She pushed them open enough to slip through them while he stood rooted. He should go with her, but he was trying to drive her away.

There hasn't been a riot in a week. Maybe she'll be fine.

He hesitated, torn. He wanted to be at her side, a shield against any harm, but the way she'd looked at him ripped at his heart. He glanced at the sun. It was two hours from noon. A warm, bright day.

Qasigh, let your protective Tone resonate around her, he prayed.

As he returned to his waiting men, ignoring their questioning looks, worry hummed through him. He felt plucked by it like a lyre tuned too much, his string on the verge of snapping.

9

"Doesn't even think I can walk through Kash alone," Avena muttered as she marched across the Tendril Bridge into the Breezy Hills Slums.

Wreathed in anger, she hardly noticed the street urchins and neighborhood youths who flocked around her, crying out her name or calling her fair lady. Without thought, she pulled the purse out of her pocket, scattering the brass glimmers, the smallest denomination of Lothonian coins, to them. The coins could buy them a day's food. It was the least she could do.

It did little to satiate her rage.

"He knows I can fight," she hissed at herself, barely over her breath.

The children were laughing and swarming around her, wearing worn shirts and ragged dresses, dirt streaking cheeks. She cast out another spray of glimmers, the brass coins falling like seeds cast from a farmer's hand.

From her father's hand.

There was another man who didn't want anything to do with her. Who didn't think she was good enough. He was a hazy memory now. She hadn't seen him since she was seven. Thirteen years had muted her memories. She could see Evane like a bright flame, and visualize her mother alternating as a warm sun or a dark void.

That terrible day played in Avena's mind as she marched through the slums, leaving behind the empty leather purse and the children to play their games. It had been one of her mother's dark days. The darkest. Mostly, her mother was a bright and happy woman, but sometimes the Black would creep into her. She would sit listlessly, sometimes not even getting out of bed. Father would ignore Mother, performing extra chores around the farm, working himself to the bone until his knuckles swelled and he collapsed exhausted at night in the chair by the central hearth, stained from working in the field. When Mother brightened, she'd do the work of two women, laughing and playing, full of life and energy.

That day, Avena and her twin sister had sought to bring flowers to brighten their mother's dark day. Only something had gone wrong. Their mother had been utterly replaced, like a darkling had crept into her skin and wore it like a puppet. She'd wanted to make Avena and Evane clean.

She'd drowned Evane in whitewash while Avena stood by frozen with fear and disbelief that their mother could do something so awful. Father had saved Avena's life by killing Mother. Then he'd walked away. She'd never seen him again.

Avena wasn't good enough for her father, and now she feared she wasn't good enough for Ōbhin. She didn't know how to prove herself if he wouldn't let her train. Wouldn't take her on secret missions against those who threatened Dualayn.

When Ōbhin had asked her to come with him to seize Creg, a rush of euphoric joy had filled her.

She rubbed at her head, feeling for the wound. She felt whole, mended by the topazes. Not even a scar remained. She kept rubbing the spot and, for a moment, her nerves fuzzed like they had when she'd first awoken. Avena stumbled and struggled to remember what she'd done to cause her injury and lose Ōbhin's trust in her.

"You okay?" a man asked her, his voice soft.

She blinked and realized she was on her knees. She didn't remember falling. She shook her head and looked up to see one of the city guards. He wore a tabard of green and blue with Lothon's white stag.

"You all right, madam?" he asked, gray hair peeking out beneath the leather cap he wore. He helped her stand.

"Just . . ." A shiver ran through her. She couldn't remember falling. "I'm recovering from an injury. Thank you for your assistance."

He nodded. "My pleasure to help."

Then she realized she'd walked the length of Angle Road through the Breezy Hills and Roida Slums to reach Patience Gate. The stone archway, piercing through the thick curtain walls which marked the original bounds of the city, were painted yellow. Traffic flowed in and out, farmers pushing handcarts laden with fresh produce, laborers in rough clothing, skilled craftsmen carrying canvas bags laden with the tools of their craft. A carriage trundled out, the coat of arms Duke Mesayn Thastom painted on the door, the guard sitting beside the driver holding a crossbow.

She gave the helpful guard a smile as she headed into the city itself. Ostensibly, she was delivering a letter for Dualayn. He'd left it outside of his lab labeled for Refractor Charlis. Avena needed her bosom friend's advice so had leaped at the chance to deliver the letter.

How could she show Ōbhin she was useful without driving him away? Fingers's warning echoed in her mind. She had no idea. *How can I show him I'm strong again if he won't let me near him? It's an impossible snarl.*

Patience Gate led into the southern half of old Kash. The Ustern bisected the city. She could see the Pillar, the ancient tower from which the kings of Lothon used to reign, thrusting gray over all the buildings. The smaller Rainbow Belfry marked the location of the Temple of the Seven Colours, the seat of Elohm's temporal power. There, the new high refractor sought to quell the fracturing chaos threatening to send her country into another civil war.

Or an external one with Roidan.

The Rainbow Belfry itself was a thing of wonder. An artifact that existed before Kash's first brick was laid, a tower made up of a spiral of white, red, blue, purple, green, orange, and yellow stones that were all melded together to form a solid whole. Every hour, the tower resonated a loud note that chimed across the city. It could often be heard out in Dualayn's manor.

The houses inside the curtain wall were older, often made of stone with their walls painted in white colors and with scrollwork patterns along the trim. The first floors were given over to shops where goods were sold or workshops where common goods, or exquisite ones for those with coin, were produced. The second, third, and sometimes fourth floors housed residences. Some were single-family homes, the shop beneath owned for generations; others were tenements where three or four families dwelled. Public houses lay on every third or fourth block, serving their neighborhoods. In alleys, she spotted the occasional ruffian. Though she was in the more prosperous part of Kash, the gangs had their presence.

The entire city was divided a hundred different ways. Most gangs were Lothonian, but the Onderian laborers, Roidanese migrants, and Tethyrian vagrants had their own thugs, all warring and battling over a few blocks. Some were allied with the Brotherhood, others the Rangers. It was said the gangs could switch sides at any time as new leaders rose and fell in their vicious, pack-like hierarchy.

The sooner she and Ōbhin could extract Dualayn from the Brotherhood's grasp, the better. *Maybe his Demochian friend could assist,* she wondered as she passed St. Jettay's Square and the Temple of the Seven Colours. A group of people prayed in the center of the large plaza. *Should I suggest it to Dualayn?*

It did disturb her how easily Dualayn agreed to work with the Brotherhood and their patron, the enigmatic White Lady.

Past the temple, she came to the Grand Course north. The wide boulevard led to the Houses of Parliament. The legislative body of her country, who should be a check against the king's abusive powers instead of enabling them, lay before her. It was built along the southern bank of the Ustern, rising five floors tall with windows set at regular intervals. The exterior stones were Homphrial marble, characterized by its blue and red veins. The windowsills and frames were gilded gold and stylized to resemble antlers meeting to form a box. As she neared Rower's Square where the street terminated, the shape of the long building became more and more apparent. It was really three separate structures connected by two narrow wings. Each was one of the three Houses.

The central one was the House of the Serfs, representing the interests of the common men and women of Lothon. Any who owned land could vote for its members or run for the seat. To the right lay the House of the Peerage; its members were nobles who inherited their seats from their ancient bloodlines. The left held the House of the Clerics, the refractors and priests appointed by the high refractor to represent the church. A law had to pass two of the three houses with a greater majority, though each also held their own area of responsibility.

Right now, the House of the Peerage and the Serfs were enabling King Anglon to levy new taxes.

Rower's Square, a large plaza, lay before Parliament. In the center rested the fountain of Lovineth the Rower, who'd famously rescued members of

Parliament from King Loshen Briflon's wrath three hundred years ago. Lovineth had used his rowboat to ferry them to safety. They'd commissioned a statue of him standing on the prow of a boat surrounded by maidens pouring water into the fountain to keep his vessel afloat with the love and hope of Lothon. Above him billowed the nation's flag, the white stag on a field of blue and green divided horizontally.

A crowd milled in the square, men wearing the green and white cloths, some holding signs written with charcoal on scraps of lumber, begging Parliament to give relief to the taxes. Some held oars, a show of support to Parliament against the Crown. Rivermen, they'd call themselves, inspired by the actions of Lovineth. Avena threaded through them without any fear, and not because of the line of city guards at the base of the steps up to Parliament's entrance. The protesters glanced at her, rough men, some with gaunt eyes and shoulders bowed by unseen forces.

Pity stirred through her. These were her people. She was a farmer's daughter. She would never forget her roots. What King Anglon was doing wasn't right. He should care more for his people than his ambition. She'd heard the rumors buzzing through the house of war with Roidan, their neighbor to the east. Ondere might take advantage of such a conflict to reclaim the Colonies, their land lost to Lothon years ago.

Another triple war. The last time the three nations who shared the large island had fought, it had led to chaos and suffering.

But what can I do to stop it? she wondered as she approached the guards. They glanced at her clothing and parted for her without a word.

She held her skirts as she climbed the steps. Her satchel swung on her hip from her shoulder. It held an earthen gauntlet and binder. If another riot broke out, she wouldn't be defenseless. *If I fight my way out of chaos, will that prove to Ōbhin I'm not a liability?*

She swept inside the building and spoke with a young man sitting at a desk. He wore a well-tailored jacket of bright blue with silver trimming, his cheeks covered in rouge as was the current fashion among the young nobility. He was some lord's son serving as a page to Parliament for the prestige.

He gave her directions to Refractor Charlis's office.

Unsurprisingly, it lay in the House of the Cleric's wing. She strode down the grand hall connecting the three buildings, the floors polished marble with a runner of orange carpet down the center. The Colour of Compassion *should* remind the lawmakers, a body of mostly men, to remember the suffering of the poor.

She passed oil paintings of "important" men striking dramatic poses. Some appeared proud in armor, shiny breastplates and pauldrons, sitting gallantly upon destriers, resplendent and martial. Others wore the fashion of their time, some in curious garments that Avena had never seen before: jackets of velvet with puffy sleeves, thick scarves wrapped about necks, voluminous pants that almost resembled skirts divided for riding.

Refractor Charlis's office lay on the fourth floor. She felt only lightly winded when she'd finished her climb instead of a dizzy spell, glad her stamina returned to her. Each office had a brass nameplate affixed to the darkly polished doors. She passed several, belonging to other priests and refractors, before she found the one she searched for.

She opened it onto a smaller office, an antechamber with a desk covered in parchment, its chair pulled back as though its occupant had left it in haste. The walls were painted in rainbow hues, the seven colors forming chevron patterns that spread out from the middle and vanished behind a shelf. It held a complete set of religious tomes upon it.

"Deffona?" Avena asked as she glanced around the small room. A small coat rack stood by the door. She hung her satchel from it and frowned. There was no place in here for her friend to hide. "Hello?"

The door to Charlis's office opened and a smiling Deffona stepped out, her cheeks rosy with delight. She adjusted her veil and then clapped her hands together. With a girlish squeal, she rushed around her desk to Avena.

Avena matched her gleeful excitement.

The two embraced as words poured out of their mouths, both speaking so fast at and at the same time, their words merged to form something akin to birdsong. Avena greeted her friend while Deffona apologized for not visiting her more while she recovered. Their excitement echoed through the room as they rocked together in a tight hug.

Finally, Deffona broke the hug and took a step back. "Why are you here? Did you want to take me to tea? There's this wonderful tea house nearby. They serve a delightful Relashim oolong."

"No, no," Avena said. She turned to her satchel and pulled out the thick envelope. She thrust it at her friend. "Dualayn's answer to Charlis."

"He's been expecting this," Deffona said, hugging it tight. "We're trying to head off the king's mad ambition to seize all of the Border Fangs for himself."

Avena smiled. She felt like a tiny link in a jewelchine network, not unlike the one she'd built for her earthen gauntlet. She wasn't an important cog, but her turning had done something to arrest this looming disaster. A war with Roidan over something as petty as jewels made little sense to her when the two countries traded all the time.

Deffona set the envelope on her desk, then her eyes flicked up and down. Her gaze narrowed. "Is Ōbhin being delicate?"

"That's a word for it," Avena answered.

"Yours?"

"Disappointed in me and reticent to see my weakness get me injured again." A weight pressed on her. Avena's good mood evaporated.

"Weakness? You? He said that?" Anger flashed across Deffona's face. "I thought he had *some* sense. Maybe he's as blind as a cockroach in the sun, but surely he could have recognized you're not weak."

"I'm not strong," Avena said.

"I don't mean physically!" She waved her bare hand in the air, her yellow sleeve rustling. "That's not the strength that counts, and you know it. Look at you. The only time I've seen you look more miserable was after Chames's death." Deffona's face tightened. "I should have been clearer with him. Maybe it was the rosebush metaphor that confused him."

"Rosebush?" Befuddlement rippled across Avena's expression.

"You know that it isn't *your* weakness he's worried about."

"Fingers said he's scared of seeing me get hurt, but I wouldn't have gotten hurt if I didn't mess up. I just can't remember *how*. It's all jumbled up in here." She tapped her head. A fuzzy ripple ran through her body, a strange disassociation. She felt unreal for a moment. Alien.

"You okay?"

"I just . . . I still get dizzy sometimes," Avena muttered.

"You did have a sword stuck in your head. It's a miracle that you're alive. Elohm's Colours healed you through His gems."

"Through Dualayn." Avena swallowed. "How can I prove to Ōbhin that I'm strong if he's running away from me? He won't let me train. I need to get better so I won't mess up again."

"Why do you think you messed up?"

"I took a piece of steel in the head." She rubbed at the spot, feeling for any leftover damage. Her fingers caressed whole skin over hard bone. "How else could it have happened?"

"I don't know." Deffona cocked her head, her veil rustling over her wimple. "Even if it was your fault, that's not why Ōbhin's acting this way. He doesn't want to see you get hurt again." A smile blossomed on her lips. "He wants to keep you safe like a prized treasure."

Avena furrowed her brow. "You *really* need to stop reading those books. They're not realistic. I don't want to be his prized treasure. I want to be at his side."

"Even though it's dangerous?"

"How can I keep him safe if I'm not beside him?" Avena asked and then blinked at her words. They shocked her. "I . . . I don't want him to go off and do dangerous things when I'm not around."

"You're finally realizing it, aren't you?" Deffona clapped her hands together and sighed again. "Love."

Avena sank down into the chair beside her. She shifted her skirt out of habit. She went to reach for her braid of hair but found nothing, instead brushing one of her small tails. "A month ago, I was afraid I couldn't love anyone at all."

"You were just confused. Now you love him, and he's trying to drive you away. That's not good. He shouldn't hurt you like that."

"He just doesn't want me to get injured, but I can't just remain behind. I can't be helpless." The emptiness in her swelled. "Never again. Maybe I should be more careful in a fight, but I know I was useful during the raid. I can remember fighting the local gang. My invention worked. It was exhilarating. I was so happy. He *trusted* me to watch his back, and I don't want to lose that."

"You can't let him push you away. You have to defy him. If he tries to run, tackle him."

"What?" Avena gasped. "Like grab his legs or something?"

"Yes! I know it's romantic that he wants to keep you safe while he goes out and fights evil, but you're not that type of woman."

Fights evil? Avena favored her friend an exasperated look.

"You'll have to be persuasive. I know he can be a delicate man, but rosebushes are resilient. You don't let him get away. You beat it through his thick skull that the best way for him to protect you is for you to be at his side when things are most dangerous." Deffona sank into her own chair on the other side of the desk. "Fighting monsters and braving evil together. And when you're not fighting, when you return to your bower, you can share in other delights."

"My life is not one of your novels," Avena muttered, her cheeks warm. She'd seen Ōbhin shirtless a few times. Memories of his brown, strong body flashed through her mind. Then the way he'd touched her bare face after Ust had attacked.

"My novels aren't this exciting. The women in them just wait to be saved. You have to be proactive about it."

"I don't need to be saved. He's already done that, remember?"

"I know." Deffona's voice grew airy and distant. "You are so lucky." She sighed again. "So, this is what you have to do. March up to him and give him a talking to. Let him know that you will not be wrapped up in swaddling cloth. That you'll do . . . whatever it is you two are doing."

"Protecting Dualayn," Avena said, her cheeks burning.

"Right, right. Tell him that you're there until the end."

"I will," Avena straightened in her chair. "When I get back. I'll corner him."

"Try the grove by your house." Deffona leaned forward, resting her cloth-wrapped chin on her bare hands. "Alone. You can kiss and make up once you have this all worked out."

"Maybe," Avena said. Her mood lifted, she glanced at the door behind her friend. "How is this new job?"

"I like it," Deffona said. "It's so different from working at the hospital, but Refractor Charlis's work is important. We're the bulwark against the king and his madness. There are clergy who are taking bribes. It's disgusting."

Avena grimaced. "They're holy men."

"I know." Deffona shook her head. "Holy men can be weak, too. Charlis fears our new high refractor is being influenced, but I'm doing what I can. Our high refractor is a great man."

"And his stance on the war?"

"He's talking about being neutral on this matter of war," Deffona said. Then quickly added, "Not supporting it, but he's not denouncing it, either. You have to understand, he's the holy leader of Roidan and Ondere, too. And those nations on Busil if they'll ever stop being heretics. He can't play favorites."

Avena gave a slow nod, though she would appreciate a more proactive high refractor. "Well, I've heard the other nations think our church is too influenced by Lothon."

"Exactly!" Deffona said.

"But if he's not denouncing it, then other clergymen in the House don't feel as pressured to make a stand. Right?"

"Charlis is trying to make a coalition with those in the House of the Serfs who recognize this for the true danger it is. Conscription and chaos. It could be another ten years of war if this spirals out of control."

"I hope he's successful." Avena shifted. She owned no property, so she couldn't do much to influence the House of Serfs, and she had no title to petition the the House of Lords.

"Tomorrow, the House of Clerics is going to pass Charlis's bill," Deffona said, her voice breathy again. Her cheeks were bright with her excitement. "The high refractor himself was in here just a little while ago to lend his support. I'm not supposed to talk about the details, but you won't gossip."

"Of course not," Avena said, leaning in. Excitement quivered through her at being included.

"It'll say that peace with Roidan is necessary and will ask for a lessening of tariffs. To lower the cost of buying gems from them and encouraging them to purchase our jewelchines." Deffona tapped the letter. "That's what is in here. Information to help sell this idea."

"Wonderful. I'm glad you're happy here. You look alive. No bags under your eyes."

"No Eldest Sister Anglia harping about every fault I have. She was furious that Charlis hired me, but she couldn't say no to a refractor. I even have my own room at his church." Deffona gave Avena a studious look. "You should come to mass. Being a good person isn't enough if you don't attend any."

"His church is so far from the estate. There's one I go to when I can," Avena said, shame skittering through her. When had she last gone? Dualayn never bothered, but many of his servants went to a small church in the Breezy Hills Slums. "I'll try to come and visit yours so we can talk after mass."

Deffona beamed.

They chatted for a little longer before Avena's eagerness to confront Ōbhin and put this entire mess behind them grew too much. She embraced her friend, the pair exchanging kisses on the cheeks, then Avena departed.

Ōbhin occupied her thoughts. Being around him was exciting. A joy. She didn't feel that bit of her scraped out by Evane's death around him. Like with Chames, Ōbhin filled something in her. What she'd felt for Miguil was a pale thing. She'd been tricking herself into thinking she loved him.

If Ōbhin had kissed me that night in the inn . . . Avena smiled. Maybe once they had made up, they could start doing things like kissing. Maybe other things. She swept out of Parliament and navigated through the protesters.

There seemed like more of them than before.

She reached the street, her skirts rustling as she moved through the afternoon traffic. The day's heat roiled around her. She fanned her face and shifted her satchel. When she was about halfway to the city gate, the Rainbow Belfry chimed. A loud note washed over her. This close, she felt it dancing across her skull.

She swayed, almost disoriented by the sound of the artifact ringing in the house. The fuzziness returned to the tips of her fingers. She gasped as a dizzying wave flooded through her. She stumbled, clutching at her temples. Her fingers felt alien as they squeezed her skull. Sounds grew muted, like she'd ducked her head underwater. Her legs wobbled. She lurched to the right. She stumbled into an alley before catching herself on a building's wall.

Cool darkness.

She staggered forward two steps. The world swam as she passed a stack of old crates. She grabbed one for support. Darkness rippled across her vision. Fear gripped her in slimy hands as her flesh felt more and more unreal.

Her thoughts were mist about to blow away.

She sank down the wall to crouch, whimpering. The world spun around her, the alley flipping topsy-turvy. Her body felt remote. Distant. Then she felt shorn from it. Darkness plunged over her as she lost all connection to her flesh.

Her thoughts drifted through a void until a bright, white light gleamed. She tumbled towards it, drawn to it like a diamond lamp illuminating a dark street. She reached out for it, touched it, and fell into a dream.

10

"She hasn't returned yet?" Ōbhin demanded of Cerdyn as he stood guard at the main gate. The sun was sinking to the west, shadows growing long, the world staining red.

"No," Cerdyn said, the grim-faced guard scratching at his neck. He wore his chainmail coat, a binder hanging from his left hip, a backsword on the other. His brows knit together, squishing his thick, black eyebrows into a single, fuzzy line. "Would've told you."

"Niszeh's Black Tone!" Ōbhin spat, icy fingers clawing at his guts. He'd heard the Rainbow Belfry chime five times since she'd left.

"No sign of riots," said Smiles. "Maybe she's stayin' in Kash. She's meetin' with her friend. Least wot my Jilly said."

"She wouldn't stay the night." Ōbhin rolled his shoulders. His leather jerkin clung to his sweat-soaked skin. "She's just delivering a letter, right?"

"Accordin' to my Jilly." The fake Smiles rubbed the back of his neck. "Maybe we should go look for her. Night's fallin'. She gotta pass through dangerous slums to get back."

Ōbhin nodded. He wanted to avoid Avena, but he couldn't let her get hurt. *I should have just gone with her. If she's hurt . . .*

Pain punched him.

"Let's go," Fingers said, stepping out. "Light's fadin'."

"Right," Smiles said. "I can get my binder. Be back in a lightnin's fart."

"No," Ōbhin said, glancing at the guards. Bran and Dajouth stood nearby, both looking worried. "Bran and Fingers, with me. Smiles, you have the command." The words tasted bitter, but Smiles was here to protect Dualayn, or so Ōbhin believed. Until Dualayn stopped being useful to the Brotherhood, Smiles wasn't a danger.

When that day came . . .

"Ain't nothin' gonna happen here," said Smiles. "Unless there's another bandit chief you done pissed off and who knows a sorcerer to enchant him."

"Only one of those," Ōbhin muttered.

The Rainbow Belfry's resonating note drifted through the air from Kash.

Ōbhin marched out of the gate, his shadow stretching long before him. Fear squeezed his chest. He struggled to breathe as he marched forward. He shouldn't have let her go off alone. He should have gone with her or sent Fingers or Bran to be a second pair of eyes.

Bile tickled the back of his throat with every step he took. The pressure crushing his chest grew and grew. Panic nibbled on the edges of his self-control. He forced his back straight as he tromped across the Tendril Bridge and entered the Breezy Hills Slums.

∽

Avena kissed a man in her dreams.

She held him tight as she lay beneath him on a bed. The sheets were sleeker than anything she'd felt. Smoother than the Demochian silk gowns that hung uselessly in Bravine's wardrobe. The cloth set her skin alive; almost as exciting as the man upon her.

He had brown skin and coal-dark hair. She shivered in his embrace. They were naked, bodies pressed tight. She felt the cooling heat of passion dying in her nethers. For a moment, she thought it was Ōbhin she kissed, but when he lifted his head and opened his eyes, they were sapphire. A pure blue instead of Ōbhin's dark brown. This man had delicate features, handsome, almost beautiful.

He spoke; his words were musical, a language Avena didn't understand, but they were reassuring words. Loving words. He stroked her cheek as he stared down at her. Then his fingers drifted to her hair.

He brought a lock to his lips, kissing not her familiar brown strands but a white-silver lock. He said something that made Avena laugh in delight. She pulled him back to her lips, kissing him, joy bursting through her mind.

The dream slipped from Avena.

She woke up on something far harder, the stench of sour dirt in her nose. She blinked. Eyes focused. She lay in a dark alley on her side behind a stack of crates. She groaned, pressing herself up. Detritus from the alley's cobblestones smudged her cheek. Some spilled off as she sat up. Confusion swirled through her.

"Dark?" she muttered. It had been early afternoon when she'd left Parliament. She could remember the strange dizziness that had beset her. She stared down at her fingers, flexing and closing them.

They felt real. Solid. *Her* hands.

She leaned her head back against the stone wall, drawing in breaths. A cold terror nestled in her belly. She had passed out in the middle of Kash. She gasped, feeling for her satchel that held her binder and her earthen gauntlet.

Missing.

She suddenly felt dirty. She bolted to her feet, violated by being robbed while she lay helpless. Her skin crawled. Whoever had burgled her could have done much, much worse to her. She patted herself, probing for pain, new bruises, finding none. Acids churning in her stomach, she darted out of the alley and almost crashed into a man in a waistcoat and felt hat.

"You okay, madam?" he asked.

"I'm fine," she lied, wanting to get away from here. Back to the safety of Dualayn's house. He had walls.

Ōbhin.

"Do you want me to fetch the guard? You look . . ." The man's delicate tone trailed off.

"I'm fine," she said. "Just fell, that's all."

"If you say so. Perhaps, I can escort you home?"

She shook her head and pushed from him. She rushed forward with the flowing traffic down the street, feeling so naked. She'd lost her weapon. Her glove to strengthen her. Night was falling. She'd have to walk through the Roida Slums in the dark. Defenseless.

I passed out in an alley. Anyone could have violated me. I'm lucky to have only lost my satchel. Fear slithered through her. *What's wrong with me? Am I not healed? Dualayn said there could be issues. Is this it?*

She chewed on her lower lip as she walked at a brisk pace, skirts swirling about her legs.

It's a warm day. Maybe it was just the heat. Her throat felt sore, in need of refreshment. *I didn't drink enough. I pushed myself too hard. That's it. Just passed out from heatstroke. I'm fine. I made a full recovery.*

She neared Patience Gate. Even as the sun set, traffic still streamed both ways. Those who worked outside the wall returned home, and those who worked inside left to do the same. A deep purple stretched across the sky. Compassion shone above her, the orange moon half-full. Behind her, Forgiveness would be rising near-full.

She had to hurry.

She paused at the gates. They were large, open maws leading out into danger. She hugged herself. *What if I pass out again?*

Avena pushed that thought down. She could still defend herself even without a weapon. Ōbhin had trained her. She just had to march out there and not be afraid. She'd never let fear hold her back. No way she would start now.

Despite her confidence, she couldn't move. Her body had betrayed her, made her helpless once more. Flashes of all the horrid things that could have happened to her in the alley assaulted her mind. A sickly ooze bubbled through her veins. It spread throughout her body, congealing her blood and weighing down every bit of her.

She wanted to vomit. To scrub herself clean.

You've walked this way a hundred times! she told herself. *You're losing daylight. You have no money. What are you going to do? Stand here? Do you think this will be any safer after dark? Stop being useless!*

People passed her, leaving the city without any concern. Her bodice constricted tight about her chest. Breathing grew more difficult. Spots danced on the edges of her vision. She felt on the verge of fainting as she struggled to control herself.

You didn't need weapons before to walk from Kash to Dualayn's household. Why now? Just take a step forward.

She glanced down at her dark-red skirts. The layers of petticoats she wore beneath gave her dress a bell-like shape. They fell to her ankles, a hint of the lacy underskirt peeking out. She lifted the fabric just enough to stare at her heeled shoes made of stiff, fuzzy suede. She just had to move one of them.

She hated this so much. Why did her body have to betray her and make her helpless?

With a grunt, she took a step.

She could do this. She had to.

Ōbhin will never let me rush into danger with him if I panic over this!

Another step.

She strained to do it. The yellow-painted gates leaned closer. This fearful rush built and built in her. Frustration washed through her. She hated this weakness. It wasn't who she was. She'd leaped before bandits with only a dagger to defend her patient. She'd stepped up to face an angry mob to support her friends. Ōbhin!

She'd fought an entire gang of ruffians.

I had my binder then. My earthen gauntlet. Now I'm alone. I could pass out at any time.

Bitter gall burned her throat. She threw back her head, about to screech her frustration, when a loud voice called, "Avena!"

She lowered her head to spot Bran rushing forward. The youth had a huge grin on his face as he pushed between two laborers who cursed at him. He didn't care. He stopped before her, his smile almost swallowing his face.

"We were so worried!" he said, pink touching his cheeks. "We practically ran hoping to find where you'd gone."

"We?" she asked, already feeling safer just with his presence. He wore a linen shirt, open in the front to show off the chest hairs he was so proud of growing, and leather pants. He had a binder hanging from his belt.

"Fingers and Ōbhin."

Her breath caught at Ōbhin's name. He approached slowly, wearing his leather jerkin and pants, his hands wrapped in black. He stared at her, his face intense, his eyes flicked up and down her, scanning her. This breathless relief fluttered through her. She didn't have to be afraid. If she fainted, they—Ōbhin —would protect her.

"Why were you out for so long?" he growled, his face suddenly full of anger.

For a moment, she wanted to march to him and throw his anger back into his face. Then the helpless fear curdled in her. She squirmed, embarrassed to admit what had happened. He stopped before her, scrutinizing her.

"You're dirty," he said. "Your dress is stained. Are you hurt?"

"I'm fine," she said. "I just tri—"

"Where's your satchel? Were you . . .?"

Her cheeks burned. He was seeing how weak she was. What if she *was* weak? What if she had been fooling herself? Had she truly fought all those ruffians by herself? Or had Ōbhin helped her? Her memories of that day were so fragmented.

Dualayn told me there would be . . . differences. What if I never was who I think I am? What if I'm not strong? She shuddered. *What if I'm just a burden to Ōbhin? I want to stand with him but . . .*

I can't even walk through Kash without passing out and being robbed.

"I'm fine," she said. "They didn't do anything to me. Just . . . It's okay. Can we go? I want to return home."

"Of course," Ōbhin said, his voice growing gentler. His eyes held pity she couldn't stand.

She'd rather he would be angry with her, defiant. That he thought she was strong enough to withstand it. He'd reined in his temper when she'd revealed her weakness. Tears hovered at the edges. Emotion choked the back of her throat. She feared breaking down and crying right here, crushed by how wrong this day had gone.

All her plans to confront him had evaporated. Even if she had fought all those ruffians by herself, she couldn't trust her body now not to faint at the wrong time.

Ōbhin offered his arm, the pity remaining in his eyes.

A little bit of fire kindled in her. She marched ahead towards the gate like she hadn't been too terrified to approach it. The men fell in around her, Fingers on her right, silent but relaxed. She wanted to take his fatherly arm, but she didn't.

She could be strong enough to walk with three men around her.

Pain stung through Ōbhin as he lowered his arm and caught up with her.

This is what you wanted, he reminded himself. *To set her free.*

He didn't know how she could have been robbed. The thieves must have come on her fast, overpowered her before she could draw her binder. It could happen to anyone. Of course, she wouldn't let it affect her. She marched back straight.

She didn't need him. She was strong enough without him around. She would walk her own path, a bright one. One where he wouldn't get her killed. That was good enough. Love wasn't for him. He did foolish things for it.

Terrible things.

The sun descended as they passed through the Roida Slums, returning to the estate in silence.

11

Sixth Day of Patience, 755 EU

Avena's consciousness escaped her alien body again. She slumped into dreams.

She stood before a diamond. It was massive, as tall as she was, and shaped in such intricate ways. A bewildering array of facets that reflected broken mirrors of reality. A network of fine, gold wires ran from it, some embedded in the gem itself. A faint hum emanated from it, a light glowing in its heart.

She glanced at the man on her right. The lover from her dream, brown skin and blue eyes. He wore a shirt with shiny buttons, the fabric possessing a silky sheen, the stitching fine. It fit him well. He smiled at her, a gesture of reassurance.

He spoke to her in that musical tongue, his words a light tenor. He stood before a black gem. She had never seen its like. She knew of no black gem but obsidian, only this didn't look melted and glassy like the few bits of the forbidden stone she'd seen. It had a smoky quality to it and hummed like the diamond but at a different note. He placed his hand on it.

She pressed her hand on the diamond. Smooth. Cool. Waiting.

There were others in the room. On her right glowed a massive ruby. A woman stood before it, blonde like a Roidanese, her skin as pale as Avena's own. Then a sapphire, the woman standing by it half-obscured. All the gems were here arrayed in a circle, each humming and glowing, each with a person placing a hand on the faceted surface.

Avena glanced at her own hand. It was alien, not her own, but it felt right. Like she belonged in this body. The fingernails were painted a soft pink, their ends long and finely shaped. Her arms were bare to her elbow. She didn't wear a dress but tight-fitting trousers of some stretchy material that hugged her thighs and rear. Her blouse had pleated ruffles following a V-cut neckline which showed off a generous swath of her bosom.

Pale-white hair spilled down her face.

She glanced around the room. The eight gems and their controllers, for want of a better term, were arrayed in the center of a room with walls and floors and ceilings of a waxy stone made of pure white. It was a substance unlike anything she'd seen before. The place had a sterility about it, a level of cleanliness Avena didn't think was possible.

The room vibrated. The gems all hummed louder. Something resonated through her body, reaching into her bones.

Avena's real eyes snapped open.

She awoke, back in her body. The alien feeling that had descended on her right before the dream swallowed her had passed. She blinked and realized she lay slumped on her side on the carriage bench. The clatter of wheels over cobblestones echoed as she sat up. Drool stained her left cheek.

Dualayn appeared enraptured with the Primer the White Lady had given to him. It must be his hundredth time he'd studied it. It held the guide to deciphering Old Tonal, the primordial language spoken before the Shattering.

He didn't notice that I passed out?

She shivered, glad it had happened while she was in the carriage, safe from harm. They were returning from a visit to the hospital. They had three patients —a man and two women—who seemed beyond normal jewelchine healers to help. Dualayn would work on them in his lab. She glanced at the window and saw they were almost home.

She had passed out right after leaving.

The dream remained with her. The handsome man, the lover of the white-haired woman, burned in her memory. If it wasn't for his blue eyes, she would call him a Qothian like Ōbhin. And the woman . . . *The White Lady?* Avena had never seen a young woman with white hair before, and she'd felt young in the dream, her body healthy. *And who were those others? What was that room? Those jewels were huge and linked together. Why?*

She shivered, focusing on the dream instead of her body betraying her again. Whatever fanciful delights her mind had conjured, no doubt gleaned from studying the primer and the Recorder with Dualayn for the last week, was better than dwelling on her weakness. She needed to accept that her mind hadn't been fully healed.

Dualayn had *still* accomplished a miracle.

Living with the occasional fainting spell was better than death. It had just stolen away standing by Ōbhin's side. She couldn't trust herself in a fight not to faint and be a burden. He might get hurt trying to protect her unconscious form.

"Anything useful?" she asked as they turned off the road onto the driveway of his estate.

"Very," he said. "I am intrigued by your earthen gauntlet. It's a remarkable idea. I hadn't thought of attaching them to the outside of the body. Imagine if we used other gems beside emeralds. Suits that could make someone immune to fire or maybe to breathe underwater. Imagine exploring the bottom of a river or the sea."

She smiled. Research with Dualayn was where she could best serve. It wasn't as exciting, wasn't with Ōbhin at her side, but it was something to feed the emptiness inside of her.

Little morsels to keep despair at bay.

Ōbhin climbed off the carriage seat as it pulled up before the manor house. In the week since Avena's mugging, she hadn't tried to join the training once. Hadn't come near him at all. She just drifted like a ghost around the yard when she wasn't inside the lab becoming a second Dualayn.

The carriage door opened and a pale-faced Avena stepped out. She had a frailness about her, a tremble in her fingers as she took Miguil's larger hand to help her step down. She held her dark-green skirt with her other hand, her twin tails of brown hair bobbing with her movement. A hollowness echoed in her eyes when they met Ōbhin's.

Hers darted away.

"Let's get the patients inside and see what we can do with them," said Dualayn. "Avena, I'll need your help with the initial exams. I think one of the women shall be easy to heal, but I have reservations about the man and the other woman."

"Of course, Father," Avena said, her voice soft, almost a whisper.

The fiery rose bristling with thorns who'd stood up against the bandits had been replaced by this wilting violet. She vanished inside the open doors of the house, leaving the hot sunlight behind. Ōbhin wiped sweat from his brow, disgusted at what he'd done.

"What's wrong with her?" Miguil asked in a low voice. "I've never seen her like this."

"I was too hard on her," Ōbhin muttered, lashing himself. Trying to keep her safe only hurt her worse.

"I never thought anyone could leash her." Miguil closed the carriage doors. "Feels wrong."

"She's not resonating with a healthy tone," Ōbhin said, staring down at his sable gloves. *I managed to destroy her in a different way.*

Avena slipped out of the lab. Of the three, the younger of the two women was recovering. Avena needed help to get her into a guest bed and out of the lab. Dualayn planned to work hard on the other two. She could already see the manic delight in his eyes.

He had ideas. Tests. He would do all he could to heal them, working day and night, pushing himself to unhealthy levels. She should object, but this timidity weighed on her. She couldn't trust herself any longer. She felt betrayed by her body. Her mind. It had her off-balance, withdrawn.

The emptiness hadn't felt this close to her in years. It was swallowing her bit by bit. The more she worried about her fainting spells, the less strength she had to keep away that hollow void in her.

She hovered on the edge of becoming that silent girl again, too scared to be noticed. For two years after her mother murdered her sister and her father abandoned her, Avena hadn't spoken. A patient woman named Daughter Heana had coaxed her out of this unfeeling void. She'd brought Colour to Avena's world.

Every day it paled more and more.

Dualayn had worked a miracle to save her, and it wasn't enough.

She should talk to someone, to Dualayn, to Ōbhin, but none of them had noticed anything was wrong with her. Dualayn had his patients, and Ōbhin saw her as useless, not worth his time. She'd lost him.

"Avena?"

The sound of her name drew her introspective attention. She looked up to see Fingers and Dajouth lounging in the servants' dining hall off the kitchen. A row of well-maintained, if simple, tables with study chairs. They were eating noodles with chopsticks in a broth of pork and onions.

"The cook made something this late?" Avena asked in surprise.

"She thinks it's supper," said Dajouth.

"Oh, Avena, there you are," said Kaylin. The fleshy woman wearing a sleeveless sleeping gown and a heavy apron over it strode out with a bowl of steaming broth with thin noodles. "I don't know where everyone is. They should be sitting down for supper."

"They're busy with something important," Avena said. The woman had been confused since her husband's death two years ago. Dyain had been the butler before Pharon. The man had fallen and broken his neck. Grief had ruined the older woman's mind. She dwelled in a shadowy version of the past.

"I bet that's Dyain's doing. That man's always tryin' to ruin my careful work." She said it with a fond smile. Then she glanced at those two. "Kadayn and Bran, eat up. Now. I didn't slave away for you to just push it around with your chopsticks."

"Right away, ma'am," Dajouth said. "The bounty of your kitchen is only matched by the beauty of your face."

Kaylin arched an eyebrow. "What would a boy know of beauty? If your mother heard you say those words, why, she'd wash your mouth out with soap." Then she turned to Avena and blinked. "What are you doin' here so late? Sneakin' food out of my kitchen?"

Kaylin snatched the bowl back and marched back into the kitchen, muttering under her breath.

"She's gotten worse," said Fingers.

"Yeah. Who's Kadayn?" Dajouth asked.

The older man snorted. "You think my mother named me Fingers?"

"It fits you," Avena said. "Better than Fingers. If you two are not busy, I need a patient carried out of the laboratory."

"I am always at your disposal, lovely Avena," Dajouth said, rising with smooth grace. He swept her a bow.

Through the heavy dullness draped over her, a small giggle bubbled out of her. For a moment, she felt mirth at his flowery attempts at flirtation. The laugh died, swallowed by her malaise. Her face relaxed into uncaring.

"If you flirt with every woman you meet, they'll all hate you," Fingers said. "They talk, women do. You do something to one, and the rest will know in an hour. All judgin' you."

"How can they be mad if I pay them all compliments?" protested Dajouth as he rose, setting his wooden chopsticks across the bowl.

Avena grimaced at his poor manners.

She led them back through the house. She hadn't remembered walking into the east wing. They passed white-plastered walls decorated with the occasional painting or bust. A runner of red carpet ran over the marble flooring to protect its finish. It was Homphrial marble, quarried from up north. Blue and red veins ran through the stone, giving it a unique, and expensive, look.

Fingers and Dajouth took up the stretcher with the woman. She slept thanks to a distillation of poppy. She would wake up in the morning recovered. Then she'd be on her way with a small purse of silver rays to aid her.

Avena supervised as they transferred the woman to the bed, not jostling her. She was young and clean now, the dirt washed from her face with patient care by Avena earlier. The woman had a mix of Lothonian and Tethyrian blood, her skin a light tan, her hair pure black. Her mixed heritage gave her a delicate cast to her high cheekbones.

"You okay?" Fingers asked.

She nodded.

"Perhaps you'd care to go for a walk, Avena?" Dajouth asked. "The night has cooled off and the moons are out. They're bright tonight. Along with the stars."

"If you have the energy to ask a pretty girl to a promenade, then you can check the perimeter for any sneak thieves trying to crawl over the wall or swim across the lake," Fingers growled.

"But . . ." Dajouth snapped his jaw shut, a petulant twist curling across his lips. "Right away, sir."

Fingers shook his head as the young man stomped off. "You'd never think Bran was the younger of those two. You might only have a winter on Dajouth, Avena."

"Maybe," she said, a tingle fuzzing her hand. It felt distant from her, alien. She rubbed at it, struggling to remember it was her hand. The smothering weight grew, the emptiness widening to embrace her.

"Are you really okay? I'm worried about you, lass."

The tingles raced up her hand. Her body felt remote again. She wondered if she was about to drift off into another strange dream while untethered from her flesh. What if she wasn't real at all? Was she actually Avena? Did she belong here?

"Avena!"

A strong hand seized hers. She gasped, suddenly aware of all her flesh again. She was half-crouched. She shook her head, her breath coming in ragged gasps. Fingers gripped her, the rough pads of his digits anchoring her. She felt tethered to her body.

"You almost fainted."

"The heat of the day was too much," she said as she straightened.

"No, that's not it at all."

She paused. She normally didn't speak of it, but the words tumbled out. "My emptiness is getting worse. I think it's devouring me. I don't think my mind healed right."

"Nothing Dualayn can do?" Fingers asked, guiding her out of the guest bedroom.

"He saved my life. I shouldn't be here. I should be grateful for what I have." She forced a smile. That was what she should do. It took such effort. Nothing seemed to matter much at all. Helping people was important, but she didn't have anyone *to* help. She just had herself.

That wasn't nearly enough.

Ōbhin would be . . .

"I just need to sleep," she told Fingers. "Would you walk me to my room?"

"Of course," he said with gentleness, pain in his voice.

He's thinking of his wife again. How could this tender man have hurt her?

Avena didn't know. But she was grateful for his presence. He had a solid aura about him. Stout and dependable. How had she never noticed this quality about the man? She'd thought him crass. Lazy. A man whining about an unfaithful wife and running away from responsibility. A coward.

Yet he had this core. A foundation. Something good could have been built upon him. How had it gone wrong? The thought stayed with her after she bade him a blessed night, closed her door, and sunk onto her bed in her dressing gown.

How could good lives go wrong?

12

Eighth Day of Patience, 755 EU

After two more days of watching Avena drift like a ghost, Ōbhin had to do something to help her.

He hadn't been protecting her. He'd crushed her. Fingers joked about a wife who cuckolded him because he hated himself for hurting her. Ōbhin understood. Each time he saw Avena's pale form, he despised himself a little more. He thought he loathed himself for killing Taim, but this was worse.

He loved her and caused her this misery.

He lounged at the main gate, taking his turn at watch. A bead of sweat ran down his forehead despite being in the shade provided by the arch. The sun sizzled. No rain had come for a week. The gardeners carried wooden pails full of lake water. Its shores had retreated, exposing drying mud dotted with pools. Those swarmed with tadpoles trapped in dwindling life. The gardeners poured the water to keep alive the rhododendron bushes while the lawn yellowed.

Avena emerged from the front door, left open to move air through the house in an attempt to cool it. She wore a lighter dress than normal, pale pink without her usual layers of petticoats to give volume to her skirt. She drifted down the path towards the stables.

You have to do it, Ōbhin told himself. *You have to let her know you made the second biggest mistake of your life. Invite her to train. Remind her that she's got passion. She'll hate you, but you deserve it.*

"You got the gate, Bran?" he asked the youth leaning on the other wall.

The boy grunted, his face a mask of sweat, lank hair matted to his forehead.

Ōbhin stepped into the sunlight. Summers grew warm in Qoth, but they were short affairs, a few weeks of heat between a cool spring and autumn. Winter ruled the mountains. He kept his back straight against the sun as more sweat trickled down his face.

Avena emerged from the stables with Miguil. He nodded to her and headed back inside. She glanced at Ōbhin then jerked her gaze away. Her pace quickened on the way back to the house. He broke into a jog, leather jerkin clinging to his sweaty chest.

"Avena, may we talk?"

She stiffened. She turned to face him, no color in her cheeks. A sheen of sweat glistened on her forehead. Her light dress clung to her in several damp spots, perspiration bleeding through beneath her armpits. She wasn't wearing any of the cosmetics she'd normally applied, subtle rogue and a brightening to her lips.

Even so, she made his heart beat faster.

Her eyes wouldn't rise to meet his.

"What do you need?" she said politely.

"We have to talk," Ōbhin said again, his tongue growing leaden. His throat tight.

"You said that. About?"

A loud clatter and jangle drew his attention as Miguil led out one of the draft horses pulling the small cart he used to fetch supplies from town. The groom gave Ōbhin a supportive look. Everyone was worried about her. Fingers fretted while the thing pretending to be Smiles spoke endlessly about Jilly and the maid's concerns. Only Dualayn, still locked up in his lab with the two sick patients, had failed to notice Avena's transformation.

A shadow hung over her. Thick, obscuring her brightness.

"Listen, I wish to apologize," he said, his words stiff. "I was . . . harsh when you recovered. Too harsh."

She shook her head. "I let you down on the raid."

Confusion rippled over him. "Let me down?"

"I can't remember what I did wrong." She looked up. "I try, but my memories aren't clear, so I can't fix it. Besides, I can't trust myself anyways. So you have nothing to apologize for. I do not belong in your world. Women shouldn't fight. We don't have the temperament for it."

Ōbhin's jaw dropped.

She started to turn, but he grabbed her shoulders in his black-gloved hands. "You didn't do anything wrong on the raid. You didn't make a single mistake; I did."

"What?"

"And if anyone has the temperament for fighting, it's you. I've seen men with far less of a backbone than you possess. Plenty of cowards slink through the world. I don't think your sex is a hindrance. Niszeh's Black Tone, you invented a jewel machine to give you more strength than a man. I saw the aftermath. You took on two dozen ruffians and left them bound and with broken bones. They'll be nursing their injuries for weeks more. Some of them pissed their britches in terror of you. I could smell the stink of it."

"But . . ." She stared at him. "How did I get hurt? I took a sword to my head. I must have done something wrong. You were disappointed in me. Like you were after I got Smiles injured during the riot." Her eyes swam with tears.

"I pushed you away because *I* got you injured." The pain tore at his heart. His words grew tight, emotion burning the corners of his eyes. "I heard you racing up behind me when I was dueling Creg. He swung at me, and I cut his sword in half and dodged the severed end out of instinct. I could have taken the blow on my shoulder, but I let it spin past. You had the bad luck to step in the way as you were trying to help *me*. When I turned around and saw you on the ground, it was the most terrifying moment in my life. I had to run and run holding you as you twitched. I didn't think Dualayn could do anything, but I had to try because I couldn't be the one to get you killed.

"If you died because of my mistake, how could I live with myself? I drove you away because I didn't want to destroy you."

∽

Avena trembled as she stared at Ōbhin. His eyes gleamed with pain. He gripped her shoulders as he trembled. A strange sense of foolishness swept through her. Fingers had explained to her what Ōbhin was doing, and Deffona had agreed. It wasn't Avena's fault at all, but after she lost control of her body, she'd accepted her fears that she was too weak. A hindrance.

After all, she'd collapsed in an alley and was robbed. She could have been violated. Murdered. It still terrified her. Even now, she could feel that emptiness swelling in her. The alien feeling prickling through her. She swayed again.

"I'm so sorry for making you feel worthless," Ōbhin groaned. "I never wanted to hurt you. I wanted to keep you safe. Keep you away from me. I only hurt those around me. I dragged Foonauri from her home only to abandon her in a foreign city. Can I even blame her for having to find other ways to survive? And you . . . I just wanted to push you onto another path, not crush your spirit."

"It's not just you," Avena said. She grabbed at his leather jerkin with foreign fingers. The numbness was spreading. "There's something wrong with me, Ōbhin. Something that terrifies me."

Confusion spread across his face.

"I'm losing control of my body and . . ." The fuzziness slithered down her flesh. Her fingers went numb. It prickled across her cheeks. Her lips. "Ay ahm pahshing auwt." Her words slurred, tongue thick. Her mind retreated. The fear built inside of her as she struggled to hold onto him.

"Avena!" he shouted, his voice so distant as she retreated further and further away.

The senses from her body grew muted. She forced out a final word, a croaking plea: "Help!"

"Avena!" His words sounded so far away, echoing through a misty expanse. "Someone! I need Dualayn!"

She sank into those strange dreams, a refuge for her terrified thoughts cut adrift from her body.

Her last word had come out clear but soft. Help.

Avena slumped against him. Her entire body was limp. Her eyes were open, pupils dilating so wide they swallowed her brown irises. Her arms fell limp down his body, her fingers no longer clutching him. If he hadn't been hugging her, she would have struck the ground.

"I need Dualayn!" Ōbhin cried. This frantic fear rose in him, a dark tide. He shifted her weight and lowered her to the grass. Her chest rose and fell with soft breaths like she slept, but her eyes stared up at nothing. He lightly slapped her cheek to rouse her. "Avena! What's wrong?"

He grabbed her shoulders, shaking her. Her head flopped to the side, limp. Her eyes stayed open. Horror squeezed his heart, a mighty fist threatening to crush the pounding organ into pulp. He shook her harder.

"Avena!" His shout cracked, half-choked by the fear clawing at his throat.

"Ōbhin?" a motherly voice said. "What's wrong with Avena. Is it the heat?"

Ōbhin shook his head as Jolayn, Bran's mother and nurse to Bravine, appeared. She knelt down, skirts rustling. She tilted Avena's head to face the sky and gasped. "Her eyes are open."

"I know," growled Ōbhin. *Dualayn said there might be complications. Is this what he meant?* His mind struggled to parse thoughts, to remember what to do. Shock rooted him in place. He hadn't trained himself for Avena to collapse mid-conversation.

Heavy footsteps thudded up and then stopped. A hoarse groan burst from Fingers as he stood a cubit away, hands balling into fists, accentuating red, swollen knuckles. A few popped as he trembled, color draining from his weathered face.

"Is she . . .?" Fingers asked.

"She's alive," Ōbhin muttered. "She's breathing, but I can't rouse her."

"Elohm's damned Colours," groaned Fingers. "The other night, she almost passed out on me. I thought it was just fatigue. She'd been working in the labs with Dualayn, and you've seen her. She ain't been right since she was healed."

Because I made her think she's weak, echoed through Ōbhin's mind.

"We need to get her to Dualayn," Jolayn said.

Her words were the first that made any sense to the addled Ōbhin. *Think! Where is Dualayn?*

Where he always was.

Ōbhin scooped Avena up in his arms. She weighed even less than last time. Her arms dangled limp. She didn't spasm. She didn't have a length of metal sticking out of her head, but the same fear gripped him. A hopeless terror.

He couldn't lose her. Wouldn't.

He raced across the lawn, booted steps pounding for the house. Jolayn and Fingers followed, her skirts rustling and his steps heavy thuds. Ōbhin reached the open doors and burst into the cooler interior, his boots squeaking on the polished marble floor as he changed direction for the lab. He swept by the stairs and hurtled toward Dualayn's door.

The sign hung from it asking for no disturbances.

The world melted in Avena's dreams.

Disharmony burst through the notes, assaulting Avena's ears. She tried to pull back from the diamond right before her. It resonated with a single tone, singing against the shattering chaos that exploded all around them.

She glanced at fear at her dream lover. He screamed but she couldn't hear the sounds he made. The obsidian gem bubbled and flowed, spilling over his hand. Across the walls of the pristine room, cracks appeared. Rents of darkness that split apart reality.

The screeching, off-tune note cracked through the air. The other seven gems blazed with their light. Seven stars shining against the black chaos surging all around them. The ground shook beneath their feet, a mighty shattering bursting through the room. Wires connecting the gems sizzled and snapped.

The black rents didn't rip the walls apart, but the very fabric of the world. She could see something alien on the other side, segmented eyes, chitinous bodies. Mandibles twitched. Avena tried to pull her hand free of the diamond and reach her lover. The obsidian ran over his arm like oily water.

He howled while her diamond grew brighter and brighter. Its note surrounded her, resonating with truth and light. It swept about her as the world shattered around them. She could see beyond this room as the walls split apart physically now, destroyed by the umbral cracks. People fled from the spreading chaos. Some were touched, their skin blackening into obsidian, hardening them in place. The roof exploded outward, revealing the sky above.

Stars twinkled and whirled. The cracks burst upward, soaring high up into the sky, reaching for the heavens. Something hung over the world, a shadowy orb blocking out the stars around it. She could see a faint outline of it, almost shiny, like looking at obsidian in a dark room.

A black moon?

Her lover fell to the ground, engulfed by the molten obsidian. It coated him and flowed for her. It hit the light of her diamond and sizzled, smoking away.

The diamond glow protected her from the cataclysm. She didn't understand what she witnessed.

The humming from the diamond buzzed through her bones. She gasped as her skeleton harmonized with the gem. She rang with that same tone. She could feel all two hundred and six bones in her body vibrating. Her flesh screamed in agony. The shaking threatened to melt her flesh, to tear her sinew apart at the most basic level.

The black moon above exploded in a burst of dark fire. She didn't hear a sound, but she could see the pieces spilling off of the massive shape and streaking across the sky. Rising on the horizon, Honesty appeared; only her white face was pristine. It lacked the crater-like valleys Avena had seen every other time she'd gazed upon the white moon's face.

The diamond hummed louder as the cracks tearing apart the world widened. The things she glimpsed thrust sharp limbs through, black-armored flesh covered in hard, bristling hairs. They pulled themselves *through* into her reality.

Avena screamed in horror, trapped in a cocoon of liquid truth.

Ōbhin kicked the door and shouted, "Dualayn! Open up right now! Dualayn!" He kicked the door harder, rattling the solid oak. He distantly felt pain throbbing through his big toe. "Come on! It's Avena!"

"Dualayn!" bellowed Fingers, his tone almost frantic. The big man came up alongside Ōbhin and pounded a balled fist on the stout door, rattling hinges. "Elohm's Colours, open the door. She's dying!"

Dread struck Ōbhin. She couldn't be dying. She'd just fainted, but those words set a panic. A frantic fear he needed to master and couldn't. He kicked the door again. It held. But Dualayn should hear them. The lab was a converted dining hall. It wasn't *that* large.

"Take her!" growled Ōbhin, thrusting Avena into Fingers's arms.

He took her with a gentleness, cradling Avena's limp form.

"Why isn't he answering?" Jolayn asked, her voice tight.

Ōbhin shook his head as he drew his resonance blade. The tulwar whisked out of its sheath. He pressed the button on the hilt. The emerald flared green, the sword humming, blurring the edge. With a series of quick slashes, he cut around the lock, slicing through the door and the stone frame. He slammed his shoulder into the door and burst it open, the locked knob clattering to the floor.

Ōbhin swept into the lab and cast his gaze around. A bloodstained sheet was draped over the large, central table. Discarded bandages lay about the floor. A few gems were strewn on counters and the workbench. The vault, where Dualayn kept all his jewels, was unlocked and open, the shelves lined with the precious stones, many bound in wires.

"Niszeh's Black Tone," Ōbhin muttered as he deactivated his sword. "Where is he? The door was locked. He has the sign out."

"I'll go look through the house," said Jolayn. "Maybe he's in the kitchen getting food."

Her footsteps pattered off as Ōbhin moved through the room, wondering if the old man had collapsed on the other side of the table or in the vault. His eyes scanned the floor. His brow furrowed as he realized something else was missing.

"Where are the two patients?" he asked.

"Don't know," Fingers said. "Never thought it'd be so drafty in here."

Cool air ruffled across Ōbhin's face, teasing a few locks of his black hair. He glanced at the vault. Its rear wall had swung inward, revealing a staircase descending downward. Ōbhin swallowed at the dark gullet.

"Did you know there was a basement?" Ōbhin asked.

"No," Fingers said. "He must be down there."

Those words animated Ōbhin. He pulled Avena from Fingers's arms and rushed ahead without thought. Without even fear of descending into the black. He hadn't allowed himself to be underground in two years. No dread of repeating his harrowing afternoon in the mines beneath Gunya would hold him back.

His feet pounded down the stairs. They were wide, running straight to a floor two stories beneath. The stone walls and steps were cut from bedrock. A chill bled from them. His bare arms prickled with goose-pimples. The steady glow of diamond light spilled across the bottom landing.

He reached the bottom and stepped through a doorway into a storeroom. Jars lined the shelves, sealed like fruit preserves. Many had topaz jewelchines inserted into their lids and were half-covered in wax.

Their contents horrified Ōbhin.

Organs.

Lungs. Livers. Kidneys. Stomachs. Hearts. Brains. Eyes. Bits of flesh he didn't know the name of. He held Avena tight to him as he stared at them. Each had a label on them written in the clear script of Dualayn. Names and dates.

Some were almost a decade old.

Fingers retched behind Ōbhin. Everywhere he looked in this terrible room were body parts taken from someone and stored in liquid. Some of the bottles bubbled, sapphires and topazes glowing in the brine. A lung in one seemed to contract and expand like it breathed, a yellow heliodor shining on its surface.

One jar had its own shelf with nothing near it. It held a brain in amber brine wrinkled in the same manner as Avena's. There were four topaz healers placed directly onto the surface, attached to it by wires of black. The forbidden metal.

Black iron.

Cursed iron.

It was said to come from only a few spots in the world. Places of terrible destruction. Leftovers of the cataclysmic Shattering three thousand years or more ago. It was the only wire you could use with obsidian, or so it was said.

Dualayn had used obsidian with this specimen. He could see the glass-like material thrust out of the wax-sealed lid of the jar. It was shaped into a thin spire as long as the span from Ōbhin's outstretched thumb to his little finger. Inside the jar, a network of black wires descended from the bottom of the spire and thrust into the wrinkled crevasses of the brain.

The name on the label froze Ōbhin's heart: *Avena, extracted the Forty-Third Day of Forgiveness, 755 EU.*

He glanced down at the girl he held limp in his arms. He remembered the surgery, the sight of her mind exposed. Wrinkled like the brain in the jar. Ōbhin shook his head. He couldn't believe this. It made no sense. If her brain was in this jar, then how was she alive? How could she control her body?

Fingers's retching grew louder. Fury filled Ōbhin. He needed answers. He shifted Avena so he could seize the jar in a tight grip. Its heat bled through the leathers he wore. A small ruby jewelchine lay at the bottom, little bubbles rising from it. A sapphire lay next to it, both glowing as they did *something* to the liquid.

The storeroom had a second doorway, the source of the diamond light. He carried Avena through it, his blood boiling. It opened into a room larger than Dualayn's laboratory upstairs. There the walls appeared directly cut out of the bedrock of the mansion was built upon. Only the lakeside wall was different. It appeared to be fused together into a smooth surface. Three tables covered in white cloth dominated the center, two holding bodies.

Dualayn worked on one, his back to Ōbhin. The furious Qothian could see the man's chest splayed open, ribs cracked back while Dualayn performed his grisly work. The second figure lay naked, a glowing healer resting on her stomach, reknitting a cut across her belly. Her breasts rose and fell with steady breaths.

Ōbhin needed answers. Demanded answers. If he wasn't holding something precious in his arms, something delicate and vulnerable, he would have already flown across the room in a rage. With care, he set Avena down on a chair by the doorway. It lay by a stretcher studded with heliodor jewelchines.

He marched forward, jar in hand, and roared, "Dualayn, what is this?"

13

Dualayn gasped and whirled around, his round face bursting with surprise. He clutched a bloody hand to the heavy apron he wore, smearing crimson across the yellowing linen. His jowls shook as he let out an explosive breath.

"Ōbhin, what are you doing down here?" he said, gathering himself. "I'm working. Did you not see the sign?"

"Working?" demanded Ōbhin. He looked around the room. Several diamond jewelchines hanging from the ceiling spread an even light across the room. The walls were covered in diagrams drawn upon large sheets of parchment. They depicted human bodies splayed open in various ways, documenting muscles, bones, viscera. The one nearest Ōbhin's right had the face of a man he recognized from the hospital.

A patient who'd died a few weeks ago.

"What are you doing here?" growled Ōbhin.

"Research. To find new ways to save those who are badly sick or injured. You know that. I am trying to save this man's life, but . . ." He shook his head. "I fear I won't be successful. I do not quite understand what is wrong with him. I have been vivisecting him all day and can't find the cause. I cannot apply the resonating topazes directly without locating what is killing him." He glanced at the other patient. "Now, she'll live. I found a large tumor in her stomach, removed it, and she is regenerating nicely."

"And what is *this*?" Ōbhin demanded, branding the jar holding Avena's brain in the scholar's face.

"Gentle with that!" Dualayn gasped. "That's her mind. If you dislodge those wires, her body will stop functioning."

"Stop functioning!" roared a familiar voice.

The dream of the cataclysmic destruction and alien creature ripping through a rent in reality faded from Avena. Her awareness sank into her body again. She flexed her hands and fluttered open her eyes. She moaned, feeling grounded in her flesh again. No fuzziness at her fingertips.

"You mean she'll die?" Ōbhin was snarling.

She focused on him. His back was to her, the light of a diamond jewelchine falling across his shoulders. He held something in his hand, a jar with something black thrusting out the top. It was full of liquid. An amber light glowed inside of it.

"Bastard," another voice growled.

She jumped to see Fingers standing beside her, wiping at his mouth. His face looked sick. "What he did to you . . . Pus-filled roach!"

"Did something happen to Ōbhin?" she asked, bewildered.

Then she noticed what was in the jar Ōbhin held. A human brain. Confusion rippled through her. She pushed herself up to her feet, feeling unsteady only for a moment. The last thing she remembered was trying to tell Ōbhin about her problem before she'd collapsed into his arms.

"You took her mind out of her body!" growled Ōbhin. She realized he yelled at Dualayn. He wore a surgical apron, blood smeared across the front.

"Yes, and you will harm her if you keep swinging her about," Dualayn said, reaching out to take the jar with gentle hands.

A sinking dread filled her as she struggled to decipher what was happening. Where she even was. It looked like Dualayn's lab, but it wasn't. There was far too much space. More tables. The walls were covered in anatomical drawings. Then she noticed two patients he'd brought from the hospital were each on a table, the man's chest spread open.

Normally, that wouldn't have disturbed her, but she wasn't prepared to see a man's innards on display. She clamped a hand over her mouth, a sudden surge of bile in rising up in her throat. She turned away.

"Dualayn," she croaked when she had control over her rebellious stomach. "What is this place?"

"You brought her down here?" Dualayn said in exasperation. "Child, it's okay. I was just waiting for you to be ready to understand the full breadth of my work before sharing it with you."

"Like taking her brain out of her body and attaching it to obsidian jewelchines!" snarled Ōbhin.

Avena's head whipped around to Dualayn. She focused on the jar. On the brain. She found herself crossing the distance without thought as she stared at it. A human mind, the brain stem disconnected from the spine. No eyes attached or auditory nerves. It was suspended in some brine with a ruby and sapphire jewelchine to maintain the environment. It was an idea Dualayn had told her about once, a way to remove an organ and revitalize it before returning it to the body.

But if the body needed that organ to live . . .

She touched her head. "That can't be my brain."

"Yes, child, it is," Dualayn said, a smile crossing his lips. "Remarkable, yes? You think your thoughts are happening in your head, but they are actually occurring right here in the jar. That's the seat of your identity. Where your soul resides."

Black iron wires drilled down into her brain, penetrating her wrinkled gray matter. The topaz healers were equally connected, keeping her mind alive. She squeezed tighter at her head, her stomach churning.

"Then what . . . How is it . . .?" She struggled to speak. "How can my body work without my mind? How am I talking?"

"You have an exquisite device inside your skull. Before I broke off my partnership with my colleague in Democh, he sent me two of his prototypes. His obsidian minds. They are amazing devices. They can control a human body just as well as a regular mind, only these ones can receive *signals*. He wants to use them to control his soldiers like automatons, but you . . ." Dualayn smiled. "You are being controlled by your own brain. See?" He touched the spire thrusting out the jar's top. "Here is the antenna. It's wired to your mind. It sends your thoughts and commands to your body through the immaterial in the same way that the eight Harmonic Tones resonate through the world and power jewelchines. Your body responds in a similar, though more complex, fashion."

"But . . . you healed my brain," she said. "Why did you take it out of my head?"

"I saw him using topazes to heal the wound to your brain," Ōbhin said.

"But it wasn't enough, right?" she demanded, staring at Dualayn. "Right, Father? You had to remove my brain to heal me?"

She stared at him, the man who'd taken her in at fifteen and given her a job. The man whose son she would have married if tragedy hadn't befallen Chames. She studied with him. Worked at his side. He taught her how to treat the sick and build jewelchines. She'd investigated the Recorder with him. He had to have an explanation. A logical reason.

"Please, Father," she said, her words rough. She felt on the verge of falling apart. Her eyes implored him.

"Child," Dualayn said, "this was the perfect opportunity to test everything. I had already removed the top of your skull. Once your brain was healed, I took advantage of this fortuitous event and replaced your brain with the obsidian mind. I didn't know that there would be any deleterious side-effects. I had been meaning to ask you if everything felt the same, but I fear I'd gotten distracted."

A cold fury ignited in Avena, a blizzard howling through her soul. She felt the emptiness widening to engulf her in a cocoon of safety. She could withdraw, flee this betrayal, but she refused. She wouldn't be helpless. She embraced the pain as she snatched her brain from him. She held the seat of her awareness cradled to her breast as she glared at Dualayn with loathing. An odious, pain-filled rage swelled in her.

"She's passing out, you gloveless snake!" Ōbhin snarled. His black-gloved hands seized Dualayn's bloody apron. Ōbhin thrust the rotund man back into the table, bending him half over the man with the splayed-open chest. "She went limp, like she'd passed out, but her eyes stayed open. Sightless."

"I feel like this isn't my body!" Avena snarled. She held up the jar with her mind, the warmth from the ruby bleeding through the glass. "Because this is my body. You put me in a jar! You ripped me from my flesh and stuck *obsidian* in its place. I feel strange all the time. I thought I was weak because I didn't heal properly. But, no! You butchered me, you feckless bastard!"

"Now, Avena," Dualayn said, his voice tight now. Sweat beaded his brow. "You must understand that I had tested this all before. Yours isn't the first brain I've removed, just the first I successfully hooked up to the antenna. I was certain you would be fine. In fact, you are. Mostly."

"Mostly!" Ōbhin growled through clenched teeth. His jaw tightened, fury on his face.

"You're a pus-filled roach, Dualayn," Fingers growled. "How could you do this to her? She sees you as a father! You were supposed to *cure* her!"

The horror swirled through her more and more. "Fix me! Put me back! I want my mind back in my skull."

"That wouldn't be advisable," said Dualayn. "Most die. The one time I succeeded, well, she hasn't been the same. Confused. Forget what year it is."

"Who do you . . . Kaylin?" asked Avena in dawning dread. "You're speaking of Kaylin? When she was saddened with grief for Dyain, what, did you remove her mind? Did you kill him, too?"

"I don't kill anyone!" Dualayn protested. "I try to save. It requires pushing the boundaries of flesh, to try new things. I had to be shown this, too. Sometimes . . ." He shuddered. "Regrettably, it doesn't always work, but you . . . Look at you. You're talking. You're thinking. You have all your memories. So you get a little woozy at times."

"Woozy! I passed out in the street for hours! I was robbed. Could have been killed! Raped! I was helpless because *you* removed my brain!"

"I am sorry about that," Dualayn said. "With any new procedure, there are bound to be some kinks to be solved. But we can do experiments. Refine the antenna to produce a clearer signal. That must be what is causing the blackouts. Your signal strength wavered. You weren't getting enough information to your body. You shut down to your most base operation level. Breathing. Heartbeat. Digestion. I tried to match the Recorder's depiction of the antenna, to shape it perfectly, but I must be off in some way. Please, please, let me think, Ōbhin."

Ōbhin released Dualayn with a sneer and backed off. Avena shifted the jar in her hands, staring at it in horror. The wires were burrowed into her mind. She struggled to feel them worming through her thoughts. They were conduits to the Black.

Is the Black infecting my dreams? she wondered. *No, no, it's more like I'm living one person's memories. One woman with white hair like . . . Raya? The White Lady has naturally white hair.*

"You have thought of something," Dualayn said, his hand reaching out to her.

Revulsion roiled through her stomach. She backed away, twisting her body to shield her mind from his touch. A fury greater than any she'd ever felt towards her mother seized her. At least her mother had the excuse of madness; melancholy had broken her mind.

Dualayn was just . . . just . . . evil.

"Don't you *ever* lay a hand on me again!"

"But, child," Dualayn said, pain in his eyes. "Don't you see what this means? I'll be able to fix my wife." He reached for her again. "We can solve your fainting proble—"

Her hand flew without thought. She slapped him so hard his head snapped back. Her handprint blazed across his cheek. She wished she'd worn her earthen gauntlet so the blow would have broken his neck.

"Do not talk to me like you didn't violate me to my core! You stripped me from my body and then expect me to be grateful?"

"Child," Dualayn said, staring at her with betrayal on his face.

It infuriated her more. He looked at her like he loved her. She'd thought he did. How could he love her and do *this* to her?

"You don't understand. Your mind will never die. Your thoughts shall outlive your body. I have made you into something beautiful. Something wonderful. Why don't you understand, child?"

A steely rasp echoed through the lab. Ōbhin drew his sword.

The blade hummed to life in Ōbhin's grip as he raised the vibrating edge towards Dualayn's throat. The man flinched back from the resonance blade. He backed into the table, trapped. He arched his head back, leaning over the patient to keep the sword from finding his flesh.

"Fix her," Ōbhin said, his voice colder than the glacier topping Mount Purity. "Put her brain back into her body."

"I told you, I can't." He stared down at the blade. Sweat poured off his brow. "Please, Ōbhin, you don't want to do anything rash. I have made breakthroughs. I will save so many lives. Please, don't kill me."

"Fix. Her."

"The risks and complications of restoring her brain are too great," he said, his voice shrill. "Reconnecting the nerves is delicate. They have to be aligned just right. At the moment, the obsidian mind in her head is interfacing perfectly. She has full control."

"No, she doesn't! She can't trust her own body because of you. She could pass out at any moment. It could get her killed!"

Avena nodded, her face fierce. The fire he thought had snuffed out blazed inside of her. The woman who'd marched with him into the house in the Greenlet, who'd stood by his side to face the mob, and who'd helped him defeat Ust stood before him. He'd been wrong about who would destroy her. Whose hands were truly stained Black?

He brought the vibrating blade closer to Dualayn's throat, a finger's width away.

"There's a way!" Dualayn croaked. "A way to make sure she doesn't pass out. I can't put her brain back, I truly can't, but I can make sure the signal's strength never fails. She won't feel alien. So long as her mind remains safe in the jar, she'll be normal. She'll have all her senses. Her full faculty. She won't have to fear losing control."

"How?" The words came out a deadly whisper. The rage brimmed in Ōbhin. He would cut this Black-damned snake down if he said the wrong thing.

"We need a proper antenna." An acrid stink filled the air. Snot bubbled from Dualayn's nose. "We can find one in Koilon, the ruins where we met. But if you kill me, you'll never discover it. I know where they can be found in the city. I know what they look like. How they work. Kill me, and she'll be vulnerable for the rest of her life. Please, please, just let me fix her. Let me make her whole. I want her to be whole."

"You just said you can't make her whole!" The sword's humming edge came within a hair's breadth from Dualayn's pudgy neck.

"But I can make her functional," Dualayn said. "What's the difference?"

Ōbhin glanced at Avena. Her brown eyes burned, emotion gleaming across the whites of her eyes. Flecks of gold reflected in her irises. Pain swam in them.

She loved him like a father, and he'd butchered her. How could *another* parent betray her?

With almost no effort, the resonance blade would part Dualayn's head from his body.

"I can make it so you never notice your brain isn't in your body," Dualayn said. "See the other jewelchines? They will never run out of charge. They are balanced perfectly to sustain your mind for the rest of your life. Let me live, let me save my wife, and I will fix you. Please, child, I only did what I thought was best."

"You're a selfish, lying roach scurrying through pig excrement!" she snarled. "I should have Ōbhin step on you. How many others have you butchered?"

"Saved!" he insisted. "All I have done was to save. To improve. I can fix you, child. Trust me."

Avena's lip curled in a snarl. She glanced down at her brain held to her chest. Then she nodded with savage finality.

"Deal!" Ōbhin spat, disgusted he'd ever desired to protect this man.

He wrenched his blade from Dualayn's throat and turned off the emerald. The man collapsed to the floor, panting, the front of his pants soaked with his urine. He brought a shaky hand to his head, rubbing at the sweat.

"Here," Avena said. She placed the brain into Ōbhin's black-gloved hands, entrusting her very essence to him. "Let me see if I can save the poor man on his operating table."

"Filthy, pus-filled, dung-eating roach," Fingers snarled. He seized Dualayn and hauled the man to his feet. "Let's go tell everyone upstairs what you've done to poor Kaylin and Avena."

Ōbhin stared down at the brain of the woman he loved. Tears misted his eyes. "We'll fix you."

14

Despite everything Avena tried, she couldn't save the last patient's life. She covered him with a blanket in the secret laboratory she never knew existed. There were other rooms off this one she was scared to open. She didn't want to know what horrors they held. The storeroom disgusted her enough.

She felt Ōbhin's eyes on her as she headed to the washbasin and the aquifer. She activated the sapphire in the faucet; the cool stream of water fell into the basin. It had a drain that must lead somewhere. She shoved her hands into the stream; watched the blood spill away.

How many died unnecessarily down here? she wondered. She heard the thoughts in her own head even though her mind was twenty cubits away in Ōbhin's hand.

"We'll see he's buried," said Cerdyn.

Others had come and gone. Jilly had taken one look at the storeroom and vomited in the corner. Then she'd ordered every maid to stay away. The guards had filtered in, Bran looking as green as kelp while Dajouth fought to keep from adding his own lunch to Jilly's. Fingers and Cerdyn had carried the female patient upstairs for her to recover.

"We'll bury him on Blackberry Hill," Fingers said as he guided the strange stretcher they'd found. It was covered in heliodors. When activated, it floated, explaining how Dualayn brought his patients down here alone. Avena had no idea such a jewel machine was even possible. "Okay, Avena?"

She nodded, emotion brimming in her. She kept washing her hands, keeping her back to the two men. Cerdyn and Fingers worked with only the occasional grunt. Then their heavy footsteps thudded away, the yellow glow from the heliodors dwindling and then vanishing.

She shut off the aquifer and turned around, her hands dripping with water. Her eyes found Ōbhin's, unable to fight the pain of what had been done to her. She ached for the numbing paradise of her emptiness. She understood why she'd retreated as a child into the hollow silence of her soul. It was so much easier than facing the betrayal from a person she'd thought loved her. Cared for her.

Ōbhin set down her jar with care on the vacated table. He crossed to her in moments, arms opening. She collapsed into his chest, pressing her face into his leather jerkin as her entire body shook. A keening wail, a long, piercing shriek of violated horror burst from deep inside of her. His arms were around her, strong, protective.

He rocked her, one hand stroking her hair at the back of her head, the supple leather rasping over her silken strands. The tears flowed. Her throat choked with emotion. She couldn't breathe through her nostrils, sucking in ragged breaths from her mouth between the shuddering sobs. More and more grief poured out of her like pus from a suppurating wound. She had taken another painful gouging to her soul.

Her arms tightened about him. She clung to his solid frame. An anchor against slipping into that unfeeling emptiness. To retreat from the pain of this world meant fleeing from him, too. From what she felt with him. What she desired.

It would mean Dualayn had taken one more thing from her. She wouldn't let him hurt her any longer. Rob her of anything else.

"I'm sorry," Ōbhin whispered after an eternity.

She stiffened at his words. "For what?" she croaked, her throat raw. She stared up at him, viewing him through a world blurred by her pain. "For what he did to me? Or that you got me injured?" Their conversation from before she'd collapsed sharpened in her mind. "Because *that* was an accident, you hear me?"

Avena seized his face.

"I'm not going to let you run away from the chance I *might* get hurt, Ōbhin!" She stared into his dark eyes. She tightened her grip on his cheeks, her pale fingers brushing across his brown skin. "You hear me? You don't get to decide what's too dangerous for me. I do. I'm not going to let you go with Dualayn while I just stay here waiting and wondering. It's my existence that's in peril. It's my life that's going to be impacted if something goes wrong. So, what are you sorry for, Ōbhin?"

She awaited his answer.

∽

He stared into her fierce, hazel eyes. The little flecks of gold glimmered in the diamond light. The stubbornness thrust out of her soul. A half-buried rock which would break your toe if you kicked it, thinking it would move where you wanted.

His emotions harmonized into a single melody. "I'm sorry that he betrayed you. You didn't deserve what he did to you. It's a crime. If I could, I would strangle the life from his body. I would leave him gloveless in a blizzard and the door barred against him."

"That's it?" she asked, her eyes searching his. Her fingers seared his face, her touch setting his heart to pounding. "That's the only thing you're sorry for?"

"I won't stop you from coming."

Her expression softened.

"I'm also sorry for trying to put you in a cage," he continued. "I can't protect you by locking you up. You're not a songbird to sing for me when I want it. You're a falcon. You should fly free over the mountains and use those talons of yours. I'm sorry for the things I said to you after you were 'healed.' It was inexcusable how I treated you. I was a coward running from my own fears."

Her forehead furrowed. Her lower lip quivered. A noise rose in Avena's throat. Then her hands tightened on his cheeks. She jerked his head down. Her mouth claimed his with a fierce passion. He closed his eyes, melting into the kiss. Her hands slid from his face to his hair, clutching at his short locks and pulling his mouth against hers.

His arms were around her again. He held her in his arms, rejoicing at the feel of her pressed against him. The taste of her. Feel of her. A sweetness he didn't deserve. He squeezed hard, knowing she wasn't a glass diamond, fragile and easily shattered. She was the real thing. Hard. Her soul bright and clear.

His gloves creaked as he gripped her back.

A salty flavor seasoned the kiss. Tears spilled from her eyes. She kept kissing him, refusing to let go as her body shuddered in his arms. Through the joy of this moment, a dark rage sang a sour note of discord.

He hated Dualayn more than anything in the world. A man who deserved to be killed.

A man he couldn't kill.

He wasn't sure how long they kissed before she broke it and pressed her face into the hollow of his neck. Her entire body shook as the grief spilled out of her again. He kissed the crown of her head, feeling her silken strands on his lips.

"I love you, Avena," he whispered, giving words to all those feelings that had been swelling in volume, the joyful tones resonating through his soul.

She tightened her arms around him, clinging to him.

Avena held Ōbhin in her embrace. The alien sensation rippled through her body. Her brain was only a few cubits away, and still she could feel the connection between her mind and flesh growing tenuous. She held tight to Ōbhin.

She could trust him to protect her if she went limp.

"I love you," she said, her tongue feeling numb, sluggish.

He squeezed his arms around her. The fuzziness surged throughout her flesh. Every nerve in her seemed to prickle like she'd slept on not just her arm but her entire body. She clung to him.

"I'm here," he said, such care in his eyes. His gloved hands stroked her back. "If you fall, I'll catch you."

She smiled.

The sensation passed a moment later. She felt firm again. In control. She sighed in relief and kept holding him anyways. His arms around her made her feel safe. They would be heading to Koilon soon. Tomorrow. Maybe even today. There were still hours left before the sun set. Soon, they would venture into those red-stained woods and down into the ruins. Last time, she'd only ventured in a short distance. This time . . .

It would be dangerous, but what choice did they have?

15

"There!" hissed Jilly. She threw down a pile of clothing before Dualayn and spat on them. "There's the clothes you'll need."

This was the sight that Avena found when she emerged from the lab with Ōbhin. Her face was still sticky from the crying despite her best attempts to wash her cheeks. Dualayn stood before the doors, rubbing his hands together as he faced Jilly and the other maids. They were all on the stairs, looking fierce.

"Pack them yourself," said Jilly. "Layni, the trunk."

The plump maid heaved a traveling trunk past Jilly. It hit the floor. The wooden frame, wrapped in leather, bowed in place as it slid across the marble flooring.

"How could you harm Kaylin?" hissed Thoni. She and the other kitchen-workers stood in the hallway leading to the east wing of the house. "She's so sweet!"

"She's a dear!" a cook named Avinane snarled, her eyes rimmed red. She threw a turnip at Dualayn. It missed and burst into pulp against the far wall.

"Kaylin wasn't my most successful attempt," Dualayn said, "but she's mostly fine." He put on a smile. "She still cooks just as—"

Angry screeches burst from all the cooks. A young one named Hajina, her hair in a pair of long braids, brandished a sharp knife, murder in her eyes.

Dualayn shrunk back, stepping on the pile of his clothing thrown down by the maids.

"I was just doing it all for the betterment of mankind," Dualayn protested. "I made mistakes with Kaylin, but I learned."

"And with Avena!" demanded Jilly. "Makes me wonder how your wife ended up as an invalid. What experiments did you perform on her?"

"I never harmed my wife!" Dualayn roared, a sudden anger seizing him. He glared at them all. "You work for me! All of you. I pay you. Put a roof over your heads. This is how you thank me for the fair wage I've given you? For mending your wounds? How many of you had relatives I fixed? For free! Tell me!"

"Wot did you do to them?" hissed Chobay. "When you healed my ma, did you cut her open and play around with her insides before you put her back together? Is her brain down in that horror collection? Joayne told us all about it!"

"Disgustin'!" screeched the cook brandishing the knife. "My uncle died when I brought him to you. Did you really try? Or was he just another victim of your madness?"

"I have never deliberately harmed—"

"You cut out my brain!" hissed Avena, marching up and leaving Ōbhin behind. She stalked out before the rest of the servants clustering around Dualayn. "Don't spin your lies and pretend you were just helping us. All you care about is fixing your wife. That's why you did it. That's why you experimented on those you were healing."

"For the good of—"

She slapped him. Her pain fed the rage in her. The stinging mark blazed across his cheek.

"Don't even speak those words," she growled. "You are a selfish, disgusting, loathsome man. You had us all fooled—all of Kash and the rest of Lothon with your noble savior act—but you're just a roach scurrying in the dark. You run through excrement and filth, then tell the rest of us that you don't stink. You are stained by the Black worse than anyone I've met."

Dualayn wilted, the piggish pain in his eyes only infuriating her more. What did *he* have to feel pain for? Grief? He stared at her like *she'd* betrayed him. She wanted to keep slapping him. To drive him to the floor and vent all her fury on him.

I'll be better than you.

She whirled around and faced the servants. "Ōbhin, *him,* and I are traveling to the Upfing Forest. We'll be gone for a while. Maybe a half-month. Thirty or more days." She didn't know how long they would be roaming through the ruins to find her antenna. "Until we return, you can live off the estate. Joayne, will you manage that?"

"Of course," the nurse said. She was at the top of the stairs. "I can't abandon my charge no matter *who* she's married to."

"Joayne," Dualayn groaned, wincing.

"Ōbhin and I have locked the vault," Avena continued. "What's down there is disgusting. None of you need to see it. Before we leave, I'll have Dualayn write you out letters of recommendation so you may find new jobs." She whirled around to face the man shoving his clothing into his traveling trunk. "Glowing letters. Right?"

He gave a sullen nod, his upper lip bleeding.

"Joayne will see that you each receive severance pay to help you out until then," Avena continued. "You are, of course, free to keep working for this pus-filled roach. I won't."

"I want to go with you," Smiles said.

Her stomach tightened as she turned around to find all the guards crowding the porch, watching through the open doors. Behind them, the summer sun shone bright on the withering lawn, a few sheep nuzzling for some shoots to eat. The fake-Smiles, at the front, looked so much like the man she'd known for the last three years; that friendly face, broad smile. A new anger burned through her, one tinged with disgust and horror.

"Me, too!" Bran said, standing beside the impostor. "We'll make sure you get better, Avena. Won't let that Black-cursed bastard do nothin' more to you."

"He's a knave," Dajouth added. "I am horrified that he would do somethin' so foul to one as beautiful as you. You have my pledge to guard you and protect you until such a time as you're made whole and fair."

"I'm not fair now?" she asked, exasperated with his flirting, especially after kissing Ōbhin. She no longer had any doubts about her ability to love another. She knew she'd loved Chames, and now loved Ōbhin. Perhaps had loved him since their first encounter when his contradictory presence had captured her attention.

"I didn't mean that," Dajouth said. "I mean, you are fair, but you'll be . . ."

"It's a trap, boy," Fingers muttered. Then he stepped up and declared, "I'm goin', too."

"You're not leavin' me behind," Miguil said. He pushed up past Fingers. Her former promised stared at her with pain in his handsome face. "I know the horses. I don't trust this bastard with them. Who knows what madness he'll try? Won't let them out of the stables without me."

"They're my horses," protested Dualayn.

"Keep packing," Avena hissed. She studied her former promised. They couldn't let Smiles come. They couldn't trust him. Which meant they couldn't let any of the guards come along with them, but Miguil . . . "Of course you can come, Miguil. Thank you. I know you'll take care of the horses."

"Then it's set," Smiles said.

"You're not coming," Ōbhin said. "None of the guards are. There are still riots in the city. For now, the cooks and maids will be living here. They need watching over. Especially your wife, Smiles. She's pregnant."

The thing pretending to be Smiles gave a sheepish grin. "You're right. Sorry, Jilly, my love, I got a bit carried away."

"You do that," Jilly said, a fondness in her tone. "It's one of your redeemin' qualities. But we'll be fine. Go 'n help them."

"No, Ōbhin's right." Avena glanced at Smiles. "Who's going to cause us problems? Ōbhin's more than capable of protecting me."

"True," Fingers muttered. "Still . . ."

"No," Ōbhin said. "You accepted coin and contract. You work for Dualayn. And he put me in charge of you. You stay here."

"Fine," Cerdyn grunted. "We'll stay."

"But . . ." Bran said, his eagerness fading from his face. "We can be helpful."

"Would anyone care for my opinion on the matter?" Dualayn muttered.

"Not one bit," Fingers grunted. He looked Ōbhin up and down. "Fine. No arguin'."

"But," Bran said again. He quivered. "They'll need our help. They're goin' to dangerous ruins and—"

"The front gate's unguarded," Fingers cut in. "Return to your post, boy. If you make me march over there, I'll grab you by the scruff of your neck and drag you like a pup."

"Fine." The youth slouched off.

"We'll pack food and supplies, Avena," said Hajina. "Kaylin got it in her head to cook up a feast." A sad expression entered her face. "She won't know what to do with herself away from here." Then her face tightened and she spat on Dualayn as he stuffed the last of his clothes into the travel chest. The cooks whirled and marched into the east wing.

"I'd like to leave tonight," Ōbhin said to Miguil. "Could you hitch the horses to the wagon?"

"Tonight?" Dualayn protested. "But we'll only get a few . . ."

His words trailed off as Avena glared down at him.

"Sorry, sorry, forgot." He rose. "I'll go write those letters."

Avena gave a satisfied nod.

They wouldn't get far, but Ōbhin wanted to be away from the mansion. It no longer felt like a home. Discovering the horrors in Dualayn's basement laboratory had broken the place. Despite the warmth lingering as the sun lowered to the western horizon, a chill seemed to gust out of the house. Like a last, wheezing gasp of something dying.

Ōbhin thought he'd found a place to protect. To belong. Where he could walk a path that would lead him from the misty darkness of his crimes of two years ago. But it wasn't ever this place.

It was her.

Avena.

He glanced at her sitting on the wagon bench beside Miguil. She wore her hair in those two tails, looking adorable. He found himself smiling, admiring the porcelain white of her pale neck, its graceful curve vanishing into the neckline of her airy dress. She wore a light blue one with no petticoats.

Excitement rippled through him from the kiss. The same giddy delight he'd experienced in those days after first making love to Foonauri. That freshness of new romance. He wanted to keep kissing Avena, to find a quiet place and share something majestic with her.

But he couldn't do that *here*. Not where she'd been so thoroughly betrayed by her mentor. His gaze slid to the sulking, portly man sitting by his traveling trunk in the wagon bed with Ōbhin. He held his primer for the Recorder in one hand with his journal spread open on his lap.

Miguil drove the team towards the open gates where a sullen Bran and cheerful Smiles awaited. Ōbhin slipped onto the edge rim of the wagon bed, the narrow board digging into his backside, and studied the thing masquerading as Smiles.

"We'll hold down things here, don't you worry," said Smiles. "Me 'n Jilly will make sure you 'n Avena got someplace to go once you return."

Ōbhin nodded, coldness swelling inside of him. The thing was here to guard Dualayn, and yet hardly gave any resistance to coming along. It had pretended to be the devoted husband. To be Smiles. The real one wouldn't have abandoned his wife.

"I know you will," he said, almost wanting to believe that the real Smiles wasn't dead. It was so easy to slip into that delusion. "Take care of your wife and the others."

Smiles grinned back in his friendly, relaxed manner. Ōbhin fought back the pain.

"You sure I can't come?" Bran asked. "I get not bringin' Dajouth, but I'm not annoyin' like he is. Am I, Avena?"

"No, no," she said. "But you need to watch out for your mother and the others. Be strong. Maybe you'll impress Hajina."

His back straightened. "Really? Has she ever said anything about me?"

"Maybe," Avena said in a coy way. "We'll return as soon as we can."

Ōbhin glanced at another travel chest, this one bound tight in iron chains and secured with an amethyst jewelchine lock. In a swaddle of soft sheets and pillows rested her brain. If anything happened to that box . . .

We'll fix you, Ōbhin thought. *Lausi, let the winds sing to us with your Swift Tone and guide us to the answer we need to save her.*

Miguil flicked the reins. Goodbyes shouted around them from the maids and cooks. Ōbhin found Fingers lingering in the back, arms folded, watching with stoic grace. Their gazes met. A single nod was all that needed to be said.

Then Miguil turned them west onto the lane and they were clattering away from Dualayn's estate.

The road would bend to the north and skirt the Porcelain. There it would intersect the main highway heading west from Kash. After three or so days of travel, they'd reach the Upfing Woods. Another day to travel south into its heart and find the ruins.

As they rode, Ōbhin glanced at Dualayn. He was going from book to book, examining something. "You do know how to find this antenna, right?"

"Yes, yes," Dualayn said. "In the Hall of Communication." He lifted his gaze, his upper lip swollen from Avena's slap. "You see, the gems function through a signal that resonates through the immaterial. Eight standing harmonics."

"The Tones," Ōbhin said. "What was once one was broken by disharmony and separated."

"That is . . . *a* creation myth for them," Dualayn said with care. "Either way, the Tones, these standing harmonics which are probably amplified by the moons, each vibrate at their own specific frequency. Not one any human can create. Luckily, they don't use all the possible ones. Not even close. There are plenty of frequencies not in use. Hundreds of them. Thousands. Other . . . musical notes being played."

"Okay," Ōbhin said, struggling to understand. He knew music scales. There were more than eight notes. "Your point?"

"That she is broadcasting on her own frequency. No one else uses it, so there shouldn't be any signal interference," Dualayn explained. "What she's experiencing is degradation since I did not fully sculpt the obsidian antenna correctly. That is my mistake, but I only have the work of my friend in Democh and my translations from the Recorder's description. Once I have my hands on the proper antenna found in Koilon, she won't have any of these problems. I promise. She'll live a normal existence."

"Except I'll have *obsidian* in my head!" snapped Avena from the driver's bench. "I have the Black's forbidden gem in my skull connected to my nerves by black iron. It's going to leach into my blood and taint my soul."

"Superstitious nonsense," said Dualayn. "Perhaps I should have done a better job of stamping out these beliefs you picked up from the Daughters of Compassion. Obsidian isn't forbidden for any logical or sound reason. It is no different than any other gem."

"Except you *have to* use black iron wires to make it work. The poisoned metal that scars the world! The Black unleashed it in the Shattering."

"Child, no one possibly knows fully what happened back then. It was three thousand years ago. Yes, *something* happened to change obsidian and separate it from the other seven gems, but it's not some mythical clash between invented beings."

"Invented?" Avena's head whipped around while Ōbhin shifted. "Elohm is *invented*? The Creator of All, who put that miserable, shrunken soul into your body and filled you with all the Colours to give your existence meaning, was *invented*?"

Dualayn sighed and glanced at Ōbhin. "You see, the Daughters who raised her indoctrina—"

"Ōbhin, gag him, please. I'm tired of hearing his offensive speech."

Ōbhin didn't necessarily disagree with Dualayn about Elohm. The Tones were the truth. The harmonic resonances that powered the gems had their own . . . Well, "personalities" wasn't quite the word. Their own quirks. They were elemental forces personifying Fire or Water or Fatherhood. However, his stomach curdled listening to Dualayn's constant attempts to justify his actions.

Ōbhin found a rag and rolled it into a gag. Dualayn stared dully at him. "If you gag me, people will wonder. All I have to do is make a commotion, and you shall be arrested. I have powerful friends, and I don't just mean Grey and his Brotherhood. I want to help Avena as much as you do, but there are limits to what I will endure."

"Then don't antagonize her. And if you do draw attention to us, remember, I can draw my blade in a heartbeat. I've killed better men than you."

Dualayn shivered. "Indeed. My apologies. I forget. I just keep hoping that we can put this past us."

"I doubt that's possible," Ōbhin said, tossing the gag at the man. "She's the only thing keeping you alive. Remember that the next time you claim her god isn't real and that what you did to her was no different from setting a broken leg."

Dualayn stared down at the gag and sighed.

"We will find it," Dualayn said. "The antenna. While we didn't excavate far, lucking out and finding the Grand Library from the start, there were passages leading from it. I hope we can find intact streets. It will be dangerous, but I am willing to do it."

"Facing death's always a powerful motivator," Ōbhin said, sitting down on the scholar's traveling trunk. He leaned over. "Keep studying your notes. Make sure we find it fast so we can be done with you."

"You shall understand once the anger dies down," Dualayn said. "I promise. We will one day—"

"Ōbhin," Avena said, her voice low and deadly.

His hand dropped to his sword. Dualayn swallowed and clamped his jaw shut.

For the next two hours, they rode in silence. As darkness descended, they approached one of the small farming villages outside of Kash. It lay far enough away that they weren't in danger of being swallowed by the avaricious city and its ever-growing need for land.

Ninth Day of Patience, 755 EU

Avena sat beside Miguil as he drove the wagon west again, the sun rising behind them. She hadn't slept well at all. She had spent much of the night staring at the traveling chest containing her mind, half-afraid that if she fell asleep, she'd wake up in a jar, merely a disembodied brain divorced from the world. Forever blind and deaf, bereft of touch and taste and scent.

She gazed in a groggy daze at the fields they passed. Mostly buckwheat and barley with patches of vegetables: squashes, edamame, turnips, and radishes. The plants appeared wilted, stunted. She hadn't realized how little rain had come this year. Drought gripped the region.

Every house had green flying from pendants hanging off the eaves of thatched roofs or pinned to doors. Children in rough-spun linens raced by, the boys waving flags of ragged green or holding knots of verdant color tied to makeshifts swords they swung at each other. Girls wove the emerald cloth into the twin braids falling in bouncing tails of browns. Farmers tied the cloth to the sleeves of dusty felt coats or linen shirts, and wives pinned green ribbons to their aprons.

People glanced at them, brows furrowing. A simmering anger brimmed in the air. Worry over her own body and her mind losing connection with her flesh dwindled. The king was increasing taxation when he should be giving the commonfolk relief. At least here. Maybe in the Colony, the lands to the south, or in the farms to the north of the city where she was from, the fields were prospering. But the central lands were not faring well. Ponds were little more than puddles, lily pads drying on cracking mud. Instead of rills, gullies held puddles teaming with tadpoles wriggling for life in increasingly dwindling spaces.

Something had to be done. She leaned back, remembering the work Deffona and Refractor Charlis were doing. Attempts to stop both the riots and the king's ambition to control the mines of the Border Fangs. Those mountains were a dark haze on the horizon. They would grow sharper as they traveled farther west.

Dust on the horizon announced a column of riders approaching. Her stomach tensed. She glanced back in the wagon where Ōbhin sat, his hand casually resting on his sword as he gave Dualayn a meaningful look. The odious man swallowed and then looked back at his books as he leaned against the wall of the wagon bed.

Would he say something? Metal glinted. The riders wore armor. As they neared, the pendants with Lothon's colors snapped from atop lances: the white stag on the field of blue and green. Crown knights wore full plate armor with tabards adorned with their personal coat-of-arms. Behind them marched a column of infantry soldiers in chain armor, shouldering long pikes that bristled like a forest.

"Good day, sir knight," said Miguil when they reached the column.

The captain reined up before them, his troop passing. He had the visor of his bascinet helmet raised, his ruddy face dominated by a bushy, brown mustache. "Goodman. How have you found the road?"

"Dry and dusty."

The knight-captain glanced at them. "I don't see many goods. You returning from the market?"

"We are heading to the Upfing Forest to conduct a scientific inquiry into the nature of the Red Heart of the Forest," said Dualayn without looking up. "I am Dualayn Dashvin of Kash, financing the expectation. These are my servants."

"I see," the knight-captain said. "A foreign bodyguard? Can you rely on a Tethyrian not to be too inebriated to swing a sword?"

"He is Qothian, Captain," Dualayn said. "A loyal and honest man. He has served me well. I have no complaints about him or the protection he has given me."

Avena held her breath, noticing Ōbhin's hand casually resting on his sword pommel. Then she glanced at Dualayn. A fuzzy tingle rippled through her fingers. She clutched at her skirt, a bead of sweat running down her face, catching the dust that billowed up from the soldiers tromping by.

"Dangerous going into the woods that deep," said the knight-captain. "And the road west is growing unsafe these days. I could provide an escort, at least until the forest edge. More and more farms are lying fallow as farmers think there's more profit to be found in robbing the merchants who come to buy their crops."

"That's not necessary," Avena said, her voice tight. "We'll be fine. Ōbhin is more than a match for brigands."

"Quiet, woman," the knight-captain grunted. "I'm speaking with your master." His gaze slid back to Dualayn while Avena bristled. "I am sure your man is good, but he is only *one* man. I would be glad to give you an escort. A pair of knights."

A pair? Avena's hands clutched at her skirt. Her heart pounded fear through her veins. If Dualayn could get alone with those knights and reveal the truth, he could be spirited to safety. He'd escape justice then.

"It is a tragedy," said Dualayn, "that so many have been driven to hardship by drought and taxes."

The knight-captain snorted, ruffling his mustache.

"But I do not wish to separate your command. I am confident in Ōbhin's skill. He used to protect the kings of Qoth, you know. He is versed in tactics that would surprise even you, Captain."

"I am loath to let you pass without an escort. I fear I must insist. For your own safety."

Avena's stomach sank when she heard the gallop of hooves. One of the knights trotted up, his armor jangling. He waited for the last pikeman to march past then swung around the wagon to reach the front and confer with the knight-captain.

A tension mounted in Avena. Ōbhin could take off Dualayn's head in a heartbeat, but he couldn't fight a column of soldiers. There would be no putting off this knight-captain. How long before their escort discovered that Dualayn was their prisoner? They would all hang if the twisted, disgusting man said the wrong word. She didn't want to see Ōbhin die. She racked her brain for something to do. To say. Anything that could let them travel on without an escort.

"There are three armed men we detained who claim to be your servants, Master Dashvin," the knight-captain said. He pointed down the road where another pair of knights escorted three riders. Avena squinted and blinked at Fingers, Bran, and Dajouth. All three wore their uniforms of padded gambeson, Fingers at their lead.

"Oh, yes," said Dualayn. "I asked them to catch up. Sent them on an errand. As you can see, I have four guards to protect me. All skilled men who've fought bandits and protected me during the Troubles. So there's no need to waste the time of your two knights."

The knight-captain studied the three guards. Fingers rubbed at his sweaty forehead, his knuckles swollen, Bran had an excited smile on his face as he almost bounced in his saddle, while Dajouth grinned as his eyes fell on Avena.

She groaned beneath her breath.

"Very well," the knight-captain said. "I will entrust you to your servants. I hope you are not stained by the darkness in the Heart of the Forest."

"My thanks for your concern, Captain. Next time I am in Kash, I shall recommend you for an award for your diligence, um..."

"Knight-Captain Dovayn," he said, fighting a smile then inclined his head. "My thanks." He heeled his destrier and clattered down the road, his three knights falling in behind him. They cantered towards the column to catch up, leaving a drifting pall of dust behind them.

"What are you doing here?" demanded Ōbhin once the knight was out of earshot. "I told you three to stay and protect everyone."

"You told us not to leave *with* you," Fingers said then shrugged. "Besides, I don't work for Dualayn no more. I'm a free agent. Decided I'd ride this way. Check out the red forest."

"Yes, yes!" Bran said, bouncing in his saddle. His horse snorted and looked back at him. Bran didn't seem to notice. "We have supplies and food and our armor and binders. We can be a big help."

"No Smiles?" Avena asked, a yawning pit opening in her stomach. "I thought he would come if you four did."

"I asked him," Fingers said, "but he's got his wife to worry about. They got a child on the way."

"Indeed," said Dajouth. "Jilly is a flower that any man would stay behind to protect, though she dims before your radiance, Avena."

Ōbhin shifted. "You spoke with him, Dajouth?"

"I did," said Dajouth. "Right before I finished packin'. He asked me to take care of you all. He and Cerdyn will watch over the women. But the three of us were worried about Avena and wished to see her made whole."

"And to see the ruins and fight darklings and crystalmen and bogarts!" said Bran, his face bursting with delight.

"Crystalmen fought darklings," Avena muttered, a chill running through her. She glanced at Ōbhin.

His eyes met her. She could see the truth in her lover's eyes. Smiles had taken on a new form. Either Fingers, Bran, or Dajouth lay dead in a ditch or thrown in Lake Ophavin. The shapeshifter's mission was to protect Dualayn, so, of course, it wouldn't be that easy to keep him away.

We should have let Smiles come. She looked away to battle her grief and guilt. If they hadn't rushed their leaving, they would have realized what the thing would do.

Which one is it? Which two can we trust?

"Get us down the road, Miguil," Ōbhin said, his voice tight. "As they said, they're free to ride where they want. We can't stop them."

Bran whooped his excitement.

16

Worry itched at Ōbhin as he studied the three riders following the wagon. Bran cast his gaze around with boyish enthusiasm. He ogled the passing farms, the oxen pulling carts, the fields of withered crops while grunting men hauled buckets of water from shrinking ponds or from deep wells. Dajouth waved his hand before his face, batting away flies, his brow glistening with sweat. Fingers rode slouched, hand resting on the pommel of his horse, face flushed.

One of them was a threat. Which one would the thing masquerading as Smiles have chosen to be? Which had the monster killed and replaced? No way to answer the question without revealing Ōbhin's suspicions. No good way to send them back, either.

They wouldn't go.

Need to be on my guard on how I treat Dualayn. Ōbhin stiffened at that thought. *Unless that's a way to reveal the impostor.*

"Fingers, look alive," Ōbhin said, moving to the back of the wagon.

The older man lifted his head. He blinked like he was coming out of a nap. His horse snorted at his shifting weight. It tossed its mane of black hair as Fingers mopped at his sweaty brow. The sound of cicadas buzzing grew louder as they passed a small stand of willow trees around a muddy pond.

"What?" Fingers asked, blinking.

"If I'm not around, you're in charge of watching Dualayn," Ōbhin said. He hated suspecting one of his men, one of his friends, of being a monster. It horrified him no matter which one had been replaced. "If he tries to get us captured, break his neck."

"With pleasure," Fingers said, a vicious grin spilling across his face. It made him look ugly and monstrous, his brows knitting. "I'll strangle him with my bare hands."

"I'll crack him so hard with my binder across the head, I'll split his head right open!" declared Bran.

Dajouth spat to the side. "You hear that, old man? We all want to gut you for what you did to the fair flower. You don't get to pluck her petals and stick 'em on another plant. You're lucky you didn't destroy her radiance."

Sour disappointment churned through Ōbhin. All three wholeheartedly wanted to eviscerate Dualayn. The thing was good. Too good. How to detect a perfect mimic? It could heal wounds. Fast. If he could get any of the three alone . . .

His stomach turned queasy. What if it had replaced Avena or Miguil? He struggled to remember when he'd last seen Smiles as his head snapped around. He stared at the two on the driver's bench, his spine crawling with the terror of not knowing which was the fake.

No, no, Smiles saw us off. The thing was there. It's not Avena.

Relief relaxed tension. He leaned against the wagon's side.

"You okay?" Fingers asked.

"Just the Black Toned heat," he muttered. "It doesn't get this hot in Qoth."

"Nor is this usual in Lothon," groaned Fingers. "Bad summer to be a farmer."

"You've been through droughts?"

"Oh, I remember one before . . ." He shifted. "Well, before I ran from my wife. Couldn't get anythin' to sprout. Lost a whole crop o' turnips. My buckwheat was barely hangin' on. Spent hours haulin' water until my back broke just tryin' to save enough to feed us through the winter, never mind sellin' it and payin' my landlord rent. Had to pawn my ma's jewels that winter just to keep the farm. Not that my wife ever noticed." His eyes grew distant.

Ōbhin shook his head. The emotion was real. Spoken with such conviction. It lined up with everything Ōbhin knew of the man, and it wasn't enough to prove if he was the real Fingers. Somehow, the thing filched memories. It stole everything about a person; the worst sort of chameleon.

Scenarios played through Ōbhin's mind as they road west. He broiled through the afternoon, drinking warm water to keep the parched burning at bay. His leather jerkin grew sodden with sweat. Avena drooped even with her bonnet shading her face. Miguil held the handle's reins in a relaxed grip. Bran slouched, his excitement vanished beneath the hot sun. Dajouth's flowery compliments dried up after an hour, his lips growing chapped.

Ōbhin pondered ways to "accidentally" injure the three guards. Tripping and plunging a knife into their arm. Dropping something heavy on a foot. Even punching them in the face in a pretend fit of anger to see what happened. They had jewelchine healers with them. If he hurt the wrong person, the damage could be repaired.

And potentially tip off the thing.

Right now, the impostor believed to be fooling everyone. How would its behavior change if revealed? Would it strike hard and rescue Dualayn before they ever got to the ruins? Or perhaps it wouldn't do anything so long as he didn't try to cut off Dualayn's head.

Ōbhin didn't know. He knew next to nothing about it, even how to kill the disharmonic thing. It was tough, healed swiftly, and could run faster than him. Was it stronger? A better fighter? What if he was wrong and it killed him?

Replaced him?

What if it tricked Avena like poor Jilly? She'd spent more than sixty days living with a thing and not realizing it wasn't her husband. It was such a good actor, Avena would never realize the difference between the real Ōbhin and the fake. She would trust it. Love it.

Ōbhin hated it more and more with every passing hour while despising his helplessness.

As the sun set, they stopped at one of the farming villages. They all lay about the same distance apart, a day's walk between each. This one was a little larger, bedecked in green pendants and flags. The town constable marched up and down the main road in ill-fitting armor with a pike in hand, his eyes hard on theirs. The defiance in the village seemed baked into the soil by the unrelenting heat of the summer sun.

They found hospitality at a nameless inn. Dualayn retired to his room to eat his meal, a sparse affair of buckwheat noodles in a thin turnip soup. It was served cool, left in the inn's root cellar all day to keep the summer heat away. Ōbhin fumbled with the chopsticks. He still hadn't mastered the strange eating implements the others used with casual ease.

"How much longer 'til we get to the ruins?" Bran asked before he scooped up several noodles and slurped them into his mouth.

"A few days," Ōbhin said. "Three, if I remember right."

Avena nodded, quiet. She sat beside him, her bonnet off and short hair falling loose about her face, freshly scrubbed clean of the day's dust.

"We shall purloin the ruins and find wot you need, don't you fear, Avena," Dajouth said. "Why, my mother always said my father was part miner. It explains why I got no fear of venturin' into the caves. Know a thing or two 'bout bein' underground, I do."

Avena rolled her eyes. Ōbhin smirked.

"Nothing quite like bein' underground," said Dajouth. "You can feel the weight above you. All that earth o'er your head, but it can't touch you 'cause the cave is sound. Things echo, too. Your voice can live for a while, y'know, amid all the drippin'."

"Drippin'?" Bran asked.

"From the water." Dajouth leaned back. "Always drippin' in caves. And dark, too. You don't wanna be trapped in the dark."

"No, you don't," Ōbhin muttered. He remembered the sunless mines beneath Gunya, the capital of Qoth. That day, he'd felt the weight of the city above. The mine's walls had felt fragile after the quake. He kept thinking the rocks possessed the same strength as rotten wood.

"How do you stand it?" Bran asked before slurping up more noodles.

"You just have to be brave and keep your head on when things go dark," Dajouth said, glancing at Avena. "Once, my torch just went out. Not sure why, but I was all alone in the dark. I wanted to panic, but you can't do that. Gotta keep your head."

"Wot did you do when you lost it?" Bran asked, leaning forward. He had a piece of noodle plastered to his chin.

"Fouled his britches," Fingers grunted. He leaned back in his chair, the piece of furniture creaking. "Wot else you gonna do?"

"Didn't foul my britches," Dajouth said, his cheeks pinking. "I kept my head. I felt the air movin', that slight breeze from the entrance. The inhalation. Deeper in the cave, there's the exhalation, but near the mouth, air flows inward. I just moved forward slowly, feelin' the current on my face until I found my way out."

Bran shook his head, still oblivious to the noodle. "I hope that don't happen in the ruins. Our torches goin' out."

"We'll have jewelchine lamps," Avena said. She stirred her chopsticks through her broth before picking up her bowl in her left hand. "And we'll be together, so if one of ours does go out, it won't matter." She drank from her bowl, draining the broth.

"True," Dajouth said. "Though, I took this girl down into the caves and turned off the lights on her. Y'know what happened?"

"She screamed her head off and then slapped you like the idiot you are for scarin' her," said Fingers. "Don't even claim you flipped up her skirt and doused your wick."

"Her screams can still be heard today," said Dajouth. His eyes slid to Avena still drinking her broth. "Some women won't be scared, though. They know how to face the danger and appreciate a man who can give her a taste."

He winked at her.

Ōbhin snorted with laughter.

Avena set her bowl down with a hard thump. "I'm going to retire. This was a long day." She rose and then bent over. "Blessed night, my bright diamond."

The words surprised him, but the kiss was welcome. Her lips tasted of the turnip broth, but he didn't mind. Blood spilled hot through him. Bran sniggered; Ōbhin did not care at all. Avena broke the kiss and had a smile playing on her lips.

"Blessed night," he said, his voice hoarse. His cheeks burned from such a public display. Kissing in Qoth was for the bedroom when a woman could remove her mask.

Dajouth scowled. "So you and her finally . . ."

"Yep."

The younger man leaned back. "Well, I had to try, y'know? I could see she was buildin' a fire to warm you, but so long as you didn't sit at it, I thought it might warm me just as well. You can't know wot will turn a woman's affections. Like to be chased, they do."

"They do?" Bran glanced at one of the barmaids, a girl not much older than him. She was pleasantly plump with a bright smile. She drifted through the room, chatting with the locals.

He stood up and darted over to her, boasting about their adventure to the heart of the forest and the buried ruins they would dive into. The barmaid had a patient look on her face as she listened.

Dajouth shook his head. "He don't know he's got a noodle on his chin."

"Just matters that he tries," Fingers said, nodding in approval. "Boy needs to grow up. Have his first woman."

"I don't think she's impressed," Dajouth noted. The woman's attention wandered as Bran kept animatedly speaking to her.

"Nope. But he's tryin'. As you say, Dajouth, you can't know a woman's heart. All you can do is throw yours out before her and see what she does with it. Like baitin' a trap. You never quite know wot beast'll wander into it. Maybe wot you expected to catch, maybe somethin' surprisin', or maybe they'll just snatch the meat and run."

"You think women are like wild beasts?" Dajouth said. "No, wait, 'course you do. You think your wife's tryin' to kill you."

Fingers grunted. "Just sayin', Bran's a good kid. Want him to find some happiness. We're goin' into trouble. This ruin sounds dangerous."

"Yeah," Dajouth said, glancing up at the ceiling. "Is it really a good idea to take that untrustworthy bastard with us?"

"We'll never find what we're looking for without him," Ōbhin said. "The only reason he's still breathing."

"Just sayin', goin' underground is dangerous enough. It might be safer to leave him above. Have someone guard him while the rest of us go spelunkin'. You know, don't risk the guy who can actually fix Avena once we find it."

Ōbhin studied Dajouth. *Is it you?*

Fingers chuckled as Bran led the barmaid across the room to a private corner. "Good for him. He sold that adventure and danger. Farm girls get bored."

"You sound proud of him. Like he's your son or something," Ōbhin noted.

"Never had a son. Bran's about the closest, I guess. Known him since he was, oh, ten or so. Good lad, if a little excitable."

"If Bran can get a barmaid to talk," Dajouth said, standing up, "I might try with the other. She's got a nice smile."

Fingers grunted as Dajouth slipped from the table.

"I thought you never had children." Ōbhin furrowed his brow. "You said that, right?"

"Huh?" grunted Fingers, still watching Bran. He'd settled the barmaid sitting at another table. He leaned over her while her eyes looked more animated now.

"You said you never had a son, but it's like you were implying you had daughters."

"Never had daughters. Never had sons." He shrugged. "Good thing. Woulda made leavin' my wife harder. I'd mighta hurt her worse if'n there was a child or two tyin' me in place." He stared down at his hands. "I know I woulda hurt her worse if we had children. Small blessin' we didn't, I suppose."

"You ever going to stop pretending to the others why you really left her?" Ōbhin asked. Fingers had confessed to Ōbhin before Ust's attack that his wife wasn't the village whore like he claimed.

"No." He shook his head. "Never gave me a single cause to think she mighta strayed. A good woman. Too good for a bastard like me. But if I don't make myself hate her, I'd just hate myself for hurtin' her. Then all I think 'bout's the rope. Got to tie that knot right, y'know. Or it'll go bad."

The casual admittance chilled Ōbhin's blood.

"Some days . . ." Fingers stretched his back. "Well, not much to live for save these kids I've grown fond of workin' with at Dualayn's." He spat on the floor. "There's 'nother monster walkin' around lookin' human like me."

"We'll fix Avena," Ōbhin said. "And Bran will find himself a good woman. Someone that can calm him down."

The barmaid stood up from the table and left a bewildered Bran behind.

"Not tonight." Fingers chuckled. He glanced at Ōbhin. "I'll see you in the mornin'. Try n' sleep while it's coolin' off. I can't wait to get to the ruins. Least we won't be roastin' when we're underground."

Ōbhin nodded. As Fingers stood, Ōbhin's gaze drifted to his sable-gloved hands. The last time he'd ventured beneath the earth had ended badly.

17

Avena gasped awake at the first tingles racing over her fingers. She could feel it, the control slipping from her body. Interference assaulted her even with her mind so close. The trunk lay beside her bed holding her awareness. Thoughts. Feelings. Soul. She stroked the lid, hardly feeling the trunk's wood through the fuzzy prickles rippling up her digits.

She rolled off her bed, her chemise clinging to her body. She lurched to the door, her feet too heavy, her gait thrown off by the numbness spreading up them. She fumbled with the latch of the door, pulling up on the handle twice before she managed to get it open.

Terror seized her. She hated this. Dreaded collapsing. Her body should always be under her complete control, not stolen away at a moment's notice. She leaned her bare shoulder against the rough walls made of logs caulked with dried mud. She slid down it, using it to keep her upright as she stumbled for Ōbhin's door. She reached it, knocking hard, her fingers curled into tight fists.

"Ōbhin!" She knocked again.

Her mind threatened to abandon her body. The hallway spun about her.

The door opened. He stood before her, illuminated by a pure silver-white. Honesty's moonlight flooded through his window, revealing him wearing only his breechcloth. A sheen of sweat covered his muscular body, skin dark brown. She fell into him, pressing her face into his warmth.

"It's happening!" she whimpered, her entire body shaking. She hated this. Hated her fear. Being helpless.

Ōbhin's arms engulfed her. "I have you."

Three simple words, but the fear that had filled her already retreated. She closed her eyes and pressed her cheek against his chest. She felt the fine down of wiry hairs above his firm strength. His heartbeat thundered in her ear.

Despite the impropriety of it, she didn't care, asking, "Can I sleep in your bed? If it happens . . ."

"I'll be here," he said, his bare hand stroking down the back of her chemise. His other slid through her short, fine hair. "You have nothing to fear."

The tingles in her fingers dwindled. The fuzziness retreated. For now.

He led her stumbling across the room. With each step, his strength seemed to flow into her, reinforcing her legs. Her normal grace and control returned to her by the time they reached his bed. His blankets were rumpled but still tucked in. They sank down onto the hay-stuffed mattress. The bed's frame creaked. She stretched out on her back, her toes twitching. He lay on his side, watching her.

His hand slid up to her face, touching her with the bare pad of his finger. The intimacy sent a momentary shiver through her. She knew what this meant for him. His eyes caught a momentary gleam of Honesty's silvery moonlight as he leaned down.

She shook her head, her heart still racing. "I didn't come here . . . I mean . . ." Her cheeks warmed. "I'm too shaken to even think of that. I feel like I could just slip away at any moment, lose my body and fall into those dreams."

He smiled at her. "I couldn't resist stealing one kiss." His finger reached her lip. He caressed her. She kissed the calloused tip, reveled in the control of her body, but the tingles still lingered in her extremities. The excitement his touch should stir in her couldn't find anything to kindle. "I'll be here, Avena. When the snows come, I'll be your shelter."

"Something they say in Qoth?"

He nodded. "Something said during certain ceremonies. A promise. When the mountains quake, I'll be your support."

"Tell me about Qoth." She stared up at him. "You don't speak of it much. You miss it?"

"I do."

Avena's fingers tightened on Ōbhin's hands, the prickling almost numbing the feeling of him away. "What sort of gloves did you wear before black?"

"Uh . . . the last pair I wore were rose gloves with flame-hued circles on them." He shifted, his voice tight. "It was the day of my duel with Taim."

"Rose?" She blinked. "That's an unusual color."

"They were a statement of my innocence. I was accused of assaulting the personage of Foonauri. The circles were the color of flame. That indicated I possessed a great love and desire for someone."

"Colors mean that much in Qoth? I thought you were all about the Tones."

"We are, but the colors of the gems and their related hues have come to mean things. Usually, men only have one or sometimes two colors on their gloves, but women can get quite elaborate with their masks."

It intrigued her. Was there a trace of Elohm's Colours found in the pagan beliefs to the east? It stood to reason since He had created the world and established the jewels, each a different aspect of Him. Just like a prism broke light into different colors, so did Elohm's light refract through every human being.

"What does . . . orange mean?" she asked, going with the Colour of Compassion and topazes.

"Orange is the color of mothers and life," said Ōbhin. "A woman will paint it on her mask to indicate her hope of having children while on a man's gloves it's a boast of his virility."

"Oh," she said, her cheeks warming up. "I think we call those codpieces."

He chuckled and she found herself giggling.

"One of the daughter colors of orange is amber. It's used by women to represent motherhood. They will mark their masks' cheeks with accents for each of their children they are proud of." He let out a heavy sigh. "I suspect my mother has one less adorning her mask."

"You don't know that," Avena said, not wanting to open old wounds. Those could bleed the worst.

"I killed the son of our satrap. Our king."

"Well, green then," she said, wanting to get away from that color. It seemed safe. The Colour of Forgiveness, emeralds, and strength.

"Men who work outside in the forests wear green gloves. It means they're close to the mountains and Vatsim, who is the Tone of the Mountains and the Earth. Viridian, a daughter hue, is seen as a deeply masculine color. It's a common one for soldiers to dye their gloves. A woman who paints it on her mask is declaring her independence and her self-sufficiency."

"So you wore viridian gloves normally?" She pictured him with that bright and happy color. The shade of grass and the leaves of the rhododendron bushes dotting Dualayn's estate.

"Purple, actually."

"Oh, really?" she said, fascinated by this. "Purple? I never would have pictured you in that shade."

"It's the color of fatherhood and protection," he said. "It's the other color soldiers wear. To express their desire to protect."

That was the Ōbhin she loved. That desire might fill him *too* strongly sometimes, but it made him special. Focusing on this helped to keep her anchored in her body.

"Women rarely wear pure purple, but mauve is often used by virgins to declare they are protecting their virtue." He snorted. "It was seen as provincial in Gunya, the capital. Something country girls wore who didn't know the delights the flesh offered."

She bit her lip, for a moment, as the desire to experience those delights rippled through her, but the unease lurking in her belly won out. She wanted their first time to be special, not when she hovered on the cusp of losing her mind. She clasped his hand tighter, fingers fuzzing.

"Still, I have a hard time imagining you in purple," she said, a smile playing on her lips.

"It's a very manly color," he said, masculine pride rearing through him.

"Maybe in Qoth." She brought his hand to her lips and kissed it. "I'd like to see you in purple anyways."

"Maybe," he said, staring up at the ceiling. "I do miss it, Avena. Every direction you look, peaks rise around you. They all have names. Histories. I grew up in Dhoseth Valley in the shadow of Mount Qaari. He wasn't the biggest mountain. Certainly not one of the Seven which ring Gunya, but every morning as a child I woke to see him out my window. Looming there, perpetually capped in ice. He wore it like a man wears his gloves, never taking them off. Sometimes, clouds would surround his flank, and other times, a dome of them would hover over his peak. He's a fire mountain."

"A volcano?" Avena asked. "Did you ever see it erupt?"

"Only belch the occasional burst of steam. They're deadly when they erupt." His expression darkened. "The day I killed Taim, Sunset's Tower erupted. It shook the ground so much the arena where we were dueling cracked. The sand flowed like water and dragged us into the old mines beneath Gunya."

"How dreadful." Avena studied his face, hating the way his eyes shadowed.

"Yeah." Ōbhin glanced at the window. "I marched onto the Sands of Truth thinking I would prove my innocence. I believed Taim was a villain who'd forced my beloved Foonauri to be his wife. I learned the opposite in those dark tunnels. I learned what sort of man I am."

"Was." Her hand touched him over his heart. She spread her fingers wide, feeling the heat of him. The pounding of his life. "That's not who you are. You've changed, Ōbhin. You've almost polished the stains from your diamond-bright soul. I can see it."

"Maybe," he said. "I wanted to kill Dualayn." He pulled her hand away from his chest. He brought her palm to his lips and kissed it. "Just like I wanted to kill Taim for what he claimed about Foonauri."

"Taim wasn't lying, but Dualayn is a maggot writhing through the muck." She turned her hand and entwined her fingers with his. "What sort of man, what sort of person, wouldn't want to inflict pain on him for the things he did? But you didn't act on the impulse."

"Only to save you." Ōbhin shifted.

"You. Didn't. Actions matter." She felt the strange tingles fading. The interference was ending. "What will you do when he *repairs* me?"

"I don't know."

She squeezed his hand. "I do. You're walking a better path, Ōbhin." She lifted her head. "You could steal another kiss. I wouldn't mind some pleasant dreams for a change."

He smiled and leaned down. Hot lips seized her. She squeezed his hand tight, her eyes closing. The exhaustion of the day's travel weighed down on her. She broke the kiss and murmured, "Blessed night, Ōbhin."

"May your fire burn strong through the night," he whispered.

She rolled onto her side, still holding his hand. He pressed into her from behind, spooning her. She had no fear as she surrendered to her dreams.

After some time, she found herself walking with Chames. The dream didn't surprise her. She accepted it as she clung to his arm. He was young and handsome, standing tall, his hair combed back and gathered in a short tail at the nape of his neck by a dark-blue ribbon. He wore a matching waistcoat, a frilly cravat tucked into it and wrapped about his neck. He wore the knickerbockers that were in style, pants she'd chosen for him, exposing the tight socks fitting his calves. She wore a fine dress of dark-red, the neckline scooped to show off her upper chest and adorned with blue beadwork across her bosom. The layers of petticoats gave volume and shape to her skirts.

"This is the perfect spot," he said as they reached a secluded part of the lake. The high bank behind them shielded them from the view of the near estate. The thick layers of reeds warded them from the view of the rest of the shore.

A scarlet dragonfly buzzed past to hover over the green water.

The first good day of spring had arrived.

Ōbhin stood in the water, his chest bare, watching her with arms folded across his chest. His hands were naked. She smiled at him as Chames spread out the quilted blanket on the shore. She didn't resist as he pulled her down.

"You know I'm glad," Chames said.

"Oh?" she asked, glancing at Dualayn's son. She could see the older man in the younger's face, though Chames lacked the round jowls and soft cheeks. He had the brash angles of youth.

"That you found happiness," he said, opening the basket and revealing the contents: purloined food and a bottle of strawberry currant. "You deserve to be happy."

"Chames . . ." She blushed and then leaned against her promised's shoulder. "You make me happy."

"For now," he said. "But not forever."

Lightning crackled on the horizon. A storm lurked on the far side of the lake beyond the watching Ōbhin.

"I wanted it to be forever," she said, taking his hand. Her fingers slid in them. "This moment here."

"I did, too." He smiled at her. For some reason, he looked soaked, like a deluge had swept over him. He wore only a shirt, his waistcoat around her shoulders. "I wanted this spring to never end."

"But you got sick," she said, memories intruding. She wanted to banish them.

"Don't blame yourself," Chames said. "It's not your fault I died. You know that."

She nodded and leaned her cheek on his wet shoulder. "Part of me wishes we never came out here."

"And the other?"

"Remembers that hour here as the happiest point of my life. What if the storm never reaches us?"

"Then you would be stuck in a dream." He stroked her hand. "Be happy. Don't let my father steal any more from you. He's a bastard who's caused you enough pain."

"I won't," she said, staring at Ōbhin. "I won't forget you just because I found someone else."

Chames stroked her head. "Just be happy. If I could have warned you about my father sooner, I would have. I didn't know. Not until it was too late."

His lips kissed hers. As the dream fled, her body waking, she clutched to the fading Chames. She didn't want to let him go, but he became mist, the foggy vapors from Lake Ophavin that melt away in the morning sun. Her fingers passed through him.

She opened her eyes to see Ōbhin lying beside her, sleeping. She glanced out the window. Dawn lightened the horizon. She sighed and rested her head on his chest. Ōbhin breathed in sharply and shifted, groaning.

"Morning?" he mumbled.

"Yeah." She chewed on her lower lip. "I dreamed of Chames."

"Dreams are a resonance of the tones," Ōbhin told Avena after listening to her dream of her past lover. A strange jealousy danced around the edges of his emotions. Nothing sharp. Nothing like he'd felt with Taim. Ōbhin knew he had nothing to fear. Chames had died. She only had her memories of him. She didn't want to lose those.

He could understand that. Respect that.

"He said his father was a bastard," Avena said. She sat beside him, her chemise hanging off her shoulders and falling down her body like mist risen from the snow higher up the mountain and spilling down its forested slopes. "It felt so real. Like he was there. He wanted me to be happy."

"Maybe it was him." Ōbhin shifted. "In Qoth, we believe that sometimes our souls don't melt into the harmony of the Seven Tones. Our music still lingers. Wanting to communicate. Or maybe just the echoes of strong songs reverberating around through the immaterial."

"Through where Tones broadcast. My mind." Avena's brow tightened. "If Chames thought his father was a bastard, did he know about the secret lab? Did he witness something? The last time I saw Chames, his father took him in there and . . ." She shuddered. "No, no, Dualayn loved his family. His wife and son. He wouldn't hurt them."

Ōbhin's stomach sank. The lie spilled easily from his lips. "Of course not. But if Chames's soul is lingering, watching you, then he knows what his father would do. I'd hate my own father if he'd done something like that."

Does my father hate me for what I did? Shame for killing Taim had driven Ōbhin from Qoth. He had taken Foonauri with him, promising her a new life. He wondered about her. Had she found happiness in Guirreu, Ondere's capital, to the south? Did that rich man she'd seduced shower her in jewels and luxuries? *Do you hate me, Foonauri, for dragging you across the world?*

I hate myself for doing it. I should have left you behind, but I'm selfish. I cling too tight. He glanced at Avena. She'd become his reason for escaping the darkness. She made him feel too much to stay in the mire, but if she were to die, would he be lost?

He'd have to be careful with Avena. Too much could destroy her as would too little. A balance. He'd have to find it or repeat past mistakes.

18

Twelfth Day of Patience, 755 EU

Obhin studied the three suspects as they left behind the village, the Upfing Woods a dark smear on the horizon. After three days of traveling, he still wasn't sure which one was the impostor. Fingers, Bran, or Dajouth.

His eyes flicked between each of them before frustration drove his attention to Avena. She sat on the wagon's driver bench beside Miguil. He leaned back, a wide felt hat on his head cocked to the side to shield his eyes from the sun rising on their left. Avena hadn't donned her bonnet, her loose hair swaying in the breeze.

He smiled as he watched the strands dance around the back of her neck.

Avena hadn't shared his bed since that night. She'd had no more signs of signal interference. He ached for her. It had been two years or longer since he'd been with a woman. With Foonauri. What had been minor urges now consumed him. But Avena was a modest woman. He would be patient with her.

It made her kisses all the more special.

If she were Qothian, he was certain her mask would have the purple-red hue of rose as an accent proclaiming her love and commitment to a man. The color of a maiden's promise. He closed his eyes, picturing her in a mask, only her brown eyes peeking through, a mystery begging to be unwrapped.

His fingers remembered the feel of Avena's face. He flexed them beneath his gloves, the fire swelling in his veins for a moment before a cough from Fingers snapped his eyes open. The sound stretched a tightness taut across his shoulders like the skin of a mountain bear mounted on a frame of alder being scraped off all the fat and flesh clinging to it.

Who was the impostor? The grumliicho who'd stolen his friend's face? What would happen to them when they reached the Red Heart of the Forest and the ruins of Lost Koilon? Legends abounded of the great cities destroyed in the Shattering and places in the world where strange events supposedly happened. In Lay, a country east of his mountainous Qoth, there was said to be a valley stained an unnatural orange that hummed with a note whenever Mother, the orange moon, shone full. Those who ventured to the Shattered Islands often uncovered bits of strange architecture, stones shaped in impossible ways, alloys of metal stronger than steel and lighter than tin.

After an hour, the edge of the woods appeared, marked first by a swath of stumps surrounded by the grass before the thick edges of the woods. The lane narrowed and grew rougher. Only woodcutters ventured this far to coppice the trees, cutting them down to near their stumps and allowing them to sprout new growth to be harvested in a decade or two.

Ōbhin straightened and climbed over the bench, settling on Avena's left. She scooted over closer to Miguil to give Ōbhin room, favoring him with a smile. A foolish grin spilled across his lips. There was something to a woman showing off her face all the time, to witnessing her emotions shining bright.

"There'll be a sidetrack coming soon," Avena said. "We'll want to take it."

"Yes, yes," Dualayn said from the back. "She is quite correct."

Avena stiffened. "Thank you for thinking I'm a dullard. You might have cut out my brain, but it still works just as sharply."

"I meant no offense, child, I jus—"

"Avena!" she hissed. "My name is Avena. Not 'child.' Not 'daughter.' Not 'girl.' Avena."

"Ah, yes, I forgot. Old habits are easy to fall into." He chuckled.

Ōbhin stared ahead, ignoring the foul man. If he didn't, his hand would start to drift to his sword, his mind considering those darker paths. No justice would ever be delivered on Dualayn if Ōbhin didn't kill him when this was over. He had too many powerful friends protecting him from the courts and proper justice.

It would be so easy, a part of Ōbhin thought.

He knew it for a treacherous lie. Killing never was. Oh, plunging a knife into a heart or cutting off a head took no more effort than swinging an ax to fell a tree or wielding a hoe to weed a field, but the weight lingered. A man didn't think about the tree he felled for firewood to keep his family warm or the field he furrowed to provide food.

But the man he killed . . .

Ōbhin thought about it over and over and over, an echo trapped in the cave of his thoughts resounding time and time again. Sometimes, it was worth it. Necessary. Would Dualayn's death be another echoing in him?

Near noon, Bran gasped, "The trees! They're really red!"

Ōbhin looked up to see the same oaks and alders and spruces they'd ridden through, only now their barks looked leached from brown to white and their leaves stained by violence. The brush held the same scarlet hue.

"This is amazing!" the boy shouted, ripping off the first oak leaf he rode past. He held it in his hands, marveling over it.

～

"So many rubies were used in Koilon that I think their essence has leached into the soil, affecting the plant life," Dualayn was saying as they traveled through the Red Heart of the Forest.

Avena rolled her shoulders as she sat between Miguil and Ōbhin. She had to hone her anger against Dualayn. She had spent many years living with him, respecting and even loving him as her father. He would have been her father-in-law. If she wasn't careful, she would forget what he'd done to her. She'd fall into old patterns, wanting to hear what he had to say, to learn from him.

She seized the pain of the betrayal. He had violated her as surely as if he'd crept into her bed in the dark hours of the night. At least then, she might have fought back. She'd been helpless, at her most vulnerable. Unconscious, entrusted into his care.

The sickest part was the sincerity in his voice. He believed he'd done something marvelous to her. Given her a gift. That she should be happy to accept what he'd done to her. He'd done it out of love. Because he cared for her. A sick, twisted, perverted love. It nauseated her stomach because a part of her wanted to forgive him. The part of her that cared for him. Loved him. It shone with brilliant Green. She refused to accept it.

She would not forgive what he'd done. Even if he apologized with sincerity, she wouldn't. Couldn't. He made her body an enemy. Something she couldn't trust any longer.

She couldn't let herself weaken around him. If she became vulnerable near him, what was to stop him from doing the same again?

She stared ahead at the woodcutter's path moving through the crimson woods. Bran rode at the lead, his head snapping around in awe. Dajouth wasn't much better. He'd found a red-stained wildflower, some sort of daisy which had lost its usual yellow. He had it tucked behind his ear like a youth out courting.

"Didn't think there were enough rubies in the world to do that," Fingers muttered. "The lost city is truly beneath us?"

"Truly," said Dualayn. "The rise and fall of the land around us are probably the remains of buildings covered up by detritus. The eons can bury cities, turn streets into catacombs. This city was badly damaged by the Shattering and what I can only translate as darklings, but they sound more diverse than our mythology suggests. Darklings of Water. Darklings of Fire. Darklings of the Night and of the Earth. Like that. Perhaps they do not even refer to darklings, but it is the best word for it I can decide upon. Something evil. Dangerous. Interlopers."

"The enemies of the devas," said Avena. Devas were the heavenly beings who served Elohm and fought against the darklings. They were led by Reylis, the Archon-Supreme of the Devas. Avena suspected the White Lady *was* the Archon-Supreme. Raya was so similar to Reylis. She had white hair and exuded a presence of Honesty. Yet she worked with that dark sorcerer, Dje'awsa, and had hired Grey's crime syndicate.

Avena absently rubbed at her forehead. It tingled for a moment, perhaps in memory of the kiss Raya had planted there at their last meeting the morning after Ust's attack. Thinking of Raya led her mind to those dreams of being a white-haired woman. Of having a lover and witnessing some cataclysmic event.

Was it really the Shattering? Did I dream the moment the Black invaded our world and broke reality? Were you there, Raya?

She'd been meaning to talk to Ōbhin about it but hadn't found the right time to. She wanted to be alone with him, and though she'd spent one night in his bed, that had been out of fear of her body failing. She yearned to share her Red with him, but marriage was also important. A swearing of oaths, a promise. It was special.

The intimacy men and women shared was something that she didn't think should be so easily traded away else it would lose its value.

Should I give him my promise? She'd given her Red to Chames on that wonderful afternoon, her blood full of the heady strawberry currant. If she slipped into Ōbhin's room again, when she wasn't afraid of her body, she knew where it would lead.

Was she ready to commit to Ōbhin? Was he ready to commit to her?

She glanced at him. He still wore the black gloves, but she knew he was striving towards polished light. She told herself, *once my mind is repaired, we can talk of promises and futures and dreams.*

"See, there it is," Dualayn said. "That's the largest gem I've ever encountered. The ancients could *create* gems, Fingers. That is why they had so many rubies here. In fact, this might be the place where they manufactured that particular gem. Something about a, 'Harmonic confluence with the Realm of Absolute Flame,' which is my best translation."

"Wait," Bran said and heeled his horse ahead. He craned his neck. "Is that a solid ruby?"

"It is," Dualayn said.

Avena peered through gaps in the crimson foliage to glimpse the crystal pillar. It thrust at an angle out of the earth in the clearing where they'd excavated into Koilon. The ruby pillar had always intrigued her. It seemed impossible. Too large to be real, and yet it was. Ten cubits in length and who knew how much more was buried.

"Though it is crooked now," said Dualayn, "it once thrust erect and upright. Called the Ruby Lodestone, perhaps. Or the Ruby Guidestone may be a better translation of Old Tonal. Tricky word to translate. They used the root for magnetism in the word for it, but I do not think that is what it meant. It was supposed to provide guidance through the Harmonics of Reality."

"What are the Harmonics?" Avena asked, staring at the pillar, a tingle of awe rippling through her at seeing the impossible artifact again.

"The immaterial through which the Eight Primary Tones vibrate, child. As well as your thoughts. It also has something to do with the Warding holding back the darklings."

Avena nodded and then realized she was slipping into her old behavior. She piled sandbags around her soul to keep the floodwaters of familiarity from weakening her anger. She would not forgive this man and accept his violation no matter how much the Green in her heart begged.

The trees broke around them and the clearing emerged, their old campsite appearing. The mound of dirt from their earlier excavation now had tufts of red grass growing across it. There was no sign of Ni'mod's body, though she could see the rusting half of his strange, hooked blade lying in the grass. They hadn't buried poor Ni'mod, the Bloodfire who'd guarded them.

Ust hadn't allowed it, impatient to leave.

She glanced at Ōbhin sitting beside her. He'd killed Ni'mod in the fight. The scar on his left cheek looked paler than usual. He'd shed his past of being a bandit and the crimes he'd committed while lost in dark fog, but here was a reminder. How would he react?

She nudged her shoulder into his. He glanced at her and she smiled, warm and reassuring. His gloved hand tightened on hers. He gave a slow nod and a long exhale. She saw, or so she hoped, acceptance in his eyes.

"The hole is still uncovered," said Dualayn. "Good, good. And I don't think any of the villagers we hired have come back to disturb it."

"They were frightened enough being here," Avena said. Dualayn had dismissed them once they'd found the Recorder. If Ust's bandits had attacked hours earlier, would there be more innocents dead?

Probably, she thought, not sad at all Ust had died.

Ōbhin said, glancing at the sky, "Let's set up camp and ready the ropes. At first light, we'll descend."

"I have maps," Dualayn said as they sat around the campfire after their supper. The tents were set up; Avena had her own while Ōbhin was sharing one with Dualayn. Bran, Dajouth, and Fingers had brought lean-tos for themselves. The skies were clear. Ōbhin doubted there'd be rain anyways.

"What I have pieced together of the layout of Koilon before this present cataclysm. I do not know how much use they will be, but . . ." Dualayn pulled out of a satchel two rolls of parchment. He handed one to Avena and the other to Ōbhin. "I did not prepare more. But this way you two can see I am not holding back."

"Very considerate," she murmured and unrolled hers, her brow drawing down.

Ōbhin opened his own. Though Lothonian used a similar alphabet to Qothian, a few letters were different and there was one they didn't have in his own language; it was still difficult for him to read. They used the letters to represent different sounds from Qothian, their words looking strange compared to how they sounded. But he deciphered most of it. A building labeled "Grand Library" was circled. A second, "Hall of Communications" lay to the east and south. There was a sketch of street layouts, other buildings that were labeled with strange names like "Flame Manufactory," "Wave Resonance Beacon," "Hall of Illumination," "Crystal Sheriff Hall," "Hall of Assemblage," "Hall of Markets," and "Offal Reclamation." He could puzzle out some; Hall of Assemblage sounded like some sort of government building, but he didn't know how you could manufacture flame. The Flame Manufactory lay to the north of the Grand Library by a point marked, "Ruby Guidestone." The Wave Resonance Beacon was south of there, a medium-sized building. Offal Reclamation rested on the edge of the town.

"I have marked what street names I could decipher that appear to be by the buildings," Dualayn continued. "I hope there will be signage once we're underground to help us out. If you look carefully, I wrote the names in Old Tonal and with the very characters they used."

Ōbhin noted the finer script beneath.

"I cannot wait to find the Hall of Communication," Dualayn said. "Imagine being able to speak across the world. To converse with my friend in Democh without having to wait half a year for his response to reach me. It'll revolutionize things. Knowledge will be at everyone's fingertips."

Ōbhin studied the Hall of Communication. It was a large building, dominating what looked like a square. It was near the Hall of Assemblage, the Hall of Illumination, and the Crystal Sheriff Hall. Ten or so blocks of travel, if the map could be trusted. It wouldn't take long above ground, but below it could be days of exploring.

"We need to be wary of loose stones and weak ceilings," Ōbhin said, looking up from the map. His gaze turned to the darkness. To the excavated hole. Memories of his time trapped beneath Gunya hovered on the edge of his awareness. The deep black, the thick dust, the earth shaking from aftershocks. "We need to be careful not to bury ourselves in there."

"Yes, yes, and mark our path," Dualayn said. "I have spent some time ripping up old shirts into strips of cloth. We should leave them in suitable places to help guide us. One knot means we went that way. Two knots to indicate that it leads to a dead end. I think that should help us keep from getting lost and covering ground we've already searched."

Avena gave a slow nod. She drew up her knees to her chest and stared into the fire.

The weight seemed to press down on all of them. Tomorrow, they would venture into the black earth. Even Bran's enthusiasm seemed muted. He picked at the lace of his boot. Ōbhin's chest rose and fell with deep breaths. They were venturing underground with two people he couldn't trust.

And he didn't know who one of them was.

It wasn't long before they began peeling off to find their bedrolls, Avena first, Bran shortly after. Dualayn crawled to the tent and soon his snores echoed. Fingers drifted off then Dajouth threw his flower into the fire and crawled into his lean-to.

Alone, Ōbhin stared into the dying flames as he leaned against a stump. He found himself sinking into sleep. Into dreams. They were blurred, a mess, a replay of what had happened in the mines over two years ago. He plunged the knife into Taim's chest over and over and over again. The shock in the plump prince's face never failed to add new cracks to Ōbhin's soul, letting the filth of guilt seep in and stain him from the inside.

Where the polishing cloth could never reach.

He woke up as dawn lightened the horizon, his eyes sandy. He would have to make better choices this time. For Avena. For himself. He couldn't keep cracking his soul. He would splinter himself beyond even Avena's skill to repair.

I guess you get to live, Dualayn, he thought. *Fix her. Give her a life without fear of losing control of her body, and you'll walk away alive.*

With a grunt, Ōbhin stood and started rousing the others.

19

Thirteenth Day of Patience, 755 EU

The diamond light swung from his hip as Ōbhin descended the rope into the ruins of Koilon. His black gloves rasped over the rough hemp. A dry scent filled his nose, old dust, a smell not unlike entering a study which had been empty for a few seasons. The rot of paper long since disintegrated away. The dancing light illuminated ghosts of shelves rising around him, covered in the moldering remains of knowledge lost to the ravages of time. A thick layer of gray dust coated the floor, disturbed with footprints, preserved traces of Dualayn's last expedition.

Ōbhin reached the bottom, heavy boot crunching on the fine powder. More drifted through the air, stars orbiting an aimless pattern through the space illuminated by his lantern. He adjusted his backpack full of food and supplies before plucking his lantern from his belt. He held it up and peered around. His nose tickled, a sneeze building, eyes watering.

Something scurried in the darkness, black-furred body vanishing into a pile of gnawed leather.

"Ōbhin?" Avena called from above.

"Come on down," he said, not seeing any danger. Not sure there would be any.

The rope swung at the edge of his vision. Avena descended next, her trouser-clad legs wrapped about it. She wore her fighting clothes, one of Bran's old shirts tucked into her sturdy, canvas pants. Thick-soled boots rasped against the fibers. Emeralds sparkled on the earthen gauntlet vanishing into her right sleeve. A binder swung on her left hip, thumping into her leg. She landed in a puff of desiccated books, the fine dust swirling around her feet.

To his delight, she planted a quick kiss on his lips.

"I'll be fine," Dualayn said from above. "You don't need to tie a rope about my waist, Fingers."

"Just wanted the joy of droppin' you the last few feet and seein' you soil your britches," Fingers answered, a pleased rumble to his voice. "Not hurt you, but..."

Bran burst into laughter. "He'd squeal like them pigs they take into the cannin' factories. Big ol' hogs, all afraid."

"Your mother would not be pleased with such sentiments coming from you, young Bran," Dualayn said.

"I'm supposed to take advice on right and wrong from you?" The boy laughed again. "Get down the rope before I volunteer to lower you. And I got skinny arms."

Dualayn grumbled something. The rope shook again as the old man groaned. Ōbhin ignored the complaints and moved through the library. The floor sloped at an angle that deepened the farther north he moved. Through gaps in the dust, he could see gray stone beneath his feet. It was all one piece, cracked in places, but he spotted no joints where stone met stone. It had a smoothness, obvious even with the pits gouged into it. There were traces of a fine carpeting in spots, the edges gnawed ragged.

"What is this stone?" Ōbhin asked.

"The ancients called it cement," said Avena. "Made of crushed limestone and gravel. They poured it into the shapes they wanted."

Ōbhin shook his head in amazement.

Dualayn grunted as he reached the bottom of the rope, his lantern shedding more light. Bran descended next, chortling in delight, his voice echoing through the room. Ōbhin grimaced at the thick cobwebs stretched between the shelves before him.

A loud clatter exploded through the room. He whirled around to see Bran leaping away from a shelf crashing to pieces in a burst of dust. The boy thrust his hand behind his back, his padded gambeson flexing about his body.

"Do not destroy things more than they already are," Dualayn said, his voice pained. "All their great books . . . All their works of knowledge . . . All lost to time's rotting touch and the Black-cursed rats. You can see their runs along the edges. Generations of the foul things have nested and devoured it all. If the ancients hadn't encoded their wisdom in the Recorder . . ." He shook his head and wiped at his brow. "And that assumes it held *everything*. There could be priceless knowledge contained in the droppings of a rat who died centuries ago."

Avena stood before a pile of rotted wood. It looked to have been a table once, now collapsed. "We found the Recorder here," she said. "It was placed, we think, in the center. Though it's hard to tell." She looked around. "The walls had crumbled along the south, and there is a gap in the floor to the west."

"Where did you spot that exit?" Ōbhin asked, peering through the gloom. The spiderwebs spread across the shelves made the world misty beyond. Thick clumps of dust clung to the strands. The desiccated corpse of a small rat hung in one.

He shuddered. *How big are the spiders creeping through here?*

"That way," she said, pointing before her. "That dark shadow is it."

The floor had half-collapsed in the direction she pointed, bowing in the middle and then rising back up to the wall. An opening lay in the wall marked by a frame of rusting metal; a portal leading to deeper darkness. Ōbhin batted away cobwebs before him, the dusty silk clinging to his gloves.

"This is eerie," said Fingers as he came up behind them. "Feel like I'm walkin' through a crypt. Do you smell it? That dry scent of bones?"

"I just smell dust," Ōbhin said.

"Exactly," grunted Fingers.

"Come, come," Dualayn said. "That door should lead out to a street, hopefully."

Ōbhin reached the collapse in the floor, the cement slab broken. A pile of rubble lay at the bottom along with a pool of dirty water. It had a thick consistency, a soup of dust. He skirted around it, Avena on his heels. He swept more cobwebs out of the way. Rats, or other vermin, scurried through the detritus before them, claws clicking on stone and fur whisking over decay.

Avena squeaked behind him.

He whirled around to see her eyes wide. "What?"

"On your shoulder. There's . . ." A shudder of revulsion spilled across her expression.

He glanced at his shoulder and flinched. A spider sat perched there, body milky white, eyes black and reflective. It was the size of a child's hand, legs spindly and hairy. With a bark, he smacked it away, flinging it off into the dark. Revulsion spilled down his skin, every hair on his body rising.

"Elohm's Colours, that was big," Fingers groaned. "Spiders shouldn't grow that big. Ain't natural."

"They grow bigger in the Kon'veyth Depression," said Dualayn. "Hopefully, these are not venomous."

"Venomous?" groaned Miguil. "Wish I'd brought a prism."

"Yeah," Bran said, his voice tight.

"Just a cave spider," Dajouth said, his voice light and carefree. "Only the rats have to be afraid of 'em. And Bran, since he's so small."

"I don't want to end up like that," Bran said, pointing at another rat caught in thick cobwebs. It was the size of Ōbhin's hand, its black fur looking fresh. Lurking in the shadowed recesses near it was something pale and spindly.

Ōbhin beat down the disgust and animistic fear spilling through his veins. He pressed on, sweeping through more of the cobwebs as they worked past the collapse and through the rotten shelves tumbled around them. He felt a thousand faceted eyes watching him, salivating for his flesh. He could almost hear their legs as they scurried around them.

The deeper in they went, the less sunlight came from the hole. Soon, only their lanterns shed illumination. It was bright and steady but traveled only a few cubits before falling off, swallowed by the darkness around them. Memoirs of those terrible moments plunged into mines beneath Gunya filled him.

True black had a weight. A suffocating pressure that squeezed around you, crushing you as surely as a bug beneath a Ka'voyith elephant. The scant lantern he held before him provided little protection against it, a fragile nimbus straining against the mammoth bulk lurking all around them.

He peered at the umbral portal. His light didn't seem to penetrate beyond it, like the doorway swallowed everything. A glacial waterfall poured down his spine, the melt chilling him. What if his lantern failed?

You found your way out of the mines, he reminded himself.

Taim didn't, another voice accused, harsh and cold.

Not because of the dark or spiders.

He felt Avena behind him, her warmth and light spilling around him. He wasn't alone. He had his friends, even if one was a traitor. He even had Dualayn. He didn't face the crushing weight of umbral black alone. He wasn't a single bug beneath the elephant's massive foot.

He reached the portal. His light spilled through. The room beyond was wide. His light had nothing to reflect upon. No unnatural barrier was swallowing it. The illusion must have been fear's work. The confusion caused by dread, like a morning fog spilling off the high peaks and transforming the world alien.

He stepped through it. This room held tables and chairs, some rotted to the point of collapse, others gnawed by the hungry teeth of the devouring rats. The ceiling had collapsed on the far side, the floor tilted at a sharp slope to the right.

They advanced to the buckled flooring. He hunched his head, the cracked ceiling descending. Remnants of tarnished wires ran across the concrete, some leaving stains of decayed metal behind. Others vanished into fixtures, perhaps made of silver or some other shiny metal. All were now black with patina.

"There's a diamond in one," Dualayn said. "They must have used them for light like we do. The others must be lost in the debris, popped out when the ceiling half-collapsed. Remarkable."

"So there's a small fortune buried beneath the dust," Fingers said.

"Not why we're here," Ōbhin said as he stepped onto the sloped floor, his boot's sole gripping the concrete. "Once we find the antenna, feel free to loot this place all you want."

"Maybe I will," Fingers said.

"Imagine what else we'll find down here!" exclaimed Bran, his voice echoing back a moment later.

" . . . down here . . ."

" . . . ere . . ."

"And keep your voices down," Ōbhin hissed, glaring behind him at the boy. "Whisper."

Bran winced. In hushed conciliation, he said, "Sorry. I forgot."

Ōbhin ducked his head lower. He scrunched down, half-crouching on the slanted surface. The collapsed ceiling was held up by some sort of crushed plinth that may have once held a bust. A doorway lay in the wall. He placed his free hand on the stone floor, his body a low angle. He almost had to slide across the slanted floor.

"Why couldn't the floor and the ceiling be slanted in the same direction?" muttered Dajouth.

Bran gasped. Boots scrambled. The youth floundered, his feet struggling to find purchase as he slid on his side. His hand had grabbed a crack in the floor. Dust spilled down towards the dark shadows at the bottom of the collapse.

He held tight and managed to get his foot beneath him. His dust-streaked face burst with relief. "Didn't want to find out wot's down there."

"Spiders," Fingers said, low voice rumbling. "Nest of 'em. I can feel 'em watching us, Black-cursed bastards."

"Don't say that," Avena said, her voice faint.

The last few cubits, Ōbhin had to travel lying on his left side, his feet struggling to hold his position as he scooted along. The collapsed ceiling brushed his right shoulder. His chest tightened. If that plinth collapsed, the massive stone would pin him. He'd be trapped for what remained of his life, howling in pain. Worse, Avena would be caught up in it. And his friends, too.

The floor leveled out the last cubit. He slid onto his belly and crawled forward. He shoved his arms through the doorway and hauled himself through into a small antechamber of some sort. The ceiling here had panels set in it, some missing. The tiles appeared to be made of talcum stone and had periodic recesses for lights that were spaced among them. Shards of glass lay shattered amid the layer of dust coating the floor.

He took a step forward.

SNAP!

He flinched back to see a rib bone shattered beneath his foot. More lay scattered through the room, peeking through the dust. The rounded joint of a femur. The smooth plate of a skull. A few finger bones piled in the corner. It looked like a scavenger's kill site, the body pulled apart and feasted upon thousands of years ago then left to lie here undisturbed until now.

"Elohm's Colours," Avena said. She joined him, staring around. "Fingers was right."

"They've been dead a long time," Ōbhin said.

"A dead city," Dualayn said. Dust streaked his rotund face. He wiped it off with his heavy cotton shirt then slapped at the canvas pants covering his thighs. Clouds of gray burst from him. "I think the city was still inhabited

Ruby Ruins

when the darklings came and the Warding was sealed. The event appeared to have been . . . cataclysmic."

~

Cataclysmic . . .

The dream Avena had witnessed the last time she'd lost all control over her body filled her mind as she and the others stepped out of the library through a wider portal. The memory of the world melting away, walls torn apart by darkness. The strange demons reaching through from a black void. The darklings who had spilled through the world.

I really witnessed the Shattering, Avena thought. *I dreamed about it. The moment it happened. Something in that room, what they were doing with the gems, invited it. Did they sin against Elohm? Did they accidentally awaken the Black? They* had been *using forbidden obsidian.*

She shuddered, feeling that cursed jewel in her mind. What did that mean for her? She would live the rest of her life with an obsidian mind, a proxy for her brain they'd left behind in her tent. It was too fragile to bring on their exploration. She gripped her lantern tight in her left hand, the bite of the metal handle digging into her palm. She clenched until it almost hurt.

She could still sense it. She was still in control of her body.

"I think the top of a building's fallen over us," Ōbhin said, holding his lantern up.

She lifted her gaze. The facade of a red building, its walls made of bricks mortared together, not poured cement, ran at an angle over their heads from its base ten or so cubits before them. Some of the windows set in it were still intact, the glass smeared in dust.

In one, a skull grinned, peering out at them.

"The rest of the street's collapsed," said Fingers. He stood to her right before a wall of crumbled brick. "We need to go this way, right?"

"Regrettably," said Dualayn. "I was afraid of this. I do not know how far we can get into the city via this method but excavating to find the Hall of Communications could take years."

Avena shivered. She didn't want to spend years worrying about when she'd next lose control of her body. How could she live? She could never go out alone. Never do anything dangerous. If she were to ride a horse and pass out, she could break her neck from the fall. To fix her, she was risking all their lives. Ōbhin, Fingers, Bran, Miguil, Dajouth, and even Dualayn. The collapsed buildings and crushed rubble around them reminded her of the danger. She shuddered, feeling the weight of the forest above them. There were twenty or thirty cubits of soil burying the city.

"There's a door into the building," Ōbhin said. "Let's see where it goes. Maybe we can get out on the other side."

"The building's collapsed," Avena said. "Is it safe?"

"Nothing we'll do down here will be safe," he said. He grabbed the mangled edge of the metal door, bent and warped in its rusting frame. He grunted and pulled. The steel squealed as he dragged it a cubit open, revealing black beyond.

"Maybe I should go on alone," Avena said. "I can find the . . ." Her words trailed off as Ōbhin stared at her. Warmth flushed her cheeks. "Right. I'd be a hypocrite to ask you to go back and stay safe. Still, I don't want anyone to get hurt trying to help me."

"No one does," Ōbhin said. "You can't control people. Trying to do that only destroys them. It's like telling a miner, who knows his earth and rocks better than you, where to dig. You can guide him, advise him, but if you try to dictate where he drives his shaft, he'll run into weak rocks, fault lines, and unstable caverns. That could collapse the entire mine, creating sinkholes above. The devastation can ripple."

"He might still find that bad rock on his own," Avena said.

Ōbhin nodded. "Then you just need to be there to help dig him out." He took her hand. "You're not changing where we're driving our mine shaft."

"We're here to make you as right as possible," Fingers said, his voice a deep rumble. It reverberated through the confined space. His lantern spilled light across his face in strange ways, highlighting chin and cheekbones but shadowing his eyes.

"Even I am, Avena," Dualayn said. "I hope that I can earn your forgiveness."

Avena sighed. "Let's continue on. We only have so much food."

She shifted her pack on her back, reminded of its weight, then she went forward. She pushed the door farther open with her earthen gauntlet with ease. Her shoulder joint ached from the increased strain.

Dualayn tied a cloth to the door as she peered around inside. Decay had ravished the room. It looked like water had once flowed through here, staining the floors with a waving pattern of grime covered in a growing layer of dust. A pile of furniture lay piled against an opening, more bones wrapped up in the remains along with strangely shaped crystals covered in the tarnish of ages. They were narrow and long, twisted in the same manner of the Recorder and made of the same two stones.

They cleared the rubble out of the way, throwing wood to the side. Many pieces broke apart. Strange worms burst out of one, writhing and wiggling in the sodden pulp. Avena grimaced. Sweat trickled down her face. Ōbhin heaved a large plank to the side, throwing it over the pile. It snapped in half with a loud clatter. Something scurried from the wreckage.

She hated the sounds. As they penetrated deeper into the building, she could hear creaking above. Groaning protests of stone grinding on stone. Fine dust sifted down from the ceiling, landing on her face. Her skin itched. She felt like a thousand centipedes crawled over her body, their little legs prickling her.

They moved down a hallway with doors leading off into small rooms. In one, a half-collapsed bed held a nearly intact skeleton draped in cobwebs. Bony arms clutched something which had long decayed away to spindly bones. Things slithered just out of sight. Insects and spiders and other nasty things fled their light. Bones littered the hallways or thrust out of the buckled doorway of the apartments they moved through. Skulls grinned at them from amid piles of rot and filth. A large pool of water flooded one room, the floor sagging and buckling from the weight. The water rippled as something wormed beneath the surface.

They came to a metal door at the end of the hallway after several bends and twists. The ceiling groaned over their heads. Long shafts of diamonds were inserted into the metal frames. Each jewel had a wire running through them lengthwise, the ends corroded and damaged.

Dualayn muttered as he pried one from the ceiling, turning it in his hand while Ōbhin wrenched at the door. It was painted entirely black and pitted in places. He threw his shoulder into it. Metal resounded. The door held.

"Come on," he grunted and slammed his shoulder into it again.

"Frame's buckled," said Dualayn, his voice distant. "It's seized the door in place." Then he let out a groan of awe. "To be able to *grow* crystals. They created this with the wire running through it. I imagine this must shine with a remarkable amount of light. And look at the shape, designated to spread it over a wider area, I suppose."

"Does that matter?" Avena asked, irritation bubbling through her fear.

A distant moan reverberated from above, rocks shifting. The top of this building had collapsed. The walls weren't straight. Many were bowed in places, the ceiling sagging. The weight of the forest above pressed down on them.

"Let me try," Avena said after Ōbhin's third shoulder slam.

He glanced at her earth gauntlet and stepped aside. She pressed her hand against the exit, fingers spread wide. The emeralds shone across the dull surface of the door. In spots, Ōbhin's impacts had smudged the patina, revealing a silvery-gray metal beneath.

She pushed. Her shoulder joint ached from the strain, not enhanced by the glove's strength. Only her arm has increased power. Her boots slid on the filthy floor. The metal groaned. She gritted her teeth, facial muscles tensing. Sweat broke across her face. Stones moaned above.

"Wot's that?" Bran asked, his voice squeaky with fear.

"Just the earth settling," Dajouth said. "It's fine. Happens underground. Or in buildings. I wouldn't worry."

"No, those thuds. They sounded like footsteps."

"What would be walkin' down here?" asked Fingers. "Everything's dead."

"Rats ain't," Dajouth said. "And I've seen some big spiders."

"Saw a roach the size of my hand," Bran said.

Avena shivered. She hated disgusting roaches. Brown bodies crawling through dark spaces, surprising you when opening cabinets with their flat bodies and beady eyes. She pressed harder on the door, the throbbing in her shoulder joint increasing.

"It's not budging," Ōbhin said.

"Maybe we can backtrack and check out the rooms," Fingers said. "They gotta have windows. Someone of 'em might lead somewhere."

Ōbhin drew his sword. Emerald flared bright from it. Avena gasped and stepped back. He swung, the humming pitch of his blade rising and falling. He cut through the door in four quick, practiced slashes. The lines appeared, flakes of corrosion falling away from his slices. The metal stayed lodged in place.

Until he kicked it.

The large section he'd cut out popped through and crashed to the floor on the other side. The clang reverberated around. Avena winced at the clatter, half-expecting the ceiling to collapse on them. Ōbhin muttered beneath his breath about being an idiot.

Nothing caved in on them. Stress relaxing, she raised her diamond lantern and peered through the dark portal. A stench rippled out, putrid, worse than the smell of offal from an abattoir.

"Elohm's Colours," cursed Fingers.

Avena's eyes stung from the strength of the rot. She breathed through her mouth and tasted the foul aroma. It clung to her tongue. Dajouth spat beside her. Dualayn groaned and clapped a hand over his mouth and nose.

Ōbhin stepped through the opening he cut and cursed in his musical tongue.

"What do you see?" Avena asked, holding her free hand over her mouth and nose, struggling to hold down her breakfast. She stepped through after him.

Her boot step on something squishy and wet. Humid air wafted about her, the room significantly warmer. A finger's width of brackish liquid rippled about her boots, the floor beneath soft like she'd stepped into a swamp. The lantern light fell on shiny forms rising out of the foul water, piles of bloated rot wrapped around bones.

Hundreds of bodies. They were piled on each other, mounds of decaying flesh. She clamped her hand over her mouth tighter, bile rising up her throat as she realized what they walked through. The dead had liquefied. The walls were covered in rivulets of black slime oozing downward, the deposits of an endless cycle of evaporation and condensation, the contents in this room never escaping.

"Elohm, bless us with the brightness of your Colours," Bran whimpered. "Maybe we shouldn't be here."

"You can find your way back," Dualayn said, his tone queasy. "Colours bless me, the putrefaction is . . . astonishing."

Ōbhin nodded. He stared down at one corpse. "This one has scales."

Avena's stomach clenched. The body he stood over was larger than any human. Its skin had rotted black but held an impression of snake-like scales. A pebbled hide. One long arm reached across the foul puddle, fingers ending in flesh-rending claws.

"Elohm, shine bright Your Colours and fill this world of Black with Your radiance," Avena muttered. "Is that a darkling? I thought they were more . . . human."

"There's another door," Fingers growled. "Ōbhin, cut us out of here."

Ōbhin sloshed across the room to where Fingers pointed. Emerald light flared. The sword hummed. Avena stared down at the monstrous corpse before her with a sick fascination. She felt a greater warmth on her face, like the thing shed *heat*.

"Utterly fascinating," Dualayn said, stepping up beside her. "A true monster. Proof they are no mere legend."

"I already had proof monsters existed," Avena whispered.

Emerald light danced. Metal clattered. A breeze howled through the room and gusted about her. The air smelled fresh compared to the death around them. A promise of escape, but she couldn't look away from the darkling.

Dualayn nudged it with his foot. The skin sloughed off, exposing bones of ruby red beneath. Not *made* of ruby, but possessing the same scarlet hue. They seemed to have a faint glow. The heat increased. A shiver ran through her.

"That should not be possible," Dualayn said. "Where is it getting the energy to produce heat? This thing has been dead for three thousand years."

"Don't care," growled Ōbhin. He was already out of the room. "Come, there are stairs leading down. The air's rushing up from it. Smells a whole lot better than this putrid rot."

Avena nodded and skirted around the darkling and its hot bones. She stepped through the corpses of humans melded into blobs, their flesh mixed together in death. Had that thing killed everyone in this room? Had they been trapped in here with it?

She exited into the fresh air and leaned against a metal railing pitted with black patina. The wind up the stairs felt refreshing. Many runners were crumbled, broken. Above them, roots poked through the cracks in the stone, frilly and thick and red. Small things crawled on the roots, little specks of scarlet.

"Ants," Fingers muttered, studying the roots. "I've seen this type before. Should be black."

"Whatever stained the trees would have affected them," Dualayn said. "It must be in the soil. Though there is surprisingly little red down here. I thought Koilon was the Ruby City."

"Maybe it's the pillar that stained the soil," said Avena. She took another deep breath of the dry, dusty air flowing from below. She felt soiled. Her boots had a rind of decayed muck around them. Her hair felt damp and stiff, like the very putrid rot had filled the atmosphere with minute particles of liquefied flesh. "Let's just keep going."

"I hope we are making progress," Dualayn said. "I do not know which way we travel."

"North," said Ōbhin. He led the way down the stairs.

Avena followed, the soles of her boots sticking to the floor with a tacky sensation. Her toes wiggled in her dry socks, glad none had seeped through. She ached for a bath. To dunk her head in the deepest, hottest pool of water she could find and then scrub herself with the harshest brush ever made.

She would scour her skin clean of the filth they'd just plunged through.

The stairs had a landing and another flight that descended in a zigzag. At the bottom, they found a hallway. Rusting pipes, dripping with water, hugged the ceiling. Puddles formed in the dust, a layer of mud around the little lakes. Footprints disturbed the detritus, small, clawed. They looked almost canine. In cracks in the wall, insects scurried, vanishing into reddish dirt.

The hallway led not far, twenty cubits before opening into a much larger room. Their light fell away, unable to reach the far end. Support columns of grime-coated concrete rose twice as thick as Avena's waist to the ceiling over her head.

More pipes and slots for diamond lights crowding the busy ceiling.

"Listen to that sound echo," said Dualayn. "This room is vast."

They stepped out into it and their footsteps echoed back at them, sounding loud. Avena winced at it. She raised her lantern up. The air stirred in here. A fuzziness rippled over her body. She swayed, a momentary loss of control. She staggered into Ōbhin, barely holding onto her lantern.

"Avena," he said, steadying her. "Is it . . . ?"

"Sorry," she muttered, the feeling retreating. "Just momentary dizziness. It's going away."

He opened his mouth when something rumbled beneath them. Avena felt the quivering in her boots. It vibrated up her bones to her back molars. She stared down, a chill racing across her skin. She tensed, waiting to see what would happen.

A loud boom rose up beneath them.

20

"Wot's that?" Miguil asked, trickles of dust falling from the ceiling above them. "Cave-in?"

Ōbhin stood tense, ready to dart away from falling debris. Pressure squeezed around his heart, a mighty fist of fear seeking to crush it. A liquid fear melted through his bowels. Flashes of the earthquake and the terrifying plunge into the mines beneath Gunya filled him. The flowing sand gripping him, dragging him deeper and deeper into the earth.

"I think we're fine," Dajouth said after a long period of silence. "If it was going to collapse, it would've by now."

"Elohm's damned Colours, I hope you're right," Fingers said, his voice a low whisper.

"There are main support columns here," Dualayn said, padding up to a thick column of pitted stone. "The ceiling looks strong. I don't think we need to worry about collapses here."

"Yeah," panted Ōbhin, the fear slowly trickling from his guts. He edged forward, gripping his lantern. Sweat soaked his gloves.

The light fell on what looked like a carriage of some sort. It had metal wheels wrapped in rotten, black leather. It had glass windows on all four sides, its body painted a deep red that had weathered the ravages of time better than the exposed metal. Where the paint peeled, rust ravaged the steel beneath. It was sleek and lean and like no carriage he'd ever seen.

"How'd you hook the horses to it?" Miguil asked. The groom moved to the front, his effeminate face streaked with dust. "There's no tongue. Not even a single hitch."

"There's more," Fingers said. "This one's blue and shaped differently."

His lantern light fell on another carriage, taller. More rotten leather surrounded its rusted wheels. The glass had shattered. A skeleton lay inside of it, a hand gripping a wheel sheathed in more rotten leather. Fabric covered the seats, mostly gnawed and devoured by insects. Something scurried out of sight, fleeing the light.

"We're in a carriage house," Miguil said as he drifted to the right, staring at the other carriages.

They were green and yellow and blue. One looked silver. Some had intact glass, others had bodies inside of them. One had its door ripped off. It lay nearby, the metal half-melted. The interior of it looked burned, the frame warped in places from a great heat.

"Hundreds of them," Avena said. "So many in one place. Who would need so many carriages?"

"The people who lived in the tenement above," Dualayn said. "They must each have had their own."

"But they're so poor," Dajouth said. "Those apartments weren't that big. Who could afford their own carriage if they lived in such a small space?"

"Leather wheels?" Miguil asked. He kicked at rotten black that burst apart. "They wrapped the metal rims in them."

"Metal wheels are impractical as it is," said Fingers. "But put leather on them? Why not wooden wheels banded in iron?"

"Bugger me Black," Bran hissed and leaped back.

A shadow burst out from beneath a car and lunged at him. Fingers kicked it. The small shape, the size of a cat, rolled across the dust before gaining its paws. Fur bristled. It barked like a small dog before darting beneath another carriage.

"Like a lapdog," Fingers muttered. "Noblewomen in Ondere have them. Mebudese Lapdogs or some such nonsense."

"Must be living off rats," Ōbhin muttered.

"Poor things," said Avena. She crouched down, shining her lantern beneath one of the sagging, rotten carriages. A piercing yelp echoed. Claws scratched across the stone floor as one of the dogs fled. Its yipping barks echoed through the vast space.

More answered. Snarling growls and screeching challenges. They echoed around Ōbhin and his companions like flurries of snow driven through a narrow mountain canyon. Eddying and swirling, whipping around and assaulting them from every direction. But the barks held fear.

"How big is this place?" Dajouth asked. "I've never found a cave this big. How far does it go?"

"This wasn't a cave originally," Dualayn said. "These thick support columns have held up the roof remarkably well. The engineering here is fantastic."

"Big space to search," Finger said. "Maybe we should split up. Find the way out faster."

Ōbhin studied Fingers. *Are* you *the shapeshifter? Did you murder Fingers and slither into his skin?*

"Okay," Ōbhin said, the tension squeezing about his heart. He had to be careful here. He casually rested his hand on the pommel of his sword like he often did. He set the lantern down on the roof of one of the carriages and gazed around.

Avena studied him, the diamond light picking out the gold highlights in her eyes. Dust streaked her face and darkened her loose hair. Emeralds glowed around her hands, giving her enhanced strength. Her hand drifted towards her binder.

"Dualayn and Dajouth with me," Ōbhin said. "Avena, lead Fingers, Bran, and Miguil."

He studied Fingers, searching for any sign that the man objected to the decision. Or showed disappointment.

Fingers glanced at Avena. "Well, girl, which way you want to go?"

Bran grinned, nodding while Dajouth shrugged and shifted over to join Ōbhin. Dualayn let out a wounded sigh, understanding why Ōbhin chose him. The hurt expression on his face stirred not an ounce of pity in Ōbhin's heart.

Avena caught his gaze then flicked her eyes to Dajouth. He gave the slightest nod. Had he inadvertently selected the impostor? Bran bounced eagerly beside Avena, boasting about how he'd find the exit while Fingers held this paternal air. Miguil, above suspicion, only looked on with unease. He'd come here to help Avena. Their relationship had gone from betrothed to friends with surprising ease.

Love and lust can easily be mistaken for the other, Ōbhin thought, Foonauri lurking in the back of his mind. He'd obsessed over her from the beginning. Too much love destroyed as easily as too little. A balance had to be struck. If he clutched too tight, he would strangle Avena. Not strong enough, and she'd slip out of his grasp.

He cupped her cheek with his black-gloved hand. "Be safe. We'll be within shouting distance."

She grinned. "You're the one who needs to watch out. Dualayn might decide to carve out your kidney and stick it into a bucket so you can piss better."

"Piss?" Ōbhin asked in amusement.

"I've been spending too much time with coarse and vulgar men." She raised up on her toes and brushed his lips with hers. Heat sparked in him.

Bran sniggered.

Avena broke away and marched to the left. "Remind me to laugh hard the next time you flirt with a tavern maid. I remember a host of stories from when you were younger. I'm sure they would love to hear about them. Like the time with the ducks."

Bran's chortles cut off. "You wouldn't."

Avena shrugged as she passed between two carriages, one of the dogs snarling from beneath it.

"Dualayn, lead on," Ōbhin said. "Dajouth and I will make sure none of the dogs bite your ankles."

Dajouth snorted with quiet laughter. He wiped a hand through his blond hair, dust spilling off the fine strands. "Yep, we'll keep those intact at least."

"You two are droll," Dualayn said and headed in the opposite direction.

Ōbhin glanced a final time at Avena. Every instinct told him to go with her, but she had Miguil, and if Ōbhin were wrong about Dajouth being the impostor, then she'd have either Fingers or Bran to protect her. But none of the three objected.

Dajouth must be the one who'd been killed and replaced.

Maybe I'll have an opportunity to do something about you, Ōbhin thought, his insides hardening like an aardvark's plates. Dajouth had been one of his men no matter how annoying his flirtation was. A reckoning was fast approaching with the changeling.

∼

The dogs growled and snarled around Avena's group. They scurried through the dark, desiring to protect their territory. But the humans were bigger and had lights. She shuddered, realizing generations upon generations of these dogs had existed in the dark. Breeding, living, dying in oppressive black. Their eyes must have atrophied to the point that the lanterns were as blinding as the sun. Their world had been turned upside down with the invasion of light and the intrusion of strange creatures their ancestors had once loved.

She worked her shoulders. *Humans do not belong here. We fled this place during the Shattering. We left it to the bugs and rats and these dogs, abandoning them to their own affairs. We've only returned because now it matters to us.*

It reminded her of the same arrogance of King Anglon and his taxes. How he'd exploited his people suffering in the drought to finance his ambitions to control the Border Fangs. How many wars had Roidan and Lothon fought over those mountains? Some of the bloodiest battles in her nation's history had been in those passes. Thousands dead, choking the mountains to serve the vain ambitions of men.

These dogs suffered from their light. She wanted to apologize to them as they moved deeper.

The light from Ōbhin's group dwindled to a faint glow, like the sun about to peek over the horizon. The darkness of the vast carriage house pressed around them, wanting to swallow them. They followed the wall, the stone buckled and cracked in places. Broken pipes ran along the ceiling, some burst open, others dripping water from seams. Corroded masses of wires snaked above. Some went to lights, but others led to hybrid gems of topaz and amethyst. They were nodules twisted around each other.

Healing and protection? She couldn't understand why the wires would run to them from the lights. How would a network of jewelchines like those work?

After perhaps a quarter-hour of moving through the rotting carriages and occasional blocks of rubble, the wall glittered ahead. Something made of scarlet glass flashed, reflecting their lanterns' lights. She gasped to see a vein of red passing through the wall. It continued along the floor and ceiling. It crossed one of the carriages, transforming the metal and interior upholstery into ruby. The rest of the vehicle had rotted, but the ruby sections had remained perfectly shaped, untouched by the ravages of age beyond a coating of dust.

"Elohm's Colours," Bran muttered, studying it. "Wot caused that?"

"Reality warped," Avena said, remembering her dream of the experiment and the tears of Black rending and melting the room around her. Had something happened here like that, only with rubies? What had she witnessed in her dream? The moment of hubris when mankind had unleashed the Black? *Then why is it* ruby *here?*

"Is this wot's stained the trees above?" asked Miguil. He prodded the vein of ruby running across the floor, scuffing away the dust coating it.

"I don't know," Avena said. "Maybe." She struggled to get her bearings, to follow the twisting path that they'd journeyed to reach here, but she was hopelessly turned around. She had no idea how far they were from the library. Did this garage run back underneath it? Away from it? This room was larger than the building that they had passed through to find it. This underground structure, this carriage house, must support multiple buildings.

"Don't matter," Fingers growled and stepped over it. He didn't touch it, his longer stride clearing the cubit-and-a-half-wide strip. "Let's keep movin'."

Avena nodded while her curiosity itched at her. She glanced to her right and spotted the distant glow of Ōbhin. For the first time in days, she wished to hear Dualayn speak. Would he know what had caused this . . . rubyification? How did it happen? He'd taught her so much, how to heal, how to build jewelchines, how to think through problems. He'd understood her need to learn after Chames's death.

Her heart softened towards Dualayn for a moment. She recoiled at that. She hardened her emotions against him, reminding herself why she was here. She had *obsidian* in her head. Foul and dark. Who knew what effect it would have on her in the future? He had mutilated her for his own knowledge.

She marched ahead at a brisk pace, ignoring the dogs.

Her footsteps stomped along, dust bursting around her boots. She licked dry lips, wanting to stop and drink from the aquifer she had stored in her bag, but refused to stop now. She wanted to find the Hall of Communication and get as far from Dualayn as she could.

I was like your daughter!

Below, a large crash boomed.

She froze. Miguil groaned. She peered down at the floor as a loud thudding sound echoed again. The skin down her back crawled, like a thousand baby spiders scurried up and down her flesh. Her heart tightened as she listened.

"Wot was that?" Bran asked.

"Somethin' shifted?" suggested Fingers. "We disturbing things?"

"But comin' from below?" Miguil asked.

"I don't know," Avena said. She peered ahead. "Is that an opening? It's darker than what's around it."

"Let's find out," Fingers said, his voice tight. "I don't like this. We shouldn't be here."

Avena nodded her agreement and pressed on.

The booming sound didn't return as they crossed to the darkness. It led to a stairwell that had collapsed, rubble choking the stairs. Water dripped through it, oozed along the floor as a small rivulet, and vanished into a crack in the floor. A sign was set in the wall written in Old Tonal. She wiped at it with a handkerchief, smearing away the dirt.

"Wot's it say?" Bran asked, staring at her.

"I don't read Old Tonal," she said. "But I memorized some of the place names. Let me see. It's hard to decipher."

She held her lantern light closer and buffed the sign again.

"This leads to the library, I think." She looked up. "We're back where we started, only lower in elevation."

Fingers grunted and spat. "Figures." He popped his knuckles. "Well, least we know this is the wrong direction to be headin' in. Don't think we wanna be poppin' out behind the library."

"Didn't see much choice," Avena said, her stomach sinking. "It's huge. Maybe there are better places it comes out."

Fingers shrugged. "Let's keep movin'."

"Just . . . I need to drink," Miguil said. He unslung his pack and began digging around.

Avena's stomach rumbled. Her throat burned. Sighing, she surrendered to her needs. She pulled out her aquifer, a small sapphire set in a wooden handle. There was a leather-wrapped button sticking out a hole carved in the side. She brought it to her mouth and pressed it.

A cool stream of water gushed out. A gem this small would produce enough water a day to keep her alive. She savored the liquid as she gulped it down. The wet flowed down to her stomach. A refreshing chill washed through her for a moment. She let some spill over her face, crossing the dust coating her sweat-damped features.

Drinking the water reminded her of another biological necessity. She looked at the alcove then at the three men. "Could you give me some privacy?"

"Why?" Bran asked.

"She's got to piss and don't want you watchin'," said Fingers, hooking his arm around the younger guard and pulling him along. "Let's go see if we can't get them dogs to bite your ankle."

"Wot?" Bran gasped.

Miguil put away his aquifer and nodded to her.

She passed her water quickly. When she emerged, she grimaced to see fresh, steaming puddles soaking into the dust just around the corner; the men hadn't gone far to relieve themselves.

She found them clustered around one of the carriages. The metal body in the front was missing, exposing a mass of rusting metal congealing together. Fingers rubbed his hand over the central mechanism, a ruby and an emerald fused together into a jewelchine the size of a horse's heart. The corroded ends of wires stretched out of it in a dozen directions.

"No wonder there's no place for a horse to hitch up," Miguil said in awe. "Machines that drive themselves."

"How did they get the wires inside the jewelchine?" Fingers muttered. "I don't get that."

"They grew them," she said, staring in fascination. "Dualayn is studying the Recorder to learn that secret."

Miguil shook his head. "Did everyone in Koilon own one of these? Were they all rich?"

Avena gave a hopeless shrug.

"You can see some of the mechanism," Miguil said, lowering his lantern into the compartment. "See, down there, that box has rods leadin' off to the wheels. They must work like gears in a watermill. You have to use them to change the speed the mill rotates compared to the flow of the river."

"You know about waterwheels?" Avena asked.

"My father owned one. He had to sell it when I was young."

"Oh, I never knew that." Heat rushed through Avena's cheeks. They'd once been promised before she'd learned what Miguil truly craved in a partner. As a woman, she could never fill that desire. Still, she should have known more about his past.

Miguil shrugged like it didn't matter.

She opened her mouth to ask more when the thud of heavy footsteps echoed through the carriage house. She turned towards Ōbhin's light. She was surprised by how far away it was. The footsteps sounded so close.

"Strange how sound echoes in here," Fingers muttered. He popped his knuckles by clenching his fist. "I'd swear those are close."

"Yeah," Avena said, her fingertips growing fuzzy. "Ōbhin?" Her voice echoed through the carriage house. "Ōbhin!"

The footsteps thudded closer. She bit her lower lip, frozen for a moment, then she rushed from the wall towards Ōbhin. Those footsteps were too heavy to be any human being.

∽

"... bhin ..."

The feminine voice echoed around Ōbhin. His ears pricked up and he glanced out to his left to the distant glow of Avena's group. Her lantern seemed to bob and wink out for a moment, blocked by an object. He frowned as he wondered if she was coming closer.

"This definitely leads up," Dajouth said, peering up the sloping ramp they found. The wall to their right had collapsed, heavy stones crushing a metal carriage, part of its mangled body thrusting out from it. "I can hear space up there."

"Yeah," Dualayn agreed. "We should attract the others' attention."

"I think they're coming towards us," Ōbhin said. He could hear their footsteps, distant but thudding closer and closer.

"Ōbhin!" Avena shouted, her voice clearer. She was crossing the carriage house fast.

"Something's wrong," Ōbhin said, his hand on his sword. "Avena!"

The thudding grew louder and louder. It boomed with heavy steps. It seemed to echo all around them for a moment and then it was behind him. He turned his head, confused by what was causing it. He thought it was Avena and her group. The thudding grew louder, echoing from near the collapsed wall.

He frowned. The sound came from a dark spot he hadn't noticed before. Something *glowed*. A faint red and green, like the mixed moonlight of Firedrop and Earthheart shining at the same time.

"What is that glow?" Dualayn asked, backing up.

A figure made of amethyst stepped into the carriage house. It held the rough shape of a man, its body faceted. It stood a head taller than Ōbhin, its conical crown just clearing the ceiling. A ruby glowed in the center of its chest while emeralds shone in various spots around its body. For eyes, it had diamonds. It creaked as it lumbered forward, the floor shaking from the impact of its step.

"Crystalman," Dualayn croaked, voice as choked as Ōbhin's throat felt.

It seemed to look right at Ōbhin and pause. He drew his weapon, breathing labored.

An ear-splitting shriek burst from the figure before it boomed words in a musical language Ōbhin didn't understand.

Dualayn groaned.

Ōbhin activated his resonance blade.

21

The ear-splitting alarm blaring from the crystalman assaulted Ōbhin's ears. The world grew woozy, the sound knifing into his balance. Diamond eyes flared bright, focusing on him. The gemstone figure thundered towards Ōbhin.

"He called us 'crystal flawers'!" Dualayn shouted. "I think it means intruders or something bad."

"Niszeh's Black Tone," Ōbhin curse, dropping his lantern with a clatter, the diamond light winking out. The crystalman's eyes shone brighter as it advanced.

Dajouth's binder burst with amethyst light. Avena shouted his name. Ōbhin let it all fade as he focused on the hulking automaton lumbering at him. The ruby jewel in its chest, where its heart would be, drew his scrutiny. It had to be important. He shifted his stance, dropping out of his guard position to ready a strike.

Sweat dripped down his scalp as he waited for the perfect moment to attack. The ground shook with each of its steps. The diamond lights blazing from its eyes were almost blinding. The siren shrieked louder, his ears throbbing from the volume.

The crystalman entered his range.

He lunged forward, pushing off with his back foot. His sweat-soaked jerkin creaked around him. He slashed hard, the pitch of his sword humming louder. The crystalman's arm drew back to deliver a punch, gemstone fingers curling into a fist the size of Ōbhin's head.

His sword arced down into the chest and struck solid crystal.

The resonance blade *should* have cut through the amethyst with the same ease of a seamstress cutting through a bolt of linen. Taking no effort. Meeting no resistance. Instead, Ōbhin's sword hit the gemstone and rebound though no barrier of amethyst energy had been thrown up. The shock of the impact shivered up the weapon and into his hand. Jarred up his humerus. His fingers went numb and his blade fell from his hand and clattered to the floor.

"Niszeh's Black Tones!" he cursed in Qothian as the massive crystal fist barreled down at him.

He threw himself to the side out of desperation. The fist clipped his thigh. Bruising pain burst through his leg. The blow spun him. The dark world of the carriage house spun around him. He hit the ground hard on his belly. The loud smack echoed around him. Air burst from his lungs.

He coughed, gasping for air, dust billowing around his face.

The ground thudded. The crystalman loomed over him and drew back its arm for another fist.

"No!" someone shouted.

Avena dropped her lantern as the cry burst from her lips.

She didn't think. Couldn't think. Her lover lay on the ground. The crystalman—*what else can it be?* she'd thought when she'd seen it—prepared to deliver a fatal blow. She pushed the activation button on her earthen gauntlet. Green light flared around her arm.

She threw herself before the crystalman and thrust her right arm before her, palm open, fingers fuzzed numb. She had greater strength. Emeralds enhanced her limb. She felt it as she caught the fist threatening to kill Ōbhin.

Pain exploded in her shoulder. Though her arm had the strength to take the punch, the enhancing energy ended where the glove did. Thought it had a long sleeve, extending nearly to her shoulder, it didn't reach there. Ligaments ripped. The ball of her humerus dislocated from her shoulder socket. The force of the impact threw her off her feet. She hurtled backward, howling in agony.

Her back struck the hood of one of the autonomous carriages. Metal groaned. She flipped and tumbled over it then fell off on the far side. She landed on the unyielding, dusty floor in a ball of groaning pain.

"Avena!"

Fingers knelt beside her, setting down his lantern. Bran and Miguil raced by, Bran's binder out. Fingers grabbed her upper arm, giving her a squeeze, perhaps to comfort. It delivered only agony. She screamed as the ball of her dislocated humerus ground in the socket of her shoulder. Fingers ripped his hand back.

"Healer," she groaned through the pain. Her legs spasmed. Her lower back throbbed, felt prickly and numb. "In my pack!"

"Sorry," he groaned. "This is going to hurt."

She nodded as he sat her up. Bone ground on bone. Her head threw back while teeth clenched down hard, clacking together. Her entire face strained as she growled her agony. Legs spasmed. He drew off her pack and then stretched her onto her back. The pain retreated to only moderate torture.

Fear surged over the throbbing fire of her injuries. Ōbhin was fighting that thing. She'd witnessed his sword's ineffectiveness. How could they beat it? She struggled to think, but the pain drowned out her thoughts.

Fingers produced the topaz. He activated it with a press, the orange light bathing her face with the gentle love of a mother's kiss. Memories of her mother on a bright day, when she was smiling and loving, flowed through Avena's mind. *"There are my two otters,"* her mother said, scooping up Avena and her dead twin, Evane. *"Look at you, just drenched."*

The topaz rested on her shoulder, soothing away the fire as, for a moment, she felt like she was in her mother's arms with Evane and nothing bad had ever happened.

The blaring shout from the crystalman shattered that moment of peace: *"PSADZEF ACHIE!"*

∽

"Avena!" Ōbhin groaned as he scrambled to his feet, his thigh throbbing from the punch. He spotted Fingers kneeling down where she'd vanished. He wanted to rush over there, but he couldn't bring this thing anywhere near her.

"Ōbhin!" Bran shouted, the youth looking serious as he raced around one of the carriages, Miguil on his heels.

Ōbhin retreated as the crystalman swung blows at him. It slammed its fist into the ground. Dust burst around it. A loud snap. A crack raced across the floor's smooth surface. The automaton advanced, its diamond eyes shining at Ōbhin.

Bran darted in to swing the binder, but the crystalman pivoted and swung a fist. A chime-like tinkle echoed as it moved, its crystalline structure resonating. Bran squeaked out in fright and threw himself down. Dajouth rushed in, his blond hair glowing in the diamond lantern shining behind him. Dualayn held it as he pressed himself against the wall.

"Ōbhin!" Miguil shouted. He snatched up Ōbhin's weapon and tossed the humming blade at him.

He cursed and flinched back as the curved tulwar tumbled through the air, emerald light flashing. It hit the concrete floor at his feet, slicing through the stone. He yanked back his foot, narrowly missing having his toes severed. The crossguard hit the stone, stopping the blade from cutting deeper.

"Sorry!" Miguil groaned, wincing.

The crystalman rang, "*PSADZEF ACHIE!*"

The sound echoed through the room. Dajouth flinched back and shook his head. He looked dazed. Bran shoved him to the side, throwing him out of the way of being crushed by a fist.

"Hey!" Ōbhin shouted, wanting to protect his men. "Over here!"

He backed past one of the thick support columns. The crystalman turned, its diamond eyes shining focused beams across the carriage house. They landed on Ōbhin and focused. Its entire body pivoted and marched at him. He had to figure out a way to kill this thing. To deactivate it.

His eyes flicked around, searching for something.

"Where else you hurt?" Fingers asked, the ground shaking beneath Avena.

"Shoulder's dislocated and back might be broken," she groaned.

"Is there another healer in here?" Fingers asked, digging around. He had a frantic look on his face.

"No," she said. She closed her eyes, the soothing bliss of the topaz radiating through her. The numbness in her back retreated. "I need you to pop my arm into place. The topaz can't do that."

"How?" he asked.

"Grab my arm and yank," she said. "I'll let you know when the ball of my humerus is back in the shoulder socket."

He grabbed her hand, squeezing her through the earth gauntlet. The emeralds still shone, spilling verdant light across his fatherly features. He stood up and then planted his boot on her chest beneath her shoulder joint.

"This is gonna hurt?" he asked.

She nodded and tensed. She held the topaz to her shoulder with her left hand. "Do! It!"

He pulled. Hard.

She screamed. The love flowing from the topaz couldn't blunt the pain of her torn ligaments twisting and her humerus's ball sliding over her shoulder socket. Bone ground on bone. It popped into place.

"That's it!" she snarled through clenched teeth.

He let go. Her arm flopped down. She panted, sweat soaking her face. She closed her eyes, drawing in ragged breaths, rubbing the healer over her shoulder, letting it repair her. She relaxed as the pain flowed out of her.

"Better?" Fingers asked.

"Yeah," she said. She flexed prickling toes. A humming fuzz danced over her thoughts. "Now go. You have to help Ōbhin."

Fingers's brow furrowed. He glanced over the carriage towards the fight and then back down at her. "You're hurt."

"I'm fine," she said. "I'll be up soon and . . ." Her words trailed off as the minor prickling she felt intensified in her toes. A surge of panic rushed through her. She squeezed down on the topaz, her digits feeling thick and useless. Her grip didn't feel as sure.

"It's happening?" Fingers asked, kneeling down beside her.

She didn't want to admit it. She didn't want to think it was happening now. Her obsidian mind wasn't receiving a clear signal, distorted by a hiss, almost a whisper. A wave of fear washed through her. The ground shook from the crystalman, Ōbhin and her friends fought for their lives, and she was about to be rendered helpless.

"I hate this, Fingers," she said, her eyes stinging with tears.

"I know," he said, his hand covering hers, holding the healer. Her eyes

Ruby Ruins

focused on his swollen, red knuckles. "I'm here for you. Ōbhin will figure out how to defeat that thing. You got nothing to worry about."

"Thank you," she whispered with numbing lips and a thick tongue. She stared into his eyes as she fought to stay in her body.

∽

Ōbhin's sword could do nothing against the automaton. He retreated, leading the crystalman from where Avena had fallen. The orange light of the topaz glowed over there, giving him hope for her. Injured, but not dead. He had to believe that, or what was the point of any of this? Dajouth and Bran flanked him.

"How do we defeat this?" Ōbhin asked, throwing a glance over at Dualayn at the mouth of the ramp, two diamond lanterns at his feet.

"The, uh . . ." stammered Dualayn while Ōbhin slashed at an incoming fist, deflecting it to the side as he retreated. Bran and Dajouth both swung their binders, trying to hit the arm. Dajouth's landed, a burst of energy binding about the arm.

It did nothing to hinder the crystalman.

"Let's see . . ." Dualayn muttered as the hulk lumbered on, forcing Ōbhin and his two companions to scatter as it swung massive arms down at them.

The impact shook the concrete floor. Dust and rust sifted down from the pipes overhead. The shaking ground tripped up Ōbhin. He fell hard onto his side. He groaned, landing on the bruised thigh. The simmering pain soared to a sear. He growled while Bran seized his wrist and hauled him to his feet.

"The ruby jewelchine!" Dualayn shouted with excitement. "That has to be the power source driving the rest of it. The emeralds are giving it strength, and the amethyst gives it a natural warding."

"I already figured that!" snarled Ōbhin. He darted to the right, a crystalline fist slamming down at him. Air rushed over him from the force of its passage. It hit the metal side of the carriage. Rust burst off the door and glass shards, clinging in the frame, crashed to the floor. "*How* do I destroy it? I can't cut into it with my blade!"

"Come on, Dualayn," Miguil said, hanging back by the older man. "Think!"

"I am trying, young man," Dualayn snapped. "You work for me, so remember to—"

"I don't work for you!" Miguil seized the front of Dualayn's work shirt. "Give us a Black-cursed way to stop this!"

"Okay, okay!" Dualayn muttered, pushing back Miguil. "Let's see . . . Brute force might do it."

"What level of brute force?" Bran asked as he rushed in. He struck his binder against the crystalman's torso. The metal hit with a resounding chime, the entire automaton seeming to vibrate.

"Well, the ceiling collapsing on it," Dualayn said. "If we have some tuning forks set to the resonance frequency of an amethyst, and if they were sufficiently large, we could cause a harmonic shattering to destroy it."

"Do we have those?" asked Ōbhin. The diamond eyes fell on him. He pushed himself from the carriage.

Metal crunched behind him as he rushed past the automaton. He roasted in his leather jerkin. Sweat spilled down his face. The back of his throat burned for water. Fatigue nibbled on the edges of his limbs. The hulk lumbered on.

"We do not," said Dualayn. "I will keep considering options."

"Yeah, do that," muttered Dajouth.

Bran rushed forward, shouting, "Let's see if this works."

He moved fast, his scrawny legs carrying him beneath a swinging punch. He ducked low and slammed his binder into the crystalman's right side. Purple energy sprang up and seized both of its legs. For a heartbeat, Ōbhin wondered if it would topple. The thing seemed to sway, its legs pulled tight together.

"*PSADZEF ACHIE!*" bellowed from the entire construct like the sound was produced by the crystalline structure vibrating in harmony.

The purple binding snapped as Bran struggled to get clear. The binding vanished from about the automaton as its leg kicked out. With sufficient strength, even a human could snap an amethyst binding. The automaton had no issue breaking free.

The foot connected with Bran before he could react.

Ōbhin screamed in horror as the young man flew upward and slammed into the ceiling with a bone-crunching impact. He slid across it for a cubit, thrown hard by the force of the kick, before rebounding and landing broken on the roof of a carriage. Metal dented from the impact. His body bounced. Spun. His arms and legs bent in unnatural ways. He fell off out of sight on the other side of the vehicle, landing near where Fingers attended to Avena.

"Bran!" Dajouth shouted in shocked horror.

Ōbhin swayed for a moment. The youth couldn't survive such an impact. The force would have snapped his neck and broken every bone in his body. A sick feeling built in Ōbhin's stomach. He'd have to tell Joayne that her youngest son had died because he hadn't had the strength or knowledge to slay a legend.

Roaring in fury, Ōbhin whirled on the crystalman bearing down on him. He would find a way to destroy this thing.

22

Metal crunched.
 Bran flopped off the side of the autonomous carriage and crashed into the hard floor behind Fingers. Avena clapped fuzzing hands over her mouth. For a moment, the shock of seeing the young man slam into the ground drove back the whispers interfering with her body's control.

Bran spasmed. His head snapped around, his skin rippling white and pudgy. A new horror seized her as she witnessed the same doughy flesh molding back into Bran's face. It was what she'd seen when Smiles hit the wall after Ust's head-cracking punch. Bran's broken limbs popped into place, straightening back into their proper shape.

Fingers looked behind him. "Elohm's blessed Colours, you alive?"

"Yes," Bran croaked as he lay there. "I just . . . got the breath . . . kicked out of me . . ."

The traitor. The changeling. Poor Bran had joined Smiles, the boy lost in some ditch or anonymous grave, someplace where the body wouldn't be found and spoil the impostor's ruse. Hatred burned through Avena as she held the topaz to her shoulder.

Sweet, innocent, energetic Bran. Full of life, eager to go on an adventure. To show Ōbhin all his skill and prowess. All stolen away by that monstrous changeling. As Fingers went to help the thing masquerading as Bran, she wanted to snarl a warning.

The fuzziness struck her body hard. She gasped and swayed. Sagged against a rusting carriage door. Spots of darkness danced on her vision. Through it, she watched Fingers help Bran stand. The fake-youth flexed digits.

"You can't be okay," Fingers said. "That blow you took, boy . . . Let me get a healer on you."

"Doesn't need one," she struggled to say, but her tongue grew numb. The signal interference worsened. She had to stop Fingers from helping the thing. She had to expose the vile creature. She struggled to stand.

Ōbhin swung his blade hard at the incoming attack. He struck the fist, deflecting it to the side. He flowed forward, now within the crystalman's reach. He slashed with his sword, using all his strength and weight, to strike the automaton's chest. He held tight to his hilt, not expecting his blade to cut through it. He landed hard, square on.

His blade didn't so much as scratch it.

"Perhaps if we had diamond," said Dualayn. "It's harder than amethyst. It's how we actually shape gems. Use smaller ones. Isn't that fascinating?"

"Not really," barked Miguil.

Ōbhin pivoted to his right to dodge a kick and ducked an elbow slamming down at his head, feet shifting. He cleared the crystalman's reach and whirled around. As he backpedaled, he struggled to think through his boiling rage. Bran might have annoyed Ōbhin with pestering questions, but the youth had a bright future before him. Ōbhin would have gladly answered the youth's every last query, patiently describe every last fight, just to let the boy have that unsoiled life.

Dajouth gripped his binder in two hands. Shouting, he slammed his weapon hard into the forearm of the crystalman. A loud chime rang through the carriage house. The energy bound the arm to the torso. It lasted not even a heartbeat before the crystalman broke the energy and lashed out.

The young man was already moving, but not fast enough.

The blow struck Dajouth's arm. Bone snapped. A blood-stained shard thrust out his arm and through his gambeson. The impact spun him around.

He hit the ground hard, screaming. Blood soaked red through the quilted armor.

"Dualayn!" Ōbhin barked. "Help him!"

"Right," Dualayn said and darted forward.

Miguil picked up Dajouth's binder and stood trembling as the crystalman advanced on Ōbhin. "I don't know how much I'll help, Ōbhin, but . . ."

"I appreciate it," said Ōbhin. The groom had only a basic amount of training. He had courage, though.

Rage wasn't helping Ōbhin. It burned through him, powering his attacks, but it also distracted him. He needed to focus. He couldn't make any mistakes. He had to think. There had to be a way to kill this thing.

Brute force . . . Bring the ceiling down?

They were fighting near the ramp. There were three support columns that held up the roof near him. It was insane. He could kill them all, bury them in rubble, but what choice did he have? He glanced over his shoulder to spy the nearest one.

He backed towards it as the crystalman thundered after him.

"Fyungerz," Avena's numb tongue slurred. Her lips felt as fuzzy as a yellow-spotted caterpillar.

She stood by, brazing her left shoulder against the carriage. Her legs quivered. Fingers dug around in his pack, searching for a healer. A loaf of hard bread spilled out. He scooped it up and shoved it back in.

"Fyungerz, hez nyot Byranj," she struggled to say.

"What, Avena?" Fingers asked.

"I'm fine," Bran protested. "Attend to Avena, she's having trouble."

"You are not fine, boy! Sometimes you don't feel injuries right away."

Avena opened her mouth to speak when the lumbering crystalman drew her attention. It advanced on Ōbhin. He lay trapped against a support column. Primal terror rippled through her. She swayed and screamed out his slurred name.

The crystalman swung a powerful fist at her lover, a blurring streak of amethyst.

Ōbhin dived to his right.

It was a mistake.

The amethyst fist crashed into the support column behind him as he landed on his upper back, head tucked down, and rolled into the rotten wheel of a carriage. Metal bolts thrusting out of the rusting wheel jammed into his back through his leather jerkin, bruising skin. His head smacked into the metal fender. Flakes of rust burst off, bloody snow dusting his shoulders.

The column didn't collapse. The crystalman's punch left a small dent, hardly more than a chip. Some stone crumbled away, revealing a braided chord of steel running vertically in the column. The thing could punch it a dozen times and do nothing.

The crystalman turned to face him, diamond eyes shining. He had nowhere to go, trapped by the vehicle, the column, and the automaton. He scrambled to his feet, his back sliding up the frame of the vehicle. He felt an opening. The window was missing.

He dropped his resonance sword and squeezed himself into the carriage. He landed on a rotting seat. The leather burst beneath his touch, mildewed stuffing erupting along with metal springs. He coughed as the padding filled his mouth. He spat out the dusty filth while scrambling to the other side.

The crystalman seized the carriage and lifted it.

Ōbhin seized the other window with black-gloved hands. He gripped hard as he suddenly dangled from it. The crystalman lifted it over the carriage head, prepared to hurtle it. A burst of cold energy exploded through his veins, pumping frigid necessity through his body.

He hauled himself upward. The carriage was almost touching the ceiling. He pushed himself out of another window as the thing tossed the vehicle. He fell down the back of the crystalman. The concrete floor rushed up. He raised his left arm to brace himself.

Pain burst through his wrist. He rolled to his side as the vehicle hurtled through the carriage house. He seized his discarded sword, blade half-sunk into the floor, and scrabbled to his feet. Metal crashed behind him as he formed a new plan.

To Avena's relief, Ōbhin spilled out of the back of the carriage before it hurtled out from the crystalman. Then she realized it soared in her direction. Perhaps the automaton had sensed her and wanted to kill them both. Perhaps it was bad luck. Her body struggled to move, but the numbing interference gripped her.

She couldn't even scream.

Bran darted around Fingers in a blur of inhuman speed. He slammed into her and threw her back. She hurtled to the ground, landed hard. The topaz spilled out of her hand, rolling behind her, flashing orange light. Her vision swam, darkness pulling at her.

The carriage slammed into the vehicle she'd stood behind, bounced and struck Bran's head. His neck snapped as he was thrown to the ground. The carriage tumbled past, crashing into the side of a third and pushing it into a fourth. Bran hit the floor, his flesh bleeding white.

Fingers let out a strangled cry as he witnessed Bran's head snap back into place.

Avena fought to hold onto her body, but the interference won. The last thing she saw before being ripped from her body and thrust into her dreams was Bran standing up, his face white clay molding back into shape.

Ōbhin ignored his sprained wrist and slashed through the column the crystalman had punched. He sprinted past it, expecting the ceiling to crash down on it. He threw a look over his shoulder to see the automaton turning around and focusing diamond eyes on him.

The column remained standing.

"There's too much weight for that to work!" Dualayn shouted. "You need to do more than cut through it. You have to do it in such a way that the weight causes it to buckle."

The solution flashed through Ōbhin's mind. "Like felling trees!"

He'd seen it enough growing up in the mountain valley. Lumberjacks didn't cut through a tree, they cut a wedge into the trunk. That caused it to topple over in the direction they wanted. He pictured it in his mind. If he made two diagonal cuts, one slashing downward and the other upward, the force of the ceiling would shove the piece out to the side.

The crystalman advanced on him as he rushed towards the next column, closer to the ramp where Dualayn had dragged Dajouth. The older man pressed a healer onto the younger man's broken arm. Miguil stood warily nearby, tracking the crystalman, looking for an opening.

This had to work. Ōbhin could see no other way of getting out of this alive. The crystalman thudded after him. Not as fast, but relentless. It knocked a carriage out of the way, metal screeching. Ōbhin reached the column.

He made his first slash high on the column and cut at a downward angle, leaving a thin line just visible in the gray. Then he attacked low. The crystalman closed the distance. He sliced upward, creating a wedge that would pop out of the column and, hopefully, bring down the ceiling.

The column groaned. Stone ground together. The wedge barely shifted before its slide stopped. It was still held in place by the fast weight above. Ōbhin stared in shock at it, almost forgetting death bearing down at him for a moment. Why hadn't it worked?

"You have to overcome the coefficient of friction!" Dualayn shouted. "You need to hit the column with sufficient force!"

The crystalman swung at Ōbhin.

He threw himself onto his belly out of desperation. The fist roared over his head and struck the column. The blow knocked the wedge a hand's width to the side. Stone cracked overhead. A pipe burst as more of the wedge shifted out of the way. The ceiling sagged.

Ōbhin scrambled to his feet as the wedge popped out of the column. The weight of not just the ceiling, but the building above and the forest on top lost its support. It all came crashing down in a roar of hungry chaos.

Chunks of the ceiling broke free and hurtled down. The failure spread in a wave over him. A large piece crashed into the crystalman. He threw a look over his shoulder. Jagged slabs crushed carriages. Dust billowed. Fingers scooped up Avena and ran away from the devastation before they were lost to Ōbhin's sight, obscured by the collapsing debris.

It rained around him and the crystalman. Pieces crashed on the floor beside him. Sharp fragments peppered his legs, knifing through his leather pants. Chimes rang as large chunks hit the automaton. The ground shook. The earth groaned. A cloud of chalk burst around him.

Ōbhin ran.

He took two steps when something slammed into his lower left leg. Pain exploded as he fell face first. The ceiling roared over him. The wave of destruction rushed at him. His ankle throbbed, twisted in the wrong direction.

Broken.

"Niszeh's Black Tone!" he groaned as he struggled to stand.

"Ōbhin!" Miguil burst out of the dust and seized his arm. He pulled him upright. Ōbhin gripped the groom, leaning on him as he hopped on his good foot. They staggered for the ramp, death crashing down behind them.

A great rush of dirt poured down through the ceiling, spilling from above. The scent of fresh loam and pine trees chased them as they rushed for the ramp. Dualayn dragged Dajouth up the sloping surface. The entire world shook and growled. New clouds of dust surged around them.

Miguil and Ōbhin reached the ramp, debris choking the world behind them. The groaning slowed and stopped. Miguil sank Ōbhin down. He stared back at the devastation. A mix of broken stone and dark soil separated them from Avena and Fingers.

A chill swept through Ōbhin as he gazed out at the terrifying sight. Fingers was the impostor. Dajouth broke his arm and didn't heal. Bran was dead. That left only the older man. He was alone with Avena. He had her.

What would he do with her when he didn't have to pretend?

How could Ōbhin find her and protect her now?

23

Beings of light stood around Avena as she dreamed.

They all glowed with a pure, white radiance. They were human-shaped, men and women both, with hair of liquid starlight. She stood amid them, her body vibrating with Honesty. It soared out of her and fed into the beings around her.

They must be devas, she thought.

Across from them, they faced nightmarish horrors. Insectoid demons, their bodies covered in waxy carapaces. They scuttled like ants but stood taller than Ōbhin. They held swords of hardened black, the air thick with an acrid reek. They writhed out of torn rents in reality and crashed into her army of light.

And hers weren't the only armies fighting. They battled on a great plane. The sky overhead looked murky. No clouds, but the sun didn't shine as bright. Falling stars burned across the gloom in flares of orange-red, always streaking from the east and south and flashing towards the west and north.

She cried out in a language Avena didn't understand, giving orders, marshaling her troops. She was giving them power. It flowed out of her and gave them the strength to drive back the demonic ants. These foul insects.

Darklings? These are nothing like the lizard things we found in Koilon.

The demons crashed into her lines. They tore at her army of devas with scything mandibles. Hacked with jagged blades. Blood spurted golden-bright.

She felt each one of them die, a tiny shifting in the harmonics singing through her body.

To her right, humans of midnight black fought. They swept out shadows that splashed like acid on the demons. They were led by the man from her dreams. Her lover in this past life. He stood among them, wearing armor of glassy obsidian. No, he didn't wear it. The obsidian had melted around him, almost like a prison.

He glanced over at her and, despite the distance, the smile on his lips for her heartened her resolve.

Her truth resounded greater than the distance separating them.

She smiled back at him, forgetting about those who died connected to her power for a moment.

A vast, chittering screech broke through the barrier. A dozen of those connected to her, the devas, snuffed out. Their contribution to the symphony resounding through Avena's bones vanished. Her head whipped around, pale-white hair flying. She witnessed the ant-like demons surging out in a coordinated action. They all chittered at the same time, moving with the same precision, striking and attacking in communal harmony.

Up and down the line, they attacked. The demons met the flaming people led by the blonde woman. Beyond her forces, watery figures sent waves crashing into the attacking demons. Their leader was also a woman, the one who'd been channeling the Sapphire during the Shattering. Waves of amethyst force slammed from the purple-glowing beings beyond the dark warriors, their commander radiating strength and power. He stood strong.

Like Ōbhin. A warrior. A defender.

Avena pulled something from a pocket. It was a device made of shiny metal with an obsidian shaft thrusting out the tip. She depressed a button and it crackled. She shouted into it, a cry of urgent need as more of her beings of light lost their harmony.

A humming noise thrummed from behind her. Then metal insects, like massive dragonflies, swooped overhead. Their wings were fixed, thrusting out from the side and had blurring circles whirling above them. Air slammed down at her, whipping at her hair. They banked over sharply, cutting their forward speed and turning. Some of the demons with swollen abdomens spat sizzling ichor that splattered along the hulls of the metal dragonflies. One, soaring before the amethyst fighters, spun in a smoking circle and crashed in a burst of red and yellow light.

Doors slid open along the sides of the dragonflies. Crystalmen stepped out of them. They dropped fifty cubits to the ground, bright heliodors glowing in their bodies to slow their fall. But not enough that their landing didn't crush the demons. Crystalline hailstones hammered into the monsters. The automatons then battered into the enemy with mighty sweeps of amethyst arms. Broken chitin burst through the air. The ground shook from each impact while her devas cheered and surged forward, unleashing their light on the black insects.

Their attack drove back the demons towards the huge rift, the fracture of Black rising into the air. More fiery streaks shot overhead. One was brighter than the others. It burned across the sky. Its massive trail blazed behind it as it vanished over the horizon. A heartbeat later, a bright glow exploded, a sun dawning to the northwest.

She shouted and pressed her devas forward while her lover and his shadowy army surged towards the enemy with ferocity. Avena just knew they had to drive the enemy back into the rift before the world was completely shattered.

24

Ōbhin hardly felt the throbbing pain in his ankle as he stared at the collapsed debris. Avena lay on the other side in the arms of the thing posing as Fingers. Ōbhin's deactivated resonance blade rested across his lap. Useless to protect her.

"Miguil, can you make a splint?" Dualayn said, his voice a distant buzz intruding on the turmoil of Ōbhin's thoughts.

"Yeah."

"Good. Bind the topaz to Dajouth's arm when you do. Place it over the break."

"Sure," Miguil answered, sounding sullen.

Footsteps thudded behind Ōbhin. He didn't look away from the debris. Avena was just beyond there, helpless in that thing's arms. What would it do to her? Had he trapped her alone with the impostor by caving in the ceiling? Had he killed them all—her!—in his desperate gambit to defeat the crystalman?

"I wouldn't brood on Avena," said Dualayn as he knelt beside Ōbhin. The older man pressed a topaz healer against Ōbhin's foot and activated it.

Orange light flooded up Ōbhin's leg. The pain he'd been ignoring retreated before it. Ōbhin let out a sigh and glanced dull eyes at Dualayn. A drained lethargy weighed on him like a diamond-belly egg snake had crept into his nest, cracked his shell, and sucked all the yolk out of him. It left him hollow, on the verge of collapse.

Brittle.

"This is going to hurt," Dualayn said as he grasped Ōbhin's ankle. "I need to set the break so the Topaz can restore the bone properly."

Ōbhin shrugged. "I don't—"

Dualayn wrenched his ankle with a hard jerk. Pain exploded. The agony shot through Ōbhin's dazed thoughts, focusing his awareness on the grinding bones. He leaned back on his hands, head snapping back. His scream echoed around the ramp. It shouted back at him again and again. Then the topaz's gentle tone soothed the pain.

The touch of a mother. Of Aliiva's healing song.

"Avena is smart and capable," Dualayn said as he bound the topaz to Ōbhin's ankle. "She has the map and knows how to read the characters of Old Tonal. She'll find her way to the Hall of Communication on her own." He smiled. "She might even find it before we do."

"And if she can't?" Ōbhin asked, his mind working as the pain retreated. The topaz soothed him the way his mother's lullabies had as a small child. She would take off her mask to sing to him, exposing her face, her smiling joy and shining eyes, to her child.

"She can always leave. Unlike us, she has a path she can follow back out. We're the ones who might never find our way out."

Ōbhin glanced at Dualayn. "Fingers was carrying her. I saw that during the collapse."

Dualayn nodded. "I saw her standing before the ceiling came down. Perhaps she was injured by the car the crystalman threw, or perhaps she suffered more interference." He finished tying the knot and then clapped a hand on Ōbhin's shoulder. "She has a healer in her bag. Fingers knows how to use it. He cares for her. She'll be fine." Dualayn grinned, his gaze growing distant. "She's brilliant, you know."

The smile on Dualayn's dusty lips comforted Ōbhin. It shocked him a moment later. Dualayn didn't feel like a monster. At that moment, his thoughts cleared by the jewelchine driving back the pain, Ōbhin realized what angered him the most about Dualayn. Not just the betrayal, but the man's caring attitude. He genuinely wanted to help people. He was almost a good person who was too driven to accomplish his goals.

Too willing to cause a little pain.

It unsettled Ōbhin at how pernicious it was. This man would gladly spend all night fighting to save your life and the next day decide that chancing your death would aid him in understanding more about healing and jewelchines.

"We need to keep moving," Ōbhin said. He rose with a grunt. Putting his weight on his left foot flared the agony. The topaz healed him, but the bone felt fragile. He limped on it, keeping his weight on his right as much as possible. "How many packs do we have?"

"Three," said Miguil. "Only your pack was lost."

Ōbhin nodded. "Dajouth? Can you walk?"

"Better than you," the young man said, his face tight. "Black-cursed roaches and rats! Hurts to move my arm wrong."

Ōbhin almost laughed. "Eat rations, drink water, and then we'll find where this ramp leads."

The dream of the ancient battle against the ant demons—*are they the darklings?* she wondered—faded. Avena became aware of her body cradled in strong arms. Not Ōbhin's. She could feel a padded gambeson stretched over a large frame.

"Fingers?" she whispered.

"Yeah," he said, his voice hoarse. He slowed and stopped. "You okay?"

"My shoulder still hurts," she groaned.

"Lost the healer," Fingers said as he set her down.

"The ceiling collapsed on it," Bran said.

Her insides stiffened.

The impostor Bran stood nearby, holding a pair of diamond lanterns. He had his backpack on, a fine layer of gray dust covering his entire body. His eyes were shiny holes through the grime. The same coated her. She grimaced, feeling the grit in her mouth. Her lungs.

She coughed, leaning against Fingers while her insides broiled. She couldn't help but stare at Bran. The impostor. He looked at her with delight, a boyish smile crossing his lips. All a lie. That exuberant, bright lad snuffed out by this *thing*.

Then Avena blinked. "Where are the others? Ōbhin?" Her voice echoed down a tunnel. Water dripped from overhead. "Ōbhin!"

"He collapsed the roof of the carriage house on the crystalman," Fingers said.

"It was amazin' to watch," Bran said, his eyes bright. "He slashed the column." He mimed the swings while making swishing sounds. "Just like that. Then he baited the crystalman to punch it and . . . BAM! The ceilin' came down and crushed it."

"I ran carryin' you," Fingers added. "I followed the dogs. They were fleein' and they led me to this tunnel. Bran . . ." The older man studied the impostor with a strange look. "Bran followed us."

Fingers saw that final change, Avena thought, remembering Bran's neck getting twisted about by the impact of the metal carriage.

"I'm sure Ōbhin's alive," Fingers added.

"He was runnin'!" Bran said. "I saw that. He's gonna be fine. Him and Miguil and Dajouth." The impostor's dirty face tightened, brow furrowing. Caked dust cracked across his forehead. It had the consistency of cake frosting. "Dualayn's probably fine, too."

"I see," Avena said, her emotions battling. She wanted to draw her binder and beat the thing pretending to be Bran to a pulp. Nauseated disgust rippled over her. She pushed down impulses of revenge and anger. That wouldn't help. "Ōbhin will find me—us!—so let's keep going."

She focused on her mission while she struggled on what to do about "Bran." They continued down the tunnel, Avena taking a lantern from the impostor. Emeralds gleamed on her earthen gauntlet. It was still intact. She had her binder on her belt. She wasn't helpless.

Ideas bubbled through her mind, her rage simmering deep inside of her.

The tunnel led to a set of stairs covered in dust-laden cobwebs. Fingers just sighed and swept his hands through it as he led the way upward. The stairs were rusting metal, creaking beneath their feet. Tight and narrow, not the broad sweep they'd descended to the carriage house. With every step, Avena's stomach lurched.

The staircase shifted.

"Pus-filled roaches and crap-eating rats!" Bran cursed at one lurch, gripping the railing so hard his knuckles whitened.

Fear? Avena wondered. *Is it real? How can you fake posing as Bran so well?*

What are *you?* She was positive that foul Dje'awsa had created the impostor with magic, using crystals with blood and foul obsidian in ways that violated the natural laws of jewel machines and crystal harmonics. *Ust was brute work done fast in a few hours, but this thing must have been labor. A feat that took days or weeks to create.*

Fingers shouldered through a door. It squelched open, metal scraping on metal. A street lay before them, the middle buckled and sagged, massive cracks rending through the stone. The surface looked poured, like the concrete but different. It was black, almost like hardened tar. One of the jewelchine carriages lay crumpled beneath fallen debris. Some sort of arch lay over them like the street once had a ceiling for a short way. Part of it had collapsed. Red tree roots dangled down like frozen waterfalls.

"There's a sign," Bran said. "Can you read it, Avena?"

"Yes," she said, voice tight. She pulled her map out of her pack and studied it. She recognized one of the names. "Hall of Assembly is that way." She pointed off towards the darkness. The tunnel led that way for a short stretch. "That's where we should be going if Dualayn's map is accurate."

Fingers grunted. "He's a piss-drenched bastard, but he's not often wrong."

Bran spat, a look of disgust on his face.

Avena folded her map and led them forward; the dull throbbing in her shoulder continued. It hurt to move her arm, but she had full range of motion if she had to swing her binder or use her enhanced strength. The emeralds were dull right now, not active. They couldn't operate for too long despite being networked together to spread the load amid the smaller emeralds.

The tunnel ended at a pile of rubble, forcing them into another building. This one appeared to have been a shop of some sort. It contained rotting shelves. The items they held were long gone, scavenged by rats or maybe the dogs. Thick strands of cobwebs ran between the aisles, and a thick layer of dust covered the floor. A vein of ruby ran through the center preserving boxes on the shelves affected. One had only partly been transmuted, the side rotting away, revealing its contents to be some sort of clumped noodles or maybe twisted yarn.

It was hard for Avena to say.

They passed through a storeroom of decayed crates and a smattering of bones. Teeth marks from small animals decorated the remains, one bone gnawed for its marrow. Avena shuddered, her fingers twitching with revulsion.

Something whispered to Avena's right. She cocked her head, struggling to make out the sound. Was it a current of air caressing over cobwebs?

"A door's over here," said Bran. He grabbed it and twisted the metal knob. Metal clang and it came free in his hand, parts tinkling as they hit the floor. He threw it down and slammed his shoulder into it. The door slid a few inches outward into darkness.

thud ... thud ...

Avena froze. Bran whimpered. Fingers cursed.

thud ... thud ... Thud ... Thud ... THUD!

"Down," Avena hissed at the sound of the crystalman's approach. Was it the same one that they'd fought in the carriage house? Or were there more? Avena pondered these questions as she slid to her belly on the floor and killed her diamond lantern with a panicked thought.

Bran, crouching against the wall by the door he'd partially opened, turned his off by pushing a button on its top. The last Avena saw of him was a face full of fear. Dust filled her nose, tickling her nostrils. She clapped her hand over her mouth and nose, fighting against it. The thudding came closer, drowning out the whispering hiss.

"Elohm's blessed Colours," Fingers muttered nearby.

A glow filled the window. Soft. Red and green tinged with a purple hue. Fuzzy tingles rippled around Avena's fingers. She grimaced at the alien feeling assaulting her. Her mind recoiled from her flesh, wanting to flee it. This wasn't her any longer. She was a brain in a jar.

This is my body! screamed through her wavering thoughts as she fought against her mind's rejection of her flesh.

Fingers and Bran whispered as the signal interference built and built.

Ōbhin limped up the ramp. Despite the topaz healer bound to the outside of his left ankle, each step hurt. He gritted teeth as he followed the others up the ramp. It had a curving sweep that opened onto a street cracked and pitted. The road had sunk lower than the ramp's terminus, creating a drop Ōbhin's height. Dualayn scrambled over the edge, grunting and groaning while Dajouth leaped down.

Ōbhin slid off the edge, gripped it with his hands, and landed on his right leg, fighting to keep from putting weight on his left. Off-balance, he crashed to his right only to be caught by Miguil.

"Got you," he said, his strong hands gripping Ōbhin's arm. "I got you."

"Thanks," Ōbhin said, leaning on the other man for a moment. He cursed in his native tongue against the fresh wave of pain.

"Now that is promising," Dualayn said. He had picked up something from the ground. A sign of some sort. It was stamped into a silvery metal that didn't tarnish like others. "Hall of Communication is to our left."

Ōbhin limped on.

The sides of the collapsed road revealed broken pipes buried beneath the street. Some were big enough for a child to crawl through. The trench ran for nearly four hundred cubits, a makeshift tunnel before it ended at a ramp leading up.

They found a small void created by collapsed debris. In it, a door rusted in its frame. It didn't budge. Ōbhin's sword cut through it. On the other side lay a barricade of rotting furniture. They hauled clear a path and entered.

A dozen skeletons, with bits of flesh remaining, were strewn through the room. Some seemed to be huddled together in fear. At the stairs, they found another demon, warmth radiating from its scaled hide. Traces of red bled through the black decay of its scales.

"Fascinating, the way it still radiates heat," said Dualayn as Ōbhin limped past to head upstairs.

"Not why we're here," he reminded him, worry gnawing at him for Avena.

The next floor was a mess. Fighting had happened here. Sections of walls didn't look like they had collapsed but had been battered down. Bones lay scattered everywhere, dozens of skulls, and the bodies of two more demons. Other walls looked charred, and the debris littering the floor looked like an inferno had swept over them. The upper floors were gone, perhaps burned.

"Do you hear that?" asked Miguil as they neared an exit on the far side of the building from where they entered. "Thudding."

Ōbhin knelt down. He pulled off the glove of his right hand without hesitation. There were no women around, so no need to maintain his modesty. He pressed his naked palm to the floor, fingers pushing dust out of the way.

It vibrated with a rhythmic pattern. Footsteps. He swallowed as he glanced up at Dualayn. The man looked like he was straining to hear, hand cupped over his ear. Miguil's face, despite the coat of gray dust, had a green tinge to it, his free hand clutching his stomach.

"Crystalman," groaned Dajouth. "That's what you're hearing, ain't it?"

Ōbhin, over his pounding heartbeat, heard the distant thud with the vibration. Something large and heavy trudged near them. A cold, slick sweat broke out across his flesh. Avena was out there with the impostor. What if they ran into a crystalman?

"Elohm's blessed Colours," Dajouth whispered. "Not another one of those Black-cursed bastards. We barely survived the first."

"This worry has been gnawing at my mind," Dualayn said. He unslung his pack and opened it. He produced his map and pointed at a building he had marked on it. Crystal Sheriff Hall. "The crystalmen were created for law and order. They must have survived the death and collapse of this city and are still continuing their work."

"Three thousand years later?" muttered Ōbhin.

"Jewelchines, theoretically, can run forever. They will continuously be recharged by the Tonal Harmonics. The crystalmen were built to either have jewelchines that can power them all day long or to operate in shifts." Dualayn shifted. "The only limiter in lifespan is corrosion of the metal wires, but they have theirs buried inside the jewelchines or are using gold, which doesn't corrode."

"So this Crystal Sheriff Hall is their base?" Ōbhin asked. "So we need to avoid it."

"We need to reach it. That's where they are controlled." Dualayn looked up, tracks of sweat clearing streaks through the gray dust on his pudgy face. "We cannot defeat them in a fight. We were lucky you brought the ceiling down. We have to deactivate them. If they find us again . . ."

Ōbhin nodded. "Okay, how do we get there?"

"If we veer a little to our right, that should take us to it," Dualayn said.

"Uh . . ." Dajouth glanced out a broken window into the dark. "I think that thudding's comin' closer."

Fear squeezed Ōbhin's chest. "Lights out. No moving."

The three jewelchine lanterns snuffed out. Darkness crashed over Ōbhin. Black's weight pressed him down on his belly. His cheek rubbed into the dusty floor. The sounds of ragged breathing surrounded him. He was trapped beneath the earth again. Just like that day.

Panic fluttered through him.

He wanted to see. He moved his hand before his face, saw nothing. No flex of his wiggling fingers. His breathing increased into ragged wheezing. His heart fluttered with the intensity of an avalanche crashing down the mountainside.

The floor shook.

THUD! THUD!

The crystalman stomped closer. Light bled through the dust-smeared window. Scarlet and green. It didn't bring any relief. Death stomped closer and closer. His sword was useless. He couldn't hurt it. Couldn't fight it.

If it found them . . .

Diamond beams flooded on. The intensity blinded Ōbhin. He closed his eyes as the brilliance poured through the window. Light, it turned out, had just as much weight as darkness. It pressed down on his body, crushing him.

The crystalman stood right outside their building.

25

The thudding retreated.

An explosive exhale burst from Avena, her hot breath swirling around her hand. She pulled it away from her mouth, her need to sneeze dwindling. She rolled onto her back, panting as the darkness deepened. The glow from the crystalman dwindled as it marched farther away. The tingles in her digits retreated.

"Elohm be praised," Bran groaned. She heard movement.

"Don't move," Avena hissed. "Don't turn on the lanterns. Let's make sure it's far away from us."

"Yeah," Fingers answered, his voice hoarse and tense. "Elohm's Colours, I almost pissed myself."

Avena understood; her insides felt liquefied. She could have soiled her pants in a whole manner of different ways. She pressed up from the floor, the dust tickling at her nose. She sneezed three times and groaned, her shoulder throbbing from the violent expulsions of air.

"I can't hear them any longer," Bran said. The door creaked. "I think we can go on."

Avena hated agreeing with the impostor. "Yeah. One lantern for now. I wished we had diamond torches and not lanterns." Torches shone light in one direction instead of all of them. "Maybe we can rig up a cover for the lantern, so it only illuminates forward."

"Maybe," said Fingers. "But with what? I don't have any spare clothing."

"Just socks," she said. Her hand swept through the darkness until she found her lantern.

Brilliant light flooded the area. She winced against it, eyes squeezing shut. It shone through her eyelids, a red glow that still hurt. She looked away from it and opened them again, blinking a few times as they adjusted.

They crept out of the building, Avena's ears straining for sounds. They moved slowly, no one stepping heavily. Every step was placed with care. They found a branching tunnel. The crystalman had come from straight ahead and had gone left past them. Luckily, going straight and away from the crystalman was where they needed to go.

Patches of ruby became more common as they crept forward. The veins came every ten or so cubits, each thicker than her torso. They preserved the tunnel's original look, the pipes along the ceiling, the walls made of mortared blocks. They found a rat once, frozen in mid-scurry through the tunnels.

Crystal spiders lurked in recesses in the walls, scurrying away from their light. She felt their beady eyes peering out at the interlopers. Her hairs stood on end. The tunnel ended at a jagged break and spilled out onto a street almost entirely made of ruby. The buildings around them were transmuted, with only small gaps of normality between the transmuted city.

"We must be near the epicenter," Avena said, "of whatever caused this." Flashes of her dream rippled through her mind, the melting of reality.

"Poor bastards," said Fingers, nodding to the figures frozen in the jeweled street.

There were hundreds of them; men, women, and children. They looked frightened, their final moments captured on crystalline faces. Some held hands as they ran. A mother cradled a swaddled infant to her chest. A few of the carriages were in the road, their window panes made of ruby so thin they were translucent, revealing the shadows of the occupants inside.

The rubble above them seemed to be held up by poles that ran along the street with ruby wires strung between them. A few chunks of rock had fallen past the makeshift supports and crashed down to the street, some shattering a few of the statues.

Avena shuddered as they threaded their way through the frozen horde. A boy lay on his belly, struggling to stand while his father bent to help him. A woman supported a man who looked to be limping. Their clothing was strange, the women in dresses that fell to their mid-thighs and were often sleeveless. Others wore pants that fit them tight, hugging legs and buttocks. Men wore pants, some with shirts, others had jackets. A girl in a smock rode her father's shoulders. She looked behind, her awe captured on her cherubic face.

Every step broke off another piece of Avena's heart.

"What caused this?" Bran whispered, voice hoarse, his eyes gleaming wet. He stared down at a kneeling woman sheltering two small children with her body.

"The Shattering," Avena answered.

Fingers looked lost as he gazed at a young woman being pulled along by a man. She'd lost one of her heeled shoes, her skirt's swirling frozen forever.

Avena touched his arm. "Fingers?"

"She just . . . reminds me of my wife," Fingers said, voice thick. "She's got that same nose, you know." He glanced at her with red-rimmed eyes. "Same cheekbones."

"It's not her," Avena said. "Your wife's fine. She's back at your village." *With the miller,* Avena thought. *Happy without you.* After Miguil betrayed her with Pharon, Avena understood the bitterness a cheating lover or spouse could engender. "Let's keep going."

"Yeah," he croaked.

They left behind the crowd, passing the last few stragglers running from the transformation. The buildings on either side of them were all ruby, their tops lost to the destruction that had buried the city. Some final cataclysmic event had plunged the city underground and allowed the Upfing Forest to spread over it.

Fatigue gnawed at Avena's muscles. A hollow pit rumbled in her stomach. She wanted to keep going, driven more by her fear for Ōbhin. She wanted to find him before the crystalmen did. She needed to reunite with him more than she needed to fix her mind.

Finding the antenna wasn't worth the dangers. Not with those things lumbering around.

She glanced at Bran. He looked weary, too. He wiped sweat from his forehead with the padded sleeve of his gambeson. He'd lost his backpack, but they still had hers and Fingers'. Not enough food to last them more than a few days, and their two aquifers wouldn't produce quite enough water. They would be pushing themselves.

As fatigue mounted, she wanted to push herself through it and keep marching down the crystallized road. They passed scarlet buildings, the roofs buried. Signs led them on. They were approaching the Hall of Assemblage. From there, they could head towards the Hall of Communication. Ōbhin would be fighting his way through the ruby ruins to it.

"We should camp," Fingers said. "Choose a building, let's hole up in it, and get some rest."

"Has it been a day?" asked Avena. "How long have we been down here?"

Fingers shrugged. "I need the rest." He studied her. "I'm not as young as I used to be and not too stubborn to admit it."

Indignation flared through her. "I'm not stubborn."

Bran snorted in laughter. "I remember when you bullied your way into training with us."

"I didn't bully my way in," she snapped, rounding on the impostor. The fact he knew that disturbed her. "I insisted, and Ōbhin recognized the wisdom in training me."

"He recognized a battle he'd lose," Fingers said. "How 'bout that building? Looks good to me."

"Sure," Bran said and darted over on his long legs.

"Fine," Avena said. "We should set a watch after we eat then douse the lanterns."

"We'll be in the dark," whined Bran. A noticeable shudder of fear ran through him. Was it acting, or was the thing repulsed by the dark?

"Let's cover the lantern and leave a slit so we get *some* light," said Fingers. "If we face it away from the door, it should be fine. I don't think I can sleep in pure darkness. Not down here."

Avena relented.

The building had no intact door. They entered and found more statues, a family huddling beneath the table, the father in front, his children behind him held in his wife's arms. Avena blinked back tears as they passed deeper into the house into what appeared to be a kitchen. Half a loaf of bread sat on a cutting board, the knife resting beside it. Glasses and plates lay nearby, covered in square shapes, slices of bread with maybe meat or vegetables sandwiched between.

All rubyfied.

～

The crystalman's light swept over Ōbhin.

He lay flat, terrified to move. The crystalman tinkled like wind chimes as it scanned the room. Every ringing ding washed a cold wave of fear through Ōbhin. The skin of his arm crawled. A prickling sensation crept towards his wrist.

A pale spider moved across his skin, rustling the fine, dark hairs on his forearm. Revulsion rippled through him. It glittered in the light scanning the room. Its every step itched his skin. He wanted to bat it away.

Panic nibbled at his guts. Were other spiders crawling over him? He felt prickles tickling across his skin. Was a nest of the skittering things scurrying over him? Had they gotten beneath his leather jerkin? He wanted to thrash, to smack the filthy things away.

He squeezed his eyes shut. The spider neared his wrist and paused. A tremor raced through his arm, fighting to knock it off. Chimes tinkled. He couldn't move. He had to stay still. His jaws clamped tight against a primal snarl.

Leave! screamed through him. *Leave us alone! Niszeh's Black Tone! Disharmony curse you and your creators! Leave! Leave! LEAVE!*

The spider resumed its crawl. The back of Ōbhin's neck tingled. Was another creeping up to his hair? His breathing quickened. Unmanly terrors, shameful fears, swept through him. He wouldn't flinch. He would endure.

He'd once kept watching through a blizzard, guarding his post at the palace. Snow and cold hadn't stopped him. He'd endured it wearing only his winter *sherwani*, a long jacket that fell down to his knees, made of the finest Raqob wool, and heavy winter gloves, dyed the majestic purple of the warrior. An honorable hue to wear.

Not the filthy sable on his hands now.

The spiders itched all over his body. He wanted to scream. He forced slow breaths. The scanning lights bled through his eyelids. How long should it take the crystalman to search? Either it would notice them or move on. It had to pick one of those options.

Leave! Attack! Do something!

The lights snuffed out.

THUD! THUD!

The crystalman lumbered away. Ōbhin bolted upright, his hands slapping at his body. He smeared wet guts across his arm; one spider dead. He slapped at the others, voice cracking. He remembered his dead friend Carstin's fear of the damned things and understood why the man had once thrown his blankets into the fire in a panic.

"What's wrong?" Dajouth asked.

"Black-cursed spiders!" snarled Ōbhin.

"Elohm's blessed Colours," Miguil groaned. "They're in here?"

"They are everywhere," said Dualayn calmly. "We need to find the Crystal Sheriff Hall. It is our only hope. We must deactivate them. If we are caught again . . ."

Ōbhin nodded, his fear retreating. The spiders were gone. Dead.

They crept out of the building and moved through the street. It wasn't long before they found the strangest sight yet: a vein of ruby slashing across the ruined tunnel they wandered down. Dualayn paused, touching it in awe.

"Transmutation," he whispered. "It was thought impossible. Scholars in Abriss often delve into alchemy. They're always seeking a way to turn common stones into jewels. Diorite into emeralds or andesite into sapphires. Things like that. And yet . . . This has changed everything. The stone walls and floor, the metal pipes."

"There's another one," Miguil said, lifting his lantern and hurrying down the hallway.

Ōbhin limped after. His foot felt stronger by the hour, but still had a burning ache. Soon, they came across a second line of ruby rippled across the hallway. He glanced at it and frowned. They both seemed to point back in the same direction. *Radial? Do they all come from the same point?*

"This is clearly unintentional," Dualayn continued. "It's haphazard. Some force unleashed. Perhaps this is what caused the Shattering."

"Or it was done by that scaly demon we saw," Ōbhin said. He pulled off his glove and touched the transition from crumbling stone to smooth ruby. Hard, slick.

"Elohm's blessed Colours," breathed Dajouth. "There's a piece of a person here. A foot that ends at a sheer line. It's in a shoe. All ruby." He held it up in his left hand. The orange glow of his healer bled through the bandages of his splint. "He must have been running when this happened."

"Poor bastard," Miguil muttered. He drew the four points of the prism before him.

"Let's keep going," Ōbhin said.

"Yes, yes," said Dualayn, rising. "I hope this effect hasn't struck the Hall of Communication."

A new fear added to Ōbhin's worry for Avena.

As they pressed on, they found more transmuted structures until it grew so thick, everything was ruby. They emerged from a building onto a street crowded with statues. They were packed in, all fleeing in the same direction, running from the effect.

Chimes rang. White light sprang on.

Ōbhin cursed and threw himself back into the building, pushing Miguil with him. They all pressed against the walls as the crystalman plodded closer. Ōbhin's face tightened. *Has it been standing stationary? Niszeh's Black Tone, did we activate it?*

His stomach churned with bitter acids, but the automaton stomped by without stopping. It marched up the street and then its sounds retreated as it moved farther away. Ōbhin swallowed, mouth dry. He shook as he stepped out onto the road, Miguil muttering behind him.

Dualayn led them across the street, through the frozen people running in terror, and down an alley. The collapsed debris above their heads was held up by the tops of transformed buildings and streetlamps. The transmutation made things easier to move around.

On the other side, they opened onto a vast lawn, perhaps a park. The jeweled blades of grass twinkled in their diamond lanterns. In the center of it where there were no supports, the debris had buried the park, but along the edges was a line of some sort of broad-leaf trees holding up the rubble.

Another crystalman rumbled down a side street. They couldn't tell if it was a new one or one they'd seen. They crouched behind a wall of low hedges trimmed to form a boxy barrier. They waited with bated breath in the dark.

When it lumbered away, they crept down to another street. They could hear faint thuds echoing in the distance, reverberating through the place. They peered down the street. A large building lay reduced to ruby rubble. What remained of it was still standing, shattered pillars with stubby and broken arms like trees shorn of their branches, and had been transmuted into gleaming jewels. People seemed to be fleeing from it, caught up in the explosion.

"That's the Wave Resonance Beacon," said Dualayn as he paused to read a sign. The letters could just be made out in the diamond lamplight. They were slightly raised from the surface. "Perhaps the epicenter of this calamity."

"What does that mean?" Miguil asked. "Wave Resonance Beacon?"

"I am not rightly sure," admitted Dualayn. "I think it was a means of strengthening the Tones. Of enhancing their effects. Perhaps with so many jewelchine engines in one place, they absorbed so much harmonic resonance that it weakened its strength in this area. Jewel engineers have always thought of it as a resource you could never deplete, but that is not how the laws of entropy work. Energy, you see, is just the potential to do work. It is never lost, just changes into different forms."

"What?" Ōbhin asked, frowning.

"The jewels store potential energy in them. When turned into machines by the application of wires, they unleash that energy in different forms: thermal, kinetic, restorative, conjuration. It only makes sense that the universal Tones are generated by something and it is putting out a steady amount of potential work. The more jewelchines taking that potential, the less there is at any given time. So if you could generate your own potential work, much like we can make a fire to generate heat and light, that would be a boon."

"So it overloaded or something?" said Ōbhin, shaking his head. "And killed all these people?"

"And probably unleashed the demons on the survivors," Miguil muttered. "I haven't seen any scaly things frozen."

Dualayn nodded.

"Let's keep going," Ōbhin said and limped forward. The soothing love from the topaz faded. The soreness in his ankle swelled as he walked. His boots crunched on the dust and detritus covering the ruby road. His limp worsened.

"Perhaps we should camp," Dualayn suggested. "We're all tired. We can take a few hours rest and push on. I think we are still some distance away if we are near the Wave Resonance Beacon."

Ōbhin paused. Avena was out there, alone with the impostor. She might be hurt. Dying. She needed him to find her, but he had no idea how to do that. How could he locate her in this maze? He could only keep pressing on to the Hall of Communication and pray that she'd found her way there.

"I think he's right," Miguil said. "My feet are throbbing and my legs feel like lead. Your limp is worsening, Ōbhin. It's not smart to keep pressing on." The groom clapped a hand on Ōbhin's shoulder, pulling him up short. "If we're tired, we'll miss things. Set off a cave-in. Maybe blunder into one of those crystalmen."

Ōbhin stiffened. Fatigue nibbled at his thoughts. He could feel the effect of its drain on him. He wanted to keep pressing on; he did. He wanted to find Avena and hold her in his arms, but he was never going to do that if they got themselves killed.

"Fine," he said, a bitter taste staining the back of his mouth. Failure and fear. He felt like he was abandoning her to a cruel fate by giving up, but a dull ache throbbed across his skull. His ankle burned with every step.

She's smart. She'll find you. She'll deal with the impostor, too. He smiled for a moment as he thought, *She's too stubborn to let anything stop her. Not even losing her mind holds her back much.*

Avena couldn't sleep.

Not since Fingers gave Bran the watch. Their soft talking had roused her from exhausted sleep. She lay on her back, the hard floor providing an uncomfortable bed. She rolled onto her side, and she spotted the impostor. A dark figure crouched in the dark. They'd covered the lantern with Fingers's gambeson, wrapping the padded garment around it. Only a sliver of light bled out, a razor-thin strip of light spilling across the ruby floor.

She glared at the dark figure. The impostor.

Fingers's sawing snores rumbled through the kitchen. The thing that had killed two of her friends now stood watch over her. Avena didn't like having her life resting in the monster's hands. Bitter rage and grief swirled through her. Thoughts of pregnant Jilly and motherly Joayne danced through her mind.

She'd have to tell both women the truth. *I did nothing about this thing, and now Bran is dead.* She focused on him with such intensity, wishing her eyes could become flaming columns and immolate him. *Give me ruby jewelchines for eyes, and I'll roast his foul flesh!*

The figure shifted. "Avena?"

She didn't answer.

"Avena, is something wrong?" It crept towards her. His features grew sharper as he stepped out of the shadows. Bran's boyish face, smeared in places with dust but wiped mostly clean, became visible. He wore only a loose linen shirt, his gambeson stripped off. He crouched by her. She could smell his sweat. "Avena?"

"Yes?" she hissed.

"You're staring at me like you're mad," he said. "What's wrong?"

"What's wrong?" Her anger flashed hot through her. She felt like an igniter activated, heat sparking to life inside of her. She bolted upright and glared at the youth before her. "You want to know *what's wrong* with me?"

"Well, yeah," Bran said, wounded pain in his voice. "Why wouldn't I?"

"Who are you?" she demanded.

"What?"

"I asked who you *really* are!"

"I'm Bran." He smiled. "Who else would I be?"

"No, you're not Bran!" Her voice echoed through the room. Fingers's snoring stopped. "You murdered Bran just like you murdered Smiles! Who. Are. You?"

"I'm Bran," he said again with complete confidence.

She balled her right hand into a fist and pressed the activation button. The emeralds on her glove flared to green life as she threw her punch. Bran gasped in shock. She struck him before he could pull back. The shattering of his jaw resounded through the room. He stumbled back and fell, pulling the gambeson off the lantern.

White light flooded the room, shining with the Colour of Elohm's Honesty.

Bran's jaw rippled white. The bone popped as it set back into place. He worked his jaw, grimacing for a moment. Then he was whole again. He rubbed at his face and gave her a sullen look, full of shocked pain.

"Bran couldn't do *that*!" Avena hissed. She grabbed her binder and stood up. The amethyst flared to life. "What are you?"

Fingers sat up, his face half-shadowed.

"Tell me! Who are you? Who made you?"

Bran shrugged. "I'm No One."

"You killed him, didn't you?" Her voice cracked. Grief fed her anger, the emotion shining through her soul. An ugly light.

"I became him." The impostor smiled in that boyish fashion. "I am Bran."

"No, you're not!" She leveled her binder at him. "You're a thing posing as him. You were planted here to protect Dualayn by the Brotherhood!"

The impostor grimaced. "Yeah, but I don't like it." The thing spat. "I hate Dualayn for what he did to you, Avena. And to Kaylin. She used to be stern, but she slipped me sweetmeats and pastries when I was a child."

"You are not BRAN!" Avena boomed. Her rage echoed around them. She didn't care about the consequences. "Don't talk like you are."

"Avena," he said with such sincerity in his voice. He pled with his eyes, staring at her like a youth who knew he was in trouble but only wanted to earn forgiveness.

The look in his eyes, like the pair of them were friends, offended her. This wasn't Bran. This wasn't the boy she'd watched growing up. "Stop pretending you are him! That you have any feelings for me! Drop this act!"

"I do care for you. I saved your life, remember?" His head cocked. "I pushed you clear of the carriage. It hurt real bad when it hit my head."

Fingers stood and drew his binder. He activated it.

"You don't care for me!" she snarled. "You just saved my life because it was part of your mission."

"My mission is to protect Dualayn. I saved you because you're my friend. You—"

She swung the binder at him as hard as she could. It hissed through the air, emeralds blazing on her gloves. He moved back with a blur of speed, retreating faster than Bran—a human—could. His face twisted with pain. Emotion shone in his eyes.

"I'm your friend, Avena," he said. "I'll always be your friend."

"You killed my friends!" she rushed at him, tears spilling down her cheeks. He retreated and hit the wall.

She slammed her binder down. His cheekbone shattered as the purple bond snapped around his face. His flesh went white and modeled like clay. He kept staring at her as she drew back the binder.

"You murdered Bran just like you murdered Smiles, didn't you?" She swung again.

CRACK!

His arm snapped. Bone broke through the skin and pressed against his linen sleeve. The binding gripped his torso, pinning his limbs to his side. She sobbed with incoherent rage as she cracked the binder down on him again and again. She heard his collarbone snap. His forehead fractured. She broke his arm again and again and again. She bound him in a cocoon of purple energy.

Not once did he stop looking at her with pain. With betrayed hurt. His body healed faster than she could break him, than she could avenge her two friends.

She threw down her binder and punched him. Her enhanced fist slammed into the purple energy binding about his head. The force shattered it and broke his nose. Blood spurted. It splashed hot across her face as she cocked back her arm. She screamed out in pure pain and grief, vision blurred by hot tears spilling down her cheeks.

Her fist crashed into his face again and again. Green light streaked across her vision, blurred by the ferocity of her blows. She felt his cheekbones crumple. His jaw broke. He spat out bloody teeth. He sobbed, snot bubbling from his nose and staining her earthen gauntlet. Pain swam in his eyes.

"Stop staring at me like you're Bran!" she screeched, her voice echoing. "You're not him! You murdered him!"

His eye socket cracked, skin tearing across his temple.

He healed. His skin went white and molded faster than she could slam her fist in him a second time. A third. Fourth. New teeth grew to replace the ones she'd broken. She couldn't hurt him. Couldn't kill the thing that had stolen away two of her friends.

She grabbed the front of his shirt and stared at him. "Why! Why Bran? He was a sweet boy! Why did you murder him?"

The impostor Bran hiccuped through his sobs as she swayed before him. Then he jerked out of her grasp and ran for the doorway, his torso gripped by the bands of amethyst energy. Her knees buckled as he fled into the darkness of the ruins.

She collapsed.

Fingers caught her. His strong arms swept around her and pulled her into his chest. She couldn't stop the grief from gushing out of her. She could finally release the anguish for Smiles she'd buried deep in her soul. It mixed with horror for poor Bran. Fingers rocked her. She turned and pressed her face into his broad chest, her entire body shaking from the force of her grief.

He stroked her hair with a large hand and whispered soothing words. No different from a father comforting his child.

26

Miguil shook Ōbhin awake.

His eyes snapped open. Miguil's normally handsome face looked grayed and wearied, bags weighing beneath his eyes. Ōbhin groaned as he sat up. His ankle throbbed, though the pain didn't feel as bad. He was mending.

"My watch?" Ōbhin groaned.

Miguil nodded. "Been a few hours. I think. He's no help."

Ōbhin glanced over to see Dualayn at a window of ruby. The man sat in a crystallized chair, once padded and comfortable. He stared at the transformed glass as though he could see any detail through the translucent gemstone to the city of Koilon beyond.

"Wouldn't trust him if he was," Ōbhin said. "Okay, I'll take over. Get some sleep."

Miguil nodded. He stretched out on the gemstone floor near Dajouth. The younger man lay on his side. His arm was out of the splint. Though the healer had run out of energy, it had mended his bone. They were good at repairing simple things. It was the complex injuries, delicate work, that they were not so good at.

How many people did you kill to figure that out? wondered Ōbhin as he took his post by the door. He was only a cubit or so from Dualayn.

"I am glad we didn't go deeper into the ruins last time," Dualayn abruptly said. He leaned back in the chair. "I would have gotten her killed."

Ōbhin's spine stiffened. "Don't pretend that you care about Avena. You cut out her brain!"

"I had to experiment," Dualayn said. "I had to know it worked on others. I had refined my procedure to the point I was certain it would do no harm to her."

"And Kaylin?" Ōbhin asked. Everyone spoke of the cook as a lively woman before her husband's death when her mind was sound. Now she was confused about everything. Only while cooking did she have any focus. "Were you certain she wouldn't have been harmed?"

"Certainly," Dualayn said. "Another failure, I am sad to say. But I had the opportunity to use her. She came to me needing something to help her sleep after Dyain's death. It would have been a disservice to my experiments not to study her."

Disgust roiled through Ōbhin like the hurtling of snow down the mountainside. An avalanche of offended rage. "Why do you even need to cut out their brains? It makes no sense . . ." Ōbhin shuddered as a horrifying thought struck him. "You want to give your wife a younger body. You already learned from Avena that you could regenerate Bravine's damaged mind, but that wouldn't undo what the years have afflicted upon her body."

Dualayn glanced back to the ruby window.

"Maybe you would have stolen a younger body for yourself, right? Niszeh's Black Tone, that was what you were going to do. You just needed someone to perform the operation. Someone you thought would understand. Someone like Avena."

"She should understand," Dualayn said, anger thick on his tongue. "She'll be immortal. So long as the jewelchines are not disturbed around her mind. When her body wears out, she'll just have to find another. Young. Strong. Healthy."

Bile rose in Ōbhin's throat. It wasn't just horrified disgust he had for Dualayn, but that the man had worked with Avena all these years and didn't understand who she was. "You think Avena could do that? Could steal another person's life for her own?"

"Some people are better than others." Dualayn lifted his head. "A natural nobility, not one inherited from your parents, but one found in your flesh.

Immutable characteristics that make you brighter, more talented, possess skills that only a few others have. Like you."

"Me?" Ōbhin growled.

"You are a skilled swordsman." Dualayn glanced at him, eyes hard in the diamond light. They looked like agates with black pupils swallowing eternity. "It's beyond your blade. You are a master at fighting. You know how to move, when to act and react. How to read your opponents. That's a talent few others have. Avena is no different. She's intelligent. As smart as my son. If he had lived . . ." Dualayn shook his head.

"You didn't?" groaned Ōbhin. "Aliiva's Motherly Tone, say you didn't do that."

Dualayn glanced down to his lap. His hands rubbed together. "I learned a lot from Chames. I was so certain I had it all figured out. I didn't think I needed any tests. I was so wrong."

"You killed your own son?" Ōbhin croaked, his hand drifting to his sword.

"He was sick with spring fever. I had him sedated in my lab. I had it all worked out. I had practiced on cadavers. I was certain I could remove his brain and insert the obsidian mind without incident. I hadn't developed my heart pump. That's important. It's a ruby jewelch—"

Ōbhin's sword whisked out. His hand trembled as fury gripped him. Avena suffered so much guilt believing it was her fault Chames had died. She castigated herself time and time again for begging him to take her out of the house and on their picnic. All that blame she'd piled on herself. She'd buried herself in the garbage heap of self-recrimination. She thought she was as foul as the refuse she covered herself in.

She wasn't. *Dualayn* was.

"I wish the mob had killed you that day in Kash," snarled Ōbhin. He loomed over the scholar. The man's pudgy face whitened. Sweat broke out across his temples. "I wish they had torn you apart. I *killed* and *maimed* for you that day. I butchered frightened men to protect your life because I thought you were someone worth guarding. That you were making the world a better place."

"I am," he protested. "I made a mistake with Chames. Like I had with my wife. I hired the wrong man. He was supposed to fix her."

"You were supposed to fix Chames, and look what happened." Ōbhin brought the sword closer. "And Avena? You were only supposed to save her life, not butcher her. Now, look at what is happening to her. She has obsidian in her skull."

"It's harmless. Wives' tales. Superstition. The eighth gem is no different from the others."

"To her, it is everything foul and wicked, and you put it in her brain when you were healing her."

"I will fix her," Dualayn objected. "That's why we're here. I learn from all my mistakes."

"No, you don't. You still think people are just things you can play with. That you can use for your own gain."

"Progress has a price." Dualayn looked away from the sword. He trembled, sweat beading on his upper lip. "I didn't always believe that. I had to be taught this lesson. It's regrettable, but I won't apologize for it."

"I don't see you paying the price." Ōbhin's thumb rubbed against the button set in his sword's crossguard. All he had to do was press it . . .

He did.

The sword hummed to life. Dualayn flinched. He threw wild eyes at the blade.

"I can cut your brain out right here," Ōbhin said, his voice a harsh whisper. He leaned in. An intimacy had fallen over them. Something private. He moved the sword closer. "Huh? I can vivisect you right now. Let's see what I can learn from direct observation."

"Please," Dualayn said. He shrank back into the chair. "You need me. To fix Avena. To shut down the crystalmen."

Ōbhin pushed the button again. The sword's buzzing stopped. The razor edge of his tulwar gleamed in the light. He pressed it lightly against Dualayn's scalp, just enough to let him feel it. "One day, you're going to pay progress's price."

Avena's crying slowed. Stopped. Fingers held her the entire time. She found comfort in his arms; a different sort than Ōbhin gave. She held Fingers back, her arms barely able to wrap about his wide girth.

"I had a wife," Fingers said, his words slow. He broke the silence of the room.

"I know," Avena said. "She cheated on you. I'm sorry."

"No, she didn't," he said, his words creaking like a rotten floor devoured not by worms or beetles but by grief and pain. "Not ever once did she betray her promise to me. She loved me fiercely, but I hurt her. Bad."

Avena looked up at him. Anguish gleamed in his haunted eyes. "How bad?"

His body shook. "I killed her." He sniffed as he fought back his emotions, fighting to keep his pain bottled up. "I didn't mean to. I've been pretending that she's alive, that she just cuckolded me because it made it easier to live with it. I loved her so much. I still do. No matter how much she hurt me or how angry she made me. No matter what she forced me to do that day. I loved her so much, the only way I can live with myself is to make myself hate her. She left me no choice. I need to pretend I was doing the right thing when I hit her. That I'm a good husband." He snorted with disgust. It almost became a choking sob. "I even pretend that I send her money."

"Fingers," she whispered, confused. Shocked.

"But I'm not a good husband." He broke away from her and stepped back. She swayed, off-balance. "Not in the least, Avena. I killed her. I cracked her in the head with my hoe so hard I broke the haft. She collapsed. Dead."

Avena stiffened. She stared at the man before her. A sudden fear seized her, a dread to know the answer mixed with a glimmer of hope. A shining diamond beckoning her through the darkness always lurking in that empty place in her soul.

"Did you . . . have any children?" Avena asked, her voice raw and hoarse. "Daughters?"

Fingers looked away from her. "No."

Avena struggled with her memories to remember her father. In her mind, he was young and fit, tall and strong. He wasn't this heavyset man crushed by the weight of years. Her memories were blurry. She'd been so young, only seven, when her mother had drowned Evane in the whitewash and was about to do the same to herself. So young when her father had to swing his hoe out of fury.

"Are you . . . my father?" Avena asked. She trembled there, knowing the truth. She wanted to reach for him.

"No," Fingers said. "We didn't have any children." He sank down to the dusty floor, his back still to her. "Get some sleep, Avena. We got to keep going on."

"But . . ." She swallowed. "My father killed my mother like that. With a hoe. She made him furious because—"

"I'm not your Black-damned father!" He scrunched himself tighter and then the sounds of exaggerated snoring rumbled from him.

Avena's legs buckled. She sank down by the lantern. She turned it off, plunging them into silent darkness. She could feel him nearby as her mind struggled to process this revelation. She'd thought her father hated her for being too weak and helpless. For just standing there while Mother had drowned Evane. When he'd walked away after killing his wife, Avena had understood it was all her fault. By not acting, she'd forced Father to kill Mother.

Of course, he'd despised her. Hated her.

But now . . .

Fingers had come to work for Dualayn not long after she started as a maid. Had he been watching her from afar? Had he tracked her from her time at the orphanage with Daughter Heana and then to her new home at Dualayn's? Had he been close by her all this time?

Did her father not hate her? Was he merely a man destroyed by the fact he'd killed the woman he loved?

She felt too drained from her grief over Bran and Smiles to cry. She stared in her father's direction, listening to his breathing become regular, for his snoring to become real. She fell asleep listening to his breathing, and though she was in ruins, hunted by automatons, separated from the man she loved, she felt safe.

For the first time in fourteen years, her father was nearby to protect her from the monsters of the world.

27

Ōbhin kicked Dualayn awake the next "morning." Time had lost all meaning in the ruins of Koilon.

The old man started awake. He rubbed at his face, blinking in the diamond light shining down on him. He groaned and sat up. The others were already awake. Ōbhin felt rested enough. He couldn't just stay down here and do *nothing*. They had to find Avena and shut down the crystalmen before they all died in the dark.

"Break your fast then we're leaving," Ōbhin said.

Dualayn rubbed his rib. "Was it necessary to kick me awake?"

"Yes." Ōbhin faced the exit. "You're a heavy sleeper."

"We *definitely* tried to wake you up gentler," Miguil said.

Dajouth fought to contain a laugh.

"I am starting to realize there is nothing I can do to ever win back your good graces. If you could just imagine how things would be better if—"

"Don't." Ōbhin's shoulders rolled. "You're lower than a pus-filled roach scurrying through dog shit. You're a worm, Dualayn. You feed off everyone else and what you crap out is even worse."

Dualayn muttered about all the lives he saved as he readied himself to continue on.

Ōbhin tested out the healer. Aliiva's soothing Tone flooded through Ōbhin's ankle. The topaz had regained enough energy to operate while they rested. Dajouth held his own to his arm. Out of the sling and splint, he looked almost a hundred percent.

Not that they could do anything against the crystalmen.

Except collapsing ceilings. Ōbhin was lucky not to have died. If he did it again, others would be hurt.

They crept out of the house onto the crystallized streets. They soon found another transmuted crowd fleeing the destruction of the Wave Resonance Beacon. He couldn't help but stare at their frozen faces and wondered if they'd known they were about to die. There were so many families. The park nearby must have been full of parents and their children enjoying a leisurely day. Perhaps it was some sort of holy day.

A surcease from their labors.

They left the frozen crowd behind where the ruby transmutation petered out. Only strong lines radiated out after a certain point, like the energy bursting out had started out as violent spurts of focused change firing off in a hundred different directions before an explosion of transmutation engulfed the area. When they crossed the boundary out of transmutation, the ruins became choked off with rubble.

Ōbhin wondered if those past here had survived. Or were they the owners of the bones they'd found throughout the city? Had they escaped one catastrophe only to be slain by the lizard demons?

"That building, perhaps," Dualayn suggested, pointing to their left.

Outside of the transmuted area, traveling through the buildings made the most sense. They were connected by subbasements and utility tunnels that had survived the city's burial. As they traversed through a winding path, rats and other things scurried through the darkness. Perhaps some of those feral dogs watched them from hidden crevasses, waiting for the light to pass.

Perhaps an hour into their walk, a crystalman thudded on the level above them. They all froze, staring up at the ceiling of the tunnel they crawled through. Yellow centipedes scurried along it, wiggling out of cracks like they were fleeing the thing stomping above them.

"Think it knows we're down here?" Dajouth whispered.

Ōbhin had no idea. Every step prickled his skin. Avena was out there. If she ran into one of those things . . . He had to believe she was safe. That the thing posing as Fingers wouldn't harm her. It would need her to find Dualayn at the

Hall of Communication. She wouldn't retreat from the ruins. She would keep looking for them.

He would keep looking for her.

When the crystalman had passed, they continued on. The tunnel soon ended at a set of concrete stairs. The strange materials used—metal pipes and railings, stone poured to make bricks and floors—no longer astounded him. They had become his mundane existence so fast. They swept through the spiderwebs, finer than the ones created by the crystal spiders, and headed up the stairs.

It was another tenement building. They were common. They had to break through the door. They found it blocked by a pile of bones. They clinked and clattered as they pushed them apart. Devastation abounded. Parts of the walls had been battered down. Some showed signs of ancient fires. The bodies of three demons, their scales rotted black, lay scattered amid the remains of the humans. The heat bleeding from their bones suffused the air in suffocating currents.

How can they still be warm after all these years?

They crept through the room. Dajouth neared one of the dead demons. He prodded it with his binder.

"Black piss!" he yelped and jumped back.

Something hissed. Then a large, red-black snake crawled out of the body. It had an angular head marking it as a viper. Venomous. Dualayn recoiled back, bumping into Miguil. The pudgy man's lantern swung before him, sending shadows dancing.

Following the snake boiled out smaller ones. Little worms that scurried after the larger. Dajouth backed up more, his face pale. Ōbhin's muscles tensed as the larger snake slithered towards a pile of debris. Its snakelets followed and they all vanished into a hole in the wall.

"The heat," wheezed Dualayn. "They would enjoy the heat."

Dajouth shuddered, his arms shaking with violence like a dog trying to rid fur of water. "I hate snakes. Worse part 'bout goin' in caves."

Ōbhin eyed the demon corpse by him. Did its scales just move? Was another viper lurking inside? He gave it a wide berth as they crossed the room.

Hidden by a staircase, they found a crystalman had melted before cooling and solidifying. The concrete floor beneath it had cracked and warped, sagging in places. Another demon lay dead by the jewel slag. The outer layers of amethyst had melted enough for some of the emerald jewelchines inside to also run like wax across the purple gemstone. It formed strange patterns.

"Another way to fell them," Dualayn said.

"Just need a lizard demon," muttered Miguil. "'Course, you'll probably die yourself. Look at this room."

The walls were blackened with soot. The ceiling above was gone, the second floor burnt as the first. Charred bones, bits of femurs or cracked ribs, lurked in the piles of ash. Ōbhin hoped the owners had been already dead before being cooked to such temperatures.

They passed through the apartment building into another store. This one appeared to have sold clothes. Half-rotted scraps of silk or linen hung off corroded hangers. There were strange statues that had no features, only the suggestion of them. Decayed cloth draped them, appearing to display the wares. Through the center was a wide path cleared of any debris that led to a large hole battered through the wall. It opened onto a large space.

They stepped out onto a street. There appeared to be a glass roof over it. Surprisingly, it held up the weight of the earth and rubble that had buried Koilon. It spread far, supported by slender columns of rusting iron.

"Remarkable," said Dualayn. "It goes far. Hear the way our voices echo. This is bigger than the carriage house."

"What is it?" Ōbhin asked.

"Perhaps a plaza." Dualayn looked out into the darkness. "I think we are close. If I am correct, the Crystal Sheriff Hall lies in that direction." He pointed out into the murk. Their light didn't fall on anything.

"Look at the ground," muttered Dajouth. "I think he's right."

Ōbhin did, too. There was a path worn into the black, tar-like stone of the plaza, a smooth depression like a rut in a road. Something polished into the hard, rough surface by eons of travel. The width reminded Ōbhin of a crystal-man's width. He took off his glove and bent down. He touched the surface.

He felt the distant thuds of heavy steps.

"At least one patrols here," said Ōbhin. "Three thousand years walking the same path."

"It's not the only one," Dajouth said. "Look at that path leading to that hole in the building. They must have battered their way through the city, making their own streets to keep it safe."

Miguil groaned. "I can hear one. It's coming closer."

The thudding steps grew louder and louder.

～

It was quiet when Avena and Fingers broke their fast the next morning. They cut off slices of dark rye bread and ate it with the smoked chicken they'd packed. She washed it down with water from her aquifer.

Fingers wouldn't look at her. He had a tense wariness in his face, the look of an animal cornered in a trap and terrified there was no escape. She wanted to press him for knowledge about her mother and why he'd abandoned her. She feared to clutch too tight. Fingers's normal tough facade had been stripped away to reveal a fragile core, as delicate as a robin's egg.

Grasp it too tight . . .

Avena would be patient with her father. Just knowing that he had stayed close to her all this time had eased so much guilt from her. She felt lighter knowing that he had never hated her. That he still loved her.

After all, he'd descended into a black ruin to help her. He still walked with her even though he could find his way back out.

Instead, Fingers asked her about Bran. As they shouldered their packs, she explained all she and Ōbhin knew, their theory on how Dje'awsa had created him with sorcery, a subtler craft than the crude work the dark man had performed on Ust. The impostor worked for the Brotherhood, a guardian sent to watch over Dualayn. It could mimic a person so well it became them.

"Injuries are the only thing it can't fake," she said. "I don't think it can control its healing. It happens automatically. It's fast and strong, but I think becoming Bran has affected its personality. We can use that to kill it."

"Smiles is truly dead?" asked Fingers.

Avena nodded. "The night you went drinking with the new guards . . . We think it replaced him then."

Fingers spat out a string of curses. "Poor Jilly. A month with that thing pretendin' to be her husband. Wot, sixty or more days?"

"Yeah," said Avena, her voice tight. "I'll have to tell her and Joayne when we return . . ." She scrunched up her eyes. "She loved Bran."

"Doted on her youngest son," he said. Knuckles popped. "When we find that bastard, I'll help you wring its scrawny neck."

She smiled, feeling comforted by his presence. She wanted to take his hand like a little girl, to be that innocent child once again. To hold the doll he'd made for her with a face stitched on by her mother. To run through the fields with Evane laughing at her side. The other half of her stolen away.

You would have liked Ōbhin, Evane, thought Avena. The emptiness inside of her didn't feel so wide today. Fingers's revelation had filled in the pain in ways that Ōbhin couldn't. He could make her forget, but he couldn't help her forgive herself.

As they moved through the transmuted ruins in the direction of the Hall of Communication, she felt eyes watching her. She shuddered, fearing Bran lurked just out of sight. She didn't know what the thing's capabilities were. How far its abilities stretched. Did it need to eat and drink? To sleep? Could it see in the dark?

She kept glancing around, searching for the impostor. She never saw a sign, just felt that prickle at the back of her neck.

"This isn't good," she said as they reached the edge of the ruby transmutation. The debris held up by the streetlamps and transmuted buildings crashed across the road before them. "We're so close to the Hall. Another few blocks that way."

"Can't help but detour around it," said Fingers. He nodded to a building to their right. It would take them north. "That one?"

She sighed and nodded.

They ventured into the building. The collapsed floors above forced them into the basement. They found another carriage house full of the horseless carriages. A few lines of ruby transmutation knifed throughout while the floor boiled with cockroaches. They were big and brown, running across the debris in a vast wave.

She grimaced with each crunching step across the tide of the filthy things. She kept having to kick her boots to knock them off of her. Fingers slapped at his calf. One must have crawled up beneath his trouser leg.

Relief burst from Avena's lungs after crossing the far end of the disgusting migration. Here a set of stairs led upward. To reach them, they had to wade through knee-high water. It spilled over the cuff of her boots, her wool stockings absorbing the brackish liquid. It smelled worse than a swamp, all rotten muck and filth.

I'll need to take a bath for a month once we're out of here. Two full turnings of all seven moons!

She climbed out of the foul liquid onto the stairs. It led to an underground path that took them almost in the direction they needed to go. One of the lizard demons lay dead in it, head crushed by a half-melted pipe. Bones lay scattered around it. Scavengers seemed to avoid eating the demons while having no qualms about humans.

The tunnel ended at another set of stairs that led to an alley between two buildings. The debris loomed over her head. A rusting girder thrust down before them out of the stone. She slid past it and frowned at a sound drifting through the air.

Whispers.

It was like people were talking just a room over. Her head cocked to focus on the noises. Fuzzy tingles prickled the tips of her toes and fingers even as hope surged through her. Talking meant other humans. Her friends.

"Ōbhin!" she shouted.

"What?" Fingers asked.

She darted forward down the alley to where it opened onto a narrow street that seemed mostly clear of rubble. A few large piles of it had crashed down from above, but it seemed to go for blocks. The prickling spread up to her hands and itched at her legs.

"It's Ōbhin and the others!" she shouted, excitement mounting.

"Wait, Avena!" Fingers growled. "I don't think that's them!"

She burst out onto the street and held her lantern up high in her left hand. Brilliant light shone across the neighborhood. The buildings here were close enough together to provide the support to keep this area from being entirely swallowed.

"Ōbh—"

Fingers's dirty hand clamped over her mouth. He pulled her back. Indignation surged through her. She thrashed, the whispers swelling. They were so close. Why was he stopping her?

The crystalman stepped out of the next alley down the street. Its diamond eyes shone bright and swept at them. An alarm blared loud from it, ringing through the ruins. With lumbering steps, it marched at them.

Avena stopped fighting against Fingers.

28

"Idiot!" she snarled at herself as she and Fingers ran back down the alley. The booming steps of the crystalman thundered behind them. The alarm screeched and echoed through the ruins. Something groaned above. Her shoulders crawled, realizing the ceiling was shifting. It could collapse on them.

The light from their lanterns swung wildly, dancing and painting the alley with splashes of illumination and patches of night. They had to find some way to outrun it. To lose it in the maze of buildings and half-collapsed tunnels.

If they made the wrong turn and were cornered . . .

She threw a look over her shoulder. It had reached the mouth of the alley and marched down it with the implacable force of a flash flood. Nothing could stand in the way of a boiling torrent of water surging down a river, destroying docks and bridges, devouring the banks and spilling into towns.

"Door!" Fingers shouted and threw himself to the right. He slammed into a rusted slab of iron and bounced off. "Black-filled roaches!" He threw himself into it again, the metal groaning. Flakes of orange-red drifted off.

The crystalman thudded closer.

"Out of the way!" she shouted, clenching her right fist to activate her earthen gauntlet.

Emerald spilled across Fingers's frightened features. He threw himself back. Her shoulder ached, still injured from yesterday, but she could move it enough. She thrust her hand, palm open, at the door. The metal groaned as she pressed on it. The emeralds surged strength into her, resonating with the Colour of Forgiveness.

Or the Tone of Earth, as Ōbhin would put it.

Metal flexed, moaned. Patches of rust sloughed off like the winter coat of a yak. The crystalman's alarm rang in her ears. She could feel the automaton almost on top of them. Fingers screamed. Her shoulder burned, the pain a shouted warning at her. She felt the ball of her humerus grinding in the socket close to dislocation.

She roared and pushed hard.

Something snapped. Metal clattered to the ground on the other side. The door swung open, and she charged through it into a hallway covered in a thick layer of dust. Clouds burst around her feet as she rushed forward. Fingers followed, his boots stomping behind her.

"Elohm's bright Colours illuminate our souls! It's right behind us, Avena! Run!"

The entire building shook. A mighty crash of bricks were collapsing. The walls around her flexed and warped. She knew the automaton had battered through the wall to chase after them, destroying vital structural supports of this building. It held up more than just its own weight, but all that earth and the Upfing Forest above them.

She turned in an open door and darted into an apartment, passing rotten furniture she hardly had time to notice. Something yelped and darted out of her way. She plunged into another room and gasped at the debris choking the windows, blocking any escape that way.

The crystalman crashed onward in a wave of shattering masonry.

"There," Fingers pointed. "Stairs!"

She had no idea if that was a good idea. She had no time to think. Her feet were already racing for them. Her lantern danced in her hand, swinging light before her. She raced up the stairs two at a time. Sweat spilled down her face. All those mornings running laps around the manor with the rest of the guards gave her the stamina to reach the top with her breath.

She found herself in a hallway. It led the length of the building. The far end was lost to the gloom, but she thought it looked open. A dark portal through which her light couldn't reach. A way out of here and away from the crystalman smashing below.

"It's on the stairs!" growled Fingers. "Go, go!"

Avena sprinted down the hallway. Something heavy crashed below. She threw a look behind her. Dust billowed up the staircase. It flowed around Fingers, swallowing him for a moment in a dusty haze of brown illuminated by his lantern.

"Did the stairs collapse?" she shouted.

"Think so!"

She slowed as she reached the window. It was clear. Below, she could see rubble piled around the building's foundation, debris from the collapsed ceiling. There was a trough of dirt carved up into the earth above them. The top of his building and the next held up the rest of it. She could see tree roots thrusting through the collapsed ground. The tendrils seemed to be holding the soil together, keeping more of it from collapsing down on them.

Across the alley, another window loomed. Its glass had long since broken out, leaving only a few sharp teeth thrusting up, all covered in a thick layer of grime. She bit her lip and looked down at the debris. They were higher up than they should be, or the ground here had collapsed over the eons.

"Should we climb down?" she asked. "It's about twenty cubits down." At that height, they risked breaking an ankle.

"It might batter through the wall while we're doing that." Fingers looked behind him. It hadn't followed them. She could hear it crashing through the house below.

"We can go up maybe another level." Avena thrust her head out the window, peering up. Then she looked left and right. The alley on both sides seemed to end in walls of collapsed rubble. "We have to get across to the other building."

"Too far to jump," Fingers said. "Close, but I couldn't make that."

Avena shook her head. The other window was so tantalizingly close. "Let's climb down and then up the—"

A crystal fist burst through the floor a cubit from her foot. Broken concrete rained down on the automaton. It rang like wind chimes. Another fist smashed upward, erupting closer to them. The floor groaned beneath them, cracks radiating out from the blows.

Fingers growled and seized her. She gasped as the larger man lifted her with ease, thrusting her out the window. No, he didn't thrust her. He threw her. She screamed as she soared across the gap between the two buildings. She dropped her lantern. It tumbled low and broke against the wall, snuffing out.

She slammed into the lip of the other building's window. The air burst from her lungs. She groaned, her arms thrust through the opening. Her booted feet skittered on the building's face as they searched for purchase. Almost immediately, she started falling. She screamed, the frame scraping at her skin through her shirt, at her breasts.

She caught it, throbbing scratches beating pain with her heartbeat. The soles of her boots gripped crumbling brick and rotten mortar. She climbed up and spilled over into a room. She landed with a dusty thud, millennia of destructs bursting around her in a writhing cloud.

A skeleton lay beside her. She hardly noticed as she rolled to her feet and whirled to the window. "Fingers!"

He had his back to the far window. Concrete cracked. The crystalman was about to batter through the floor. She could see its amethyst body through the lower window. Fingers turned around and threw his lantern across the gap. The light soared at her. She caught it.

"Go!" he shouted. "It's fixated on me. You have a chance."

His emotions were writ across his face, that desperate love a parent had for a child. He would make sure she lived. Emotion stung her eyes more than the dust billowing around her. She shook her head. It wasn't fair. She had just found him. Realized who he was. She couldn't lose him again. Not so soon.

The whispers echoed through her mind. Numb fingers clutched the lantern. She held it high, desperate to find *something* to bridge the space.

"This is a problem," whispered Ōbhin.

They had snuffed out their lanterns. In the dark, the crystalmen appeared as faint glows of purple moving through the vast space. As his eyes adjusted to the heavy darkness, he spotted another glow even farther away. The automatons patrolled before the very building they needed to enter to shut them down.

Ōbhin's mind worked as he watched them. The open plaza appeared to be

Ruby Ruins

twice the size of the grounds upon which Dualayn's manor rested. He judged it to be as big as St. Jettay's Square before the Temple of the Seven Colours. At least two crystalmen circled it. While there seemed to be some obstructions that occasionally blocked the sight of the automatons, there wasn't much cover to hide them for more than a few heartbeats.

"There's no way we can cross that unseen," said Ōbhin.

"We must," said Dualayn. "Look. You can see our destination in the glow of the far one. Those steps."

"Can we work our away around through the buildings?" asked Miguil.

"There are more around than those two," said Ōbhin. Their presence seemed to confirm Dualayn's theory. The crystalmen were patrolling close to where they were controlled. They would stay by their headquarters. Their creators would have ordered them to guard it. Without anyone alive to give them commands, they now followed their previous instructions.

Ōbhin glanced at Dualayn. "You are certain you can shut them down?"

"Absolutely."

Just like you were certain Chames wouldn't die, or Avena wouldn't lose control of her body. Ōbhin's shoulders itched. Avena was out there. He wanted to rush out there and shut them down. To end the most dangerous threat to her life.

Being brash wasn't the solution. Slowly. Stealthily. Taking their time to reach it. Miguil was right. He couldn't let his fear of 'what ifs' drive him to do something reckless. He drew in slow, measured breaths.

"Okay, we'll work our way—"

The distant alarm echoed through the ruins. The screeching sound dumped frozen snow down his back. Dajouth groaned and Dualayn muttered beneath his breath. Ōbhin gripped the debris they hid behind.

The crystalmen had found Fingers and Avena. The luxury of time evaporated.

"I'll distract them," Ōbhin said and rose. He drew his resonance sword and picked up a lantern. His eyes had adjusted to the near night, the light glowing from the nearest crystalman surprisingly enough for him to see shadowy shapes of obstacles before him. "You rush for the building as they chase me."

"That's insane," Miguil hissed. "They'll kill you."

"He's in love," Dajouth said. "That makes every man crazy. Ōbhin, we'll do it. I'll drag Dualayn in there myself if he objects."

Ōbhin nodded and burst from his cover. He raced across the craggy surface of the plaza. He had made it twenty cubits away when he activated his sword and lantern. Light flared around him. The nearest crystalman stopped and began to turn. Ōbhin slashed his blade at it, striking its arm as he rushed past.

The ear-splitting screech, like the rising cry of a hawk that never stopped for breath, burst from the automaton. Ōbhin kept running. He leaped over a pile of rubble. Ahead, he made out a street leading into more buildings, their top levels crushed by the falling earth.

To his left, a third crystalman lurched to life and trudged out. The far one marched at him. He had three of them following him. It had to be enough. He was placing his trust into the hands of a man who had proven himself unworthy of guarding the midden heap.

It wasn't more than ten cubits separating the two buildings. That wasn't that far. Just two of Avena stacked together. She had to find some way to save her father. She ignored the whispers echoing through her head. She rubbed her tongue across the roof of her mouth.

It felt fuzzy, like it was covered in prickling caterpillar down.

She couldn't collapse. She had to keep her mind here. She fought against the signal interference, hoping the fear flooding through her body would help to keep the connection between her mind and flesh strong.

This room had debris like the rest of the ruins. The interior walls here were made of wood. There were planks. . .

Planks!

She grabbed the longest one she could spy, one end snapped off. She didn't have time to measure. To plan. She picked it up and thrust it through the window. With a mighty heave, she shoved it across the intervening space, screaming her father's name.

He grabbed the end and lifted it up. It stretched across between them. It was barely wider than Fingers's thigh. It had to be enough. She pressed her hands down on her end, anchoring it. Tears beaded her eyes.

"Please!"

He climbed out onto the window and groaned. He didn't stand but crawled across it. Dust billowed behind him. The automaton still punched. For a wild moment, she thought he would make it. He was somehow crossing the gap, his gaze locked on hers. The board creaked and bowed as he neared the middle. It slipped in her grip, wanting to slide free and fall. Nothing anchored the other end, allowing it to move.

She pressed down with all her weight. Her entire body felt light. Alien. Her vision swam. She felt on the verge of her collapse. The numbness spread up her arms. Her legs. She couldn't feel the plank shifting beneath her hands any longer.

"Hyurri," she slurred. "Fyingyers!"

The plank cracked. Fingers growled and threw himself the last few cubits. She grabbed his outstretched arms with numb digits. The board fell away. It slammed into the debris below as she hauled him back.

Her fuzzing feet tripped over each other. She squeaked and crashed to her back, Fingers on top of her. The weight drove the air out of her lungs a second time. Her vision washed black for a moment. She almost lost her body. The connection between thought and action grew tenuous, a slender thread.

The crystalman slammed into something. The wall? She struggled to move. Fingers rolled off of her and shook his head. He snatched up the lantern she'd set down to thrust the plank across. He whirled around as she fought to rise.

"Fyingyers . . ."

He glanced down at her. "Black's foul piss, it's happening?"

She nodded and managed to sit up. His right arm swept down and hauled her to her feet. She staggered against him. The world swam about her. She wouldn't surrender. She wouldn't give in to the signal loss. She would stay in control of her body.

They staggered forward, the alarm fading behind them. The whispers dwindled. With every step, more and more control returned to her body. She stopped being half-dragged by Fingers. She started placing her feet with strength.

They were leaving the interference behind.

"There are stairs," she said, the words coming clear.

"You're getting better," Fingers said.

"It's the crystalman," she said, frowning. The whispers were coming from the automaton. The thing was *talking* to something else. It was sending strong tones through the immaterial. Was the antenna attached to her brain picking up interference? Was that even possible?

She had no idea. She didn't understand how half of the hits worked. But she could feel it retreating. The whispers were muted as they descended the stairs. The fuzziness retreated down to her fingers and toes.

"I can detect them," she said, sparks of excitement bursting through her. "I can tell when they're close."

"Yeah, so can I," muttered Fingers. "Hear that one bellowing? I think it's bringing help." He frowned. "Is a second one blaring an alarm?"

Avena shook her head. She couldn't tell. The awful screeching radiated around them as they moved through the first floor of the building. Everything down here looked strangely preserved, just covered in stains of filth on the wall and a thick layer of dust. Nothing lurked in here. No bones littered the floor.

"Door," said Fingers, holding the lantern to his right.

She nodded in agreement. They crossed to it. She bit her lip. The whispers echoed through her mind. They were growing stronger again. It was like she was hearing a second voice now. Two of them. Three. Maybe four. It was so hard to tell.

"More coming," she muttered, a hunch bubbling in her mind. "The controller is directing them at us."

"Then let's move," Fingers growled.

She nodded, the fuzziness creeping up her. Was the presence of more intensifying the interference? She swallowed, unsure. She clung to Fingers as he thrust open the door. Their lantern spilled out onto a street. Large mounds of rubble littered it. One had crushed a demon, its leg thrust out from beneath blackened stone.

"Comying cloyser . . ." She held him, the whispers screaming in her mind. The alarms blared all around them.

"There's light," Fingers said, looking to their right.

The unmistakable shine of a swinging lantern illuminated the intersection. Then Ōbhin appeared and turned towards them. He spotted them as he ran at full speed, his resonance blade held in one hand, the lantern in the other.

"Run!" he shouted.

The whispers slammed into Avena's mind. Her body went limp, unable to fight off the interference. She felt her thoughts plunged into an empty void. The whispers were all around her. But there was something else. Another voice. One that she had followed before. A voice that had called to her the other times she'd blacked out.

Ruby Ruins

She entered a dream.

29

In the dream, she screamed with frantic desperation. Avena didn't understand the words pouring out of her mouth. She had her hand outstretched before her, diamond light gleaming at her fingertips. Before Avena stood a man. Raya's lover.

He stood rigid, his arms pinned to his sides. A web of darkness slowly crept over him. Thick tendrils of gleaming obsidian coated him like an invisible spider slowly cocooning him. On the edges, the darkness vanished, leaving behind unmarred reality.

It's a rent, Avena realized. *One of the rents the demons poured out of.* She could see the hole in the fabric of the world repairing itself. It wasn't a spider cocooning him, but a weaver stitching cloth together with threads of black.

He was on the other side.

She couldn't touch the threads. Some force repelled her light. She pushed and pushed. Tears spilled down her face. Raya's lover stared at her with sadness in his eyes while his face held calm acceptance. The rent knit tighter and tighter. It swallowed his torso. His shoulders and neck.

Only his face remained.

"Raya," the man whispered as the darkness wove across his face.

Then all that stood before her was the devastation of a battlefield. She sank to her knees and buried her face into her hands. She sobbed and sobbed, pouring out all her grief. Avena had felt this pain once in her life.

When Dualayn told her that Chames had succumbed to the spring fever.

I'm so sorry, Raya, Avena thought. She *was* dreaming the White Lady's memories. This had to be the Shattering when the Archon-Supreme had led the devas into driving the darklings back. The healing rent must have been a Warding being established, banishing the demons and other monsters from their world.

But why was Raya's lover trapped in there?

I'm so sorry! The words felt hollow. Avena didn't know if the White Lady could understand her nor if she could even affect anything in this dream.

Raya beat at the earth next, liquid diamonds falling to the scorched earth. She threw back her head and let out a pained cry of anguish to a sky covered in a haze of gray dust. Pure grief, undiluted by any other emotion. Her entire body shook.

Avena wanted to hug Raya. The memory of their last conversation, when the White Lady had kissed her forehead, resonated through her. The woman had mentioned losing someone and wanting to get them back. This was what she wanted.

To free her lover from this barrier.

From the Warding.

What did that mean? There had been breaks in the Warding in the past. When her ancestors had first landed at the mouth of the Ustern River a thousand years ago, they had found the darklings free. Boan Sword-Arm had to use three artifacts—supposedly, the Amethyst Band held by the Kings of Lothon, the Lost Emerald Spear of Ondere, and the Healing Staff of Roidan—to reestablish the Warding and trap the darklings back in their black domain.

In this dream, Raya's lover seemed to be at the focal point of the closure, the point where the weave between realities was completed. Avena knew the weakness of any weaving was at the end, where the tails of the threads used to create it lay. If you were to pull on one of those, you could unravel everything.

Did the White Lady seek to unravel the Warding?

Before Avena could even consider this, whispers intruded on the vision. She knew what they were now. Why she was having such problems with her body around the crystalmen. She was hearing the commands they received.

Impulses that she could almost make out. There was a single voice giving orders, and they were responding. She concentrated on them.

Her dream of Raya's life faded.

Avena floated in a dark void. A place of nothing. There were harmonics that rippled in the background. They were hard to make out, faint like the ringing in the ear after a loud noise. They were all merged together and yet separate. They had . . . auditory flavors to them.

Fiery.

Soothing.

Gusting.

Radiant.

Was she hearing the tones that powered the gems? Were these the reverberations of creation that the jewelchines tapped into and channeled?

Maybe.

But there was something else. She could hear a commanding voice over them. It boomed to her right. It came from a construction of diamond and obsidian, the two jewels merged and connected to each other via an intricate network wire trapped inside of them. The device floated with her, projected into the immaterial like her thoughts. The jewelchines went beyond any she could imagine. It seemed like magic to her.

It was sending signals to a dozen units. Four of them were close. Those were being directed to chase. To hunt. Demons had intruded. They had to be destroyed. Koilon had to be defended. In the commands were images.

Fingers and Ōbhin ran, a limp figure in the Qothian's arms.

That's me in Ōbhin's arms. We're being chased. Understanding crashed through her. *The voice gives purpose to the crystalmen. They're nothing without it. They have no minds, so the ancients* created *a mind to control them.*

Avena knew what she had to do.

30

Avena collapsed as Ōbhin reached the pair.

"Avena!" Fingers gasped, clutching her body and keeping her from hitting the ground.

Fear consumed Ōbhin's shock at seeing the pair. The crystalmen still lumbered after him. His plan to only risk himself had backfired. Now Avena was in even more danger. Fingers struggled to lift her limp form.

Ōbhin couldn't allow that. He wouldn't entrust his Avena's life to the impostor. With practiced skill, he slammed his tulwar into its sheath as he stopped before Fingers. Fear gleamed in the impostor's face, faking the older man with skill.

"I have her!" growled Ōbhin. He ripped Avena from Fingers and hefted her across his arms. He clutched the lantern still in his left hand, her legs draped over that limb. "Let's move!"

"Right!" Fingers shouted and ran the only way they could.

Away from the crystalmen.

They all blared alarms. The sounds resounded through the alley. Ōbhin's legs already burned from his run. *How long will it take Dualayn to turn it off?* Fear gripped his chest that the old man was waiting for him to be killed.

Once I'm dead, he won't have to worry about my sword taking off his damned head!

The thought poisoned Ōbhin. He held Avena tighter. He rounded a corner, carrying her limp form from the charging monstrosities. Something crashed and boomed. The road shook beneath his feet. Fingers cursed.

"The one chasing us is barreling through the building!" he shouted.

"What's one more?" Ōbhin asked with flippancy.

A dreaded certainty that he would die filled him. If he could just save Avena. If he could do one bright thing with his life and help her to find stability, he would gladly die down here. It was only fitting. He shouldn't have walked away from the mines beneath Gunya. Not alone. He'd killed the man who'd helped him escape.

No, I never escaped. I've been wandering lost in those mines ever since.

He felt so close to the light. The surface was near. He pushed through the fatigue not for himself but for Avena cradled in his arms. The strained tendon in his ankle burned, growing weaker with every step. It was one more pain he embraced. He could take it.

He took another turn, lost in the maze of buildings. If he couldn't lose the crystalmen, he had to find a place to set down her body where they wouldn't see her but lumber past chasing him. She'd be alone, but she'd wake up and be out of danger. His eyes scanned the rubble of the streets.

Everything looked so obvious. He didn't have time to do more than drop her. The crystalmen were close. He threw a look over his shoulder to see them already rounding the corner. Three of them marched with an implacable gait.

"Next left!" Fingers shouted. "Maybe we can duck into a building."

Ōbhin went right instead. He darted down the road. It was opening up. There was less debris. He passed a rusting horseless carriage and leaped over a corroded streetlamp. His feet landed hard, steps echoing around him.

"Why not left?" Fingers growled.

"Liked right better," he panted and then took the next left.

There was something familiar about this street. The light from his lantern spilled before him. The crystalmen thudded behind him. Their steps all merged together. The buildings ended as the street opened up onto a large plaza.

He'd run back to where he'd started his mad distraction. Maybe with more space, he could split off from Fingers. Then the impostor could do some good by leading a few of the automatons away so he could get Avena to safety.

Miguil and Dajouth will look out for her. Dualayn will probably shut off the machines before she's killed. He still cares for her in his own demented away.

Lights gleamed at the far end. Diamond lights. The others had turned their lanterns on, illuminating the shape of an impressive building looming behind them. Walls smooth. There was a frieze over their heads, choked with dirt and too far away for Ōbhin to make out the details. He ran towards them.

And if Dualayn doesn't care about Avena, he'll care about his own life.

Fingers thundered behind Ōbhin, puffing and wheezing. The run was taxing Ōbhin, too. He was fighting for breaths. The metallic flavor of blood filled the back of his mouth. Muscle fatigue consumed his thigh muscles. His healing ankle burst with pain. His gait became an uneven limp, but he couldn't stop. His fear for Avena dragged him along like a panicked horse dragging its cart.

Halfway across the plaza, Avena burst into squirming activity in his arms. Her sudden movement threw him off-balance. He gasped and pitched forward. He failed to arrest their fall. The diamond lantern spilled from his grasp and crashed on the ground.

Went out.

He landed a moment later. They tumbled in a heap, rolling across the cracked and worn pavement. She cried out as the world spun. Then she ended up on top of him, her knee in his face, her elbow digging through his leather jerkin into his guts.

"Ōbhin?" she gasped.

"Yes," he groaned, bruises throbbing across his back and buttocks while his left arm burned from abrasions. "You're okay?"

"I know what I have to do!" She rolled off of him.

"What?" he called, shocked that she was acting without any confusion. "Avena!"

"Distract them!" she cried as she broke into a run for Dajouth and Miguil. The pair were on the steps, both holding binders.

"Come on," Fingers growled and seized Ōbhin's arm. The impostor hauled the Qothian to his feet. "Any idea on how to distract them?"

Avena could feel the four crystalmen sending status updates through her mind. Now that she understood what the signals were and how they were interfering with her brain's connection to her body, she'd adapted to them.

Like how a one-handed man could re-learn how to dress himself and do other activities. Her mind, it seemed, had capacities to mold itself to new circumstances and forge new paths.

There were eight other crystalmen also sending reports. All their impulses converged on the building before her. The signals blaring from it were so strong this close they screamed through her mind. It was sending out boisterous commands demanding help. It had been penetrated.

A demon had intruded the building.

She could see Dualayn in the alarmed shouts the jewelchine mind broadcasted. In them, he frantically sought to utilize some sort of interface. It was made of light, like the letters projected by the Recorder into the air. They were command options he was struggling to navigate, but he didn't know which ones to press. He flailed at them.

"Avena!" Miguil shouted as she raced up the steps towards her friends, focusing her awareness back on the real world.

Dajouth grinned at her.

"Help Ōbhin!" she shouted. "Just keep them busy and please, please don't die. Not even you, Dajouth."

Dajouth knuckled his forehead. "I'd never die when a pretty girl wants me to live."

A smile spread across her lips. *If we survive today, you can shower me in all the compliments you want.*

She darted into the building, following the echoes of the artificial brain. She entered pure darkness and moved by instinct. She could *see* a map of this place in the shouts. Her mind was interpreting it, like she was imagining the layout of Dualayn's manor.

Only she'd never been here.

So much data plunged into her. It was amazing she was able to function at all in the ruins. It was so strong here. She was in the heart of it. The rest of the city had died, but the controls for the crystalmen had triplicate backups to keep them supplied with the resonating frequency they needed. She didn't quite understand the specifics, but she understood the principal.

The artificial mind needed more tonal resonance than what naturally echoed through the universe. That background hums she'd heard just weren't loud enough. The ancients had amplified it somehow to fuel their more powerful jewelchines.

She went left and right. Her boots kicked up dust. She smelled the decay in the air. In her mind, she could see the crystalmen approaching her father and lover. The two most important people in her life faced death head-on.

She couldn't fail them.

She found stairs. Light spilled up them. It flickered, oscillating shades of purple mixed with the steady light of a diamond lantern. Dualayn's mutters rose from below. She hurtled down the stairs, taking them two or even three at a time.

He'd opened a metal door, clearing the dust from the floor in a sweeping arc and leaving it piled behind the portal. The room beyond was surprisingly clean. She was shocked by how white it was. Dualayn's boots had left thick tracks across the pristine surface towards the large diamond wrapped around the obsidian. Purple letters of light floated before him. He touched one.

"Mmm, that doesn't seem to be it," he muttered. He glanced down at a notebook he'd brought with him. "Pity, that seemed to be the right word."

"Dualayn!" she shouted.

He whirled around and blinked. "Avena, child, this is a surprise. I had not expected to find you here, but I am heartened to see you're alive. Is Bran with you?"

"Just get out of the way, I need to shut them down," she said.

"That is what I am attempting to do," he said. "If you think you know better than—"

"Yes, I do! Now step aside!"

He did, a look of shock at her brusque words.

The four crystalmen fanned out as they marched towards Ōbhin and the impostor, a skirmish line bearing down upon them. He drew his resonance blade, knowing it was a futile gesture. He glanced up at the ceiling illuminated by Fingers's lantern. It now rested on a small rock and shone bright around them.

"No way to bring that down," he said. There were no support columns like at the carriage house. "Is that glass above us?"

"Diamond," muttered Fingers. "What else could be strong enough?"

Ōbhin glanced at the thing pretending to be his friend. Now wasn't the time to hate it. He had to work with it. "Any ideas?"

Fingers shook his head. "We can run in circles until Avena does . . . whatever it is."

"You don't know what that building is she ran for, do you?"

"Nope."

"So how does she know that's where they can be turned off?" asked Ōbhin.

Fingers shrugged. "She's a smart one."

"No one's that smart." Ōbhin activated his blade. The humming gave him comfort, a false hope that he could somehow do anything about the death lumbering for them. Their diamond eyes all flicked on, focusing on him.

The ground around him was illuminated. The black, tar-like rock was marred by cracks. They would give treacherous footing. He couldn't trip and fall. That would be the death of him. He slid his foot back as he fell into a guard stance out of habit.

The back of his foot slipped over one of those cracks. He heard pebbles spilling down into it. Struck metal.

Metal?

An idea kindling in his mind, he turned around and peered at the crack in the ground. The automaton's diamond light shining down him spilled down through a small hole through the plaza into a space below. He could see a horseless carriage rotting below.

There's only a cubit of stone between us and another level.

"Well, you want to run left or right?" Fingers asked. "They're getting close. Probably the best thing we can do is split up."

"Go left," Ōbhin said and spun around. He slashed at the ground before him. His resonance blade sliced a long line through the black stone. The ground shook. The crystalmen were almost upon him. Fear clutched his chest.

"Eh, Ōbhin?" asked Fingers, backing away. "This isn't the time to attack the ground."

"Run, Fingers!" Ōbhin snarled and slashed another line, forming a cross on the ground before him. He looked up to see the lead crystalman only cubits away and closing fast.

There was no time for him to escape. Shouts echoed behind him, Miguil and Dajouth crying warning. The crystalman stepped onto the ground where he'd cut, arm drawing back for a skull-crushing punch. Earth groaned. Rocks ground together. The thing took another step and raised its arm to crush him.

The plaza gave away.

The automaton dropped down into the carriage house below. It hit with a loud crash. Crystal shattered. A new alarm rang, a high-pitched screeching. It assaulted Ōbhin's ears. Through billowing dust below, he could see the thing lying on its back, its legs shattered.

"Ōbhin!" Fingers exulted and slapped him on the shoulder. "Now let's move! The others are on us!"

From Ōbhin's right, a crystalman lumbered in and swung an amethyst fist at his head.

31

Ōbhin shoved Fingers to his left before diving beneath the punch himself. The air howled over his head. The automaton shifted its stance while Ōbhin rolled from the trap he'd cut in the black ground. Fingers cursed and stumbled. Ōbhin gained his feet and took off at a run. The crystalman marched after him.

"Come on! Over here!" Miguil shouted from Ōbhin's left. He threw a rock that crashed into a different crystalman, bouncing off the hulk without marring its surface. Miguil picked up another stone. "I'm right here! Come on!"

He hit it in the head.

Ōbhin glanced at the one chasing him while Miguil took off running, leading his away. In short sprints, Ōbhin could open up the distance between them. The crystalman had only one speed: inevitable. Eventually, a human—Ōbhin—would tire out. The mechanisms powering the crystalmen had functioned for three thousand years.

A large mound of debris cut short his flight. He whirled and judged there was enough room for him to make his trap. He attacked the ground. He drove his sword deep into the black stone and sliced his first line. He tried not to focus on the amethyst behemoth marching at him. The ground shook with its every step. The first done, he slashed the second one deep into the ground.

"Ōbhin!" Dajouth shouted. "Watch out!"

"I'm fine!" Ōbhin called, hating this part. If he retreated, the automaton might miss stepping on his trap. He focused on the crystalman plodding at him. Its eyebeams blinded Ōbhin. He almost couldn't see anything else now.

"No, no, from your left!" Dajouth shouted.

Left?

He glanced over. Through the shining glare of the diamond beams falling on his face, he made out a shadowy shape. The fourth crystalman had followed him, too. It came at him from another direction. It had flanked him with its diamonds off.

Now, it was right on top of him.

~

Avena followed the whispers.

"How are you reading that?" Dualayn asked as she tapped the glowing letters hovering before her. They had a tactile presence, like touching something spun of spider silk. Delicate. Too much pressure, and they would shatter.

"I'm not," she said, hitting the next option, knowing she was working through a menu even if she didn't understand it.

She had to go faster. Two were cornering Ōbhin. He was in danger of being killed. She couldn't let that happen. But it wasn't easy as just turning off a switch. The power came from a sealed basement that was held behind a heavy, locked door. It transmitted a higher amplitude of tonal energy through the world without any wires. The power was broadcasted like her thoughts were from her brain in the chest back at their camp. Nor could she damage the artificial mind with any tool she had on hand. Diamond surrounded the mind. She could shatter brittle obsidian, but not reach it.

She had to deactivate it, and that meant inputting codes. They sang in her mind. She shouldn't have access to them, but the mind was broadcasting too much information. More than it should. She swayed, her hands moving on their own, almost directed by the words whispering through her thoughts.

Her body felt alien. A puppet.

"Avena," whispered Dualayn in awe.

"Hush," she said and closed her eyes. Her mind interfaced with sounds. Her fingers acted, mere devices. An extension of a mechanism responding to her inputs. Her breathing slowed. Her heartbeat dwindled. The feel of her body faded, her connection tenuous. Too deep, and she'd lose all control of her body.

So much to do, and death was coming for Ōbhin. She could see him from two different angles. Two different crystalmen closing in for the kill. The artificial mind had lured her lover into a trap. Ōbhin had fixated on one automaton, thinking no will directed them as a unit.

That it couldn't learn from his first trap and thus would blunder into his second.

She couldn't do it in time. He'd boxed himself in. He was turning as the flanking crystalman's fist fell. It hurtled in, too fast for Ōbhin to dodge clear.

"No!" Avena shouted.

∼

Ōbhin saw death coming for him.

Understanding fell upon him in that instant of clarity, as time seemed to stop before the fist crushed his head. He'd let himself get cornered. The crystalmen had set an ambush of their own using the first as a distraction, keeping him half-blinded with the lights. Even now, it was flanking around the trap to cut off Ōbhin's retreat. He shouldn't have stopped by the rubble pile.

He pivoted anyways, attempting to flee. He had to escape. For Avena. He didn't want to lose her. He was prepared to die to save her, but in that desperate moment facing his end, he realized he'd rather live *and* save her. To survive with her. She shone with diamond hope. The energy surged through his limbs as his body moved.

Too slow. He felt trapped, like there was heavy snow around him, an avalanche that had swept over him and pinned him in place. The amethyst fist plunged at his head. Avena's smiling face appeared in his mind, her hair in a long braid, her irises adorned with those flecks of gold.

A blur streaked before him. Something moving too fast. A figure. Slender. The amethyst fist crashed into the figure's skull instead of hitting Ōbhin. The loud crack of bone snapping resounded. The head snapped to the right, spittle flying from a mouth.

Bran's mouth.

The youth caught the wrist of the automaton even as the force of the blow pushed him back into Ōbhin. Confusion rippled through Ōbhin as he stumbled towards the other crystalmen circling around his trap. He scrambled to stand.

Bran shouted, a deep and primal roar. A bellow, full of fury. His head had twisted around too far not to snap his neck. The skin around his throat bunched up, broken vertebrae poking at his flesh. His skin rippled pasty white.

The impostor had saved Ōbhin's life.

Gripping the automaton's fist, Bran pivoted. In a feat of strength that should be beyond what any human being could accomplish, Bran heaved the automaton over his shoulder. The impostor's legs snapped from the weight placed on them. Bone shards speared out through his trousers. He collapsed beneath the bulk of the crystalman but finished his swing.

As Ōbhin scrambled to gain his balance, the automaton crashed to the ground right on his trap. The stone shattered into four triangular slabs. The crystalman rang as its hands struggled to purchase on the edge before it plunged down into the carriage house in a resounding crash. Fragments of amethyst and chunks of black stone burst in all directions, pinging against rusting carriages.

The thing posing as Bran collapsed to the ground in a cry of pain, legs bent the wrong way in three or four spots. Behind Ōbhin, the other crystalmen advanced. A boil of confused emotions beset Ōbhin—shock, rage, fear, more—but he didn't have time to process them.

The crystalman threw its punch.

Ōbhin's feet found purchase. He threw out a desperate parry with his tulwar. He struck the automaton's inner wrist with his resonance blade with a hard slash. The energy of his deflecting attack was just enough to knock the fist a fraction off-target. Ōbhin's training to dodge severed weapons gave him the reflexes to twist his head the rest of the way clear.

The attack slammed past him. Wind rippled over his hair. His back slammed into the rubble pile that trapped him. The crystalman recovered from its missed attack, swinging its arm like a club now, a sideways blow to crush his head.

"Go low!" the impostor shouted.

Ōbhin understood, his body already moving in that desperate motion. He dived forward, thumb deactivating his resonance blade. He hit the ground before the hulk. The crystalman struck the rubble as he rolled between its feet. Its legs moved; its heel struck Ōbhin's hip.

Sent him rolling.

He cursed as he tumbled for the hole his trap had made. His legs fell over it. He dropped his sword as he scrambled to seize something. Anything. He slid over the edge, the weight of his lower half dragging him down towards a twenty-cubit drop onto the ruins below.

He snagged a crack. His black leather gloves gripped it while the crystalman turned around. Bright eyes fell upon him. A heavy foot rose to crush his arms. *Better broken legs than a crushed skull*, he thought and let go.

∼

"No!" Avena screamed.

She had to shut it down. She was so close. She put in the last code as she witnessed Ōbhin hanging, about to fall into the hole. She slammed her fingers down on the light buttons as the crystalman's foot stomped down at his skull.

She hit the deactivate button.

Ōbhin let go and fell.

Avena's stomach dropped with him. Then the whispers in her mind died. The artificial mind turned off. The characters of glowing light before her winked out of existence. She lurched back, knowing she hadn't been in time.

"Ōbhin!" she shouted and whirled around to race for the stairs, terrified at what she would find.

32

The moment Ōbhin let go, the crystalman's glow died. A deep darkness fell on him as his belly slid across the stone. He was a heartbeat from dropping to his possible death. Fear surged through him. The crystalman creaked as it toppled above him in the murk.

Avena had shut it down a heartbeat too late.

Something rushed above him. A hand seized him. Iron fingers crushed his wrist. A grunt of pain. Agony flared in Ōbhin's right shoulder socket; his fall halted. The groan of the toppling crystalman grew. Then a loud crash. The wind of its passage as it hurtled past him into the hole whipped over him. An arm, or perhaps a leg, struck his right foot, sending him swinging. The automaton shattered beneath him, mixing with the fragments of its brethren.

It would have landed right on me, thought Ōbhin.

"Come on," the pain-filled voice of the person holding his arm groaned. With a loud grunt, Ōbhin was yanked out of the hole and deposited on the ground. His savior fell down beside him.

"Who?" Ōbhin asked. "Fingers?"

"No," the voice answered. Through the pain, Ōbhin recognized it.

His stomach tightened. He scrambled back from the impostor. His hands swept across the dark, grimy ground for his dropped sword. Fury burst through him. The thing who had killed his two friends now had saved his life twice.

That thought bubbled through the anger.

Ōbhin froze. He fixated on the sounds of the thing's breathing. His eyes adjusted to the dim light shining from the diamond lanterns sitting on the steps of the sheriff building. In it, he made out the impostor standing on Bran's legs. They were still bent and broken, its unnatural flesh supporting its weight. There was a pop and a crack. The figure jerked. As Ōbhin's vision grew better, he witnessed those legs straighten.

Become whole.

Can anything kill this thing?

"You murdered Bran," Ōbhin said, struggling with his emotions. "And Smiles."

"I became them," the figure answered in Bran's voice. The pain was gone. "Healing bones takes the longest. It always hurts, though."

"Becoming them isn't being them," said Ōbhin. "They're dead, right? Buried in some shallow grave or dumped in the lake?"

"I—*Bran*—liked the ducks swimming on the lake. I asked my handler to bury him by it." Sadness brimmed in the impostor's voice.

"And Smiles?" Ōbhin asked, emotion tightening his voice. As his vision sharpened, he spotted his sword. He snagged it and rose, facing the impostor.

"My handler took him away to a pigpen." Bran rolled his right shoulder. "His body can't be found."

Ōbhin's sword shook. "I see."

"I have my mission." Bran's earnest, youthful face stared pleadingly at Ōbhin. "I must protect Dualayn."

"You didn't have to save me just now."

"You're my friend, Ōbhin." The thing pretending to be Bran stepped forward. "I—"

"You killed my friend!" The resonance blade hummed to life, emerald light flaring from the pommel.

Bran's face fell. "Avena said the same thing. Perhaps I am not allowed to have friends."

"Who are you really?" Ōbhin had to know. "Did Dje'awsa make you?"

"I'm No One," Bran said after a moment. He raised his hands and backed away into the darkness. "I will keep my distance. I know you need to keep

Dualayn alive until he fixes Avena. You won't hurt him. I'm not a threat. For now."

The thing calling itself No One fled into the swallowing black of Koilon's ruins. Ōbhin's entire body trembled. Rage suffused him. He would find a way to put down Dje'awsa's foul creation. *Next time. When he hasn't just saved my life.*

∽

Avena burst out of the building onto the steps. The lantern light shone around her. She scanned around, struggling to gain her bearings. The last image of Ōbhin she'd received from the artificial mind seared in her thoughts. Terror lashed her heart to painful ribbons.

"You did it!" an excited Miguil shouted. He and Dajouth stood twenty cubits or so away over a collapsed crystalman.

"Where's Ōbhin?" she demanded.

"Went that way," grunted the weary voice of her father. Fingers trudged into the light, breathing heavily, sweat cutting streaks through the grime coating his face. "Chased by two . . . of those . . . Black-cursed bastards."

Avena looked in that direction, clutching her hands tight together. She opened her mouth to shout when green flared in the darkness to her right. Ōbhin's sword.

She darted in that direction, the glow of her earthen gauntlet spilling enough light before her to see where she stepped. He stood by himself facing the darkness. She cried his name as she ran. He turned to face her. She caught a glimpse of his face spreading with joy.

Then his blade went out. He became a shadow flowing towards her. They came together. Arms went around the other. She clutched him with desperate need. He was alive. He hadn't fallen like she feared. She'd been in time. She pressed her face into his leather jerkin and trembled.

They had found each other in the dark.

He kissed her forehead and whispered comfort to her. In that moment, she knew everything would be fine. They would find the antenna. She would adjust to the cursed thing shoved into her skull. Just like her brain had adjusted to the artificial mind's broadcast.

She would make a life.

Avena wouldn't let the butchery Dualayn had committed stop her from moving forward. She had a second chance at love. That hollow pit in her heart was almost filled. All that remained was the absence her dead loved ones had left in her life.

Evane was the largest, but she realized Chames had dug his own place in her heart, and even her mother was there. Not the woman who'd been driven mad by the Black, but the smiling woman she'd been most days. The bright woman her father had loved.

She had lost too much in her life to lose anything else.

∽

As Ōbhin held Avena, he felt the black gloves around his hands. A prison he donned every morning. A declaration not only to the world, but to himself, that he was worthless. Today, he had wanted to do more than just protect.

He had wanted to live.

He'd been willing to die to save Avena, but he found he would rather live with her. Ōbhin had found value in his life once more. The last time he'd gone underground, he had believed himself to be a noble man. A proud warrior. He had emerged a murderer. A broken man.

That dark, twisted version of himself had entered this darkness and died. The old one reborn. He was ready. Finally ready to remove these gloves and wear proper ones. Purple gloves, the color of protection, of a man who wanted to protect those he loved. And with circles on them the color of flame. A declaration of his love, his burning passion for someone else.

The person he wanted to protect most of all.

Avena had promised they would escape the grime and darkness. She'd kept her word. As he held her, he whispered the three words burning in his heart. The three words that had transformed him once more.

"I love you."

Avena's faced lifted. Her lips met his. He wouldn't be a coward this time.

∽

Avena felt a great deal of energetic joy as they resumed their search through the ruins. The crystalmen were gone. The only dangers left to them were collapsing debris. The impostor, No One as they settled on calling it, lurked out in the dark. She could feel it watching, but it stayed away.

It took hours yet, but they reached the Hall of Communications. The building, like many others, was half-collapsed, crushed by whatever cataclysm had buried Koilon. As near as Dualayn could tell, the destruction of the Wave Transference Station had unleashed the ruby transformation. That appeared to have unleashed the invasion of the strange demons with their still-warm bones. Perhaps they were birthed in the destructive energies unleashed at the moment of the Shattering. They were different from the ant-like demons she'd witnessed in her dreams of the White Lady's past.

Different breeds of demons? Are darklings one? Are other monsters among them?

At some point, someone named Ozsor had sealed the Ruby Nodule which might have meant setting up a Warding. It was the last event chronicled in the Recorder. The Warding must have buried the city, perhaps banishing the living demons back to wherever they'd come from.

Maybe she would never know the truth of the ancient past.

The search of the Hall of Communication's ruins led them to a storeroom full of the antennae. They were all made of obsidian. They looked like slender shafts of smoky black the thickness of two of her digits.

"Look at them all," Dualayn said after giving her the first one. "They are beautiful. Their shape is extraordinary. See the minute detail of their construction. The one I made for you is such a crude thing in comparison. My deepest apologies, Avena."

"That's what you're apologizing for?" grunted Fingers. She still thought of her father as Fingers. He continued to keep his distance, perhaps unwilling to face that he had abandoned her that day.

The hardest thing to do is forgive yourself, she thought. It was something Daughter Heana had told her as a child during her many attempts to coach Avena to speak again. Back then, she'd had trouble accepting it wasn't her fault that Evane had died. She didn't even need forgiveness yet couldn't give it to herself for so long.

She would be patient with her father.

"Look at the craftsmanship," Dualayn said, picking up a second. "If I can figure out how to grow the crystals like the ancients di—"

Ōbhin's sword whipped from his sheath and activated. Before Dualayn could react, the blade sliced through the antenna. The tip fell to the floor and shattered. Obsidian was the most brittle of the eight gems.

Proof of its corrupted nature, she thought. In that second dream, though, obsidian had seemed like the other gems until it had melted during the catastrophe.

"Why did you do that?" Dualayn roared. He glared at Ōbhin, but the easterner was already moving. His sword slashed across the shelves, cutting through the stockpile of antennae. Dualayn went to grab Ōbhin.

She seized the man's wrist and yanked him back. "You are not going to butcher another person like you did me."

"He's going to give you the immortality speech," Ōbhin growled. His blade sliced again. "He thinks you'll find it acceptable to hop from body to body, living forever by stealing from others."

Avena shook her head. The words didn't shock her. Nothing about Dualayn would ever again. They only saddened her. *How did we work so close these last few years since Chames's death and completely misunderstand the other? Maybe we just wanted to see ourselves in the other, a mirror to our own desires? We'd interpreted everything through our own bias.*

"This is a travesty," groaned Dualayn. "These could be used for other purposes, Avena, and he's destroying them. We could communicate across the world. Instead of taking months for messages to travel from here to Ala'i"—the capital of the Empire of Democh lay on the far side of the world—"it would be as fast as you could snap your fingers. Don't you see what you're allowing him to destroy? Progress!"

"Why would I want your ideas to spread?"

She watched as Ōbhin went through the storeroom, destroying every last one. Her mind drifted to other problems. She had to tell Joayne and Jilly about their loved ones' deaths. Then there was the dread the Brotherhood's meddling in Lothon's politics churned in her. War loomed on the horizon . . .

Something Dualayn had said when she'd encountered him in the Crystal Sheriff Hall resonated in her mind. When she'd found him by the artificial mind, he'd asked if Bran was with her. It was like Dualayn had only cared about the youth. Not Fingers. Bran. She stared at Dualayn and realized he *knew* that Bran had been replaced by No One.

Her loathing swelled.

33

Three or four days after Avena had climbed down the ropes into the ruins, she pulled herself up and out of them. Her body ached. Her stomach rumbled. Food had grown tight on their journey out of the ruins. They'd had trouble retracing their steps. Dualayn's plan of leaving markers behind had fallen apart after the carriage house.

They found the exit. Eventually. They made a few false starts, but when they rediscovered the large carriage house where they'd almost died, they'd found their easy trail back. Now, as Avena emerged into what felt like midday, summer sunlight, she whooped for joy.

She staggered and sank down onto the red grass, careful not to fall on her backpack and break the delicate antenna. Their camp was still here. The wagon was secure, the food they'd hung from a tree out of reach of predators looked unmolested. The one thing they feared was the horses, but they were still hobbled by the pool of water at the far end and looked healthy.

The red grass had not harmed them.

"I want to take a bath," she groaned to Ōbhin. Grime coated his hair and streaked his face. His gloves looked more gray than black save in cracks at the joints where they had creased. He nodded to her as he stumbled out and fell to his knees.

One by one, they climbed up until only Dualayn remained. With grumbling, they hauled the old man out of the ruins. The scholar spilled over and panted on his back. He lay there for a few minutes before he stumbled off to the water, fell to his knees, and dunked his face into it.

Ōbhin stood by the hole as he pulled up the rope. He stared down into the dark. "I doubt he'll be stopped by this," he said, "but why make it easier for No One?"

Nobody objected.

In the dark, there hadn't been much chance for a private conversation. She hadn't had a chance to confront Dualayn on her suspicions of No One nor had she found the privacy to tell Ōbhin about her dreams. But most of all, she wanted to speak with her father. To let him know she didn't hate him.

She glanced at her father who was sitting on a rock and staring at the swollen knuckles of his hand. Now wasn't the time. She needed to clean up. Put on fresh clothes. She had to feel alive before speaking of her feelings.

And she needed all the men to stay behind a small hillock so she could bathe without being watched.

Well, Ōbhin could watch, she thought and warm fantasies of bathing with him, washing the dirt from his muscular body, filled her mind.

Later, as the sun set behind the trees, she saw her chance to speak with Dualayn. The others were cooking dinner, laughing in the way of men who wanted to prove that danger and death they'd endured hadn't affected them. The scholar was sitting on the wagon bed, writing in his journal.

She crept from the fire, her skirt whisking about her legs. It felt strange to wear feminine garb after what felt like a lifetime in the dark of the ruins. The bodice felt snug about her bosom, restricting her breathing. She reached the wagon and scrambled up with ease.

"I really don't have much to say to you if you are just going to berate my methods," Dualayn said, not looking up from his writing. "I made peace with it a long time ago."

"You knew that thing had replaced Bran."

Dualayn paused. "Yes."

"That thing killed Smiles and Bran. Do you care?" She leaned forward. "They were your employees. Bran grew up at your house. He was a little brother to Chames for a while."

Dualayn closed his book. Pain flickered across his face. "I did not . . .

instruct the infiltrator to kill them and replace them. I was only made aware of what happened to Smiles after he was dead. There was nothing I could do."

"So you do care. About some things."

"I care about many things. I have failed many times. I am grieved by each one. I am not happy that your transference wasn't as seamless as I'd hoped. The interference pattern wasn't supposed to happen." He looked up. "I thought I had it all worked out."

"And those you were supposed to heal?"

"I healed more than I killed. I performed my experiments on the poorest of Kash. On the vagabonds. The sickly. The deformed. Those who were already parasites upon society. I couldn't help most of them. I ensured their deaths weren't in vain."

"Like Smiles's and Bran's were?"

Dualayn sighed. "The infiltrator is astounding. It can not only change its shape to any form, but it can adopt the *truth* of a person's life. Become them. It is my greatest work, and I can't even take all the credit for it."

Avena shook her head. "No, no. Dje'awsa made him."

Dualayn snorted. "That sorcerer? I studied what he did with Ust. Crude. Unrefined. No true artistry. No understanding of how gems can be fully utilized. His is a savage practice. It is keyed off blood, I think, and the use of obsidian. I don't fully understand it. It seems to violate all natural laws. I created something more elegant with the infiltrator. I created a network of jewelchines within him, all bound by black iron wires. That's the true key to most of his abilities. Emeralds for strength, topazes to heal him, heliodors to give him speed."

"And to change shape?" asked Avena, loathing her curiosity. She worked her tongue across the roof of her dry mouth. Why did this last revelation shock her? How could this monster produce one more hurtful truth? Memories of fatherly gestures, comforting hugs, a shoulder to cry upon swam through her thoughts. They sought to blunt her hatred, to dull it.

She honed it on fresh anger.

"That was the White Lady's doing." Dualayn shifted. "I do not understand how she did it, but it was part of my arrangement with Grey. He wanted the infiltrator for his business among other things. The White Lady pointed me in the direction and gave the infiltrator the ability to embrace another's truth."

"When?" asked Avena in confusion. "The White Lady didn't visit our estate until after Ust's attack."

"Ust delivered the infiltrator to my labs," said Dualayn. "Pharon facilitated. Let him in through the gates. He had the keys to the postern gates, you know. He liked to slip out into the grove to meet his lover."

"I . . . knew that," Avena said, her cheeks warming. Memories rose of the night she'd caught her promised locked in a passionate embrace with Pharon.

"I worked on the infiltrator for days. I hardly slept."

"Who was he?" Avena asked, struggling to remember. Dualayn had spent so much time in his lab. Especially after they'd returned. He was obsessed with his recorder and his macabre experiments. *And I was busy learning to fight so I could spend time with Ōbhin. I didn't even realize my attraction to him.*

"It was that associate of Ōbhin. What was his name . . .?" Dualayn leaned back.

"Carstin?" gasped Avena. "He died! I was there when he passed away in your lab."

"Did he?" Dualayn stared at her. "I almost thought you knew I was up to something when you questioned the ingredients I used to make the anesthesia. I taught you too well." He chuckled.

She glared at him.

"Anyway, it put him into a deep coma, and he was sustained by what the White Lady's kiss did to him."

Avena's forehead tingled. The White Lady had kissed her on the temple, and her body had trembled like a note had hummed through her flesh.

"Whatever she did to him, it let him survive being buried alive and now allows him to change into another person. He's rather unique. I tried to duplicate him several times, but it takes a healthy person to survive the implantation. The problem with using the poorest of the sick for—"

She slapped him. Hard. Then she whirled around and hopped off the end of the wagon bed in a flurry of skirts. She hadn't tried so hard to keep Carstin alive just so he could be turned into a monster with no identity. What was the point of all the anguished nights she'd spent keeping him alive? She had been taught to heal the sick by a man who secretly delighted in butchering them.

She found herself at the edge of the clearing. The red-stained birch tree rose above her, its bark bleached white as bone left in the sun. She leaned against it, feeling her forehead tingle. Had the White Lady done something to her? Was that why she dreamed about the enigmatic woman's past? How she'd glimpsed the loved one that Raya wished to save, and why she would work with dark people like Dje'awsa and Grey?

Like Dualayn?

"He understands what it means to strive to reclaim what was lost and fix past mistakes," the White Lady had once said about the man.

"Avena," Ōbhin whispered.

She whirled around. The sight of Ōbhin lit by the Virtue's red moonlight struck her. The scar on his right cheek gleamed crimson against his brown skin. He wore a linen shirt and clean pants, his hair no longer a tangle of filth. She threw herself at him.

Beneath the birch tree, away from the others, she poured out what she'd dreamed, what she knew of the White Lady, that she might have been alive since the Shattering, and that the man she wanted to save was trapped in a healing wound, surrounded by darkness.

"I don't know what will happen if she frees her lover from the weaving," Avena whispered, "but it can't be good for the world. She's working with the Brotherhood. With that pus-filled roach Dualayn. And Dje'awsa. What will *his* magic do?"

"Don't know," Ōbhin said. "Something to worry about tomorrow."

She bit her lip. She held back about Carstin. It would only cause the man she loved more pain if he knew what had happened to his friend's body. That thing, No One, wasn't Carstin any longer. It was a mirror reflecting the last person it had killed, stealing their truth. One day, Ōbhin might have to fight No One.

He couldn't be distracted. He couldn't hesitate. Not if it would cost him his life.

"There's something Dualayn told me," Ōbhin said. His arm tightened around her shoulder. "I'm sorry, Avena."

"What else did he do?" she demanded. "Did he replace the baby growing in Jilly's womb with a darkling or a grumliicho?"

Ōbhin took a deep breath. "When Chames was sick, Dualayn spent days trying to heal him, right?"

"No," she croaked as the weight of his words fell on her. She gripped his shirt. "He didn't. Don't say that. Chames died of spring fever."

"Dualayn called it a mistake. The arrogant roach thought his experiment would work. He tested on his son."

Avena kept finding new reasons to hate Dualayn. She sobbed against Ōbhin's chest as she remembered her last dream of Chames. If it had been his spirit she'd dreamed, he had tried to tell her. Warn her. She just hadn't understood.

She clutched to Ōbhin and longed for the end of pain.

∽

Twentieth Day of Patience, 755 EU

No One kept his distance on the return to Kash. Ōbhin knew it was pointless to think it had been trapped in the ruins. The thing would have found a way to claw out of the darkness. But it was a problem for the future. He wasn't looking forward to the steps he'd have to take to ensure those around him weren't replaced.

After three days in the ruins, he found it strange to be in the summer heat. No clouds marred the blue skies. The drought worsened. The fields they passed on the four-day trip back to Kash were wilted and browned. Farmers drained streams and ponds for water to keep their crops alive. They simmered in the heat, displaying defiance against the king. Green adorned every last hamlet they passed. Soldiers moved in platoons. Knights rode in companies.

Lothon boiled.

Finally, their wagon reached the outskirts of Kash. They passed the village of Reed Bend and took the turnoff at the Porcelain. The city's walls formed a dark haze on the horizon while belching smoke from the factories stained the blue sky a leaden shade. Lake Ophavin's waters had retreated even farther, exposing more drying mud.

Ōbhin rode on the wagon beside Avena and Miguil. Dualayn sat in the back. He had behaved the last few days, lost in his writing. No one talked to him. Fingers and Dajouth rode on their horses. Bran's spare mount trotted behind the wagon, looking forlorn without its rider.

Cerdyn manned the gate. The burly man pushed out of the shadows. His eyes flicked over them and a tightness increased in his face. "It didn't go well?"

"No," Ōbhin said. "We lost Bran."

"And Smiles? He went with you, right?"

Ōbhin hesitated. He glanced at Avena.

"Yeah," Avena said. "They're both dead."

Cerdyn spat to the side, his dark brows furrowing. "Elohm polish their souls and lift them to the light."

Avena nodded, her back straight, shoulders bristling. Ōbhin recognized the tension, and the anger, in her expression. Her brown hair fluttered loose about her face. It was longer, brushing the edges of her shoulders now.

He missed her braid. He almost regretted taking her to Dualayn, but she would be dead if he hadn't. Her brain might reside in a glass jar, but at least she still lived. Was still herself. The obsidian mind hadn't done anything to her personality.

It just stopped working sometimes. Twice on the journey, she'd slipped into strange dreams of the distant past. Of the Shattering. It stunned him to think that the White Lady, who looked no older than Avena, was thousands of years old. That she had witnessed the mythical cataclysm. Maybe even helped to cause it.

The wagon clattered up the driveway. Sheep wandered aimlessly across the brown lawn. The rhododendrons drooped, shriveled blossoms falling to the withered ground. On the porch, several women appeared. Jilly, Joayne, Kaylin, Layni, and Hajina. Jilly clutched her stomach, her neck craning. Joayne rubbed her hands together.

"Where is he?" Jilly shouted. She darted off the steps. "Where's my Phelep?" Her eyes were raw and wild. "What happened to him?"

"And Bran?" asked Joayne. The older woman's face paled. She trembled on the steps. "Did he . . .? Where is he?"

Miguil reigned up the wagon. He looked at his feet. Avena squeezed her eyes shut for a moment. "Jilly and Joayne, I'm sorry, can we . . .?" She swallowed the painful emotion choking her throat. "Can we talk in private?"

"No," Jilly said, shaking her head with violent jerks. Tears spilled down her cheeks. "He's not dead. My Phelep wouldn't abandon me. Us!"

Joayne seemed to flow off the porch. She took Jilly by the shoulders. The older woman's eyes grew liquid as she whispered something. Then she turned Jilly away and took her inside. Avena climbed off the wagon in a swirl of her dark-brown skirts. Ōbhin leaped down after.

Jilly's sobs led the way. They passed the others on the porch. Kaylin, the older cook, had a confused look on her face while Hajina held her hand, a fierce anger burning in the younger cook's eyes. Plump Layni reached out a hand to Jilly then pulled it back. Layni clutched her clasped hands to her breasts, looking stunned.

"Is it Dyain?" Kaylin asked. "Is he hurt? I haven't seen him today."

"He's fine, Kaylin," Hajina said.

Ōbhin glanced at the cook. She looked around like she didn't know where she was. Dualayn had removed her mind and put it back in her body, damaging her in some fundamental way. Sometimes, she knew her husband was dead, other times she looked for him. Only in the kitchen did she have any normalcy.

And she's losing that, Ōbhin thought. *I won't let her stay here. No one should ever be around that bastard.*

In a small sitting room off the main entranceway, Jilly broke away from Joayne. The young maid faced Avena and Ōbhin. She rubbed her hands together. She looked frail, made of spun glass. So delicate, a single touch would cause her to shatter. Joayne wasn't much better. Bran's mother squeezed her hands tight together. Her knuckles grew white.

"Where is he?" Jilly demanded. "He went with you. He told me he was doing that." Her gaze shot past Ōbhin. "Right, Fingers? You, Bran, Dajouth, and Phelep all went after them."

"Well . . ." Ōbhin glanced back to see Fingers standing in the doorway. Avena had revealed her suspicions of the man. Now that Ōbhin knew, he could see the resemblance between them in the ears, a hint in the brows.

Fingers cleared his throat and said, "You see, Jilly, Bran, Dajouth, and I went with them."

"No, Phelep had to have gone," Jilly said. "He wouldn't have abandoned me. He loved me."

"He did love you," Avena said. "This isn't easy to explain, but . . ."

Jilly weathered the truth that her husband had been dead for over a month. That she'd been sharing a bed with an impostor for sixty or more days. Joayne collapsed into a chair when she learned her son had been killed, his body buried along the lake.

"Dualayn's associates murdered my husband so this monster could replace him and guard that piss-soaked roach?" Jilly demanded at the end. The fragility vanished. Fury brimmed in her face. "The Brotherhood stole away my child's father for that pathetic piece of dog excrement?"

"Yeah," Ōbhin said. "We wanted to tell you, but we didn't want to reveal what we knew. Not until we could understand it. We were trying to protect everyone." *That piece of dog shit included . . .*

"I'm sorry!" Avena said; she moved close and went to hug Jilly. For a moment, Jilly looked about to rebuff Avena, but then she relaxed and the pair embraced. "I promise you, Jilly, Ōbhin and I will look after you and your child. And you, too, Joayne. We're so sorry. We didn't think No One would kill anyone else, let alone your son."

Joayne nodded as she sat on the chair. "He liked the ducks, you know," she said, rubbing her hands together. "He'd have liked being buried by the lake and . . ." She swallowed. "I think I need to lie down." Tears spilled down her cheeks. "If you'll excuse me."

Ōbhin nodded as she passed.

"And what about *him*?" Jilly asked. "What punishment will Dualayn receive? What justice will I find for my husband? None! He has powerful friends. They'll protect him. If I brought this complaint to a magistrate, they would laugh at me. He'll be free! Him and this monster and that Black-cursed Brotherhood!"

"For now," Ōbhin said. "They're getting away with it for now."

She shot him a look. "You could kill him. Right now! Just cut off his head!"

"Maybe," Ōbhin said. The darkness swirled in him. He had found his way out to the light, but it would be so easy to fall into the Black again.

A rap knocked on the door. "We should begin the procedure so you can vacate my house."

Ōbhin turned to face Dualayn standing unapologetic at the door. Ōbhin was finding standing in the light to be difficult. In the dark, you didn't have to care about right or wrong; you could just act.

As Avena and Ōbhin followed Dualayn to his lab, her father pulled her aside. She paused as she stared up at his face. It was the first time he'd approached her since their conversation in the ruins. "Can you give us a few moments?"

Dualayn sighed. "Fine, fine. We'll be downstairs. I have to get things ready." He glanced at his lab door. "I hope none of the servants have ransacked it."

"We didn't go in your horror dungeon!" spat Jilly as she stalked by.

Avena swallowed her emotions. She wanted to hug Jilly and take away her pain. Losing Chames had hurt, but Jilly and Smiles—*his real name was Phelep*—had been married for five years. They'd known each other as children. She'd had the support in her life gouged out and replaced with a monster and hadn't even realized it.

Her father shook his head as he watched Jilly vanish. "Should just unleash her on Dualayn and be done with it."

"Yeah," Avena said. Part of her wanted to let Ōbhin or Jilly or anyone kill Dualayn. However, it went against all the teachings of Elohm. It would stain their souls. She had an obsidian mind in her head now. She was already touched by darkness. If she gave in to the worse impulses of her soul, what would happen to her when she died?

Would she be too weighed down to rise up to Elohm?

And what about the cost murdering him would put on Ōbhin? she asked herself. *He would do it for me, and it would be one more burden for him to carry. How can I say I love him and do* that *to him?*

Justice for Dualayn would have to wait.

"I'm sorry I abandoned you," her father said. He cupped her chin, lifting her gaze to his face. His thumb stroked across her cheekbone.

"So you're admitting it."

He nodded. "Named you and Evane after my ma and her ma. Thought they sounded good together, you know? Avena and Evane."

"They do," Avena said. "We do."

"It's myself I hate," he continued, looking not at her but beyond her. "For Evane being dead. Your mother. It's my fault."

"It was Mom," Avena said. She seized his shoulders. "I thought that it was my fault for the longest time. That you hated me for just standing there."

He shook his head. Emotion filled his eyes. "I hate myself for abandoning you, but every time I look at you, I see Evane. I failed to save my daughter. I let her die. Your mother, Usrella, she'd said things a few times. Things that concerned me, but I ignored them. She wasn't herself when she was dark, but she usually was bright. She loved you girls. From the moment she found out she was pregnant until the last time she tucked you both in. I could see it. She treasured being a mother. She wanted more, but the birth was hard on her. She almost died bringing you two into the world."

Avena hadn't known that.

"I didn't hit your ma to save your life, I did it out of fury. At myself for ignoring those warnings. For pushing down those whispers of fear and pretending everything was fine. I destroyed our family because I couldn't face the truth about her. So I ran."

"Not far," said Avena. "You've been near me, haven't you? While I was living in the orphanage. Then you came to work here to watch over me."

"Too ashamed to ever say anything." He still wouldn't look at her.

"You're here now." She slid her hands from his shoulders to around his neck. She hugged her father. "That's enough. I can help you forgive yourself. I don't think it was anyone's fault, not even hers. She was broken, wasn't she? She couldn't help the things she said. I've learned about the sickness of the mind. Dementia, depression, grief, mania, and more."

"I could have taken her to a sanitarium. The first time she told me Elohm whispered to her and that she had to cleanse our daughters, I should have done it. The way she talked . . ." His arms went around her. "Evane could be here with you."

She would help her father like she was helping Ōbhin. Like they were helping each other. Letting go of the past was difficult. Accepting fault for your actions and not taking the blame for others was such a hard thing to do. It could destroy even a good man.

And that was what her father was. A good man who'd been broken by the terrible events of his life. She would mend him. "I love you, Dad."

He let out a sobbing groan and squeezed her tight. Her ribs creaked and she reveled in the strength of him. Her eyes closed and she breathed in his scent. Memories sparked through her of riding on his shoulder, Evane on the other, through golden fields of ripe wheat. Of kisses placed on her brow as she was tucked into bed at night, her favorite doll clutched to her side, Evane beside her. She savored this moment.

Then she broke away. "We'll talk more once Dualayn is finished."

He nodded and cleared his throat. "Don't let that bastard hurt you again."

"Ōbhin will be standing by with his sword." Her face tightened. "Dualayn thinks himself too important to risk dying."

"Besides, you're his next great work." Disgust flicked across her father's face. He glanced up. "If anything happens to her, don't kill Dualayn. Let me beat him to death."

"He won't harm her," Ōbhin answered as he stepped into the room. "He's waiting. He's growing . . . impatient."

"He's not the one about to have his chest cut open," muttered Avena. "He can wait."

A smile flicked across his face.

"You take care of her, Ōbhin," her father said.

The men exchanged stares. Ōbhin nodded. So did her father. Then they both turned away. She shook her head, at a loss for what had just passed between the two. Did men have some secret form of telepathy?

Fear tightened about her chest as she took Ōbhin's arm. In the true lab, beneath the other, she would be on the table again. Dualayn had to replace her mind's antenna, and that meant severing her connection to her body. He had to keep her alive with jewelchines, the reason they had to wait to affect the repair until they had returned to his lab.

One last time losing control of my body, she thought. *It's like falling asleep. That's all.*

∾

Ōbhin hated seeing Avena on the table. She was naked from the waist up, her body anesthetized. A long tube of leather had been forced down her airway. Dualayn called it intubation. It was hooked up to a pig's bladder and a heliodor jewelchine that kept filling it with air. The bladder was held between a pair of wooden paddles connected to a set of gears turned by a ruby jewelchine. The paddles compressed the bladder in a steady rhythm.

Her chest rose and fell with the compression.

When Dualayn made the incision down her chest, Ōbhin gripped his sword tight. He held the pommel as the blood spilled between her breasts and across her throat. Dualayn applied boiled cloths to stem the rivulets before grabbing a metal tool with teeth-like notches designed to ratchet something open.

The sounds of Avena's ribs cracking as Dualayn spread them apart would haunt Ōbhin's nightmares for the rest of his life.

There, nestled between lungs inflating and deflating, lay Avena's beating heart. Dualayn brought a ruby, no bigger than the beating organ, to it. Black iron wires wrapped about it. Four leads thrust from it. The jewelchine in position, Dualayn gave the order.

Ōbhin closed his eyes then pulled the antenna from Avena's brain, leaving it sitting in the bubbling water, kept alive by the other jewelchine. The signal to her body ended. Her heart stopped beating in an instant.

Dualayn worked fast. He pressed the four wires into Avena's heart at specific spots before triggering the ruby. It burst with red light. Her heart beat again, pumping life through her body. Dualayn sighed in relief.

"I have done this dozens of times," he said, glancing at Ōbhin, "but never with a death sentence should I fail."

"Pity," said Ōbhin. "Might be more people alive today."

"Doubtful, since what I learned from their deaths has saved countless more." Dualayn moved around the table and unwrapped the antenna they'd procured in Koilon. He hooked it up to her mind with the black iron wires, sliding them into her brain suspended in the liquid.

I'll never sleep well again, Ōbhin thought as he watched the macabre experiment.

He'd prefer for Dualayn to restore her brain to her body, but he insisted there would be side-effects. Drastic ones. This was better than nothing.

Ōbhin's anger burned.

"There," Dualayn said. "Now to test it." He disconnected the artificial heart.

Avena's real one kept beating.

"This antenna should give her a clear signal. Even if she's on the far side of the world from her mind, she'll never have any interference issues."

"Close her up," Ōbhin said.

"And me?" Dualayn asked. "Will I die once I do that?"

Ōbhin shook his head. "She doesn't want to make me into a murderer again."

"She told you that?"

"She doesn't have to." He glanced down at her sleeping face. "I know her."

Avena dreamed of the Shattering again. She watched the darkness warping the world, turning everything black. *There must be a city somewhere transmuted to obsidian instead of ruby,* drifted through her mind. *Where ant-like demons were unleashed.*

The vision of the past faded after a while and she entered normal dreams until she finally rose out of groggy sleep. Her body was coming awake. She fluttered open her eyes to see Ōbhin staring down at her. A smile crossed his lips. His hand stroked her brow.

"How do you feel?"

"I don't know," she answered. She flexed her fingers and toes. She could feel the linen weave of a dressing gown cladding her body, and the silky caress of a few strands of hair brushing her cheek. She felt . . . different than she had earlier. There was more of an immediacy about her. A pressure in her bladder. An ache in her back from lying on the hard surface. "I have to pee."

"That's how you feel?" asked Ōbhin.

"Yeah," she said. She sat up and enjoyed the sensation of the dressing gown shifting around her. "I feel solid. Real. I'm not a guest in my own body." She looked around. She was in the lab where she'd gone to sleep. They were alone. "Ōbhin, I don't feel weird. Not like I did after I woke up from my injury. I feel like me!"

She threw her arms around his neck. She hugged him tight. She held him and shook. Her mind lay in that jar feet away, but to her perception, it didn't seem that way. Her thoughts echoed in her head where they belonged. His arms held her, strong, protective.

She didn't care that she had to pee. In fact, she reveled in that simple bodily function. The fear that she might lose control had utterly vanished. This antenna was an upgrade. Dualayn was correct. She had nothing to fear from interference.

She just had to worry about the black gem being in her head. She had an obsidian mind controlling her body. What would that mean for her soul?

She should denounce Dualayn—he *should be* executed for his work—but who would investigate him? He had powerful allies, even when excluding the Brotherhood. Many nobles and merchants profited from his inventions. Magistrates would be bribed. His crimes would be overlooked.

No justice would be found, but that didn't mean that Avena would just sit by. The Brotherhood was trying to destroy her country. They had killed the high refractor, orchestrated the riots, and were driving resentment against the king. Of course, King Anglon wasn't helping with his desire for war, but one problem at a time.

Most of all, the White Lady's intentions terrified her. The woman needed something from Grey and Dualayn. Something that would free the man she loved. Avena had experienced Raya's desperation as the Warding imprisoned her lover. If that had been Ōbhin trapped, what would Avena do to save him?

How far would she go? Dualayn had been driven beyond any moral limits to restore Bravine. The White Lady said she was just like Dualayn. That he was someone who understood her pain.

"I want to do something, Ōbhin," she said. "I want to stop the Brotherhood, Dje'awsa, the White Lady. All of them. I don't want them meddling in my country. My city. I want to bring some form of justice to them all."

Ōbhin nodded. "Ideas?"

"No," she admitted. Then her brow furrowed. "Refractor Charlis. He's working in Parliament to keep things from fracturing worse. Deffona is his secretary. He's a good man, and she'll want to help us. Maybe he will, too. We're going to stop them, Ōbhin. All of them."

Ōbhin smiled. "There are those thorns of yours."

Avena smiled.

They could discuss plans later. She had to pass her water and leave this place. She never wanted to enter Dualayn's manor again. All her happy memories were sullied by this room they were in. This was where Chames had died, killed by his own father.

Where Ōbhin's friend had been turned into a monster with no identity.

She and Ōbhin left the foul room behind, her brain carried in his strong grip. They traveled upstairs and closed the door to Dualayn's lab. They would pack up and leave, find a new place to live in Kash, and then figure out how to save it from the corruption festering in the midden heaps.

Everyone was waiting outside of it. Miguil and Dajouth, Cerdyn and plump Layni. Joayne and Jilly stood by each other, one wilted and the other blazing. The poor cook looked befuddled as Hajina whispered to her and held her hand.

Everyone was here but her father.

After everyone had hugged her, Cerdyn said, "Fingers left this letter for you, Avena."

A pit formed in her stomach. Even before she'd unfolded the parchment, she knew he'd fled. That guilt had driven him away once again. She trembled as she read the scrawled words begging for her forgiveness.

She would be patient with her father. She would save him, too.

The last thing he'd written was the address to a banker in Kash. *"I've been telling everyone I'm sending my pay to my wife, but I've been depositing it in a trust for you. You're the only one who can access it. It's yours. Make something with it. The best I can give you. I ain't worthy to be your dad."*

"But you are," she whispered as she pressed the letter to her chest and fought the tears.

34

Thirtieth Day of Patience, 755 EU

The summer heat roiled around them as Ōbhin and Avena walked down the overgrown lane of the farm where she'd grown up. It lay on the outskirts of the village of Upper Kash, a few hours' travel on foot north of the city. From the banker who held the trust her father had created, she'd also been given the deed to this land. Her father had signed it to her before he'd vanished.

Ōbhin had never suspected Fingers's true identity.

The farmhouse's roof had collapsed in many spots years ago. Plants poked up through the rotting floorboards. Streaks of mud from flooding caused by heavy rains rippled across the interior. Avena wandered lost through it while Ōbhin looked around for the perfect place to hide her brain.

If they were going to take on the Brotherhood, they would have to be careful. They couldn't leave the most vulnerable part of her where it could be easily found. With Fingers's money, they had bought a small house in the Breezy Hills. Avena was popular in that neighborhood thanks to her habit of giving away her pay to the street urchins. Jilly, Joayne, Cerdyn, Dajouth, Layni, and Hajina had all chosen to help Avena in her plan on bringing justice to those who had wronged them.

Dualayn. The Brotherhood. Even the White Lady.

Ōbhin would help in any way he could.

Avena drifted from a room. Her expression flicked from fond remembrance to grief. She would pause to touch a wall or a piece of rotten furniture before letting out a heavy sigh. He left her to her exploration as he pried up the soot-crusted hearthstones, his purple gloves digging them up one by one. He didn't mind the black stains left behind.

He'd come by them honestly.

Beneath the hearth, he excavated a hole with a shovel, piling the old dirt in a small mound until he'd dug it big enough. The soil looked dry. He set the crate inside, her jar packed in sand. The jewelchines in there would keep her brain alive for eternity, or so Dualayn claimed.

Avena came up alongside him when he rose. She stared down in the hole then pulled out his old, black gloves from her satchel. His new ones were made of fine cow leather, dyed the purple of a defender. Avena herself had stitched on the circles, each the color of flame, on the backs.

"I'm home," she whispered to Ōbhin before she tossed his gloves on top of the box.

"You sure you want to put those stained things in there with your brain?" Ōbhin asked, staring at his shame. Thanks to Avena, he had finally pried them off. She'd restored his pride. His life. She'd upheld the promise she'd made to him in an alley behind a seedy tavern.

"Even stained, they protected me." His promised, as the Lothonians called their betrothed, slipped her arm around his waist. She leaned her head against his shoulder. "It's comforting knowing they're watching over the most important part of me."

When they left here, Ōbhin and Avena's war against the Brotherhood would begin. So he savored this quiet moment with her, unsure what their future would hold.

The END of Book Two

The adventure continues with
Obsidian Mind, Jewels of Illumination Book Three

ABOUT THE AUTHOR

J.M.D. Reid has been a long-time fan of Fantasy ever since he read The Hobbit way back in the fourth grade. His head has always been filled with fantastical tales, and he is eager to share the worlds dwelling in his dreams with you.

Reid is long-time resident of the Pacific Northwest in and around the City of Tacoma. The rainy, gloomy atmosphere of Western Washington, combined with the natural beauty of the evergreen forests and the looming Mount Rainier, provides the perfect climate to brew creative worlds and exciting stories!

When he's not writing, Reid enjoys playing video games, playing D&D and listening to amazing music.

You an follow him on twitter @JMDReid, like him on Facebook, visit his **blog**, and sign up for his newsletter.

BOOKS BY JMD REID

Jewels of Illumination

Diamond Stained
Ruby Ruins
Obsidian Mind
Emerald Strength
Amethyst Shattered

***

Jewels of Illumination Box Set: Books 1-3

Masks of Illumination

Mask of Guilt - May 2021
Mask of Vengeance - June 2021
Mask of Hope - July 2021
Mask of Betrayal - August 2021
Mask of Redemption - Sept 2021

Assassins of Illumination

Books by JMD Reid

Fractured Soul - Oct 2021
Shattered Soul - Nov 2021
Sundered Soul - Dec 2021

The Storm Below

Above the Storm
Reavers of the Tempest
Storm of Tears
Golden Darkness Descends
Shattered Sunlight

Ingram Content Group UK Ltd.
Milton Keynes UK
UKHW012127130423
420127UK00006B/410